Quintin Jardine was born once upon ~~~~~~~~~~~~~~~~~~~~~~ rather than America, but still he grew to manhood as a massive Sergio Leone fan. On the way there he was educated, against his will, in Glasgow, where he ditched a token attempt to study law for more interesting careers in journalism, government propaganda, and political spin-doctoring. After a close call with the Brighton Bomb in 1984, he moved into the even riskier world of media relations consultancy, before realising that all along he had been training to become a crime writer. Now, forty novels later, he never looks back.

Along the way he has created/acquired an extended family in Scotland and Spain. Everything he does is for them. He can be tracked down through his website: www.quintinjardine.com.

Praise for Quintin Jardine:

'A triumph. I am first in the queue for the next one' *Scotland on Sunday*

'The perfect mix for a highly charged, fast-moving crime thriller' *Glasgow Herald*

'[Quintin Jardine] sells more crime fiction in Scotland than John Grisham and people queue around the block to buy his latest book' *The Australian*

'There is a whole world here, the tense narratives all come to the boil at the same time in a spectacular climax' *Shots* magazine

'Engrossing, believable characters . . . captures Edinburgh beautifully . . . It all adds up to a very good read' *Edinburgh Evening News*

Quintin
Jardine

HOUR OF
DARKNESS

headline

First published in 2014 by
HEADLINE PUBLISHING GROUP

First published in paperback in 2015 by
HEADLINE PUBLISHING GROUP

2

Cataloguing in Publication Data is available from the British Library

ISBN 978 0 7553 5703 1

Typeset in Electra by Avon DataSet Ltd, Bidford-on-Avon, Warwickshire

Printed in the UK by CPI Group (UK) Ltd, Croydon, CR0 4YY

MIX
Paper from
responsible sources
FSC® C104740

Headline's policy is to use papers that are natural, renewable and
recyclable products and made from wood grown in well-managed
forests and other controlled sources. The logging and manufacturing
processes are expected to conform to the environmental regulations
of the country of origin.

HEADLINE PUBLISHING GROUP
An Hachette UK Company
338 Euston Road
London NW1 3BH

www.headline.co.uk
www.hachette.co.uk

In Memoriam

This book is dedicated to my great friend, Jack Arrundale, the closest thing to a living brother I ever had, who died on Tuesday, 19 March 2013, at the ridiculously early age of 75. Jack and I laughed, played, argued, drank and did all sorts of other things together, for almost forty years. I've missed his company, his wisdom and his chat every day since he passed away, and will do every day for the rest of my life.

And yet I won't accept that he's gone; I won't allow it. As Bruce Springsteen wrote of Clarence Clemons, a great sax player, yet one who never featured in Jack's top ten since he was a jazz man through and through, Jack hasn't left the band just because he's dead, nor will he leave it, not until the last one of us who knew and loved him is dead too.

Lately I've been contemplating the Old Testament, rather a lot.

'That's not surprising in a cop, Mr Skinner,' I hear you say, but it's not as simple as that; it goes back to something my father told me.

We think of pre-Christian values as simple, but I don't see it that way. Even Exodus and Deuteronomy are a shade contradictory. Take the sins of the fathers as an example. It's not quite clear how many generations should take the rap for Dad's transgressions. And as for that cruel trick God played on Abraham, when He let him come within an angel's whisper of cutting young Isaac's throat . . .

My Biblical tendencies come from my old man, although as far as I know, he never sinned. I saw no evidence of it when I was growing up, although he was always very tightly wrapped. He was a quiet man, never much of a smiler, never much of a joker, but kind nevertheless. I don't recall him ever raising his voice to me, or to anyone else for that matter. He was generous, no question; within reason, anything that I wanted came my way, sooner or later . . . other than him, that is. He never gave of himself, not on a personal level.

He did most of the things that fathers are supposed to do, like taking me to football matches until I was old enough to go on my own, and getting me started on golf, but we had very little interaction at home. That territory belonged to my mother, and to my beast of an older brother.

Dad spent most of his home time working in his study, next to our dining room, while Mum lived on Planet Gordon's or Planet Beefeater or wherever else her gin brand of the moment took her. As for Michael, the less I say about him the better; he's in his grave now, and he can fucking stay there. He was a Grade A sinner, that is for sure.

My father shared his wealth, much of it self-created, but he never shared what was in his heart. I'm pretty sure, no, I'm certain, that I know why. I believe it was down to his war and to the things he had to do, but always, he refused to talk about that time, refused point-blank, until I stopped asking him, until I gave up trying to penetrate the force field of privacy that he kept around him.

While no one ever really saw the man inside him, that was the way that life had made him, and I stopped resenting it long, long ago. Which, given the circumstances, was pretty big of me, for it caused me a lot of grief.

The problem for me was that Dad's introspection affected his vision; it was so profound that he couldn't see the things that were happening closest to him. He had no idea of the tortures that Michael inflicted on me, during my childhood years. He never even realised that my mother was alcoholic, not until he saw it as an underlying cause on her death certificate.

He died without ever telling me, or anyone else that I know of, about his war and the experiences that I now realise had scarred him. He left me his medal, one of those that you only won for exceptional service, and that was all. He kept no diary, and he must have destroyed any papers related to those years, for I found none afterwards.

It wasn't until I reached chief officer rank in the police force that I made any effort to fill in that gaping hole in his life story, using channels that had become open to me. Even now, much of the secrecy remains. I know that he was operational, in the Balkan region, the area that became Yugoslavia in the austere peacetime, but I don't know what he did. Those files are still closed. All I know is what he was trained to do, and that did not involve escorting prisoners to the holding area.

So what did he do, that silent man, to give me the old prophet values that have lingered in me ever since?

It happened on the day on which he was destined to die. The disease that was claiming him was in its final stages, beyond therapy and at the point where 'palliative care' meant giving him enough dope to keep him out of the pain that consciousness brought.

I expected him to go that afternoon. His nursing team had told me that it was a matter of hours. They did so to prepare me, I imagine, but in truth I'd been ready for a while. I suspect that he had, too; I hadn't seen him smile in years, not a real face-cracker, at any rate, not even when he saw his newborn granddaughter for the first time.

I sat by his bedside in his room at the hospice. There was music playing, softly: Ella Fitzgerald was singing him on his way . . . my choice, not his; he was beyond comfort, but I wasn't.

Myra had been willing to come with me, but I had talked her out of it. That hadn't been too difficult; she'd been there the previous day and it had been horrific. I had no idea what 'projectile' really meant, not until Dad sat bolt upright in bed, without warning, and fired an eruption of vomit that splatted against a wall more than six feet away from him. My poor, doomed, first wife had caught some in her hair.

There was no chance of a recurrence as I sat beside him, hunched forward and helpless. There was nothing left in him by then; he'd been a big man in his time, almost as big as me, but the thing that was killing him had reduced him to a skin-covered skeleton, with no organs functioning other than the heart that was still pumping, and the lungs, from which the stentorious breathing of approaching death sounded in the room, contrasting harshly with the velvet voice coming from the cassette recorder.

I didn't expect him to waken again, ever, but he did. His eyes flickered, then opened. They weren't seeing me, though. They were looking at a scene far away and they told me that whatever it was, Dad wasn't enjoying the view. I found myself hoping that he was seeing his past and not his future. I've suspected since childhood that any afterlife might not be all it's cracked up to be.

Suddenly the claw that had been his left hand grabbed my arm, and tugged at me. I was startled, but I eased myself off my seat and leaned over him, getting as close as I could to his corpse breath.

'Robert,' he whispered, with an urgency that scared me.

'Yes, Dad,' I said, trying to keep my voice calm.

'Be careful, son,' he croaked. 'Blood will out, always.'

And then his grip on me loosened, and his eyes closed, for what did prove to be the last time. I sat down again, and listened as the rasp of his breathing quietened, and as it slowed. Ten minutes later, it stopped, and he was gone.

I pressed the bedside buzzer; his nurses responded within a few seconds. They made comforting noises, and the older one asked if I was okay. I told her the truth, that I was, and that I was happy he was out of it. She nodded; I was sure that in her job as a door warden for the dying she'd heard the same response a hundred times and more.

As they did what they had to do, disconnecting the tubes that led into and out of his newly vacated body, a doctor joined us. He made a quick examination, shone a torch in the old man's eyes, then closed them again. 'Will there be a cremation?' he asked, the first words he had spoken. 'If so you'll need a second certificate, signed by a second doctor.'

I sensed impatience in him; I was tempted to put him to as much trouble as I could, but that would have been at the expense of the living, so I shook my head. He completed a form and handed it to me; I glanced at it, noting the words 'heart failure', 'pneumonia' and 'carcinoma', in the usual medical scrawl, then pocketed it. When I looked up to thank him, he had gone.

I picked up my dad's belongings, his wallet, watch, spectacles, and his driving licence . . . I found myself smiling at the thought of him going into a hospice thinking he'd be driving home . . . then thanked the nurses for all they'd done to make his last days as easy as they could be.

'Don't you want his Bible?' the younger one asked, indicating the black book on the bedside cabinet.

I stared at her. 'It's his?'

'He brought it in with him,' she replied. 'He read it all the time, when you weren't here.'

And then I was back with him, by his side in South Dalziel Parish Church when I was five or six years old, listening to him belt out the hymns, accepting the white King's Imperials that he slipped to me, then surreptitiously pocketing them because I didn't like to tell him that I hated mints.

I cried for my father then, the only time I ever did, and that's

5

when I put him into context: an Old Testament guy at heart. I took the holy book with me, and I have it to this day. I hadn't read much from it until recently, but I'm pretty familiar with most of it now.

Later on, once I was home and ready to talk, Myra asked me how it had been. I told her, moment by moment, scene by scene, and finally word for word.

'What did he mean?' she asked, curious.

'I haven't a fucking clue,' I told her, frankly.

I do now.

One

'What's up, Sauce?'

'Nothing,' he replied, a little too quickly, and with an edge to his voice.

'Hey,' she protested. 'Don't bite my head off.'

'I didn't. At least, I didn't mean to. Why should anything be up?'

'Because you've been home for three hours, we're on to our second bottle of red, and you haven't cracked a smile all evening. This is our first week of living together. You're supposed to be overjoyed, happy, bubbly. Or is this the real Sauce Haddock I'm seeing? Is this what you're usually like at home?'

'Aargh!!!' he shouted, suddenly, then rolled sideways along the sofa, burying his face in her lap and rubbing his head from side to side against her tight-fitting woollen onesie.

'Stop it,' she giggled. 'We've only just had supper; you can't still be hungry.' She grabbed a handful of his hair and tugged him upwards until he was left with no choice but to look directly at her.

'Who says I can't?' he whispered.

'Well, that's not on the menu, 'cos I've got my period. Go and get another Magnum out the freezer; that'll cool you down.'

'No it won't,' he said, firmly. 'You may trust me on that, Ms Cheeky McCullough.'

She let him go, and he swung himself round to sit beside her, wrapping an arm around her and drawing her to him.

She laid her head on his shoulder. 'Well, are you gonna tell me? What gave you the faraway eyes? Did you have to bollock somebody at work? Or did you get on the wrong side of your new DI?'

'Neither of those: I'm still easing myself in as a detective sergeant, not ruffling feathers, and Sammy Pye isn't the bollocking type. Yes, I've had better days, but don't worry about it. We have our deal, remember? I'm not going to bring work home.'

'But you will, love,' she countered, gently. 'You have tonight, whether you wanted to or not. You can't help it.' She squeezed his arm. 'Listen to me,' she said. 'When we were out with the McGurks on Sunday night, after they helped us move in, Lisanne and I had a heart-to-heart when you and Jack were up at the bar. She marked my card about living with a cop. And she should know; her first husband was a plod as well. "Faraway eyes," that was how she put it. "When you see those, you know that what's going on behind them isn't very nice, and shouldn't be allowed to fester. A CID cop's wife's job," she told me, "involves a lot of therapy. It involves knowing when something's hurting in there," she tapped his forehead, "and getting it out and blowing it away." So, lover boy, I might not be Mrs Cop officially, but I'm still taking the job seriously.'

'It was a call-out,' he admitted, almost before she had finished. 'Luke and me.'

'Luke?'

'The DI; it's his nickname. They call him Luke Skywalker . . . I'm not quite sure why, probably something about the Force being with him, like in *Star Wars*.' He frowned. 'Here, did you know that there are about six times as many Jedi Knights as there are atheists in this country? Official figures, from the Census, no kidding.'

Cheeky nodded. 'Of course I know. I'm one of them. And didn't you tell me that the wee pathologist bloke's called Master Yoda?'

'Aye, but never to his face. Who are you then? Princess Thingy, I suppose. Just don't copy that bloody awful hairstyle, okay?'

She grinned. 'That's a promise I'll make and keep, worry not. So . . .' she paused, '. . . this call-out; why's it getting to you?'

'You don't want to know.'

'I do. We're a couple. We share.'

He gave up the struggle. 'It was a woman,' he said. 'She'd been in the water. Her body was washed up on Cramond Island: well, most of it was. She was missing her head, her right arm and shoulder, and part of her left arm from just below the elbow down. Dr Grace said . . .'

'Who's he?'

'She,' he corrected her. 'Sarah Grace; she's the other top pathologist. She'll take over from Master Yoda . . . Professor Hutchinson, to give him his proper name . . . when he retires in a few months. She's also the chief constable's . . . sorry, the ex-chief constable's ex-wife, but from some whispers I've heard, they're pretty friendly again.'

'You mean Mr Skinner? Hold on, I'm getting confused here, I thought his ex-wife was that politician, Aileen de Marco, the one who got caught by the tabloids having an affair with an actor.'

'She was Mrs Skinner number three. Sarah Grace was number two.'

9

'That explains lots of things,' she murmured. 'Now that man, he has serious faraway eyes. I'm not sure I'd want to know what's behind them. Right,' she declared, coming back to the moment. 'I'm up to speed on the Skinner marital history. So what did ex-wife number two say?'

'That she'd been hit by a ship's propeller; there's a lot of marine traffic goes past the island, tankers and such bound for the oil terminal. She reckoned that she'd been in the water for at least a couple of weeks.'

'Oh, my poor darlin' boy,' Cheeky murmured. 'That must have been awful for you.'

'One for the Chamber of Horrors, that's for sure. And maybe the Chamber of Secrets as well.'

'How come?'

'Because she was naked. No clothes, no jewellery, no head, no hands, all adds up to no means of identification. We haven't a clue who she was and we have no obvious way of finding out.'

'What age was she? Young, old, in between?'

'Not young, but Dr Grace won't be able to give us an age range until she's done the autopsy.'

'Christ, you won't have to go to that, will you?'

His smile was grim. 'Oh aye, love. Part of the job. She did it this afternoon.'

She stood, topped up his glass from the bottle of Washington State Merlot that stood on the coffee table, and handed it to him. 'Therapeutic,' she said. 'Once you've finished it, you can look at another body to take your mind off it. I was kidding about my period, by the way.'

She winked at him, then rejoined him on the sofa. 'Hold on,' she exclaimed, as she settled herself against him. 'How come this is your job at all? People do decide to end it all, and quite often they do it in the river. A few of them jump off the Forth Bridge.'

'Naked?'

'Sure. Why not? But it needn't have been a suicide. She could have been skinny-dipping and got into trouble. So why isn't uniform handling this? How come it's a CID job?'

'Because, my love,' he sighed, 'the propeller might have mangled the poor dearie, but it didn't stab her six times in the chest.'

Two

'Sir Robert Skinner,' she murmured. 'Yes, it has a ring to it, a nice melodic sound.'

'In that case, honey child,' I couldn't stop myself chuckling, 'it's as well that I'm tone deaf, because I've turned it down. I'm sorry if it disappoints you that you'll never get to be a Lady, but it's the way I feel.'

She raised an eyebrow; it's one of her trademark gestures, and it always makes me smile. 'I'd only have got to be Lady Skinner if we remarried, Bob, and we agreed that isn't going to happen, remember.'

'I remember,' I conceded, 'but the truth is, anything Sarah wants Sarah gets, so if I had accepted and you'd wanted to be a titled lady, us getting re-hitched would have been fine by me.'

She smiled at me, across the table. 'I'm an American, remember? We're an egalitarian people.' She paused, for a second or two. 'To tell you the truth,' she resumed, 'I assumed that it would be offered, now that you've been confirmed as Chief Constable of Strathclyde. It kinda goes with the job, doesn't it?'

And then she hesitated again, as a frown gathered. 'Here, you didn't turn it down because of me, did you? To save any social awkwardness, with you having to explain why I wasn't Her Ladyship.'

I stared at her. 'What are you talking about?' I chuckled. 'You're Professor Sarah Grace, or you're about to be; that's much more impressive, and more significant than being Lady Skinner, any day of the week. No, I turned it down because I didn't like the people who offered it to me, as simple as that.'

'You mean Clive Graham, the First Minister? I thought you and he were . . .'

My nod stopped her mid-sentence. 'We are: in spite of him railroading through the legislation to create the new single Scottish police force, Clive and I are fine. No, the knighthood nomination came from Downing Street. If that lot offered me a damn Snickers bar, I'd turn it down.'

'You lie, Skinner! You're addicted to those damn Snickers bars.'

'Okay.' I couldn't deny it. 'I'd take it, but I'd insist on paying for it.'

'Aren't you worried,' she asked, 'that if you're not knighted, people will think you've been snubbed, and maybe even that there's a skeleton in your cupboard?'

My laugh was so sudden and so loud that the couple two tables away, our nearest neighbours on the restaurant's wooden terrace, turned to frown at me.

'My cupboard's full of bloody skeletons,' I retorted, not caring whether they heard or not. 'You know that, better than anyone. Put an ear to the door and you'll hear the dry bones rattling around in there. Yours, on the other hand,' I raised my voice for the benefit of the eavesdropping frowners, 'yours is full of fresh corpses, still with some flesh on them, like the one you had to finish your day on Friday, before we left.'

She winced at the memory; that was unusual for Sarah. 'Hey,' she murmured, 'I'm on holiday. I don't want to be reminded about her, poor creature.'

I took her hand. 'You know, life isn't fair. You deserve to be Lady Grace in your own right. You could be too. They have honorary awards. Isn't Steven Spielberg a knight?'

'Is he? I don't know. Anyway, I'm only interested in you. Couldn't you take another honour instead of a knighthood? A CBE maybe?'

'I don't think you can negotiate with the Honours system,' I told her. 'Besides, if I did that, took something less than a K, it really would be seen as a snub by a lot of people, and hell, I couldn't have that; my great big ego wouldn't allow it.

'Nah, Sarah love, the fact is, I don't really approve of gongs being handed out to people simply because of the job they do, whether they're good at it or not. I believe they should be earned. It took Jimmy Proud' (my predecessor as chief in Edinburgh), 'more than a decade in post before he got his. I'm hardly through the chief's office door; I haven't done my time.

'And,' I pointed out, 'I won't get to do it in Strathclyde either, seeing as my new post will disappear in a few months, when the new unified Police Scotland service comes in.'

'A service which you will head,' Sarah countered. 'I checked before we came away,' she told me. 'The bookies aren't taking bets on the appointment, not now that it's out officially that you're a candidate.'

'They know something I don't, do they?'

'The bookies always know things the rest of us don't.'

'Not quite. The job's open for applications from across the UK. There are some serious candidates in for it.'

'Name one,' she challenged.

14

'Andy Martin.'

She didn't expect that one. Her wine glass almost slipped from her grasp and into the dregs of her Crema Catalana dessert. 'Andy's applying?' she gasped.

I nodded.

'But why, in heaven's name? What's he doing that for? The whole world knows that Andy's your protégé, but it also knows that his feet aren't big enough to fill your boots, not yet.'

'Then the whole world is underrating him,' I insisted. 'If I wasn't in the running, let's say I was the guy filling the post rather than pursuing it, Andy's the person I'd appoint. He's the Director of the Scottish Crime and Drug Enforcement Agency and that more than qualifies him.

'Sure, he's been my sidekick for much of his career, so I know him better than most. However I also know the other likely runners, as members of the Chief Constables' Association, and through having worked with some of them. Being as objective as I can, I rate him ahead of any of them.'

She frowned. 'He's also your daughter's partner. Your acting son-in-law, they call him.'

'So what? That shouldn't bar him from applying for a job he could do, and I told him so.'

'You did?'

'Of course I did. I told him that he had to apply. I insisted that he did. I told him that if I dropped dead the day before the interviews, and he wasn't on the candidates' list, he'd be doing himself . . . and the whole bloody nation . . . a disservice.'

'How does Alex feel about it?'

'My daughter agrees with me.' My smile was involuntary; for a second I was somewhere else. 'She actually said that in some ways Andy would be a better choice than me.'

Sarah's mouth fell open; she closed it again firmly. 'Now I know you're kidding me.'

'I'm not. She did. She's read the enabling Act for the new force; so have I, but it took her, as a lawyer, to point out that they've made a Horlicks of it, that there's an organisational clash between the new chief constable and the new Police Authority, just waiting to happen. Diplomacy not being my strong suit, she thinks that . . .' I didn't have to spell it out.

'Yes, I see those storm clouds,' she agreed. 'And what do you think?'

'I think that should I wind up in the job, as soon as my arse is in that chair, I'll write my own ticket. No fucking quango's going to cross me. If I have to, I'll get Clive Graham to amend the legislation.'

'Will he do that?'

'If I ask him nicely. If that doesn't work, I'll ask him again.' My smile may have looked a little evil.

'Meaning you'll make him an offer he can't refuse?' she grinned.

'Something like that,' I murmured.

Sarah's good at reading me. 'Are you suggesting that you've got something on our First Minister?'

'Not any more; I did have, but I destroyed it. The very fact that I did that means he owes me one. Shit,' I chuckled, 'he owes me half a dozen and counting.'

'Sounds mysterious. You didn't catch him with his kilt lifted, did you?'

'Not personally, but someone did.'

'My God!' she gasped. 'He's supposed to be Scotland's Mr Clean. It wasn't rent boys, I hope.'

'No, it was heterosexual, and the footage wasn't graphic, no bouncing buttocks or any of that stuff, but it was enough to have finished him.'

'Wow! You'll be telling me next that he was having it off with the leader of the Scottish Opposition herself.'

I turned my head slightly, and gazed out across the marina, so that I could admire the outline of the mountains against the deep pink sunset. 'No comment,' I murmured.

My partner stared at me. 'Clive Graham and Aileen de Marco? He was bonking your ex-wife?' Our near neighbours twitched again at her raised voice. Fortunately by that time I'd gathered from their conversation and his cigarettes that they were French, and so would have no idea who either the bonker or bonkee were.

'Just the once,' I replied, 'if I'm to believe what Aileen told me . . . and I think I do. There was drink involved, on both sides. I couldn't bring the man down over a booze-driven and probably unsatisfactory shag. Besides, he wasn't her only one; everyone knows that.'

'Then it's as well,' Sarah said, severely, 'that she's gone from Scottish politics, and that you've cut all ties with her.'

'Let's just call her my mid-life crisis,' I suggested, 'and never talk of her again. Agreed?'

'Happily. We didn't come here to do that. Remind me, why have we come here?'

My eyes went back to her. 'We've come here for a new start, you and me. We've come here because L'Escala was good for us in the beginning. We've come here because I've been neglecting the Spanish house for more than a year. If Alex hadn't used it, it would have lain empty all that time. We've come here because we need a holiday, both of us.'

'Do you feel guilty about not bringing the kids?' she asked, quietly. 'I do, just a little.'

'Then don't,' I insisted. 'I'd feel guiltier if we'd taken them out of school. Besides, they have a full-time carer and their grown-up sister is going to spend time with them on the two weekends we're away, while Andy has his kids with him. He might even take his two out to Gullane, and they can all have a party.'

'Yes, Alex said that. How will their mother feel about it, do you think?'

I shrugged. 'From what I'm told, Karen will be fine about it. Everything's fallen into place in her life. Her move from Perth was brought forward, and Danielle and Robert are into nursery school. She's been able to rejoin the force, as she wanted, and at her old rank too.

'Because Andy has the kids at weekends, she's trying to work as many of those as she can, so she can be free for some of the week. It's okay; unconventional but okay, pretty much like you and me keeping our separate houses during the week.'

'Are you really not going to consider moving closer to Glasgow?' she asked.

'Not an effing chance: this job, assuming the bookies are right, will change my life quite enough. I won't let it uproot me from my home. I left Gullane once, when you and I moved to Edinburgh. Neither of us was happy there.'

'True.' She paused for a second. 'How do you see it changing your life?'

'For a start, I'll no longer be the type of cop I've always been, or tried to be,' I told her, instantly. 'Instead I'll be a desk jockey. My life will become a struggle against the bureaucrats and bean counters in the supervising authority that the legislation has set up. The bloody thing is even going to have its own chief executive, would you believe.'

'Does that mean you'll have to report to that person?'

'Over his dead body . . . or hers; but Alex says that's a battle I may well have to fight. She calls it the smoking gun in the legislation. Oh, worry not, love, I'll have my way, and I will make sure that the new force is as efficient on the ground as it can possibly be.

'But . . . my days of crime-fighting are over, to my great regret. The terrible truth is, they were the moment I accepted the Strathclyde job.'

As I finished I had the strangest sensation, as if my words were hanging in the air, then drifting off into the sultry Spanish night like smoke rings. I think Sarah caught it too, for almost a minute went by before she spoke.

'If that's true,' she said, 'I can't say that I'm sorry. It doesn't matter what rank you've reached, you've always put yourself on the line for the job, emotionally and physically. That had to end sometime, before it ended you. You must know that, Bob.'

'Sometime,' I agreed, 'but of my choosing. This isn't the way I thought it would finish.'

'But it has, and your kids will thank you for it, like I thank you now. They're going to want you around to see them through school and university and on into their adult life.

'Me too,' she added. 'I don't just want you around; I need you. I've tried living without you and it didn't work very well. I hate to remind you, but you're over fifty years old and you have a heart pacemaker.'

'Am I? Have I?' I murmured. 'Goddammit I'd forgotten!' That was almost literally true. I've had the pacemaker for a few years, to make sure that my heart rate doesn't drop too low, as in down to zero. It doesn't affect my day-to-day life, and if it wasn't for a small lump on my chest just below my left collar bone, nobody but me would know it was there.

'Well, I haven't,' Sarah murmured, with a small grimace. 'That day you fell over, I almost died with you. As a pathologist I know all too well there is such a thing as unexplained sudden death syndrome. I've seen it, too often, in young fit men. There they are on the autopsy table and there is no discernible reason why, other than the fact that their heart isn't beating any more. You may have forgotten about it, my darling, but I never will.'

I sensed a hovering presence near us. Not John, the proprietor of La Clota, where we had eaten, as I always have on my L'Escala visits, since the earliest days . . . John wouldn't have hovered; he'd have crash-landed at our table . . . but the tall young waiter who had served us. His face was new to me, but that wasn't surprising since I hadn't been in Spain for a couple of years.

I glanced in his direction, and he moved in, his order pad in his left hand, which had a large sticking plaster across the back. 'Coffee, senores?' he asked. 'Or would you like liqueurs?' His English was confident, but heavily accented.

I glanced at Sarah. 'Coffee will be fine,' she said.

'Me too,' I told the kid, once Sarah, my coffee monitor, had given me the nod. 'But let's have a couple of sambucas as well.'

'Certainly. What type of coffee, senores?'

'Americano, please,' Sarah told him.

'And I'll have a *tailat*,' I added. There's no single word in English for what I wanted, espresso with a little milk, so I used the Catalan.

He frowned at me. 'I'm sorry?'

I switched to Castillian Spanish. '*Un cortado, por favor.*'

His eyebrows rose, and he flushed a little beneath the tan. 'Of course. *Perdon*, senor.'

I'd embarrassed the lad. 'No,' I said, 'it's my fault. I shouldn't be flashing my crap Catalan. So you're not from these parts?'

'No, senor, I am from the south of Spain. There's more work on the Costa Brava than where I live; I'm here for the rest of the summer.'

'Good for you, son. What will you do when it's over?'

'I go back to Cordoba, to start university.'

'To study what?' Sarah asked.

'I will study chemistry, senora.'

She smiled, and its warmth seemed to wash over the boy. 'You could do much worse . . . What's your name?'

'Nacho, senora.'

'Then good luck with your career, Nacho.'

'Thank you, senora.'

'But before you get that far,' I interrupted, 'do you know what to do with a sambuca?'

'Of course, senor; I set it on fire.'

'That's right. But you'd be best to do it at the table, not at the bar. You might want to work here again next summer, and John will not take it too well if you burn down his restaurant.'

'That is true, senor,' he agreed, with a smile. 'I will bring matches.'

He turned and strode into the restaurant.

Sarah's eyes followed him. 'Nice kid,' she murmured.

I sensed an unspoken 'But'.

'But …?'

She frowned, then shook her head. 'Nothing,' she said. 'One of those "walk on my grave" moments, but it's gone. I had a strange feeling that I'd seen him before, that's all. But it's nonsense, for I've never been to Cordoba in my life.'

Three

'Was it a quiet weekend, Sauce?' Sammy Pye asked his recently appointed detective sergeant, across the desk in his small office.

'Yes thanks, boss. Yours?'

'Yes, quiet and pleasant. A nice counter to the way we ended last week, with that awful post-mortem.'

'Mine too. I was a bear on Friday evening. Cheeky was great, though. She saw straight away that I was struggling, and put me right. As far as she could, that is. I was still a wee bit on edge, in case we got a call-out.'

'Mmm,' the DI murmured. 'But we didn't, neither of us, and in a way that isn't good news. It means that the scientific bods haven't come up with a DNA match for our victim, and that the trawl that we put in place across the force area on Friday for a missing white female, probably in her sixties, with an appendectomy scar and a history of childbirth hasn't come up with a single possibility.'

'So we've got a murder in our hands, but with no way of identifying the victim.'

'That's the story, Sauce. Plus we've got a new boss in the city CID who's only going to be interested in keeping his clear-up rate at one hundred per cent.'

Haddock frowned. 'Am I the only one that thinks his appointment was a bit of a surprise?'

'Hell no,' Pye retorted, 'you'd be a minority of one if you didn't. "Come back, Neil McIlhenney, all is forgiven," that's the general view . . . not that the big fella did anything to forgive, before he headed south.

'I know what was behind it, though; my dear wife might not be a Command Corridor secretary any more, but she still has her sources. There are a couple of reasons. First, neither Chief Constable Steele nor ACC McGuire wanted a superintendent as their exec. The truth is, Bob Skinner only put the guy there as part of his rehabilitation after his breakdown. But on top of that, they say that ACC McGuire does not like Superintendent Mackenzie, and vice versa.'

'Uh?' the DS grunted. 'Then why . . .'

Pye laughed. 'Why did he give him a key CID job? So that he can prove himself one way or another.

'David Mackenzie might have been in a uniform for the last couple of years, clicking his heels and saying "Yes, sir. No, sir" to the high heid yins, but the arrogant bastard that ran our drugs squad and brought the nickname "Bandit" with him when he moved from Strathclyde, that guy never went away. He's always lurked there under the surface. If you ask me, what Maggie Steele and Mario McGuire have done is let him out again.'

'To piss all of us off?'

'Hardly. They'll be judged in part by his success or failure. Also, remember this; the fact is that until he crashed and burned, Mackenzie was a good detective; an arsehole, certainly, but a good detective. Bob Skinner would never have brought him through from Strathclyde otherwise, and I cannot believe that the bosses would have put him where he is now out of malice.'

'Why doesn't the ACC like him?'

'I think it's because Mackenzie misread him. When he came here he thought he would leapfrog him on his way up the ladder, so he didn't take him seriously enough, didn't treat him with the respect he was due. That was a huge mistake. ACC McGuire might be an amiable bloke, but he's very sharp, and he's a fucking monster if you get on the wrong side of him.'

'So why's he put him in the city coordinator job?'

'That's complicated,' Pye said. 'It's only a guess on my part, but I think it goes back to the time when he was head of CID and Neil McIlhenney, before he moved to London, was in the job Mackenzie has now.

'Those two are the best buddies from hell, the Glimmer Twins, they called them; because of that neither of them ever questioned the other. As a result mistakes were made. I believe that Mario's learned from that; he chose Mackenzie for that job knowing that their personalities might clash.'

'In which case,' Haddock suggested, 'won't Mackenzie wind up as roadkill?'

'No, because he's got a buffer between them, Mary Chambers, DCS Chambers; she's head of CID, remember. Mackenzie reports to her, not directly to the ACC.'

'She's no soft touch either,' the DS pointed out. 'I was in her division, till we both got moved out.'

'Mary's fine.'

'But one extra rung away from us.' He paused. 'You know, Sammy, I get the impression that the ACC isn't the only one who doesn't like Superintendent Mackenzie. I suspect he's not on your Christmas card list either.'

The DI smiled. 'They told me you were a perceptive sod . . .

unless women are involved. No, I don't like the Bandit; I'll admit that. But it's an old story, it goes back to something that happened far away from here. If you want to know about it you'll have to go and ask Bob Skinner.'

'I'll pass on that one,' Sauce laughed. 'I wish he was here, though.'

'Why?'

'He might have an idea where we go with this murder inquiry.'

'How we get a head with it, you mean?'

Haddock nodded. 'Yes.' Then his eyes widened and his jaw dropped as he caught up with Pye's black wisecrack. 'Aww, fuck off . . . sir.'

'Sorry, Sauce,' the DI said, chuckling at the younger man's indignation. 'I don't have any more inspiration than you have.'

'That's what I like,' Haddock grunted. 'The smack of firm leadership.'

'Call it delegation.' Pye leaned back in his chair. 'Seriously, where do we go? What's your thinking?'

'Limited as always, but here goes. We have an autopsy report that says the woman died between . . .' the DS paused to make a quick mental calculation, '. . . fourteen and twenty-one days before she was put in the water. She sustained six stab wounds, of which five wouldn't have killed her; the one that did ripped right through her heart, indicating that the blade was no less than eight inches long. It had a serrated edge, and the pathologist suggested that it might have been a kitchen knife.

'She said also that the angle of entry suggested that the killer stood behind the victim and stabbed her in an upward direction. She was of the opinion that the attacker was male, given the degree of force that must have been needed, given that two of the blows cut clean through ribs and a third penetrated the sternum.'

'What do you read into all that?'

'Not a lot, boss, but I hardly think this was a professional hit. Six wounds but only one meaningful. This is not an expert, surely. A pro would just have cut her throat.'

'How do you know he didn't?' Pye asked quietly.

The DS waved a finger. 'Touché,' he whispered, grinning.

'You're probably right, nonetheless,' the inspector admitted. 'Let's face it, contract killings of senior citizen females aren't exactly commonplace, not in Edinburgh, anyway.'

'No,' Haddock agreed. 'And yet, the body was dumped in the river, no clothes, no jewellery, no nothing . . . less than nothing now, thanks to that effing propeller. Whether it was amateur or professional, there has to have been a degree of premeditation, hasn't there?'

'Maybe not. Could be the killing was impulsive, an act of rage, and the guy didn't start to think about disposal until after he'd done it.'

'Postmeditation? Is that a word, gaffer?'

'If that's what happened, it is now, and I'm claiming it. Come on, Sauce,' he said, 'we need to get our brains in gear, urgently, before Detective Superintendent Mackenzie comes battering on the door wanting to know what we're doing.'

'Then why don't we get in first?'

Pye's laugh had a hint of scorn about it. 'What, are you saying I should go and batter on his door?'

'Nothing so confrontational: no, why don't you call him, and tell him we're having a press conference.'

'About what?'

'About the victim. So far the media only know that a female

body washed up on Cramond Island on Friday. Tell him that we want to call them in to announce . . . and we're going to have to anyway, one way or another . . . that the post-mortem findings have led us to open a murder investigation, which is stymied because we don't know who the hell it is that's been murdered. Then tell him that we want to ask the media for their help, by publishing an appeal for anyone who knows of a sixty-something female in the Edinburgh and Lothian areas that hasn't been seen around for a couple of weeks.'

The DI considered the proposal. 'How do you think that Mackenzie'll react,' he wondered, 'when I ask him for the okay?'

'I'm only guessing,' Haddock replied, 'but . . . from what you've said about him, he'll jump in and front it himself.'

'Then let's find out. Bugger off while I call him. One more thing,' he added, as the DS pushed himself to his feet and headed for the door that led into the CID office. 'Edinburgh and the Lothians won't be enough; this has to be a national appeal. The body was dumped in our territory, sure, but it could have been brought from anywhere.'

The young sergeant returned to his desk in the open-plan office, nodding a greeting to the two detective constables who made up the unit's complement. He was checking through their reports on their inquiries into a series of thefts from cars parked overnight in the residential dockland areas when Pye's hand fell on his shoulder.

'The Bandit reacted just as you said he would,' the DI murmured. 'We're on parade at headquarters at twelve o'clock, and he'll be in front of the cameras.'

'Brilliant,' Sauce declared. 'So when this investigation goes absolutely nowhere, as it probably will, his name will be all over it rather than ours.'

'Yup. You're not just a perceptive sod, but devious as well. Just as well I told him the media conference was your idea.'

'You fucking what???'

Four

'What's going on downstairs?' Chief Constable Margaret Steele asked. 'I saw the media beginning to gather when I came in from my meeting.'

'David Mackenzie's holding a press briefing,' ACC Mario McGuire replied.

'Mackenzie is? About what?'

'The headless body that was found on Friday: they've run out of ways to identify her so he's making a national appeal for help from the public.'

'Whose idea was that?'

'He's claiming credit, and I have no reason to doubt it'.

'Has Mary Chambers okayed it?'

'Retrospectively. He called it and then told her about it. She's not best pleased about that, but she kept her feelings to herself. She didn't want the two of them to get off on the wrong foot, and besides, she'd likely have approved it even if he had asked for permission.'

'Why's he doing the briefing himself? Sammy Pye's the SIO on the investigation, isn't he?'

'Not any more, Mackenzie's jocked him off.' The ACC held up a hand, to stall her reaction. 'Maggie, I don't like that any more than you, but let's not get steamed up about it. The guy's probably out to make a name for himself again in CID, maybe in the hope that Bob'll move him back to Glasgow when the new force takes over. Good luck to him,' McGuire grunted, 'it's the best place for him. What he's done might look like poor man-management, but it isn't going to compromise the investigation. I asked Mary to make damn sure he uses a Freephone contact number for calls from the public, so that our communications centre isn't swamped. You never know, he might even get a result.'

'He might,' Steele agreed. 'But isn't there any other means of identifying her?'

'Nah; all other routes are exhausted. The surgeon who took out her appendix didn't sign his name so …'

'Funny bugger.' She smiled, then paused for a second. 'Mackenzie's been set up, of course,' she added.

'Of course,' he agreed. 'Sammy Pye's played him, to get himself out of the firing line.'

'Not just Sammy. My former protégé Haddock's down in Leith now, and I can see his hand all over this. Mark my words, it's as well you and I have got a good head start on that boy. He's going to go as far in the force as he wants. He's another Bob Skinner.'

The big ACC smiled. 'No, he's not. There's a big difference; Bob's actually gone further in the force than he ever wanted. If he hadn't had to take the reins in Strathclyde in an emergency, he'd never have gone there, but now he has, he feels that he's got no choice but to take over as head of the unified Scottish police service. That's Neil McIlhenney's reading, and he's closer to the big man than anyone except Andy Martin. If you want to compare young Sauce Haddock with somebody, make it Andy. He still has plenty of ambition left.'

'And what about you?' the chief constable asked.

'Me? I never thought I'd make assistant chief, so I'm quite happy. I'll just sit here and see what opportunities the new set-up has to offer. Given the chance, I'll go back to CID. As for you, you've made it to the top of the tree in the outgoing system, and you'll get one of the ACC posts in the unified force, for sure.'

'How do you know I wouldn't rather take the redundancy money? There will be a lot of that on offer, remember.'

'How do I know?' he repeated. 'Mags, we used to be married. I know you.' He leaned on the last pronoun. 'You're a police officer; it's all you've ever wanted to be. Now you're a mother too, and that's good, but you're not going to stay at home until wee Stephanie's off your hands. Even if you did fancy it, you're way too young to get a pension, so you'll carry on. Don't even begin to try to kid me.'

She looked at him with a gleam in her eye. 'I never could; it was you that kidded me, remember. How is Paula, by the way, and wee Eamon?'

'They are both blooming, thanks. Being a mother . . .' his expression took on a glow of reverence, '. . . it changes women in a way I never appreciated before.'

'And men,' his ex-wife chuckled. 'Go and look at yourself in the mirror.'

'I will, after I've dropped in on Mackenzie's press briefing.'

'No,' Maggie said, quickly. 'Don't do that. Let him have his space, Mario.'

'Let him have enough rope, you mean?'

'No, I don't. He might just fool us both by getting it right. If he doesn't, I don't want him to have anyone to blame but himself.'

Five

I'm not addicted to television, not by a long way, but someone in my position does have a need to keep up to date with current affairs, and events. That's why I have UK satellite television in my Spanish place, as most Brits do, whether they're resident expats or occasional visitors like us.

Not that I was thinking of home.

Sarah and I had just come home from a late breakfast in Casablanca, a café down in the old part of L'Escala, and a couple of hours reclining on the town beach, which it overlooks. Holidays are my time for catching up on my reading list (normally I'm one of those people who take forever to get through a book, since I consume it in ten- or fifteen-minute bursts, in bed, last thing at night, before my eyes go blurry and sleep catches up with me), and that morning I'd finished the latest tale of the recently unretired DI Rebus . . . unconventional or not, with his clear-up rate he'd have gone a lot higher in my force, trust me . . . and moved on to a novel called *As Serious as Death*, the latest in a series that's set in an authentic Spanish village that I can see from our house.

'You know what?' I said to her as we settled on our sunbeds beside the pool.

'What?' she murmured.

'I love you.'

'Nice. I love you too. Now what else were you going to say?'

'Ach, nothing really, I've been thinking all morning about last night at La Clota and what we wound up talking about.'

'That young waiter?'

'Who?' I frowned for a moment; I'd forgotten all about the lad. 'Ah him,' I said. 'No, not him, the job; as always, the bloody job. You know, if the new board in its doubtful wisdom decided that they wanted someone else to do it, I've decided that I wouldn't give a fuck. There are other things in . . .'

'Ahh,' she said, cutting me off in the wise-woman tone that always brings me down to earth whenever she thinks I might be floating above it. 'We're back to buying that boat, are we?'

'What boat?'

'You know damn well. Alex told me about it. When she was a kid, you and she went for a weekend's sailing in the Clyde estuary, with your girlfriend of the time. Before it was over you were all for giving up your career, buying a boat of your own and doing chartered cruises for a living.'

'Mmm,' I whispered. 'That boat.' That weekend, that warm, lovely woman: poor dead Alison, another cop, who was even more career-driven than me, and might have overtaken me, if she hadn't got into the wrong car at the wrong time and . . .

'What is it about women, cars and me?' The thought escaped without my realising it, and once it was out there I had to finish. 'Myra, she died in a car, on her own. Alison, so did she.' I looked at Sarah. 'Can we arrange it so that we always travel in the same vehicle from now on?'

She rolled off her sunbed and on to mine, pressing her body

against me. 'Lover, I'm so sorry,' she said. 'I shouldn't have mentioned that; I'd forgotten it was her.'

She was upset, so I stroked her hair, and kissed her. 'It's all right,' I assured her. 'Shit happens. And another reason why I won't care if that job doesn't.'

'But you will. For the same reason that one phone call blew your boat right out of the water; it's what you are. Anyway, it's all academic, because the job will happen.'

She sat up, put her feet on the ground, and pushed herself upright. 'Now, before you get horny, I'm off to consider what we might have for lunch.'

I followed suit. 'And I'm off to swim, and think.' I do some of my best thinking in the pool.

I took a step towards the chair where I'd left my trunks to dry off after my early morning exercise, then stopped. They weren't there.

'Hey,' I called to Sarah, catching her halfway through the doorway, 'did you move my swim shorts?'

'No,' she replied. 'Why would I?'

'No idea, but somebody has.'

'Maybe they blew back into the pool.'

'Good thought,' I conceded and went to check. On the bottom I saw three leaves and what must have been a very careless gecko, but absolutely no garments. I swore quietly and went indoors for a replacement.

As I crossed the living area, the wall clock told me that it was just short of two twenty-five. I picked up the TV remote, hoping that the timepiece wasn't slow and that I hadn't missed the Scottish news.

I headed upstairs and changed into a new pair of Speedos. When I came back down, Sarah was standing in the middle of the room, staring at the television.

'Look at this,' she said, without taking her eyes off it. 'Hold on, I'll go back to the beginning.'

Our satellite decoder has two feeds, allowing us to pause and rewind live programmes. That's what she did, until she had found the start of the item she'd been watching.

'It's a press briefing in Edinburgh,' she said, 'about the autopsy I performed on Friday.'

I stepped alongside her as the presenter led into the piece, then felt my eyebrows rise as another face appeared on screen. 'What the . . .' I took the remote and froze the image.

'That's David Mackenzie,' I exclaimed, 'the Bandit. He's the Command Corridor exec. What the hell's he doing there?'

She looked up at me, surprised. 'Didn't you know? Maggie's moved him into Neil's old job, as Edinburgh CID coordinator. Sammy Pye told me on Friday.'

'Bloody hell!'

Since Maggie Steele had been appointed as my successor in the Edinburgh job, I'd been avoiding any professional contact, so I couldn't be accused of influencing her thinking . . . not that I could have done that anyway. I knew she'd handle some things in a different way from me, but that one took me by surprise. I'd always have put a proven team player in that job, and our David was, unfortunately, the opposite; poaching him had not been one of my better moves.

'It could have been worse, I suppose,' I muttered. 'She could have made him head of CID; that would have been a real risk. Sammy told you, you said. That means Mackenzie didn't come along to post-mortem, yes?'

'Yes, no, whatever; he wasn't there. I don't blame him; I wish I hadn't been myself. She'd been in the water for two to three weeks and quite a bit was missing.' She drew a line across her chest with her finger, from alongside her right breast to the edge of her left collarbone. 'That much, plus the left arm just below the elbow. She got tangled up with a fairly large vessel.'

Until then she hadn't told me any details about the job, but she didn't need to for me to know that it had been messy.

She reclaimed the remote and pushed the play button. 'Let's hear what he's got to say. Maybe they've found the rest.'

Fat chance, I thought. *The prop probably minced it.*

Indeed they hadn't. What Mackenzie came out with was, essentially, the losing gambler's last roll of the dice, an appeal for any information about late middle-aged women who hadn't been seen for a while, the kind that usually attract hundreds of calls to the hotline and do no good at all. When he said, 'A murder investigation,' I glanced at Sarah and she nodded.

'She was stabbed,' she explained, as Bandit wound up.

On the face of it . . . unfortunate choice of words . . . there was little or no chance of a result. In all probability the partial cadaver would stay in the freezer until the prosecutor's office authorised its burial or cremation. I knew it, and so did Mackenzie, although I knew equally well that if we were both wrong, he'd grab all the glory that ensued.

'He seemed earnest and impressive,' Sarah said, as the presenter moved on to the next item.

'Oh, he's all that on the surface, is David,' I agreed. 'We could do with him over here.'

Her frown expressed bewilderment.

'Why?'

'He might find out what happened to my swimming trunks.'

Six

'Are we both sure about this?'

Alex Skinner turned her head and gazed evenly at her partner. They were seated on the small balcony of her duplex apartment, with its vistas of the Salisbury Crags, and across the unconventional, and controversial, roof of the Scottish parliament building.

Privately, Andy Martin hated their viewpoint. He would never admit to a fear of heights, but it was there nonetheless, and amplified by the structure of Alex's terrace, which was no more than a steel frame jutting out from the building, giving him the feeling of hanging over the edge of a cliff.

Whenever his children visited, as they would do over the coming weekend, or Alex's young half-siblings, the glass door from the living room was always locked, and bolted.

'We've been over this,' she replied. 'We've had this discussion with my father. It was his suggestion that you should apply for the new chief constable post. I understand his reasoning . . . maybe better than you do . . . and I agree with him.

'In fact I agree with him so much, that I'm not going to trust you to post that completed application form. I'm going to take it to work tomorrow and in my lunch break I'm going to take it to the post office and send it off myself, first class, recorded delivery.'

'It's a huge step,' he said.

'No it's not. It's a declaration of intent, if nothing else.'

'I'm way too young.'

'Forty-two is not way too young for anything, other than a pension. You've got the service, the skills and the seniority. You're also calm, unflappable, a first-class man-manager, and a natural leader. Christ, my dad doesn't tick all those boxes. I told him so, but he knew it anyway.'

'But you want him to get the job.'

'Of course I do', she retorted, then realised that she had fallen into the pit he had dug for her. 'That's to say . . . Andy, you will sit in that office one day, I have no doubt about that, even if I believe that my father deserves to sit in it first, given what he's done in his career.'

'I know that, kid. But, go back to what you said earlier on about understanding his reasoning better than me: what did you mean by that?'

'That he wanted you to apply because you're a worthy candidate, but more than that, you'll be his safety net.'

'Against what? Acts of God and stuff?'

'Not just that; against his own ambivalence. With your application in place, he'll be free to walk away if he chooses.'

He looked away from her across to the sunlit Crags, and the Radical Road, where tiny figures walked. 'No chance,' he chuckled. 'I've known Bob for more than half your life; he's a driven man.'

'You think I don't know that? He's been that way since my mum died, and it's why he's never been very good at relationships . . . until now, that is. Please God, let him and Sarah make a go of it this time.'

He turned his face back towards her, smiling. 'You might put in a word for us too, while you're at it.'

'We don't need His help,' she declared. 'As long as we get the children thing right this time,' she added.

'You really don't want kids, do you?'

'No. Certainly not now, and I'm not sure I ever will. I'm not full of love, Andy. I've only got so much in me to share around.'

'We'll see how you feel in a few years. Either way, I'll be fine about it. I want what you want, end of story. But in a way, it's interesting that you feel the way you do.

'You think it was your mother's death made Bob what he is? I don't quite see it like that. I believe that his children are his driving forces, starting with you, of course. He wants you all to be proud of him. Even on the occasions when he's had to put his life on the line, and there may have been more of those than you know about, he's done it because he couldn't bear you to think that he was afraid to. When I first met him, you were all he talked about. Even when he was in relationships you were the absolute centre of his universe.'

Alex smiled. 'I think I knew that. When I was thirteen I actually told him I didn't fancy another woman in our kitchen full-time. Can you believe that?'

He laughed. 'Of you, sure I can.'

'It was when he was with Alison Higgins . . . not that I had anything against her, but there was someone else in the picture at that time and I didn't see her as suitable, not at all.'

'Was there? I don't remember that. Mind you, I was a new kid in town then.'

'Weren't you just! You and Mario too. I look back and I realise how young you were, the pair of you. I didn't think so then, though. You were very glamorous to a thirteen year old.'

'Come on,' Martin protested, 'we're not that old yet.'

'You're eternally young, my darling, both of you. Hey,' she

asked, spontaneously, 'do you think Mario ever had a driving force?'

'I know he did; he told me once. He joined the police to show both sides of his family that he could succeed at something that had no connection with their businesses.'

'What about you?'

'I've never thought about it, but if I did . . . You? My kids?'

'Never Karen?'

He frowned. 'No, I'm afraid not. Probably I should never have married her, or she should have known better than to marry me.'

'That's not true. It seemed right to you both at the time, so no regrets.'

'Oh, don't get me wrong,' he said. 'I don't have any. I have two lovely kids to show for it.'

'Now that is true, and they are.' Her face became solemn. 'But Andy,' she ventured, 'do you never worry about people saying that you just used Karen as a brood mare, and then came back to me?'

'Why, does that worry you?'

She pursed her lips, an odd gesture for her. 'I'm under no illusions about what people think of me, especially women. One, who shall be nameless, called me a disgrace to my gender, right to my face.'

'Then she'd better remain fucking nameless or I'll be having words with her.'

'Don't worry, I had some myself. I threatened her with a defamation action.' She winked. 'Being a lawyer has its advantages sometimes. But if she'd said anything about you, I'd have needed one myself, for I'd have laid her as broad as she was long.'

He reached over and squeezed her hand. 'Don't you worry

yourself. That thing has been said, in fact, that I just used Karen, but to her, not to me, at a women's gathering up in Perth. She told me about it, and she was spitting nails when she did.'

'Oh, that's awful. What tactless bitch did that?'

'No idea, but I do know she had her tail docked. Karen told her that, if anything, she was the user not me, because she'd wanted children more than I did. She even told the unfortunate lady that she, Karen, that is, was in your debt, because she'd always wanted to resume her career eventually, and as a serving chief constable's wife, no way could she have done that.'

'It would be nice if she really believed that,' Alex murmured.

Andy sighed. 'Look, you're never going to be her best pal, but she's okay about you. If she wasn't, she'd give me grief about you being around Danielle and Robert, or about us taking them to Bob's place at Gullane for the weekend. She doesn't mind, Alex; that's the honest truth. And also, she really is loving being back at work.'

Seven

If Detective Sergeant Karen Neville had put her mind to it, she could have hated Alexis Skinner; not for stealing her husband, but for dumping him when she had and throwing him back into the Edinburgh man pool, just as she herself was rebounding hard from a disastrous relationship.

But she believed that life was wasted if it was spent carrying grudges, plus she and Andy were agreed that they had done at least two things right in what had become, eventually, a sad, distant marriage, a point she had reiterated the evening before when he had picked up Danielle and Robert from her new house in Lasswade.

She believed also that hatred could only be destructive. She had seen enough of it in her career, and looking at the file that sat on top of the small stack of live investigations on her desk, her conviction was reinforced.

When she had applied to rejoin the police force, after her divorce and her move from Perth, she had expected to be accepted at her former rank but had assumed, more or less, that her first posting would be in uniform, somewhere, anywhere on the force's extensive area. Her interview had been conducted by Mario McGuire, with a po-faced bloke from Human Resources sat alongside him, to keep the ACC serious and on message, she guessed.

That had worked, until they reached the point of confirmation, and the HR bod had produced a list of available postings for a uniformed sergeant. The big guy had taken it from him, politely, crumpled it into a ball, and tossed it into a waste basket, ten feet away. If he had missed, it might have spoiled the moment, but he hit it, dead centre.

'With respect,' he lied, 'if Personnel thinks that I'm going to deprive CID of the services of a proven, experienced detective officer, it's got it badly wrong. Karen, do you want to go back into CID?'

Her reply had been automatic. 'Absolutely, sir.'

'Okay. I need somebody in the office at the West End. Becky Stallings is going off on maternity leave, Jack McGurk's being bumped up to acting DI, and with young Sauce Haddock . . . you probably don't know him . . . going down to Leith on promotion, I'm light on experience at detective sergeant level. If the chief constable approves, and I believe she will, are you up for it?'

'Yes please. Can my shift pattern include weekends?'

'Are you sure about that? The stuff can hit the rotor blades on Saturdays and Sundays in that division.'

She had smiled at him. 'Been there, and been splattered by that stuff; it would help with the kids, that's why I ask.'

'Then you've got it. That brings me to something else. What are we going to call you, Detective Sergeant?'

She had thought that one through before the interview, indeed as she was filling out the application form. 'I style myself Ms Martin, sir, in my private life; I'm not going back to my maiden name, not with children. I've talked it through with my . . . former husband,' she had come close to calling him

'Andy', but had maintained formality, 'and he's perfectly fine with that. But professionally, I want to be what I always was, Karen Neville.'

'Suppose he wasn't, that wouldn't matter to me, even though the Director of the Serious Crime and Drugs Agency and I go back to the last century as colleagues. Congratulations, Detective Sergeant Neville, and welcome back.'

She beamed at the recollection. Back in the moment, the huge man behind the desk opposite raised his eyebrows. 'You're one strange woman, Sarge,' he said. 'I draw weekend duty by rotation and I grumble about it. You volunteer and you're smiling.'

'How do you know what I'm smiling about, Detective Constable Singh?' she replied, deadpan. 'For all you know . . .'

'True,' he conceded, quickly. 'Do you want a coffee?'

'No, thanks; one promise I've made to myself is that this time around I'm going to drink a hell of a lot less of that stuff. Stains your teeth, rots your guts. What incidents have you got on the go?'

'Traffic passed on a hit-and-run from last night,' he told her. 'That's the most urgent. The victim's a nineteen-year-old student, a lassie. She was making her way home from not one but several pubs, along Gorgie Road, when she was hit by a car, probably blue, heading westward, out of the city.'

'Jesus,' Neville muttered, 'kids and alcohol; nothing changes. Did she survive?'

'So far, but nobody's making any promises. She's in the Royal Infirmary with serious head injuries.'

'I take it we don't have a number for the van, since it's been tossed our way.'

The Sikh shook his head. 'No, and no chance of getting one.

44

The uniforms who took statements at the scene said that the three witnesses, the girl's boyfriend and another couple, were all pretty well pished, as was the victim herself. They're emailing everything across, but the picture seemed to be that the girl stumbled out into the roadway, right in front of the driver.'

'Is it possible he didn't know he'd hit her?'

'No, because he stopped, immediately afterwards, for a few seconds. Then he drove away.'

'And still nobody got the number?'

'No. One of the lads thought it might have been a zero-eight registration, and the other girl said it began with S, but that's the lot.'

'What's the camera coverage like in that area?'

'Patchy, but there is some; not at the scene of the accident, but we can check around the time. I've asked Traffic to get all the footage they can on to DVD and send it over to us.'

'Thanks, Talvin. Have we got addresses for the witnesses?'

'Address. They all share a flat in Denholm Crescent.'

'Handy,' she said. 'In that case, let's get ourselves up there sharpish, and re-interview them. The booze should have worn off by now, and we might get some sense out of them.'

They were heading for the door when the phone rang, a direct call, not a front desk reference. Singh swore softly, but turned back and picked it up. 'Western CID', he announced.

'Who's that?' a brusque voice asked.

'DC Singh. Now it's your turn.'

'This is Detective Superintendent Mackenzie, smart-arse. You may have heard of me; I'm your boss.'

'Yes, sir,' the DC replied evenly, 'I've heard of Mr Mackenzie, and I know what he is. But how do I know that you're him?'

He heard a deep breath being taken. 'You could take my

word for it, Singh, or you could hang up and ask the comms centre to raise me on my home number. Which is it to be?'

Smart-arse, the big man thought; but he liked CID and so he chose to risk his tenure there no further. 'What can we do for you, sir?'

'That's better. I've just had a message passed to me by uniform. It came from Scottish Power. They had to gain entrance to a flat this morning to read the gas meter. They'd been unable to raise the occupant and had to make an arrangement with the owner. A lawyer looks after the place on his behalf, 'cos he's away. Anyway, a girl from the lawyer's office met the meter reader with a key, at nine o'clock. They couldn't find the meter at the front door, where you might expect to, so they went into the kitchen. There was blood all over the place, more than a cut finger would leave. Who's your senior officer there?'

'Detective Sergeant Neville.'

'Right, you and he . . .'

'That would be she, sir.'

'Of course it would, wouldn't it. How could I forget? Okay, you and she drop whatever you're doing and get round there, now. The address is one forty-two Caledonian Crescent. Check it out and report back to me.' There was a pause. 'Through the communications centre,' Mackenzie added, heavily.

As Singh replaced the phone, Karen whistled.

'You were pushing your luck, Talvin, were you not?'

He shrugged his vast shoulders. 'He called me "smart-arse",' he grumbled.

'Could be he was right.'

Eight

'I like this plan of yours.'

Her smile said that she wasn't kidding. It was warmer than I'd seen it since the early days of our marriage, and it seemed to come from deeper within her. I couldn't remember Sarah ever looking more relaxed. I hoped I looked the same, for that was how I felt.

We'd spent a whole week in L'Escala, and never left town; we'd walked, we'd swum, we'd eaten, we'd loved, we'd caught up with some friends, British and Catalan, but most of all we'd talked. We'd talked about us as a couple, we'd talked about Sarah's career and we'd talked about mine. Yes, we'd talked about the kids too, but less and less as the time went on. More and more we'd found ourselves talking about me; about what I wanted, and how I wanted the rest of my life to be.

And at the end of it all, I'd made a decision.

That plan that Sarah mentioned? Oh yes, that was a good one. We'd have an early lunch in La Clota, then take the train to Barcelona Passeig de Gracia, check into a gastronomic hotel in Placa Reial and explore the city for all of Sunday, before getting back to Scotland and the family that we'd made, split asunder, but, thank God, reunited.

Everything was good, even the calamares. I've found that squid can be a risky choice in a restaurant, because not every chef knows how to cook it properly, but I've rarely had better than I did that day. I didn't have anything else, as I wanted to keep space for dinner, but it hit the spot.

'That okay?' John, the ever-solicitous proprietor, asked, as I finished.

'It'll do,' I replied: I like to keep him on his toes.

'Good. My father-in-law caught it; I'll tell him to fish in that place again.'

'In that case I'm not going to ask where your beef comes from.'

He grinned. 'Hah, funny man. You be back soon?' he asked Sarah.

'Yup,' she told him. 'We're bringing the kids for the October school holiday.'

'That's good; we'll still be here. Maybe you can help carve the meat . . .' he laughed, '. . . or would that be too much like your work?'

I looked around; the terrace tables were fully occupied, and a few diners had been seated indoors. The staff were bustling around, doing their best to keep everyone happy.

'You flying one short?' I asked John.

'What you mean?'

'The kid who was here last weekend; I don't see him.'

'Nacho? No, he left. He said he had to go back to Cordoba. He's a good waiter even though he doesn't speak Catalan. He say he come back next year, but with kids, you never know.'

'Tell me about it! We have our dropouts in the police force too. It's a bugger when you've spent serious money training them, only for them to piss off and join private security firms.'

Sod it! He'd got me talking about work, and I had forsworn that for the rest of the break.

'Gimme a bill, please,' I asked. 'We've got a train to catch.' To speed the process, I handed him a fifty euro note.

'Thanks,' I said as he left. Sarah looked at me, puzzled.

'Thanks for what?'

'Thanks for making my life complete again. For having faith in me. For showing me the way forward when I was uncertain and confused. For loving me. Come on, let's go to Barcelona and have the time of our lives.'

We stood and I waved farewell to John, stopping him as he headed back with around twelve euro in change. Sarah took my arm and we walked off, towards Club Nautic, where our car, the one I keep out there, was parked, looking at the ranks of moored boats, and feeling the comfort of the early afternoon warmth, rather than full-on heat. In the days that we had been there the season had begun to change, as summer morphed into autumn.

'One day,' I murmured, 'we're going to spend more time here. Seonaid hardly knows this place, and the boys haven't seen nearly enough of it. That's my fault; if I hadn't messed us up . . .'

She squeezed my bicep. 'We're done talking about that. We messed us up, not just you, and now we've put us back together again.'

I kissed the top of her head as I clicked the remote to unlock the car. 'Agreed,' I said. 'I've never looked forward to growing old before, but I do now, knowing I'll do it with you.'

It was a beautiful moment, one of those you wish you could encase in plastic and keep for ever.

And then, with timing that could have come from the pits of hell, the phone rang, and I took the call that started a chain of events that changed everything that I was, and might have been.

Nine

'How far along is it?' Karen Neville asked as Singh turned their unmarked police car into Caledonian Crescent.

'I can see one of our vehicles right at the far end,' he replied, 'so I guess that's it.'

The street was less curved than its name implied. On either side, grey four-storey tenement blocks rose above them. 'I should know, I suppose,' he added. 'I lived here when I was a kid; number ninety-eight. It's changed a lot since then. We didn't have door buzzers in the streets; all the stairwells smelled like prisons.'

'Prisons?'

'Aye. You know; boiled cabbage and pish.'

He drove slowly between the ranks of cars; Saturday, so the resident parking bays were all full. There was a disabled space opposite their destination; he took it and put a 'CID on business' card in the window.

The police car that he had seen was unoccupied, and the entry door to one forty-two was closed.

'Did Mackenzie give you a flat number?' the sergeant asked.

'No, he was too busy giving me a hard time. Smart-arse, indeed,' he growled.

50

'Live with it,' she said. 'Push some buttons till we get the right one.'

Singh was about to begin the process of elimination when, to his surprise, the door clicked and opened an inch or two. The two detectives stepped into the hallway, and came face to face with an elderly lady, standing at the entrance to what they guessed was her home.

'I took you for police,' she announced.

The DC beamed. 'So much for plain-clothes duty.'

The householder smiled, gently. 'You, son, could not be anything else.' Then she frowned. 'Here, did you not live in the Crescent, what, oh, twenty years ago?'

'That's right.'

'What's your name again?'

'Talvin.'

'That's right. I used to talk to your mother. How is she?'

Unlike quite a few other neighbours, Singh recalled. 'She's fine,' he told her. 'My dad died a few years ago, though.'

'Aw, I'm sorry to hear that, son. You tell your mum that Greta McConnochie was asking for her.'

'I will indeed.' He paused. 'I don't suppose you know . . .'

'Where the other police are? Yes, they're one floor up, flat one. What is it? No' a burglary, I hope.'

'We're not sure yet. But it's nothing for you to worry yourself about. Thanks, Mrs McConnochie.'

They left the neighbour on guard duty and headed for the stone staircase. Flat one faced them on the landing; they knew that not by the number but by the black-clad woman constable guarding the door. She recognised Singh, one of those 'once seen, never forgotten' people. 'Hi, Talvin,' she greeted him. 'You got the short straw?'

'Nah, Whitney. I'm popular, that's all. This is DS Neville, she's new to the division.'

The two women exchanged nods, then the constable stepped to one side. 'In there,' she said. 'Forrest, my oppo's with the girl from the law firm and the meter reader. He's seriously pissed off with us, by the way, for makin' him hang on.'

'Tough luck on him,' Singh observed. 'We'd be pissed off with you if you hadn't.'

He stood aside to make way for his sergeant, but she nodded to him to take the lead. The windowless hallway was lit by a halogen ceiling fitment, and there were four doors leading off it. Only one was open, so he headed for it, to find himself in a sitting room.

'About fuckin' time,' the meter reader barked as the DC's shadow fell on the floor; he fell silent as he saw what had cast it.

'Sorry sir,' the man-mountain said. 'But from what we've been told this might be a crime scene. You're standing in it, so if we decide that it is, you're not leaving without giving us a statement and a DNA sample.'

'Now wait a minute,' the man protested.

'No, sir.' Neville cut him off. 'You wait, please, for as many minutes as it takes.' She turned to the room's other occupants, a girl who looked to be in her early twenties, and the second uniform, a stocky man whose tunic namebadge identified him as PC Wood. She blinked. 'Whitney called you Forrest. That is a nickname, isn't it?'

'No such luck,' he replied. 'It's for real: my nickname's "Plank". My dad was a comedian, but at least he put a second "r" in Forrest. Great name for a Woodentop, eh?'

'You are blessed.' She turned to the girl. 'And you are?' she asked.

'Tilda Trotter, from the Lesser and Syme property department.'

'Lesser and Syme?'

'Solicitors. The owner's our client.'

'But he's not the occupant?'

'No. He lives somewhere else.'

'So who is the occupant?'

'I don't actually know. This isn't one of my files usually, but I'm the junior staff member. My boss told me to come along and let this man in, that was all.'

Singh looked at the meter reader. 'Who pays the bill?' he asked.

'Search me, mate. Ah just read them.'

'We pay it,' Tilda Trotter volunteered. 'Or rather we pay it on the client's behalf. He picks up all the utility bills, and the rates.'

As she spoke, Neville glanced around the room. The flat had central heating, and a log-effect gas fire for back-up. There was a vase on the sideboard; it held flowers but they were withered and drooping. Copies of the *Daily Record* and *Hello* magazine lay on a coffee table positioned between a wall-mounted television and a cream fabric sofa, which was matched by a single armchair.

She picked up the newspaper and saw that it was three weeks and one day old. She dropped it and her eye moved on to a small side table. It was placed on the far side of the chair from where she was standing, and on it there lay an ashtray, a pack of menthol cigarettes and a lighter that could have been taken for gold, but for the pale patches where use had worn away the plating. She stepped round and peered into the ashtray; it held half a dozen white filter-tipped butts, each with traces of lipstick.

'Whoever lived here left in a hurry,' she said. 'She didn't take her fags or lighter.'

53

'Not good,' Tarvil murmured. 'Where is it?' he asked PC Wood.

'The door facing you in the hall.'

He nodded and headed for it.

'Hold on,' his DS called out. 'We don't want to piss off the CSIs, if they need to come in here. You got overshoes and gloves?'

'You're right, boss,' he conceded. 'Yes, I always carry them.'

Since he seemed to take up much of the available space, Neville waited until he had donned the sterile coverings before putting hers on. When she was ready, she opened the door and led the way into the kitchen.

'Bloody hell!' she exclaimed, as she saw what was inside.

'I couldn't have put it better,' Singh agreed.

The fitted units were modern and expensive, and the walls were tiled, white with a yellow flower motif. Above the sink, which faced the door, a rusty red fan shape spread out.

'Tell me someone's been shaking a ketchup bottle with a dodgy top,' the DC murmured.

'I wish I could,' Neville replied quietly.

She moved carefully around the small table in the centre of the room, then stopped in her tracks. The stains ran across the sink, down the front of the unit that housed it and into a pool, a thick reddish-brown pool, of something congealed and dried. There were splatters and smears all around, and indications of someone, something, having been dragged.

'Mr Mackenzie was right.'

'How?' the DS asked.

'This is more than a cut finger.'

'So let's get out.'

As they backed out, surveying the scene from the doorway

once more, Singh pointed to a broad-bladed cleaver, lying in the floor next to the mass of blood. 'Do you think that might have been used?' he asked.

'We'll let other people tell us that,' Neville replied. 'Plank,' she called to the PC, 'get on the radio and ask for SOCO attendance here, right away.' She had barely finished before the constable was speaking into his handset.

'Should we empty the place?'

She answered DC Singh's question with a shake of her head. 'Not yet, Talvin. Let those two stay where they are, but go nowhere else in the flat.' She opened the door next to the kitchen. 'Bathroom,' she peered inside. There were more bloodstains around the small basin and a blue towel lay on the wooden floor.

Singh looked over her shoulder. 'Those boards, they're rough, not sanded or stained. There's been a carpet here.'

'You're right,' she agreed. 'Stapled to the floor.' She knelt and looked closely at a metal fastening twisted as if something had been wrenched loose. There were fibres attached. 'Purple,' she murmured.

'So who's the victim?' Singh mused. 'The householder?'

'Why are you assuming there's only one? I've seen domestic homicides that looked just like this. The husband could have done the wife, disposed of her body and disappeared.'

'Take a look behind the door,' he replied, pointing. 'That row of coat hooks. There are four garments on it, they're all female and they're all much the same size.'

The sergeant winced, knowing that she had missed the obvious. 'You're right, of course. Christ, I have been away from the job for a long time. Keep on watching my back, Talvin, will you?'

'You got it,' he rumbled.

'So who is the woman . . . was, I should say?' She looked at the door for a few seconds, frowning. 'All the indications are that the place has been empty for a while, unread meter, dead flowers in the vase. I'm sure that when we look in the fridge we'll find milk that's at least a couple of weeks past its sell-by. And one other thing: where's the mail?'

She led the way back into the living room. 'Ms Trotter,' she called out. 'When you entered the flat, were there any letters behind the door?'

'Yes,' the girl said. 'I gathered them up. They're on the coffee table there.'

Singh picked up the handful of mail, and began to flick through it. 'Most of this is the usual junk,' he muttered, 'addressed to "The Householder", that's all, but, hold on, here's one . . . and another.' He held up two envelopes and put the others back on the table.

'Let's see them, please.'

He handed them over, impressed by his new sergeant's courtesy. He was used to orders, not requests.

'I. Spreckley,' she read aloud, from the first, then ripped it open. 'Bank statement. It's a current account and it's well in credit.' She paused as she studied it. 'Okay, she's over sixty, 'cos there's a pension credit here. Plus, she's claiming housing benefit.'

'She does?' Tilda Trotter, who was close enough to overhear her, exclaimed. 'She lives here rent-free.'

'Then let's hope her sins haven't found her out,' Neville muttered as she opened the second envelope. 'Miss Isobella Spreckley,' she announced. 'This one's from the NHS; an appointment under the breast cancer screening programme. Miss,' she repeated, then crossed to the fireplace, and picked up a framed photograph.

It was creased beneath the glass, as if it had been well-handled in its lifetime, and its colour had faded somewhat, lending it a pale yellow veneer. It showed a beach scene, and a woman in her thirties, dark-haired, full-bodied and not unattractive, with her arms around two boys, the older of whom could have been no more than ten. There was a clear resemblance between the trio; *mother and sons, for sure*, she thought.

'If this is Miss Spreckley . . . I wonder who these two are and where they are now.'

'And if they know where she is,' Singh added.

The DS barely heard him, for she was staring hard at the images. 'Maybe we know,' she said. 'This photo has to be thirty years old at least. Sixty-something, female, stocky build, had children. Tarvil, have you read the file on that body that was washed up a week ago? I'm not saying it's her, but she's definitely a candidate.'

Ten

'Why are you calling me, David?' Mario McGuire asked. He was in his car, with his wife in the back, beside their baby, in his egg-like seat. He had pulled into a layby when his phone had sounded.

'Because Mary Chambers is unavailable,' Mackenzie replied, his voice amplified by the Bluetooth system, 'and I need to report this further up the line. You're the ACC Crime.'

'So what do you want to tell me?'

'It's more a case of asking you, sir. I'd like to know whether you're happy about Neville having called out the bloody A team to what turned out to be a potential crime scene in Caledonian Crescent without reference to her senior officer.'

'Why should I not be happy? And why are you not?'

'I sent her down there,' he said, indignantly. 'She should have reported back to me first.'

'Why?'

'Because the householder appears to be missing, there's a possibility that she might be the Cramond Island body, and I'm the senior investigating officer on that case.'

'So I noticed when you held that press briefing. It would have been nice of you to tell Sammy Pye first.'

'With respect, I don't have to, sir. He reports to me, directly. So does DS Neville, when McGurk's off duty.'

'With respect to you, David, I don't share that interpretation. You're the CID coordinator for the Edinburgh divisions. That doesn't make you automatically the SIO on all investigations in the city; in fact, it suggests to me that you shouldn't be SIO on any. Did you give Karen a specific instruction to take no action without your approval?'

'No,' Mackenzie snapped. 'I told that big Sikh to . . .'

'Hold on a minute!' McGuire retorted, on the edge of losing his temper. 'You told who? What do you call me behind my back? "That big Mick?" or "That big Italian?" After all, in my case you've got a choice.'

'I told Detective Constable Singh . . .'

'That's better, Superintendent,' he said, cooling a little. 'You let the wrong person hear you refer to a junior officer by his religion or race rather than his rank and name, and you'll be beyond any protection.'

'Sorry, sir,' the other man replied, stiffly. 'It won't happen again. But I did tell him that he and Neville should check it out and report back to me.'

'And did they?'

'They did,' he conceded, 'but by that time Neville had called in Forensic Services.'

'On the basis of the details that PC Wood had called in, as you described them to me in your earlier call, I'd have done the same thing. As far as I'm concerned DS Neville had the discretionary authority as the senior officer attending.'

'And to advise DI Pye? Did she have that authority too?'

'Sure she did. For the last five days, Pye and Haddock have been fielding hotline calls from the public on the Cramond

Island case, all of them useless. Karen had potentially important information, and as a police officer she had a clear obligation to pass it on, directly. Blood all over the kitchen of a woman in the right age bracket, who's apparently gone missing? Come on, man, of course she did right. David,' he continued, 'cut to the chase. What's this really about? Don't bullshit me now, out with it.'

Mackenzie's sigh seemed to fill the car. The ACC looked at his wife, via the rear-view mirror and rolled his eyes.

'If you insist. I'm not happy having Detective Sergeant Neville under my command.'

'Actually she isn't,' McGuire pointed out, 'not directly. She reports to Jack McGurk, who's acting DI while Becky Stallings is on maternity leave; you've just acknowledged that yourself. That makes you her two-up boss. That aside, what's your problem with her?'

'I'm not sure she's competent. She's been away from the force for several years. During that time things have moved on, yet she's come straight back in as a detective sergeant and here she is on the ground in what might be a very important investigation.'

'You mean "high-profile investigation", don't you?'

'Well, yes,' Mackenzie concede, 'I suppose so. But that doesn't matter. In my view she should have had a probationary period in uniform and retraining before she was let anywhere near a CID office. To be honest, I don't understand why Mary Chambers didn't insist on it when she was interviewed.'

'Chief Superintendent Chambers wasn't there when Neville was interviewed,' the ACC said quietly. In the mirror, he saw his wife wince. 'She was on holiday. I did the board myself and I took the provisional decision to put her straight into CID . . . provisional, because in the circumstances, I felt it should be ratified by the chief constable, and it was. So, David, you're questioning my judgement and Maggie Steele's. Is that it?'

The car fell silent, as if Mackenzie was contemplating the ground beneath his feet and the speed at which it was rising up to meet him. 'I'm only expressing my concern,' he replied, 'and voicing an opinion. I meant no disrespect.'

'Fair enough, and I'll accept that because I know your concerns aren't based on Karen's ability at all. Your objection to her is transparent, man. She's Andy Martin's ex-wife; that's your problem. You don't like Andy. That's an open secret. You don't like him and you're concerned that she'll have his ear, and be marking his card about you.'

'No, sir,' Mackenzie protested.

'Oh but "yes, sir". And you're wrong. Karen and Andy have a civilised relationship, but they spend about five minutes a week in each other's company, when he collects the kids and drops them off. In those five minutes, there is no way that they'll share any sensitive policing issues. They're both far too responsible and too professional for idle gossip.'

McGuire paused, then decided that frankness was necessary. 'The sad truth is, David,' he said, 'that you're flattering yourself. You mean nothing to Andy Martin, nothing at all. In the unlikely event that you ever apply for a secondment to his agency, you'll be judged on your record, your performance at interview, and that's all . . . just as Karen was, incidentally. Are we clear on all that?'

'Yes, sir.' The superintendent's hostility was evident, even in those two words.

'Good. Now let's get back to matters in hand, for my Paula is mightily pissed off to be sitting in a layby when we should be at her sister's for lunch. You will call Pye and Neville, please, and tell them that if the blood in that kitchen did belong to Cramond Island woman, the subsequent investigation will be run out of Leith, with Sammy as SIO. Not you, him; that's a direct order from me. He will report to you, yes, and through you to Mary and me, but it's his show and all future public statements, press briefings et cetera, will be down to him.'

'If you insist, sir.' To Paula, it was as if the temperature in the car was growing icier by the second.

'I do, Detective Superintendent, I do. And one other thing, I want you to call Arthur Dorward in Forensic Services and ask him, as a favour to me, to put the DNA analysis of the blood from Caledonian Crescent right to the top of his priority list. I'd like a yes or no on whether it matches that body within twenty-four hours. I trust Karen's instincts, though. I'm damn sure it's her.'

'I prefer evidence to instinct.' As Mackenzie spoke, Paula saw, in the mirror, her husband's eyes flare. She mouthed the word 'No!' to ward off any explosion. 'But,' the superintendent continued, 'I'll call Dorward right away and pass on your instruction.'

McGuire exhaled. 'Fuck me! My request, David, my request. You don't instruct Arthur, you humour him. He's a prickly sod, and when he was one of us, a police officer rather than a central service person, he was often on the wrong side of insubordinate. He's got away with it, though, for twenty years because he's bloody brilliant at his job. This too: the chief constable has a high regard for him. When Stevie Steele, her husband, was killed on duty, Arthur's work led to us catching the guy who did it.'

'I didn't know that.'

'Well, you do now, so ask him gently for a hurry up on the blood from . . .' He paused. 'What's the woman's name? The missing occupant? We do know for sure she's missing, yes? It wouldn't do if she turned out to be up the shops, liked dead flowers and had an accident with a juice carton.'

'She's missing all right. The downstairs neighbour said she hadn't seen her for at least three weeks, and Neville's view is that she doesn't miss anything.'

The ACC laughed. 'She sounds like my Granny McGuire. She knew everything that happened in the whole damn street. What's her name, the vanished householder?'

'Spreckley, Isobella Spreckley.'

'Is there a husband to go to the top of our suspect list?'

'No. She's Miss Spreckley, according to the NHS, and the woman downstairs.'

'Let's hope she's not the late Miss Spreckley, but I fear she is. Let me know the outcome of this, David. Also . . . for fuck's sake, man, lighten up on your subordinates. And lay off Karen. If you put the chief and me in a position where we had to transfer one of you out of the city, don't assume it would be her. So long.'

He hit a button on the steering wheel to kill the call.

'Jesus Christ!' Paula exclaimed. 'What's that man's problem? What's with the attitude?'

'I wish I could be sure,' Mario replied. 'He may just be insecure, coming back into CID after having a breakdown last time he was there. Neil McIlhenney thinks he's jealous of me. I suspect he's jealous of every officer senior to him, and most of his subordinates as well. The bloke thought he was a whizz-kid in Strathclyde, and that us lot through in Edinburgh were just hicks beside him. He's found out that neither of those things are true and he may be having a hard time accepting it.'

'So why's he in that job?'

'Because he is a good detective: when I put him there I didn't appreciate what a bloody awful man-manager he is, that's the trouble. But it's only been a few weeks; there's hope for him yet if Mary Chambers and I point him in the right direction.'

'Let's hope so, but . . .' She was interrupted by a rising wail from the baby chair. 'Damn it! I'd planned it so wee Eamon's next feed wouldn't be due until we got to our Viola's; thanks to Mr bloody Mackenzie he's needing it now. Mario, do you . . .'

'Of course not,' he laughed. 'Eamon comes first. Plug him into the mains and I'll wait till you're done. Your Viola knows the score; she'll understand.'

He leaned back in the driver's seat, smiling as he watched her unbutton her shirt then flip up her bra, to grant the baby access to the milk supply, and knowing that he had never been happier in his life.

His mind had been in neutral, but without warning it slipped back into gear. 'Spreckley,' he murmured. 'That's a name I've heard before.'

He switched off the car's electrics to kill the Bluetooth, and dug his mobile from his pocket. The number of every CID officer from detective sergeant upwards was registered in his contacts. He scrolled through them until he found Neville, K, and called her.

He heard street noise as she answered. 'Karen,' he began, 'Mario McGuire here. Are you still at Caledonian Crescent?'

'Yes, sir. I'm just on my way to re-interview the downstairs neighbour. Am I in the shit?'

'Eh?' he exclaimed. 'Of course not. Why should you be? No, I'm just wondering about something. Other than her name, do you know anything about this missing woman?'

'No. That's why I want to talk to Mrs McConnachie again.

I don't want to start searching through the flat until Mr Dorward says it's clear, and his people have only just got here.'

'That's understood, but based on what you've seen so far, were there any hints about her?'

Phone to ear, Karen thought through the scene upstairs. 'Not really. I could see only one personal item, that was all: a framed photograph of a woman and two boys, kids, primary school age. It wasn't taken recently. The colour was quite faded.'

'Two boys,' McGuire repeated. 'Do something for me, please. Go back up to the flat, take the photo out of the frame and photograph it with your phone, best resolution possible, then email it to me. Use my force address, "accmmcguire at". Can you do that?'

'Right away, sir. Give me two minutes.'

He ended the call then reached behind him for the bag that Paula had filled with Eamon's daily needs, and found his iPad. He switched it on and waited for it to acquire a signal, then checked his email inbox. There were two new messages, one from his opposite number in Aberdeen, the second a forwarded message from the chief constable. While he waited he read both of them, and was in the act of replying to the first, when a musical tone told him that a new message had arrived. As he expected, it was from Karen Neville.

There was an image attachment and a note: 'Sir, I've checked with the nosy neighbour and she says she's certain this is Isabella Spreckley, the missing woman. Younger but definitely her. KN.'

He opened it and found himself looking at the photograph she had described, a woman with two boys. His eyes narrowed; he peered even closer, then swiped the screen to make the copied photograph larger, isolating the female face.

'Well I never,' he whispered.

'Do you know her?' Paula asked, from the back.

'I rather think I do. I can't swear to it, but if I'm right . . .' He pulled the image back to its normal size and held the tablet up. 'See those boys? If I'm right, Bob Skinner and I helped her bury one of them, going on for twenty years ago.'

He turned his attention back to the iPad, and keyed in a line, and a command. When it had been executed his went back to his phone and found another mobile number, from the personal section of his directory. The connection took longer than usual, but eventually he heard it ring, a single beeping sound rather than the British two-tone signal.

When it was answered, the first thing he heard was the sound of a seabird. The second was a familiar voice. 'Mario, forgive me, but what the fuck is it?'

'I'm sorry to break into your weekend, Bob,' he said, 'but I thought you'd want in on this.'

'Time will tell,' Skinner replied. 'You're breaking into my holiday, not just my weekend. I've got to talk on the move, though. Sarah and I are heading for Barcelona soon. Here, love,' McGuire heard him say, 'you drive.'

A car door slammed, then another; an engine barked into life.

'So tell me.'

'Just before you left,' McGuire began, 'Sarah did an autopsy for us.'

'The messy one? Woman with stab wounds and important bits missing? She only gave me the headlines, mind. I asked her not to share the details. What's up? Have you put a name to her yet?'

'Not yet, but . . .' He ran through the story of the morning's events, from the meter reader's discovery to Karen Neville's summoning of the CSI team. 'Everything fits; all my experience, and Karen's, is telling us that Cramond Island woman lived in that flat and died in it too, and that it's her blood that's all over the kitchen.'

'That's my instinct too, from what you've just told me,' Skinner agreed. 'Have you put a name to her?'

'I want you to do that for me,' the ACC said. 'I've just forwarded you a photo from the flat, by email. I want you to tell me who it is.'

'Okay, but I'll need to end this call. I'll open it, if I can, and get back to you.'

The ACC's phone went dead. He pocketed it and restarted the car, letting the Bluetooth take over. In the back seat, Paula was putting everything back in place while propping Eamon against her shoulder. The baby burped, gently, and regurgitated a quantity of sweet-smelling milk. 'Clever lad,' his father exclaimed, just as the sound of Jimmy Buffett and 'Margaritaville' sounded from the speakers.

Mario accepted the call. 'Well?' he asked quietly. 'Am I right?'

'You surely are,' Skinner told him. 'Assuming that you get a DNA match to the body, it seems that some bugger has done for Bella Watson.'

Eleven

Bella Watson!

That was a name from the past, and one that I'd hoped would stay there. On the other hand, I reasoned, if Mario and I were right in our shared hunch, then she wasn't going to be part of my future, so no real worries.

Bella's path hadn't crossed mine this century, nor had I even heard word of her. The last time I'd seen her had been in the lair of one of her men friends, a serious Edinburgh gangster by the name of Tony Manson. He had gone to hell a few years later, whereas Bella, as seemed likely, had gone to Caledonian Crescent, a better neighbourhood altogether.

If I was given to florid comparisons, I might say that Bella Watson had been to homicide in Edinburgh as Mary Mallon was to typhoid in New York. She had two brothers and two sons, and every one of them was a murder victim.

Brother Gavin and son Ryan, who was then aged no more than fifteen and a drug pusher like his uncle, had ripped off a major crime lord, bigger even than Manson, and both had paid the price of their stupidity, age being no mitigating factor with those people.

Brother Billy had set out to avenge them but had found out

that not all gunfights end like *High Noon*.

Son Marlon, a few years later, he had somehow got himself jammed between the proverbial rock and hard place, and wound up squashed.

After my second conversation with Mario, I had been so preoccupied with my thoughts about the Watsons and Spreckleys that I'd said nothing about it to Sarah, and she had left me to it, until we were on the train and halfway to Barcelona.

'Are you going to tell me about those calls?' she asked, eventually. 'All I know is that it was Mario McGuire who rang you, but I couldn't really hear what it was about once the engine started.'

'Yeah, of course,' I said. 'Sorry, love. I should have said before now; not least because you've got a professional interest. It took me completely by surprise, that's all. Mario thinks his people have put a name to that last autopsy you did before we came away, the woman in the water. It looks as if she's someone I used to know.'

I gave her a rundown on the violent life and likely death of Bella Watson.

'What a family!' she exclaimed when I was finished. 'The poor woman. How tragic can you get?'

I nodded. 'Agreed, but don't get the tissues out for Bella. She was the hardest of them all. We were never able to prove that she sent Billy out to get the crew who killed Gavin and Ryan, but I'm quite sure that she did.'

'A real Ma Barker, from what you're saying. What about Mr Watson?'

'He left them to get on with it.' I paused. 'No, that's not being quite fair to him. He was a straight guy, and didn't like what was going on. Eventually Gavin put a gun to his head and told him to get out of town. Most people, me among them, thought he was dead, but he showed up at Marlon's funeral. On the day, that affected Bella more than anything else.

'It was a bizarre event, that funeral,' I recalled. 'There weren't enough men there to take all the cords of the coffin; Jeez, there were no men left in the fucking family by that time. Mario and I, we'd gone along out of duty, no more, and we wound up helping bury the poor lad. It was surreal, with Tony Manson, the gangster Bella was involved with, and me at either end of the grave, lowering him down. I'll never forget the look on Manson's face. He was a real swine, but that day he showed me that he had a human side. He went the same way in the end.'

'Did you go to his funeral?' she asked.

'Tony's? No chance. I did solve his murder, though.'

'Did I do the autopsy? I can't remember.'

I laughed. 'No, love, you were too busy at the time, having James Andrew.'

'That's right! I do remember now; I'd forgotten the name, that was all. You showed me the photographs when I was in the Simpson Maternity Unit and I showed you how I thought he'd been killed. I told you that when you found the killer he'd have scratch marks on his wrist from where the victim had resisted him, trying to stop the last knife thrust.'

'And you were right, as it turned out.'

'They won't find any marks like that on whoever killed this woman,' she pointed out. 'He had her restrained and stabbed her from behind, over and over again, until he hit the spot.'

I've been a cop for going on thirty years and for most of that time, a detective. I've known the aftermath of violence, many, many times, far more often than has been good for me, so that now, when I see it, or when it's described to me as Sarah did then, it's as if I'm right there at the crime scene watching it happen.

'I don't get this, you know,' I told her. I wasn't puzzled by the manner of the murder, but by its motive.

'What's not to get?'

'Why would anyone want to kill Bella Watson now? Once upon a time, sure, when she was at the heart of the action and every bit as bad as her two brothers, it wouldn't have surprised me, but now, with her well into her sixties, it does. Back then her enemies would have filled a good-sized pub, but today most of them are dead and those that aren't are decrepit. She's been living quietly since her younger son died . . . and trust me, if she hadn't been, I'd have known about it one way or another.'

'Perhaps it was just a random attack,' Sarah suggested.

'After which the body was stripped of any identification and dumped in the Forth? That's more than a wee bit doubtful in my experience . . . but then again I'm not part of the investigation. I'm sure that Mario only involved me so that I could confirm what he suspected.'

It was her turn to laugh. 'Don't kid yourself. He knew it would get your juices flowing.'

She had a point, but . . . 'If that's so, it won't do him any good. It's Maggie's force now, not mine, so I can't, I won't get involved.'

I really did believe that at the time.

Twelve

'I'm glad you're on your own, dear,' Mrs McConnochie said, as she came back into her living room carrying a tray, laden with a cafétière, two cups in their saucers, a sugar bowl, a milk jug and a plate of biscuits. She may have caught a frown on Karen Neville's face for she continued, 'I have nothing against Indian people, mind. I knew his mother when they lived here, remember, a very nice woman. It's just that yon Tarvil is so big it would have been a tight squeeze to fit us all into this wee room.'

The detective sergeant smiled and replied, 'Of course. He is a family-size unit, isn't he.'

She waited while her hostess poured the coffee, and took a chocolate biscuit when it was offered.

'Well, dear,' the elderly lady began, once she had settled herself into her armchair, 'how can I help you?'

'By telling me as much as you know about the lady upstairs.'

'Of course, dear. What's happened to her?'

Karen longed to tell her that her proper title was Detective Sergeant, but the coffee was light years better than the crap in the CID room, and she was hoping for a refill, so she held her tongue. 'Nothing, we hope, but she seems to be missing.'

Mrs McConnochie ventured a small conspiratorial smile. 'She hasn't done a moonlight, has she? Were those sheriff's officers at her door?'

'No, no,' Neville assured her, 'nothing as serious as that.' She decided to volunteer some information. 'The man's a meter reader. Miss Spreckley's hasn't been read for over a year and it has to be done annually.'

'And the young woman?'

'She's from the law firm that factors the flat.'

The neighbour's eyebrows rose. 'You mean Bella doesn't own it? Well, fancy that! She told me that she did, the deceitful besom.'

'You can forgive her that one,' the DS said. 'She lives there rent-free.'

'Oh, she has a life-rent, does she? That's different.' Clearly, the old Scots legal term carried weight with Mrs McConnochie.

'How long has she been there?' She had put the same question to the girl from the law firm, only to find that she had been told nothing beyond the information she had needed for her weekend task.

'Oh, quite a long time; maybe not as much as ten years, but not far short of it.' The answer was followed by a question. 'If Bella doesn't own the flat, then who does?'

'I have no idea,' Neville replied, truthfully. 'A client of the law firm, that's all I've been told. I was half hoping you might be able to tell me that, otherwise I'll probably have to wait until Monday to find out.'

'It's important then?'

'Not necessarily, but . . .'

'Ah, so you do think something's happened to her.'

Bloody hell, Karen thought. *How stale am I? I'm supposed to be questioning this old bat, but it's the other way around.*

She yielded. 'We can't say that for certain, but it's a possibility.'

Mrs McConnochie's tight smile was more than a little smug. 'And maybe a little more than that, dear, yes? I watch television; *Silent Witness* is one of my favourites. When I had a look upstairs I saw people on the landing putting on those white paper suits, and I know what that means.'

'All it means,' the DS assured her, defensively, 'I promise you, is that we need to check some things. I'd love to tell you more, but I'm not allowed to.'

'And far be it from me to get you into trouble, my dear. Would you like some more coffee?'

'Yes, please.'

'And another biscuit?'

'Yes please. Do you and Miss Spreckley ever have coffee together?' she asked, in a near-desperate attempt to regain the initiative.

'Yes, but not regularly; I invite her in occasionally, but she never seems to return my hospitality. As a matter of fact, the only times I've ever been in her flat were when I've run out of milk and the shops have been closed.'

I'll bet you had plenty in the fridge, Karen thought.

'From what I was able to see, it's very nice upstairs. Whoever does own the place spent a lot of money on it before Bella moved in. I remember it well, the joiners, painters, plumbers, carpet fitters all coming and going. They made a lot of noise . . . not that I complained, mind you. Bella doesn't, though; she's very quiet.'

'And did she,' *Damn it!* 'does she, live alone, yes?'

'Oh yes.' The old lady's smirk told Karen that she had picked up on her faux pas. 'There's no man involved, if that's what you mean. I've never seen any gentlemen callers, not of that sort anyway, in all the time she's been here. In fact she very rarely had visitors.'

'Has she ever spoken to you about family?'

'No. Not in any detail. She did mention a sister once, and a niece. That's right,' she exclaimed, with a flash of recollection, 'there was a girl came to visit her, with a toddler in a pushchair. I had to let them in as the lassie was like you two were earlier, not knowing which button to push. She asked me where her Auntie Bella lived.'

'When would that have been? Do you remember?'

'It was this year some time, and it had been snowing; maybe February, that would be right. Oh yes, and there was a man. He came to pick them up; I'd to let him in too. A rough-looking chap he was, I didn't like the look of him. He didn't even thank me when I let him in and told him where to go.' She paused. 'Here, you don't think that he could have been involved, do you? Involved in whatever's happened to poor Bella, that is.'

Karen finished her second cup of coffee, ignoring the leap to conclusions. 'At this moment, Mrs McConnochie, I don't think anything. But when I can see things a bit more clearly, if I do need more information, then I promise, you'll be the first person I'll ask.'

Thirteen

'Do you know your trouble, David?' Cheryl Mackenzie challenged her husband. 'In your eyes, everyone is always messing you about, or out to get you. You've always been like that, and I don't believe you'll ever change.'

'What the fuck do you mean by that?' he shouted, spinning round in his chair to glare at her, his chin jutting out in a gesture that signalled sheer aggression.

'You know bloody well!' she yelled back, then paused, for second thoughts. 'But maybe you don't. I was going to say, "Just listen to yourself," but why would you do that when you never listen to anyone else?'

'That's a laugh,' David Mackenzie snapped. 'I've got no choice but to listen to you.'

'In that case, I'll carry on,' she shot back. 'You've been sitting there all day, pretending to watch the football, but really you've been brooding, quietly boiling away. I don't know what the ACC said to you yesterday, but whatever it was you've been in a foul mood ever since. It makes me glad the kids are at my mother's and not in your way. Well, do you know what? I've had enough of it.'

'Enough of what!'

'You!' she shouted. 'I've had enough of you and these bloody grudges you carry all the time. Even when we were through in Strathclyde, and your career was going well, you were the same. You could see slights where none existed, and you decided that your colleagues were jealous of you when they didn't actually give a damn.'

'You're making this up,' he said, scornfully.

'Am I? Do you remember Willie Crichton, that DI you worked with in Paisley for a while? Of course you do,' she went on, not waiting for a response. 'You never forget an enemy. Remember that police charity night we went to in the Hilton Hotel? No, probably you don't,' she conceded, 'because you got completely trousered at it. I was dancing with Willie at one point while you were leering down the tits of some young WPC, and he asked me, straight out, what he'd ever done to make you hate him. The really terrible thing was, I knew.'

'I'm glad somebody does, for I don't know what the fuck you're on about.'

'Oh no? Does that mean you've forgotten about the case you worked on where Willie was asked to give evidence for the Crown and you weren't?'

'Oh, that one,' Mackenzie muttered, his face darkening even further.

'Yes, that one. You went on about it for months, accusing him of brown-nosing McMinn, the chief superintendent, the deputy fiscal, and everyone up to the master of his Masonic bloody lodge.'

'He did too,' he growled.

'Like hell he did. You weren't called as a witness because you were off with man flu on the day when you were supposed to be interviewing the guy you'd arrested and Willie had to sit in for you.'

'That's bollocks.'

'No, it's the truth,' Cheryl insisted. 'I know it is because you were so angry about it, you even convinced me you'd been stitched up. I went to see Mr McMinn, and asked him why. He was very nice about it, when he might not have been. He sat me down and he explained what had happened. He even showed me the log of that investigation.'

Mackenzie stared at her wide-eyed. 'You . . .' he gasped, '. . . you did that? You fucking idiot!' he screamed, suddenly. 'I wondered why I was transferred to fucking Coatbridge out of the blue. Now I know.'

'Yes, now you know,' she snapped. 'And you weren't there long before everybody there was against you too. I was so happy when you met Bob Skinner, and he offered you a job in Edinburgh on his drugs squad. I thought that in a smaller force running your own section, you'd get over all that aggro inside you.

'But you didn't, no, not you. You were hardly here before you were complaining about that man Martin muscling in on one of your investigations. And that was nonsense too, because at the end of the day you got the collar and the glory that went with it.

'But as usual, that wasn't enough, so you took to the drink, big time. Skinner could have got rid of you then, but instead he gave you a second chance . . . and a promotion not much later. But in your eyes he was doing you down as well, by keeping you out of CID.'

'And he fucking was!' he hissed.

'Is that right? In that case you should be happy now that he's gone, and the new regime have put you back in there, as number two in the whole department.

'But are you? No chance; you're back to moaning and bitching about your senior officers, after only a few weeks. You know what you are, David? You're bloody paranoid, man. You need help.'

'Well, I won't fucking get it here, will I!' he roared, leaping from his chair, and leaning over her, so close that she pressed herself backwards, away from him.

'Is it too much to ask,' he bellowed, 'that you should be on my side, just this fucking once, when that fucking thick Paddy Eye-tie gorilla McGuire is trying to tell me how to do my fucking job, and threatening me with fucking Hawick if I don't do it his way? Well? Is it?'

She tried to push him away. At first he resisted, but finally, just as she began to feel real fear, not for the first time in their marriage, he straightened up.

'There has never been a time,' she told him, very quietly, 'when I have not been on your side. But you have to change or I will go to Chief Constable Steele and tell her I think you need psychiatric evaluation. I'm not going to sit and watch you destroy yourself, and me, and the children, David; I'm just not going to do it!'

As she looked at him she saw all the rigidity go out of his body, saw him relax, saw a strange smile spread across his face.

'You're absolutely right, Cheryl,' he murmured. 'You're not.'

Fourteen

'It's confirmed?' Sammy Pye said, in anticipation, with his mobile pressed against his ear.

'Yes,' Karen Neville told him. 'My missing person's become your homicide, and you're the senior investigating officer, by order of Detective Superintendent Mackenzie.'

'So he told me yesterday. There's an about-face for you. I'd never heard someone grit his teeth over the phone, but I'll swear he did. I wonder what came over him.'

'Are you kidding? I think we could both come up with the right answer for that one. Dark curly hair, become a dad recently?'

Pye smiled. 'Probably. Here, you don't have a problem with me being SIO do you, Karen?'

'Hell no. You inspector, me sergeant. Besides, this might turn out to be an overtime job and I'm not in a position to do much of that, as you know. It's much better that you lead and I give you what help I can, with Jack McGurk's approval, of course. He is my boss, after all.'

'That's fair enough; I'll square anything I need from you with him. What do you know, that I need to?'

'I was in the middle of typing up a summary when Forensic

Services called to confirm that the blood in the flat came from Cramond Island woman, now known to be Isabella Spreckley or Watson.'

'Hold on a minute,' the DI said, his tone cautious. 'Do we really know for sure that it's her?'

'One hundred per cent? We don't, not without a familial DNA match, and we've got no way of getting one. However,' she paused, and he could hear satisfaction in her voice, 'I have rousted out her medical records from the NHS. They tell me that she had her appendix out when she was forty-two, and that she had an abdominal aortic aneurysm, a condition that's one-third less common in women than men. It was being monitored by the vascular department at the Royal Infirmary. The partial remains in the morgue tick both those boxes. Do you have any reasonable doubt left?'

'No,' he conceded, 'I'm convinced. What's your summary going to say?'

'That we've interviewed all the neighbours on that stair. It seems that Miss Spreckley kept herself very much to herself. The only one who was on anything more than nodding terms was Mrs McConnochie, who lived below. If you met her you'd think it would be impossible to keep secrets from her, but Miss Spreckley managed, mostly. For example, she told the old dear she had a sister, and a niece, even though she hasn't.'

'How do you know?'

'Tarvil checked this morning with the Registrar General's office.'

'On a Sunday?'

'He's got a cousin works there. He went in and ran a trace for him. Miss Spreckley had two brothers, but no sisters. She was visited, though, Mrs McConnachie could tell us that much.'

'But not by whom? Could she tell you that?'

'It was a young woman with a kid, she said. She called the victim "Auntie Bella" when Mrs M opened the street door for her and asked her who she wanted. There was a man too; he arrived later and he was definitely not to her taste. "Rough looking," she said.'

'Is that as detailed as she could get?'

'I didn't press her. Now we know for sure what we're dealing with I can go back and try to get better descriptions of them both.'

'You could get Tarvil to do it,' Pye suggested.

'I don't think she'd be too comfortable with DC Singh. It's got nothing to do with race,' Karen explained. 'She's of a certain age, and I think she feels more comfortable with a woman than a man.'

'Understood. You've just described Ruth's granny.'

His wife frowned at him; they had been in the kitchen when his mobile had rung. 'What's my granny been up to?' she murmured.

'She got caught fire-bombing the mosque.'

'Sammy!'

'Joking, joking,' he laughed. 'It was only shoplifting.'

'Sammy!'

'It's okay; she did a runner and they never caught her. Sorry, Karen,' he said, into the mobile. 'My wife's very protective of the old biddy. As for your lady,' he continued, 'there's something else she didn't get out of Miss Spreckey, nor have you from her records. She didn't have those kids out of wedlock. She was married and her husband's name was Watson.'

'How do you know that?' Neville asked, puzzled.

'ACC McGuire told me.'

'He did? That explains a lot. He phoned me when I was at the scene yesterday, after Mr Mackenzie had briefed him. When I told them there was a picture on her mantelpiece, he asked me to copy it and send it to him. Are you saying he knew her?'

'Not just him alone; Bob Skinner knew her as well, from quite a way back. Your ex did too, so big Mario said.'

'Did he? Andy's never mentioned anybody of that name that I recall . . . either Spreckley or Watson.'

'Like I said, it was a while ago. Before our time on the force.'

'Then she must have been pretty special if they all still remember her.'

'She was part of a special family, from what the boss said. But he didn't volunteer anything. He said he'd brief me once the match was made. Were there any links to her past in the flat?'

'Sammy,' she replied, 'there were hardly any links to her present. She kept official correspondence, pension, NHS stuff, but that was all. No,' she said, contradicting herself immediately, 'she did keep some Christmas cards. There were only three of them. One was signed "Susie"; that's all, just "Susie". Another was signed simply "Vicky, Patrick and baby Susan", and the third said "Merry Christmas, Lennie". Whoever he is, he's really extravagant with words by comparison with the rest.'

'There were no envelopes, I suppose.'

'No, sorry.'

'Are the cards bagged?'

'Of course, but not dusted for prints, if that's what you were going to ask next.'

'It was,' Pye conceded. 'I'll get moving on that. Maybe they'll tell us who these people are. Every TV cop show hammers home to you at some point that nine times out of ten the victim knows the killer, but it's bloody true in the real world as well.' He sighed. 'I'm not surprised you're fine with me being SIO. So far we've got a real information vacuum; I'll need to shake some loose, if I can. Maybe the ACC will have some thoughts for me. You got anything else?'

'Only another knowledge gap, I'm afraid. Isabella was living rent-free, all bills paid, but I still don't know who her benefactor was.'

'Could it have been this mysterious non-sister, "Susie", if that was her that sent the Christmas card?'

'Possibly, but if we assume that Vicky's the so-called niece and her daughter, surely she'd have known which flat it was that her mother owned. I'll find out tomorrow, though. I have an appointment with the law firm that looks after it. They'll be able to tell me straight away.'

'Let's hope so, otherwise Mario McGuire's done me no favours by putting me in charge of this thing. It's got high profile written all over it. Great if you get a result. A ticket back to uniform if you don't.'

Fifteen

I'd taken a bit of a punt on the Barcelona hotel, but it paid off. Placa Reial is one of the city's night-time highlights and our room overlooked it. As a bonus, the chef turned out to be Michelin class. We ate there on the Saturday night, had a couple of schnapps in the square outside, then slept like logs until the sun woke us next morning, in time for a leisurely breakfast and a day spent on the tourist trail. It ended with a visit to Camp Nou, the great amphitheatre that's home to FC Barcelona. I'd neglected to tell Sarah that there was an early evening match on, but she took the news pretty well.

We found a taxi outside the ground more easily than I'd anticipated, and didn't get caught up in the post-match traffic, so we made it back to the hotel in good time. I'd have been happy to give the chef another turn, had Sarah not seen a restaurant called Los Caracoles on a television food show. When she discovered that it was two minutes' walk from our hotel and stayed open late, there was no holding her.

We even enjoyed the flight home next day, an anonymous couple on the world's most controversial airline, if not its favourite. We'd gone budget for three reasons; the cost (once a Scot always a Scot), the fact that it was a direct flight and the greater chance that nobody would know us.

We could have gone through Heathrow or City, but I can't board a flight to London these days without being hailed by someone or other, even people I barely know. With my marriage to Aileen having ended in a blaze of newspaper headlines, I wasn't keen to be spotted on the shuttle with my other ex-wife, in case that found its way into the tabloids as well.

It wasn't until mid-afternoon, when we were in an Edinburgh taxi, en route for Sarah's place where I'd left my car, that I switched on my mobile. I'd called the office in Glasgow first thing in the morning, to let my exec know that I'd be out of touch during the day, and so I was expecting most of the voicemail calls that were there when I checked. Pure tedium, nearly all of them, issues that could have been dealt with further down the chain of command, but that's what happens when you're new in post as a chief constable: your subordinates don't know you quite well enough to take a chance.

I'd barely finished sighing over the complex issue of the most efficient management of the available traffic cars in Argyll and Clyde, when the one I wasn't expecting popped up.

I confess that I was having a hard time dealing with the emotional wrench of leaving Edinburgh. I had thought everything through before accepting the Strathclyde job, and I'd been satisfied that I was doing the right thing. The time had come to move on, I'd persuaded myself, to give my colleagues, protégés and friends the opportunity to get one more promotion on their dockets before the Scottish police forces were merged into one, so that they would be as well placed as possible in the shake-up that would follow.

I'd done what I'd been sure was the right thing, but that didn't stop me being desperately homesick every time I walked through the door of HQ in Glasgow, missing my old office in one of the capital city's ugliest buildings, missing the streets I'd stalked for so many years, missing everyone, up to and including Maisie, the waitress in the senior officers' dining room, who'd served Sarah and me lunch on the day that we'd had the heart-to-heart that blew away the smoke that had been obscuring my view of her and led, very shortly afterwards, to us getting back together.

With all that emotional baggage, my stomach flipped a little when I heard Mario McGuire say, in his most serious professional tone, 'Bob, can you call me, soon as possible. A name's come up in what's now officially the Bella Watson homicide investigation, and before I let anyone pursue it, I need to talk to you.'

Sixteen

Mario McGuire, who had a dislike of the unexpected that he tried to keep to himself, looked up with a flash of annoyance at the sound of knuckles rapping on his door. If it had been the chief constable, he would have been fine about it, but hers was a much lighter touch, and in any event she would probably have walked straight in.

He frowned as he pressed the button that activated the green light in the corridor, staring at the door as it opened . . . and Bob Skinner stepped into the office, dressed as informally as the ACC had ever seen him, in light cotton cargo trousers and an FC Barcelona top.

He was grinning. 'It feels strange to see you in my old room,' he said. 'In a nice way, though,' he added. 'Sorry if I'm interrupting a private moment, chum, but your new secretary said there was nobody with you.'

'No worries, boss.' McGuire chuckled. 'Listen to me with the "boss": force of habit. Actually, I was dozing, to tell you the truth.'

'I know that, otherwise you'd have spotted me coming up the drive. That's why I always liked this room, you can see all the comings and goings from that window. How are Paula and wee

Eamón, by the way? I take it he's the reason you're nodding off on the job.'

'You take it right. He's turning night into day. But I don't care. I never thought I'd be a dad.'

'Don't miss a moment. I never thought I'd get a second chance, after Myra died. It makes your life complete.'

'You don't need to tell me that,' McGuire assured him, 'or Paula either. She's really funny, you know. She's got a wardrobe full of designer clothes and now her boobs are so big she doesn't see herself getting into any of them ever again. Does she care? Not a bit of it. She slops about in my T-shirts and looks great in them.'

'They'll fit her again. Sarah was the same, both times, but she was back to her normal cup size pretty soon after she stopped feeding.' He laughed. 'Hey, that's a hell of a subject for two chief police officers, is it not?'

'True,' the ACC agreed. 'Hey,' he exclaimed, suddenly, 'when I called you on Saturday: you and Sarah, in Spain? Bob, if you don't mind me asking, what the hell's going on?'

Skinner shot him a quick, self-conscious, sideways look, and a small almost shy smile. 'We are,' he replied. 'Sarah and me. It's early days yet and we're keeping our own houses, but yeah, we're back together, sort of. We're keeping our heads down, obviously, but we're both pretty happy about it, and needless to say, so are the kids.'

'How about the big kid?'

'Alex? She's good with it too. She's in much the same sort of relationship herself with Andy, for now at least, until she finally decides to make me a grandfather . . . although I suspect that one of my boys might beat her to it, and Mark's only just starting high school.'

He stretched some residual stiffness from the flight out of his back, then dropped into a chair that faced across the ACC's desk. 'I got your message. You sounded very businesslike so I thought I'd better come and see you rather than do it over the phone. Sorry about the gear,' he grinned and raised his right foot to display a tan moccasin but no sock. 'I'm hot off the plane.'

'You're lucky it's warm here today. It was chilly for most of last week.'

'The weather hasn't been holding you back, from the sound of your message. So that definitely was old Bella that got washed up, was it?'

McGuire nodded, in confirmation. 'Most of her; there's not a chance of us ever finding the rest.'

'And you know that she was killed in her house?'

'Her flat, yes, in Caledonian Crescent.'

'She moved up in the world then,' Skinner observed, 'from that fucking awful street she lived in. You know, Mario, for years I had this mad idea. I was going to advertise mystery tours for Festival visitors, fill up buses, then drive them round some of our worst housing schemes, to show them the conditions that the city council was prepared to tolerate.'

His friend laughed. 'Nice idea, but it would have been a crap career move. Have you always been a closet leftie?' he asked.

'I've never hidden it. I was married to a Labour politician, wasn't I?'

'True . . . but not for long. Anyway, Bella had no choice but to move up. They demolished her street twelve years ago, and there was no "down" from there. We're not sure where she lived in the period after that, before she moved into Caley Crescent.'

'I can't see that mattering,' Skinner said. 'How's the investigation going?'

The other man frowned. 'At this moment, we've got no obvious suspects,' he admitted. 'In fact we know very little about the woman's life in the years since we investigated her son Marlon's murder. It's a gap that I'd like to fill.'

'Why are you talking to me about it? I know that she worked for Tony Manson after that but she was always under the radar as far as we were concerned. I can't help you there.'

'Maybe not, but you know a man who can.'

'I do? How come.'

'Bella didn't own the flat she lived in,' McGuire said, 'but she didn't pay rent on it either. In fact, she didn't pay anything. The council tax, gas, the electric, phone, broadband and cable telly were all taken care of. She wasn't short of cash either; as well as her state pension, she had six hundred quid paid into her bank account every month, not taxable income, but an allowance.

'We only found out this morning who her benefactor was, when Karen Neville spoke to a partner in the law firm that manages the property. It's owned by a company called Dominic Jackson Investments, and they cover all the costs and forward Bella's money too.'

'Dominic Jackson,' Skinner repeated.

'That's right. The name was news to me at first, but it's familiar to you, yes?'

'Of course it is. Dominic Jackson doesn't exist; the name's an alias, set up a long time ago by Tony Manson as an alternative identity for his informally adopted heir, someone you and I both met in extreme circumstances: Lennie Plenderleith.'

'That's right; the team found that out this morning. Are you surprised that Lennie's been looking after the old bat?'

'Now you tell me, I'm not a bit surprised. You know as well

as I do that Bella didn't just work for Tony Manson. With that history, I can see that Lennie should have looked after her.'

'Do you think he might have got fed up with it?' the ACC asked, quietly.

'And had her bumped off?' Skinner exclaimed. 'Not a fucking chance. You're not serious about that, are you? Or do I detect David Mackenzie's steely mind behind the theory?'

'Hell no! Anyway, Mackenzie's warned off; he tried to grab the glory when the body was found, and I had to point out to him a bit forcefully that's not his role. I think he's in the huff. He missed his Monday meeting with Mary Chambers, and I haven't seen him since. But no, I'm not really serious about Lennie being involved, just bouncing the thought off you, that's all.'

'Who are you sending to interview him? Luke Skywalker?'

McGuire chuckled, softly. 'You know his nickname too? Sammy's the obvious choice, only . . .' He paused in mid-sentence. 'He doesn't know Lennie at all; he was just a plod out in East Lothian when he was put away. The truth is, Bob, I was wondering whether you could find some time to brief him on Plenderleith's background, how best to approach him and so on. I know that you've kept in touch with him since he's been inside, so I'm sure Sammy would appreciate any guidance you could give him.'

'I'm sure he would,' Skinner agreed, 'given the level of young Pye's ambition, but even if he walked in there with a neck-lace made out of my pearls of wisdom, in his mind he'd still be a cop interviewing a lifer looking for info on a victim's background. He might also be less ready than us to dismiss him as a suspect.

'Lennie's a very clever guy. He's been studying since he was put away and now he's got degrees and a doctorate in criminal psychology. I'm sure he'd give Pye all the facts he knows, but he might give me more than that.

'You're right, Mario. I have visited him on the inside, more often than you'd suppose. I've always done it on the quiet, to ensure that no other cons ever knew of our meetings. Last thing I wanted was to get him a reputation as a grass.'

'Yes,' McGuire mused. 'I can see how that might put him at risk.'

His former chief smiled. 'I was more concerned about the safety of anyone daft enough to have a go at him. He's been a model prisoner and I'd hate to see a blemish on his record, even if he didn't go looking for it.'

'Are you saying that you'll talk to him yourself if we want?'

'I'm probably insisting on it. It's my call anyway. The service isn't unified yet, Mario. Lennie's in HMP Kilmarnock, and you're required to inform me if you want to send a man into my patch. You've done that and I'm saying no, that I'll take care of it.'

'You'll go and see him? Have you got time for that, Bob? I know how busy you are now.'

'It won't be a problem. I don't need to go all the way to Kilmarnock. He can come and visit me.'

Seventeen

'Thanks, mate,' Sammy Pye said as he took the mug offered to him by his sergeant. 'I need caffeine at the arse end of the day, especially a day like this one.'

'Come on, boss,' Sauce Haddock cajoled him. 'We've made progress.'

'Tell me how, please.'

'For a start, we know who owns Bella Watson's flat, and pays the bills and everything.'

'Sure, but it turns out that he's a lifer. Not only that, I've just been told by the ACC not even to think about interviewing him.'

'Mmm,' the young DS murmured. 'I wonder why that was, and I wonder why it was him that gave us the message. Detective Superintendent Mackenzie's our line manager.'

'Two good questions, but all they do is add to my confusion about this whole fucking business. I've been trying to raise Mackenzie all afternoon, to update him, but he isn't answering either of his phones, landline or mobile.'

'How did Mr McGuire sound when he spoke to you? Was he in "or else" mode, or just his normal self.'

'No, he was reasonably relaxed,' the DI told him. 'He didn't bite me once! When I said we should go and see Plenderleith, he said that the guy isn't detained within our force area, and that he doesn't want to piss off Strathclyde, so he's made separate arrangements for a statement to be taken from him.'

'Would it really piss off Strathclyde if we went into a prison on their patch?' Haddock wondered.

'I wouldn't have thought so, but I wasn't about to argue the point. Also, when he told me that the guy shouldn't be regarded as a suspect without direct evidence that he might be, I didn't get the impression that was open for debate either.'

'Who is he anyway, this man? Did he tell you that much?'

'No, but I Googled him.' Pye grinned. 'It works a lot quicker than the national computer database. "Leonard Plenderleith, aged forty-five, former associate of the late Anthony Manson, allegedly a major figure in the Edinburgh criminal underworld …" I'm quoting here, mind. Tony Manson was more than an alleged villain, just never convicted.' He winked at the DS. 'Just like your bidey-in's grandpa.

'Anyway,' he continued, heading off a riposte, 'Plenderleith was Manson's enforcer. He did time for serious assault and wasn't out long before he was arrested for two murders. The victims were his wife, and a lawyer called Richard Cocozza. There was a third murder charge originally, but the Crown Office dropped that because of lack of evidence. Plus he was convicted of another, in Spain, in his absence. The Spanish agreed that he'd serve his sentence here, concurrently.'

'He sounds like a real psycho,' Haddock said.

'You could say that.'

'Then why is he off limits to our inquiry?'

'His alibi's pretty good, if a prison governor can vouch for his whereabouts,' the DI observed.

'I suppose. But even if he isn't a suspect, if he knew the dead woman, he might be able to help us identify this so-called sister and her family.'

'I made that point to the ACC,' Pye said. 'All he said was that he'd note it. I didn't push that any further either. I know I said earlier that he was relaxed, but I sensed an edge to him.'

'That leaves us sitting on our hands,' the DS complained. 'We have no leads to those people, and asking through the media for them to come forward would make us look daft. We don't have a single line of inquiry.'

'I know.' He took a swig from his mug. 'Now you understand why I need caffeine!'

Eighteen

'Is there any chance he had leave booked in and you've forgotten about it?' Mario McGuire asked the woman seated behind what had been his desk until a few weeks before.

Detective Chief Superintendent Mary Chambers, the formidable head of CID, frowned at him; it was all the reply she felt to be necessary.

He raised a placatory right hand. 'No, of course not; sorry. Then where the fu . . .' he grimaced. 'I can't have a bloody superintendent going AWOL. I'm sorry about this, Mary, I really am.'

'What are you sorry for, boss?' she said. 'It's hardly your fault.'

'I feel as if it is. I installed him as your Edinburgh coordinator.'

Chief Constable Margaret Steele pushed herself off the wall against which she had been leaning. 'We installed him, Mario, not just you. In fact it was more me than you. I didn't want the guy in the Command Corridor any longer, he had a CID background and a hankering to go back there. Yes, there were misgivings but the fact is they were yours and I talked you out of them. But let's not over-dramatise this; we can't raise the man, but for all we know he might be stuck in a traffic jam at Hermiston Gait with a dead battery in his mobile.'

'That's about a hundred to one against, but he could be,' McGuire conceded. 'On the other hand, Mary's contacted all the divisional CID offices and he hasn't visited any of them.' He scratched his chin. 'Of course there is another scenario.' He glanced at the chief. 'I think we all know what that is.'

'I don't,' Chambers said.

'No? Then Bob Skinner must have done a really good job of covering it up. A few years back, David Mackenzie was involved in an armed situation with him and our former colleague, Neil McIlhenney. It got pretty dicey; indeed, it was too much for Mackenzie, for he froze in the middle of it.

'Bob being Bob, he never blamed him, or spoke of it. I only know about it because Neil told me in confidence. Afterwards the man had a breakdown of sorts, and a drink problem went with it. He was touch and go for retirement on health grounds, but the big guy refused to let that happen and pulled him back in.'

'Why would he do that?'

'Because he had recruited him,' McGuire replied, patiently, 'from through the West; he thought he had potential and that he would freshen up our CID operation. He did for a while, until the crisis happened.'

'So Mr Skinner felt he owed him. Is that what you're saying?' the DCS asked.

'It could be,' Steele said. 'It could also be that Bob isn't great at acknowledging his own mistakes.' She winced slightly. 'Forget I said that, both of you. Not because it isn't true, but because it implies that Mackenzie was one, and that isn't proven, not yet. Tell me, Mary,' she went on, 'have you tried to make contact with his wife?'

'Not directly; I rang his home number, obviously, but there was no reply.'

'That's not too surprising,' McGuire said. 'Cheryl Mackenzie works; she's a pharmacist at the Western General Hospital.' He looked at his watch; it showed five twenty. 'She ought to be home now, though.'

'In that case,' Chambers declared, 'I'll give her another call.'

She was about to pick up her phone when it rang. She snatched it from the cradle, impatiently. 'Yes!'

'Sorry to bother you,' a gruff, and almost certainly insincere, voice barked into her ear. 'This is the reception desk. I've got a lady here lookin' for Detective Superintendent Mackenzie. She's got two kids with her as well. I've tried his number, but he's no' in. I've told her that but she'll no' go. She says it's urgent. She's a bit frantic. Can you send somebody down to talk to her?'

'Yes I can,' the DCS replied, 'but first, ask her who she is, what's her relationship with Mr Mackenzie and why she's so keen to see him.'

'All right, give me a minute.' She waited, listening to a mumbled conversation, until the civilian receptionist came back on line. 'She says her name's Mrs Austin, and that she's Superintendent Mackenzie's mother-in-law. She wants to see him because her daughter hasn't been to pick up their children.'

'Does she normally look after them during the day?'

'No, no, it's not today she's talkin' about. She was supposed to pick them up last night, but she never turned up. Mrs Austin tried callin' them last night, she says, until it was too late for her to take the wee ones home. So she put them to bed, took them to the school this morning, then called Mrs Mackenzie at her work to find out where they'd been. But it seems that she hasn't been there all day, and hasn't called in sick either. Do you want me to keep her here, till somebody comes down?'

'No,' Chambers said. 'I want you to have somebody bring her

up to my office, right away.' She replaced the phone and looked up at the chief and the ACC, both of whom were staring at her.

'What's up?' McGuire asked.

'I don't know, but either the Mackenzies have gone off on a second honeymoon without telling anyone, or there is something very seriously wrong.'

Nineteen

'You know, Ray, sometimes I feel as if my life's been stood on its head,' Becky Stallings declared. 'Not that long ago, I was a DI in the Met, with a good record and high up the promotion list; then you turned up in bloody London and look at me now. Still a detective inspector, in bloody Scotland, and up the duff into the bargain.'

Her partner beamed at her. 'Aye, isn't it great? And you look fantastic on it.' He reached out and ruffled her short, dark, grey-flecked hair. 'Quite astonishing.'

'I'm enormous,' she grumbled. 'I never thought I'd get this big this quick. I've got half a dozen dark business suits up in the wardrobe, and they're all about seven sizes too small.'

'You could always go back into uniform,' he ventured, 'then it wouldn't be a problem.'

'You what?' she retorted, loudly. 'I only came up here 'cos I got to stay in CID, remember.'

Ray Wilding nodded. The deal they had made when they realised that they were serious about each other was that if Becky could only transfer to uniform in Edinburgh, he would move south into whatever sergeant job was offered to him.

'I remember,' he conceded. 'But I knew that I was on a winner,' he added, lightly. 'Our CID would never have turned down someone like you, just as there was no chance of the Met putting Neil McIlhenney in a chief super's uniform when he moved down there, not with his record.'

'I will be able to go back, won't I?' Becky asked. 'The new all-Scottish force will be shedding some jobs. Otherwise, why do it?'

'It'll lose civilian jobs, I'm sure. But not even our fucking Justice Secretary would be daft enough to start laying off experienced detective officers. As for why do it, the majority of cops outside the Strathclyde high command couldn't give you a single valid reason.'

'Are you saying that Skinner's for it?'

'The grapevine says he isn't, but he's a pragmatist. He can't stop it, he can't pretend it doesn't exist, so he has no choice but to accept it and carry on.'

Becky eased herself laboriously to her feet. 'Quite a few Germans took the same position back in the thirties,' she muttered, as she wandered off in the general direction of the downstairs toilet.

His eyes were following her, and he was smiling, ever grateful for his good fortune, when the phone rang. He reached across the table by his side and picked it up. 'Stallings Wilding residence,' he announced. 'Ray speaking, I know my place.'

'That's good,' Detective Chief Superintendent Mary Chambers said. 'I won't have to remind you of it.'

He shifted on the couch. 'Gaffer,' he exclaimed. 'This is a surprise. What have I done?'

'Nothing, Raymond, but there's something I want you to do, and it's delicate.'

'When you say "do", d' you mean right now? I've only just got in.'

'I know,' the head of CID conceded, 'and I wouldn't ask, but you're best suited for the job in question.'

Wilding scratched his head, wondering what special skills she imagined that he possessed.

'There's a situation,' she continued. 'One of our people, our senior people, has gone off the radar. That happens, I know, but the complication is that his wife appears to be missing as well.'

He straightened in his seat. 'Who are we talking about?'

'Detective Superintendent Mackenzie.'

If she had been able to see him she might have been irked by the depth of his sceptical frown. 'Are you sure, ma'am? With respect to Mr Mackenzie, he used to be a bit on the . . . let's say the flamboyant side. A wee bit impulsive.'

'I'm aware of that, but we've no reason to believe that Mrs Mackenzie is.'

'And they've both disappeared?'

'Yes.'

'Since when?'

'Neither of them showed up for work today. Mrs Mackenzie was supposed to collect her kids from her mother's last night but she didn't. She was supposed to pick them up this evening, but she didn't turn up for that either. Her mother, Mrs Austin . . . she's with the chief constable as I speak . . . she's going quietly off her head with worry.'

'Has anyone checked the National Lottery? Maybe their numbers came up and they've buggered off. An impromptu second honeymoon up in Gleneagles, something like that.'

'Don't be flippant, Ray. This is serious.'

'Sorry, boss,' Wilding said, reproved.

'It's also very delicate. Tact might not be your strong suit, but of all the people who report to David, you're the one who knows him best, because the two of you worked together before.'

'Exactly, and that's why I know he's an unpredictable bastard.'

'But Cheryl isn't. Her mother's quite adamant that she wouldn't abandon her children. Have you ever met her?'

'Yes I have; twice, at social dos. I must admit she was a bit of a contrast to him; a sensible woman, very nice, not flash at all.'

'What was his attitude to her?' Chambers asked.

'What do you mean?'

'Was he tender towards her, or did he seem to dominate her? Did she seem under his thumb, or did she hold her own?'

'I cannot say, boss. I'm talking about a couple of squad nights out, with drink taken.'

'By Cheryl as well?'

'Now you mention it, no. She was one of the few sober people in the room, both times.' He felt himself becoming impatient. 'Look, ma'am,' he said, 'will you please get to the point. What do you want me to do?'

'Not just me; this is from the chief herself. You're to go to their house and check it out, before any alarm bells get rung. Mackenzie has a history of alcohol abuse. It's possible that he's had a relapse, and that he's on a bender.'

'Not both of them, surely?'

'From what you said that seems unlikely, and not according to Mrs Austin either. But why is Cheryl unobtainable too? I want you to go to their house now, Ray, and take a very quiet, very discreet look around.' She gave him the address.

'On my own?' he asked, as he noted it down.

'Yes. I don't want to draw any attention to this situation until we have to. Just pay them a casual visit.'

'And if nobody answers the door and the place is locked up?'

'Then you'll have the chief constable's authorisation to do whatever's necessary.'

'As in kick the door in?'

'Whatever's necessary, there'll be no comeback, I promise you.'

'My first wife promised me too,' he countered, 'to love and honour me till death did us part. Then she fucked off with a car salesman.'

Chambers chuckled. 'Maybe that's what Mrs Mackenzie's done, and maybe David's out there looking for them. Whatever, we need to find out. If the door's too solid to kick in, should you have to, call me on my mobile and I'll send a car up with a ram.'

'I'd be happier if there was a search warrant in it.'

'We don't know what we're searching for,' the head of CID pointed out. 'I'm all for doing things by the book, but the book that covers this one isn't written yet. Let me know what you find.'

Twenty

Ask me on the record if Lennie Plenderleith is a friend of mine and I'd probably deny it. I'm not sure I'd pass a lie detector test if I did.

I've known him for twenty years, maybe more, since back in the days when he was a gangster's minder, and the most feared young man in Edinburgh. At first I put him in a mental filing cabinet, the one where I kept the names of all the capital city's thugs, boxes to be ticked every time one of then got put away for a worthwhile stretch.

I'm not certain when perception of him began to change, but probably it was after Tony Manson installed him as manager of a pub he owned down Leith way. Over the door it said 'The Milton Vaults', but in the locality it served, and in the Queen Charlotte Street police office, it was known as 'The War Office'.

Its reputation as a rough pub went back for decades, but in the eighties and nineties, it got worse and worse, even after it was acquired by Manson from the previous owner in exchange for the write-off of a large gambling debt. Tony was a career criminal, but of the executive type. He called himself a businessman, and so he was loosely, but those businesses fronted for drugs, prostitution, loan-sharking and other activities.

He had two core skills: he never allowed any chain of evidence to lead to his door, and he never picked a quarrel that he even suspected he might not win. That was why he was able to co-exist in Edinburgh with a man called Perry Holmes, and his brutal and much less subtle younger brother, Alasdair.

If Scotland ever had an undisputed champion of the criminal underworld, it was Perry. In his time he was a feudal overlord of sorts, and his vassals were the likes of Manson, Grandpa McCullough, and others in their fiefdoms in Scotland's cities. His power was based on intellect, money, control of all drugs importation into Scotland, and an utterly ruthless ferocity, demonstrated when necessary by his brother, and a big beast of a man called Johan Kraus.

Those days are long gone. They came to an end when a worm called Billy Spreckley, brother of the newly deceased Bella, finally turned, walking into the Holmes brothers' Edinburgh office and starting a gunfight that was reminiscent of the OK Corral, and left as many people dead, Al Holmes and Billy himself among them. Perry survived for a few years, as a quadriplegic in a wheelchair, still with power and considerable influence, but not quite as much as before, as nature began to fill the vacuum that his limitations had created.

But I digress; back to the War Office. There came a point when the place got so bad that my old gaffer, Alf Stein, the head of CID himself, went to see Tony Manson and had a serious word with him. When Alf had a serious word, you listened, no matter who you were, and he didn't go easy on our local Mr Big. I know because he took me along with him when he did it. My brief was to say nothing, just to be there, and not to smile under any circumstances.

When I was a boy I read Damon Runyon's Broadway stories

from start to finish, over and over again. There's a character in them called Dave the Dude. When he went to a meeting he took a guy with him whose only function was to nod, whenever Dave looked at him and said, 'Yes?'

I was Alf's nod guy at that meeting, so I know that when he told Manson that if he didn't turn the Milton Vaults into the best-behaved pub in Leith then he, Alf, would make sure personally that it burned to the fucking ground with him, Manson, inside it, the message was received, well and truly.

His response was to install his gigantic young driver, gopher and general sidekick as manager. The gambit worked, in double quick time. Lennie laid down his law. He had to make believers of a couple of fools in his first fortnight in the job, and he did it so effectively that pretty soon the Milton Vaults became a place where you could take your granny . . . if she liked a pint.

I dropped in there myself a few times, just to check on the place. Lennie didn't mind. He even offered to give cops a discount, but I told him the chief constable might not be too keen on that.

It was during the chats we had in those days, twenty years ago now, that I first realised that young Plenderleith was more than just a six-foot six-inch mountain of muscle, and that there was a good brain working in there, in spite of everything.

Where Lennie was brought up, in a part of the city that isn't standing any more, kids often missed out on education, and he was one of those. His family background could not have been worse. His mother was a prostitute and his father was her pimp, he told me once, in a moment of frankness.

If only Manson had been sensible enough to keep him in the War Office full-time . . . but he wasn't. He still made use of his physical talents on occasion, and finally, inevitably, on one occasion too many. Lennie was caught in the act of passing on a message from Tony to some idiot who'd upset him and he went away for a few years as a result.

I wasn't involved in his arrest, and I was surprised when it happened, since the big lad was usually very discreet on those assignments. It took another ten years for me to discover that Lennie actually wanted to be caught. He'd got himself married to a woman in the same line of work as his mother, he was miserable, he was desperate, and he wanted to find a way out of the life.

Perth Prison helped him do that, for a few years. It also started to educate him properly. He used his time there to gain the leaving certificate that his background had denied him, and picked up more Higher grade passes than he ever would have at school.

In an ideal world, he'd have gone from the jail straight to the university, but it isn't ideal, is it? Never was, never will be. When Lennie got out, two things happened, one after the other, very quickly. His wife was murdered, and then his old boss was too. Finally, Manson had underestimated some people and it cost him his life. The wife? It was pretty obvious to us at the time that she'd pushed her husband too far.

Lennie could have run, but he didn't; he had something to do first and he did. He tracked down the guys who had killed his benefactor and took them out. But it took him a little too long, for I caught up with him.

An hour later and he'd have been gone. As it was, he tried to go, through me, but there's always someone who has your measure, and I had his . . . just. The Crown made a couple of murder charges stick, and he was sentenced to life. I could have charged him with assault and resisting arrest too, but I figured he had enough scores against his name.

That would have finished most people, but Lennie was philosophical. He saw his stretch, however long it might turn out to be, as free higher education, and he threw himself into Open University courses. The years went by until he had more letters after his name than I have (MA (Hons) QPM, as it happens). He was able to study without the distraction of family visitors, or any other sort, save one. Me.

My first visit was professional. I wanted to ask him about something I was investigating that went back to his old days. But I was so struck by the change in him that I paid him another visit a few months later, and another, and another. I never gave advance warning; I just turned up, unannounced. We never met in general visiting areas either, always in one of the private interview rooms that prisons have available.

Mostly we talked about his studies, but occasionally he'd ask me how I was getting along. He never asked me about my work, only about my kids, my golf handicap, and such trivia as I have in my life. He once asked me if I was a Mason. When I said that I wasn't, he laughed and said, 'That doesn't surprise me. You always were an atypical cop.'

I was thinking about that observation as I sat in my garden room, out in Gullane. The kids had welcomed me back, and had stayed up later than usual, until I called time and reminded them that next day was school as usual. Once they had gone upstairs, I picked up the phone and called a mobile number from my list.

'Elgin,' a brisk voice answered. The director of Kilmarnock Prison always sounds more like an insurance executive than someone who locks people up for a living.

'James,' I said. 'Bob Skinner. I wonder if you could pass a message on for me to your senior resident. Please tell him I'd be grateful if he could find time in his busy day tomorrow to call on me in my office in Pitt Street.'

Twenty-One

'I don't like this,' Ray Wilding said, aloud, to nobody but himself as he pulled up, facing a red Renault Clio.

He switched off his engine and stepped out of his car and on to the pavement in front of the Mackenzie family home. It was a villa, situated in a cul-de-sac in a new tight-built estate, the kind of street that has no through traffic and consequently little privacy, in that each new arrival can be noted easily by those of a mind so to do. He glanced around, but saw no twitching curtains.

Even if he was being observed, he would have looked like the most casual of visitors as he strolled up to the house in jeans and a Waikato rugby top, casting a long evening shadow across the driveway that led up to an integral garage. He noted that it blocked off any direct access to the rear of the house. 'Bugger,' he whispered. 'I'd rather be kicking in the back door if I have to, not the front.'

Hoping against hope that he had been sent to chase wild geese, he pressed the bronze button in the middle of the glass-panelled door. From within, eight bells chimed, in parody of Big Ben. As he waited, he looked for signs of movement through the thick obscure panes, but saw none. Checking his watch, he gave it half a minute, then rang the bell again.

He dropped into a crouch, pushed the letterbox open and shouted through it. 'Superintendent! Mrs Mackenzie! It's Ray Wilding. If you're there will you come to the door, please, otherwise I'm instructed to make an entry.'

His right knee cracked as he straightened up. Becky had been nagging him to see their doctor about it, and a sudden flash of pain made him concede that she might have a point. He looked at the solidity of the door and considered his capabilities. 'Left-footed?' he murmured. 'I don't think so.'

Yet he was loath to summon the man with the ram. In the era of Twitter, a cop's door being knocked down could become global knowledge in seconds, even in such an upmarket street.

He stepped across to his left, to the garage, examining its door. It appeared to be sectional, designed to open upwards and roll inwards. It also appeared to be locked. With fingers crossed, he grabbed the low-set handle, twisted it and pulled upwards, smiling with surprise and relief as it yielded to his strength and rolled open.

There was no car to be seen; the only wheels in there belonged to two children's cycles, one with stabilisers, that stood against the far wall, beside a door that had to lead to the back garden. The place was shelved, and those were stacked with an assortment of kitchen utensils and household items: tins of paint, a box of lightbulbs, a tool kit, a big flashlight, a power washer. The impression was one of neatness, everything in its place, with a single exception. A pile of towels had been disturbed; one hung half off its shelf and two more lay on the floor below it.

Wilding stepped inside, pulling the roller door down behind him, and plunging the space into semi-darkness. In the sudden gloom he became aware of a sliver of light, to his right, from a second doorway that was very slightly ajar.

'Oh yes?' he murmured, moving towards it, then pushing it open. It led into a small utility room, where a narrow window, set above a Belfast sink, looked out on to the rear enclosure. A work surface, with washing machine and tumble dryer below, ran from the sink to a second door, which stood wide open, accessing the kitchen. On its right an ironing table was set into the far wall, with a pile of crumpled clothes upon it, and a steam iron standing on end, plugged into a wall socket. He reached out towards it, palm up, and felt the heat of its plate from a foot away.

'David! Cheryl!' the DI shouted, but he knew it was in vain. He stepped through the open door, into a big dining kitchen and looked around. Chairs were drawn to a round table. Two people had eaten there, and had left the evidence behind, uncleared: plates, cutlery, a tall wine glass with the dregs of something white, and lipstick around the rim, and two bottles of Miller Draft, one empty, the second with only half an inch left.

He moved through to the front of the house. The living area was open-plan, L-shaped with a formal dining table and sideboard in the smaller segment, and seating in the other aligned towards a flat-screen television that was set on a swivelling wall mount. Another dead Miller Draft was perched on the wide black leather arm of one of the sofas.

'For a man supposed to be on the wagon,' he murmured, 'you're leaving a lot of empties around.'

He moved through the rest of the house, quickly. The only other room on the ground floor was a small study, with a swivel chair, desk, and an Apple computer, to which a pair of candle-shaped Soundstick speakers were attached.

The Mac's keyboard was on a shelf that rolled out from beneath the desktop. Wilding nudged it gently, and the screen sprang into life. Whoever had used it last had been looking at the P&O Ferries home page.

'Fuck!' he whispered as half a dozen scenarios jumped simultaneously into his mind.

He almost ran from the room and up the slatted open staircase. There were four bedrooms on the upper floor, and he looked into every one. The children's rooms were strewn with toys, but their beds were made and everything else about them was tidy. The third bedroom was clearly for guests, and equally clearly there had been none, not for some days, maybe weeks, maybe months, for there was a musty smell about it and a thick layer of dust on its unadorned dressing table.

There was a family bathroom, but it was unexceptional, towels on a heated rail and the kids' little toothbrushes in a glass by the basin.

He opened the last of the five doors and looked into the Mackenzies' bedroom . . . then recoiled. There were clothes scattered on the floor, and on two chairs that stood in different corners of the room. The interiors of wardrobes gaped from either side of sliding mirrored doors, and several drawers had been pulled open. He saw himself reflected in one of the doors, saw the grimness of his expression.

Ray Wilding had been in many crime scenes in his burgeoning CID career; he knew instinctively that he was standing in another. The only thing lacking was actual evidence of any crime.

He found it in the en-suite bathroom. It was as chaotic as the bedroom. Cabinets lay open, Mackenzie's Gillette razor lying by the basin, a bottle of Kouros men's eau de toilette tipped over on its side, a smear of cosmetic on the mirror. A peach-coloured bath wrap lay in the shower. He bent and touched it; still damp.

As he did so, another towel caught his eye, same colour but smaller, one of a set probably. It lay on the floor in a corner between the shower cabinet and a clothes basket, as if it had been thrown there, discarded.

He would have left it there but for the mark on one exposed corner, a mark that meant he had to pick it up. He did so carefully, with thumb and index finger, holding it aloft, letting it unfold itself, letting it reveal the stains of the blood that it had absorbed.

His pulse was thumping in his ears as he replaced it, as close to its original position as he could manage.

This was not a great idea, Mary, he thought. *Discretion or no fucking discretion, I should not be here. Dorward will go ape-shit.*

He backed out of the small shower room, and headed for the bedroom door. He was almost there when he stopped in his tracks, his attention grabbed once more, not by an object, but by the lack of one.

He looked at the bed, at the dented pillows and at the crumpled, stained, undersheet and he asked himself, 'What's wrong with this picture, Raymondo?' then replied with barely a pause, 'You know what's wrong. Where's the fucking duvet?'

Twenty-Two

'Can we keep this quiet?' Mary Chambers asked, looking through the Mackenzie living-room window into the street outside, where the unmarked police vehicle that had brought them was parked next to Wilding's car. The similarly anonymous blue van that had brought the CSI team was parked in the driveway.

'Should we keep it quiet?' Mario McGuire countered. 'We're dealing with a scene that indicates violence and suggests that at the very least a man has abducted his wife. At the very least, mind. As far as I'm concerned, if the blood on that towel doesn't belong to Cheryl Mackenzie, and a comparison with her mother will resolve that, then you are looking at the next Archbishop of Canterbury. What do we normally do in cases like this?'

She smiled at the mental image of McGuire in vestments. 'This isn't a normal case, though.'

'Tell me why not. Is national security involved? Is there any legal reason why we should hush it up? Is there any practical reason?'

'What if it isn't as simple as it seems, and they've both been abducted?' the DCS ventured.

'Why?'

His abruptness made her frown slightly but she stood her

117

ground. 'The man's ex drugs squad,' she pointed out. 'He must have made enemies in that job; it stands to reason.'

'He hasn't been on that squad for years,' he countered. 'But even if you're right, would a mortal enemy just ring his doorbell, tie him and his wife up then drive them away in their own car? Even if there were two or three of them and that was physically possible, surely the house would be a mess. It isn't; everything's neat and tidy and normal, apart from their bedroom and bathroom, and the iron having been left on.'

He shook his head, slowly. 'Sorry. I know you're only doing your job, and being devil's advocate, but as yet I don't buy any third party involvement here. I can only see this as a domestic incident, albeit a potentially serious one. The car's gone, there's blood on a towel, every other bed in the house has a duvet but theirs, and Ray found a ferry company home page on the computer.'

'The missing duvet? What's that about?' Chambers asked.

The ACC looked back at her. 'You know what I'm thinking, Mary, so don't be shy, tell me.'

'It's a kingsize bed,' she responded, 'so it must have been well big enough to wrap a body in.'

'Exactly. So,' he said, 'do you still imagine we can play this low-key forever?'

'No,' the head of CID conceded at once. 'But we can't assume it's a murder either. Cheryl Mackenzie may still be alive. But if she is, for how much longer? We've got to trace him as quickly as we can.'

'Absolutely,' McGuire agreed. 'Step one, get his car details. Can you remember what he drives?'

'Yes, it's a Honda four-by-four, but I don't have a Scooby about the number; it should be on record at Fettes, though.'

'That'll take time.' He stepped out into the hallway and called out, 'Arthur!'

A few seconds later a figure in a sterile tunic appeared at the top of the stairs. 'What?' he barked.

'Have your people cleared the study yet?'

'No, it's not a priority.'

'Well, can I go in there?'

'You're an ACC,' Dorward retorted. 'You can go where you bloody well like. But if you do,' he added, 'please wear gloves and overshoes, just in case there are forensics in there. You'll find some just outside the door. Best if you don't touch the keyboard. I don't need to spell out why, do I?'

McGuire glared at him. 'If you were still on the force rather than a central service . . .' But he knew what the provocative scientist had meant; if Mackenzie had killed his wife, then looked for ferry ports as an escape route, he might have left blood traces on the keys.

He went to the door and found the coverings that Dorward's team had left there, and slipped them on, feet first, hands second.

'What are you looking for?' Chambers asked from the living room.

'Car registration documents. I saw a filing cabinet in the office when I had a look in there.'

He stepped into the study; the wooden cabinet matched the desk and stood alongside it. It had two drawers; he opened the top one first. Mackenzie, or his wife, had been neat. Each sliding section had a subject, written on a card within a plastic clip, and they were alphabetical. 'Car' came first.

McGuire lifted the V-shaped folder from the slider, and found what he was looking for at once. There were two documents; one was for a Renault Clio. Its number matched the car parked outside, and it was registered to Cheryl Mackenzie. The other was for a Honda.

He took it out, replaced the folder, closed the drawer and rejoined the head of CID. 'The number is Sierra Lima Six Zero Delta Hotel Juliet. We need to . . .' he stopped, flashing her a small sheepish smile. 'You know what we need to do.'

'Yes, and I will.'

'Who's going to be SIO on this?' Ray Wilding asked. He had been standing quietly to one side, letting his senior officers assess the situation.

Chambers looked across at him. 'We're in Joppa,' she said, 'and that's in Sammy Pye's area. But he's got his hands full with the Watson homicide, so, my boy, that puts you in the frame. You found this, Ray, you run with it.'

'Very good, ma'am,' the DI replied, with the wry smile of a man who had just been handed a brimming chalice and knew for certain that it was poisoned. Then it vanished. 'I might have a problem, though, with my wing man, my DS.'

'Mavis McDougall? Why?'

'Because she worked with Superintendent Mackenzie for a lot longer than I did, and she got very friendly with his wife. She's going to be way too emotionally involved.'

'Ray's got a point,' McGuire chipped in. 'You might need to swap people over for this one.'

'I can see that,' the DCS agreed. 'Any ideas?'

'Just the one, off the top of my head, unless you pull in a DS from the Borders or West Lothian. It needs to be someone who didn't, doesn't, know Cheryl, and doesn't have too many preconceptions about David. That suggests Karen Neville.'

'It does, but Karen likes to have a couple of weekdays free.'

'True, but much as I like Andy, those kids of hers have got

two parents, and this force isn't carrying the whole fucking load. Daddy and Auntie Alex will help out as necessary, I'm sure.'

'No,' Chambers declared, suddenly and authoritatively, 'let's all hold our horses and think about the headlines. Sir, "Cop wanted in connection with wife's disappearance" will be a major media event. I believe we need a period of quiet, not pressure from the get-go.' She looked at McGuire. 'Unless you order otherwise, I want to keep this confidential for a minimum forty-eight hours, let's say until Thursday morning.'

The ACC frowned, then conceded the debate. 'Okay, you've got it. Ray, everything else you have on your desk you give to Mavis. You work on this alone; officially, David's having some personal time to deal with family issues.'

'With a bit of luck,' Wilding said, 'I'll have found the bugger . . .' he grinned, 'excuse me, sir, ma'am, of course I meant the detective superintendent . . . by Thursday. The only thing is, I'm going to have to look nationwide. I'll begin with a "stop on sight" order on that number, and get on to the ferry companies to check whether it's booked on any of their crossings. From what I saw on screen he could be going to any of four different countries.'

'Then you'd better make sure your passport's up to date,' the ACC told him. 'I hate to point it out but he's got up to a day's start on us.'

'What if I need help from other forces?'

'Ask for it, but don't give names, only that number and stress that it's sensitive. Don't share with anyone, not even Becky, without my authority.'

'That'll be tricky.'

'Sure but it has to be if we're to avoid the highest profile manhunt since the Yanks got Bin Laden. Go to it.'

Twenty-Three

When I confessed at a dinner party that *Blue Bloods* was one of my favourite TV shows, Aileen, my wife at that time, accused me of being a right-wing, sentimental old fart. My smile may have been a little tight-lipped, but I sat there and let it pass.

Now that she's part of my history, I want to put the record straight for anybody who was at that table and might have believed that I agreed with her description. I don't.

I know I'm not right-wing, but I don't feel that I have to prove it to anyone. I have been known to be sentimental, but it takes the presence of my children, or these days of Sarah, to bring out that side in me. A television programme does not get anywhere close. As for the last, one day maybe I'll become one of those, but not yet.

I know *Blue Bloods* is corny, but it's about cops, so that gets my attention. I know that it has one basic storyline, but the good guys always win. I know that the Irish Catholic family it portrays, the Reagans, is laughably stereotyped, but their values are my values, if not their faith.

I enjoy it, and I'm not embarrassed to say so; live with it.

One thing, though; people who know the show might assume that I associate myself with Frank, Dad Reagan, the New York police commissioner. I don't. The character with whom I empathise most is Danny, the older son, who's a New York City detective. That's why when I walked into my chief officers' meeting on my first day back after my L'Escala break, and those six uniforms stood to attention, I had a sudden flash of me, with a Tom Selleck moustache, and I thought, *Shit, this is not who I am.*

I kept it to myself, though. All I did was reiterate my edict that nobody who didn't wish to wear a uniform to my meetings should feel obliged to do so. I suspected that nobody would take a blind bit of notice, but I felt it needed saying.

The group were still, largely, strangers to me. The only two I'd known before taking the Glasgow job were the ACCs, Bridie Gorman, my very sound acting deputy, and Michael Thomas. He and I had a difficult beginning, but we'd reached a position of mutual respect, if not trust, on my part.

In truth, though, none of them was my sort of cop. The only one of the command crew I inherited that I would have chosen for that rank was old Max Allan, but no sooner was I appointed than he decided that his health wasn't up to the job any more. I couldn't complain. He'd only been hanging on to spite my predecessor. Her tenure had come to a sudden and shocking end, but that's another story.

'Nothing personal, Bob,' Max said, when he told me. 'You'll get on fine without me.'

It seemed that in my absence the Strathclyde police force had got along perfectly well without me too. There had been no serious crime, no crises and generally speaking everyone was sleeping peacefully in their beds at night. It was the sort of briefing that every chief constable should like to hear, but it left me with a growing sense of my own irrelevance.

I'd signed up for the role, though, so I thanked them all, sent them off to continue keeping the people safe, and went off to tackle my mountainous in-tray. I got so wrapped up in it that I almost broke my vow to Sarah by having a daytime coffee to keep myself awake, but I worked my way through a whole series of decisions, of which most were so damned obvious that my nine-year-old son could have taken them.

I was so wrapped up that when Inspector Sandra Bulloch, my executive officer, came into my room to tell me that a man named Dominic Jackson was downstairs in reception, saying that he had an appointment with me, it took me quite a few seconds to make the connection.

'The guys downstairs are a bit wary about him, sir,' she said. 'Apparently he's enormous.'

I smiled as I made the connection. 'That's possibly an understatement. Go get him please, Sandra.'

I was waiting at the lift door when she returned with my visitor. I'd been wondering how he'd react when he saw me on my own turf rather than on his. As it turned out he looked a little reserved, shy almost. Sandra certainly seemed to have found nothing in him to make her wary, for she was completely relaxed as she ushered him into the corridor.

'Mr Jackson,' I said. 'Thank you for coming to see me.' We shook hands; mine isn't small but it almost disappeared inside his.

'Thank you for the invitation,' he replied. 'It took me completely by surprise, as you'd imagine.' His voice was at odds with his size, but I'd known that. It was as quiet as ever, and over his years in a broad-based community much of his Edinburgh accent had worn off.

I nodded. 'Yes, I can imagine that. Come this way; my office is along here. Would you like tea, coffee?'

'I'm fine thanks, Bob. Plain water, if you've got it, but that's all.'

'Sure.'

I settled him into a visitor chair that was fortunately just big enough to take him, then fetched a couple of plastic bottles from my office fridge. I didn't sit behind my desk, but on the other side, facing him.

'Well, Lennie,' I murmured, 'this is full circle, is it not?'

'It surely is.'

'How's the course going?'

'Very well. I'm on track for graduation next summer.'

Lennie had begun a postgraduate Masters degree at Strathclyde University; he was like any other mature student in that he attended lectures and tutorials five days a week. The big difference was that at the end of the day he went home to Kilmarnock Prison, and ten thirty lights out, while the others went to their flat shares, their designer pubs and wherever else they chose to exercise and abuse their freedom.

I'd known about it from the start; in fact I supported his application when he asked me if I would. He told me that his degree and his doctorate were respected, but they were OU and that he wanted to top them up with what he had called an orthodox qualification.

He glanced in the direction of Sandra Bulloch's glass-walled office. 'Does the inspector know who I am?'

'You're Dominic Jackson to her and to anyone else in this building who crosses your path.' The university had agreed that he could study under his alias. I suppose it was possible that some of his fellow students would have heard of Lennie Plenderleith, given that criminology was in his course, but it was highly unlikely that any would recognise him. His hair was receding, and what was left was far shorter than in any photograph in newspaper libraries; also he wore a neatly trimmed salt-and-pepper beard.

'That's good,' he said. 'So, Bob, cut to the chase. Are you feeling so lonely up here that you felt the need to see an old familiar face, or is there something else?'

He took me aback. I'd forgotten how perceptive Lennie is, and maybe also discounted the fact that he's become a very well-qualified psychologist. He'd read me like a book, and also, with that single question, he'd helped me to define my feelings about the job that I'd been landed in by a combination of circumstances, and possibly by my own ego.

'Something else,' I told him, pushing the realisation aside, 'something serious that my old team in Edinburgh have happened upon, and need your help with.'

'Mmm.' He tilted his head to one side and raised an eyebrow. 'Something serious, as in something criminal?'

'Both.'

'Then I'm struggling to guess what it might be. To the best of my knowledge most of my old associates are dead, and those that aren't are in the nick or well past giving the police any trouble. Anyway, I cut all my links with that life when I was sentenced.'

'All but one.'

He stared at me. 'No, all of them, I promise you.'

'Bella Watson.'

His eyes widened. 'Ahhh!' The sound was half gasp, half sigh. 'Bella. I'm sorry, Bob, I assumed you meant my criminal associates. I don't put her in that category. What's the old bitch been up to? It must be more than shoplifting for you to be involved. She hasn't been claiming housing benefit, has she?'

'That's possible, from what I hear, but if she has, she's got away with it, because she's dead.'

Lennie took a deep breath, sucking God knows how many litres of air into his massive chest. 'People die,' he said, slowly, after a while. 'Bella must have been in the late sixties, so there's nothing out of the ordinary in her being dead; unless someone made her that way.'

'Exactly. Upwards of three weeks ago now.'

'Then why didn't I know about it? I read the *Saltire* every day. It wouldn't have missed out on a homicide in Edinburgh, on its own doorstep.'

'Have you read today's?'

'As it happens, no; I usually pick up a copy at the university, but I came straight here.'

'Do you recall reading about a body being found on the wee beach in Cramond Island?'

'Yes, but that's all it said, that and the fact that it was female and unidentified.'

'They didn't report all the gory details, because they weren't all released. They weren't told that she'd been hit by the screw of a ship, or that there were half a dozen stab wounds in the visually unidentifiable section that was washed up. It wasn't until your lawyer's girl had to go into the house on Saturday and found evidence of "foul play" that the identity of the body was established, and announced at a press conference yesterday.'

'I see,' Lennie murmured. 'Poor old Bella.' He paused, fixing me with his interrogative gaze. 'Hey, they don't fancy me for it, do they?'

I laughed. 'The thought probably did occur to a couple of the younger investigators, but I advised them to forget it. The pathologist told me that it was impossible to be anything like precise about the time of death, but I'm sure that whenever it was, your movements and whereabouts are all verifiable. Don't take their suspicions to heart, chum; they were fleeting at best. They are good enough to have asked themselves why you would kill the woman after housing her for the last nine years.'

It was his turn to grin. 'These people aren't exactly made in your image, are they? I'm sure you could have come up with a reason, in their place.'

'I'm sure I could, but I know you, Lennie. This might sound like a crazy thing to say to someone who's doing life for three murders, and got off with another, but I don't believe you're exactly a natural-born killer. With one exception you did what you did because you thought it was necessary, or just.'

'An interesting analysis,' he murmured. 'I've never tried to justify myself, to myself or to anyone else. I'm not sure I agree with your sympathetic view of the old me. What about all the casual injuries I inflicted when I was a kid, and when I worked for Tony?'

'You were part of Tony's world; you lived by its rules. So did everyone else in it and they knew what happened if they broke them. You happened, or someone like you did. Before that, as you said, you were a kid, and that was your environment. I know another man who was like you must have been then, albeit with less brain power. He saw the light before he got sucked in, joined the military and changed the course of his life.'

'I can guess who showed him the light.'

'It didn't take much. I met him again, recently. He's a fucking spook now, would you believe!'

'I'd believe anything. What was the exception?' Lennie asked, suddenly.

I gave him a long look. 'Come on,' I said, slowly. 'You don't need to ask me that.'

'My wife? Yes, I can see why you would think that. Now I'm

going to tell you something that you are not going to believe. I pleaded guilty to Linda's murder, but I didn't kill her.'

I hadn't been expecting that one. 'You're probably right, Lennie, I'm not going to believe it. I'd like to, but I was there at the crime scene. I saw the mess, I saw your bloodstained palm print on the wall, your thumb print on the bathroom mirror.'

'I found her, and I got her blood all over me, but I didn't kill her.'

I cast my mind back over a decade, to the scene. 'We found the clothes you changed out of. There was semen on them.'

'There probably was. I'd just got out of jail, and I'd been with a woman, but it wasn't Linda. She was an unrepentant whore, and I decided when I was doing my time that I wasn't going to waste any more of my life on her. No, it was somebody else, somebody I'd been involved with before I went inside.

'I met up with her and then later I went to Linda's flat to pick up my stuff, plus an air ticket and some travel money that I'd told her to get for me. I found her. She couldn't have been long dead, for she was still warm and the blood hadn't congealed. It's true, Bob; I'd like you to believe me, but . . . what the hell, it doesn't matter.'

I hadn't taken my eyes off him. Lennie wasn't the only psychologist in the room. 'Why did you plead to it?'

'Because I thought Tony had done it,' he replied, quietly. 'Linda was a seriously provocative woman; I thought she'd pushed him too far and he'd had her taken care of. I wouldn't have blamed him.'

'Do you still believe that?'

'In the absence of any other solution, or proof that it was a completely random killing . . . given that prostitution is a dangerous game . . . yes I do.'

'You were that loyal to him, that you took a rap for him even though he was dead?'

'He was the nearest thing to a father I ever had; a bad man, yes, but not all the way through.'

I wasn't going to tell him there and then, but I was inclined to believe that analysis.

'Can I ask you something, Bob?'

'Within reason, sure.'

'When I found Linda it was obvious that she'd been having sex with the man who killed her. Those clothes you found, yes, they were mine, but I'll bet you never cross-checked the semen traces on them with what was on her body.'

Good point, Lennie.

'No,' I admitted. 'We didn't. The investigating officers hadn't got round to it by the time you were caught and confessed. Because you did, the Crown Office said not to bother. They had plenty of other evidence against you.'

'Could they still do it?'

'Honestly, I do not know. If it could be done, would you want it?'

He smiled, sadly. 'If I could pay for it to be done privately, I would, but only to prove it to you. It won't get in the way of my release and I don't want to dig up the past.'

'Then privately,' I told him, 'I'll accept what you're saying. If I do so publicly, it means that Edinburgh has an unsolved murder on its hands, and my old colleagues wouldn't thank me for that.' I paused. 'As a matter of interest, what about the other woman, could she confirm that you were with her?'

'Not any more; she's dead. She was killed in a fire in her husband's car showroom, down in Seafield.'

I remembered that fire. It had been no accident. I'd known

the woman too, and wasn't sorry she was dead, but that wasn't ground I was going over with Lennie.

'Let's get back to Bella,' I said. 'Did you have any contact with her at all?'

'I sent her a Christmas card every year. Do you want to know why? Because she was the only person I could send one to. There was always you, I suppose, but your wife might have thought it was a bit weird.' He grinned. 'Or should I say your wives?'

'Touché,' I chuckled. 'Aileen certainly would have. Your contemporary socialist politician is pretty old guard when it comes to crime and punishment.'

'All politicians are; they're all things to all people. When I get out I might form a new party on the internet, and let the members determine the policies by questionnaire. They'll tell us what they want and we'll believe in it.'

'I hate to disappoint you,' I said, 'but you're too late. They've been doing that for years: focus groups, they call them. Did Bella send you a card back?' I asked.

'No. And we had no contact other than that. I've had no contact with her, in fact, since before I went in for assault.'

'Why did you do it? Why did you look after her in that way?'

'I did it because Tony would have wanted me to,' he explained . . . although I'd known the answer anyway. 'He had a soft spot for the old boot; Perry Holmes had both her sons killed, and the second one died because of him. Tony took care of her when he was alive, and when I inherited his estate, I felt that I'd an obligation to carry on doing that. She'd been living in a flat that Tony owned and left to me, but it was attached to some property I wanted rid of, so I instructed the lawyers to give her a budget and let her choose her own place.'

'I see. So you don't know anything about her life?'

'Nothing, not since the last time I saw her, and as I say that must be fifteen years ago. You've probably seen her more recently than I have.'

'Probably not; I think the last time I saw her was at her son's funeral. You may recall it; you were there, cord number three, if I'm right.' Then I remembered a later meeting, with her and Manson. 'But no, that wasn't the last; there was one more time after that.' I caught his eye. 'What did you think of her, Lennie?'

He tilted his head back and gazed at the ceiling for a few moments. He was smiling when he met my eyes again. 'Ever read *Lord of the Rings*?' he asked.

'Sure, a long time ago.'

'Do you remember Shelob, in the third book?'

'The bloody great spider that nearly does for Frodo?'

'That's the one; bloody great female spider, to be absolutely accurate. That's how I've always seen Bella: clever, cunning and utterly vicious.'

'That's a good analogy,' I conceded. 'I've always suspected that her brothers did her bidding a lot of the time, but I'd never have got near proving it. So, from all the people she mixed with back in those days, can you think of anyone who might have carried a grudge against her for a long time? After all, she was living as Isabella Spreckley, not Watson. Could it be that an old enemy had lost track of her, then came across her again?'

'It could. I'll grant you that. But if that's what happened, I can't help you with a name. Apart from Tony, nobody liked the woman, but I can't think of anyone who might get that extreme about her.'

'Look at it from another angle,' I suggested. 'People she might have had a serious down on herself.'

'Even there, I can't tell you anything you don't know already. The Spreckley family fell foul of the Holmes brothers. They made Bella's brother and son, Gavin and Ryan, let's say disappear. Brother Billy took out the Holmeses and died in the act. A few years later, Bella's second boy was killed, on Perry's orders, then Perry drowned in his hydrotherapy pool.'

'Was drowned, we reckoned,' I corrected him. Officially, Perry's wheelchair malfunctioned, or so the fiscal decided, when no alternative could be proved.

'And so did most people,' he acknowledged, 'but if you're asking, I have no idea who held him under. You're not suggesting that was Bella, are you?'

'I know it wasn't. I didn't investigate it, but I know she might have been a suspect if she hadn't been able to prove she was in Florida when it happened . . . with Tony Manson.'

Lennie whistled. 'I didn't know that. It tells me plenty. Normally Tony wouldn't have taken Bella anywhere you couldn't reach on a Lothian bus. That suggests he was behind it.'

I shrugged. 'It's academic; ancient history. I didn't care much at the time and I care nothing at all now.'

'Whatever, Bob, it just about closed the book on Bella's feud.'

'You'd imagine so, but . . . Tell me, have you ever come across a man called Peter Hastings McGrew when you were inside? He's a lifer too, doing time for two murders.'

He stared at me. 'As a matter of fact, I have. We met when he came to Kilmarnock, three years ago. I run group self-assessment sessions in prison, me and an outside psychologist. The idea is to get long-term prisoners to open up about their crimes, and to examine their motivation at the time. We don't ask them about their current perspective, for they'd all claim to have reformed. It's the job of my colleague to listen to them and reach a view on their fitness for parole. Hastie McGrew came to these sessions.'

I felt my antennae twitch. 'He came to them, you say?'

'Yes. He was released on licence a few months ago, at the back end of last year, in fact.' I felt a chill run through me, but I hid it from my visitor.

'Did you know anything about his crimes before you met him? Had you ever heard of him?'

'No, and that surprised me, until he told me that he did what I did: he accepted his culpability and pleaded guilty to save the Crown the cost of a trial.'

'Right. Now, do you remember a man called Derek Drysalter, a footballer?'

Lennie frowned and his big face darkened. 'Always. Where are you going with this, Bob?'

'Not far,' I replied. 'Drysalter was a hit-and-run victim. That's how the complaint read, and that's how it was investigated. Needless to say we never traced the car or the driver . . . because they didn't exist.' Lennie knew that I knew exactly who had smashed the guy's legs, but I had no wish to make him admit it.

'The lad was a serial gambler,' I went on, 'and very bad at it; he'd run up a big tab with Tony Manson, so certain conclusions were drawn. He never played again after his . . . accident, but he's done all right since as a manager and a pundit.'

'I'm glad to hear it,' Lennie said. 'All I will say is that I had doubts about a few of the things Tony asked me to do, but he was my patron so . . . For every action, a reaction; behind every effect, a cause. That's the way our world worked,' he observed. 'It's the way the legitimate works too, but that's codified, and those codes are the accepted mores. Now,' he continued, 'are you going to tell me what took you from Hastie McGrew to Derek Drysalter?'

I did. 'They're brothers-in-law.'

I didn't think I could ever surprise Lennie Plenderleith, but that did.

'They're what?' he gasped. 'Are you telling me that wife of his . . . What was her name again? Alafair, that was it . . . that Tony Manson was banging, was Hastie McGrew's sister?'

'I am indeed. Now, work this one out. Hastie and Alafair were illegitimate in the days before it was fashionable. They used their mother's name rather than their father's. Given that young Marlon Watson, who was Tony's driver, remember, was killed by hired talent from Newcastle while Tony and the girl were off in Majorca or wherever, who do you think Daddy was?'

It took him all of three seconds to read the script for the drama that had been played out the best part of twenty years earlier.

'Perry Holmes,' he murmured.

'Spot on, my friend. That guy you had in your self-assessment group is Perry Holmes's son.'

'And Perry had Bella's boy done to warn Tony off his daughter?'

I nodded.

'Which means that Drysalter's "accident" had nothing to do with him thumping his wife when he found out she'd been playing away, or with a gambling tab? It was Tony sending a signal back?'

'Exactly.'

'Did you know about Hastie McGrew being in my group? Is that why you asked me in here?'

'No, Lennie,' I said. 'I promise you I had no idea. I've barely thought about McGrew since the day he went away. But since he's probably the only guy alive, apart from you and me, who knows about the Watson feud, and . . .'

He raised a hand, interrupting me. 'I'm with you. Hastie's a smart guy. He could have suspected, rightly or wrongly, who was responsible for old Perry's death. What you're about to ask me was whether I ever said anything to him that might have hinted that I knew where Bella was.'

'I am indeed.'

'I'm trying to remember.' He frowned, deeply. 'Jeez,' he whispered. 'There was one session, when I steered the group towards atonement. To get contributions going, I started off; I told them that one of the people I killed had left a teenage daughter, and that I'd established a fund that would pay her way through university.

'I also mentioned that I was looking after someone else, a woman friend of Tony's who'd suffered enough loss for anyone's lifetime. I said I'd bought a place for her in Edinburgh, just off Dalry Road.' His expression changed, took on a look of anger. 'Fuck it!' he snapped.

'What?'

'My psychologist colleague asked during the session if I'd done it anonymously. I said I had for the girl, but that I'd bought the flat under my investment alias, Jackson.'

'McGrew heard this?'

'Yes. He was there. If he'd wanted he'd have been able to look through the valuation roll, to find out who was paying the council tax.'

'No,' I said, 'he wouldn't; it only lists addresses. The property register, though, that's a different matter. He could look for your name there . . . or rather for Dominic Jackson. I'll pass McGrew's name on to my old team in Edinburgh. Mario McGuire will know who he is; he was around at the time.'

I looked across at him and my breath caught in my throat. That great big guy had tears in his eyes.

'I thought I was gone from all of that,' he sighed. 'I swore to myself I'd never hurt another human being. There's a curse on me, Bob, and now I've passed it on to Bella.'

'Nonsense,' I said, firmly. 'Yours was exorcised years ago; if it wasn't, you wouldn't be my friend. As for Bella Watson, she called her curse down on her own head, before you were even born. There was a streak of badness in her that affected everyone she touched. You're not responsible for her death; she is.'

'I'd like to believe all that, but it's difficult for me. The dreams I have at night, man.'

For all his intensity, I could not stop myself from smiling. 'Listen, mate,' I countered, 'you've done some awful things in your life, but you've faced up to them. You did them because you thought it was your duty. Society didn't agree with you, but you're paying the price it exacted without complaint. I've killed people too, in the line of my duty. Society said that was okay, but that doesn't stop me having dreams that are, I'll bet, just as bad as yours.'

I let my words sink in, before I added, 'So, Lennie, think no more of this; complete your degree, and after you're released next year, you and I will work together. How, I don't know, but I can feel it; we will.'

Twenty-Four

I was still contemplating my departed visitor, after walking him to the lift, when Sandra Bulloch knocked on my door and slipped into the room. 'Your friend Mr Jackson seems like a nice chap,' she said, with a smile and a glint in her eye.

'He is,' I replied. I was amused by her reaction to Lennie; Sandra's normally a very serious person, and it was the first time I'd seen her even hint that there was another side to her.

'How old is he?' she asked, not quite casually enough. 'Late thirties?' she suggested.

'No, he's in his mid-forties.'

'He wears it well.'

'Yes, he's an ascetic. His life is almost monastic, you might say.'

'Mmm. Does that mean he's single?'

'Yes it does. You might say he lives the way he does because he's single.'

She stared at me. 'Uh? I don't get that, sir.'

'He was convicted of his wife's murder. He says he didn't do it. Yes, I know most of them say that, but I believe him. He did kill another couple of people though, no question.' I chuckled at her confusion, then explained who Lennie Plenderleith was, and had been.

'He's a charming man,' she said, her enthusiasm dampened, 'but I've heard that said about Crippen. Can we expect him to become a media celeb when he's released?'

A good question, and one I hadn't considered. 'Probably not,' I surmised, 'for that would drag up his past. When he does get out he'll only be Lennie Plenderleith to his probation officer. To the rest of the world he'll be Dr Dominic Jackson, practising psychologist. But,' I continued, 'you didn't come in here to ask for his phone number.'

'No, sir,' she agreed, 'I didn't. While you were engaged, you had a call on your private line from Chief Constable Steele, in Edinburgh. She asks if you could call her back.'

'Of course.'

'Shall I get her for you?'

'No,' I told her, 'I'll ring her myself. I've got another task for you. A life sentence prisoner named Peter Hastings McGrew was released from Kilmarnock Prison recently. I want you to find out what he gave as his address and who his probation officer is.'

'If I'm asked why, sir.'

'You can say that he's a person of interest.'

'And if I'm asked of interest to whom?'

'Then you've got my permission to yell at whoever asks you.'

As my exec left me, I picked up the phone and dialled my old Edinburgh number. Maggie Steele picked up on the second ring.

'Chief Constable,' I said, 'I'm told that you rang me. First McGuire, now you. Can't you people leave me alone?'

'You're a hard habit to break,' she laughed, 'but it's necessary. Mario told me that he'd been in touch with you about the Bella Watson murder. This is a completely different matter.'

'Formal or informal?'

'Let's begin with informal, and take it from there. Imagine the shit hitting a giant wind turbine.'

'That would spread pretty far,' I conceded. 'Tell me about it.'

'I've got a missing officer, and his wife is nowhere to be found either. A bloodstained hand towel was found at their home, and forensics have established that it's hers . . . the blood, that is.'

'How long?'

'Have they been missing? Possibly as much as forty-eight hours.'

'Is their car gone?'

'Yes,' Maggie replied, 'and the duvet from their bed. The house was tidy, no signs of a disturbance, but their bedroom was in a mess, as if someone had packed and got out of there in a hurry.'

'How do you know they used a duvet? They might have slept under a sheet in the summer.'

'We found a cover in the tumble dryer. It's a fair assumption.'

'Yes it is,' I admitted, 'but all you've told me so far is that a couple have run off. How much blood was on the towel? Was it just a pinprick or was it a whole armful, to quote Tony Hancock?'

'No, it was less than that. There was a little more in the kitchen.'

'Come on now,' I said. 'She might have been chopping onions and cut a finger; we've all done something like that. She might have had a nosebleed. It might be completely unconnected with their disappearance, yet clearly you're pressing the panic button. They could just have done a runner from a crisis situation; unmanageable debt, for example.'

'They've abandoned two children, Bob,' Steele told me. 'They were left with her mother, like, just left with her. There was no contact, no nothing. The woman is frantic.'

'Okay, I'm convinced,' I conceded. 'Something's up. Now are you going to tell me who it is? I doubt that it's a rank and file officer, or you wouldn't have your knickers in such a twist.'

'Would you like to take a guess?' she asked.

'Aw, come on, Maggie! No party games.'

'I'm serious. You've got the best instincts in the force. I'd like to know which of my senior officers you think is capable of going off the rails.'

'If you must,' I sighed. 'Well, leaving you out of it, and also big McGuire, and taking a broad view . . .'

I paused, considering the possibilities. 'George Regan's a sound bloke, but his wife has never got over losing their son, and neither has George, completely. She's borderline crazy, so is it possible that she's talked him into a suicide pact? But what am I talking about? You mentioned children, plural. George junior was an only.

'Of course,' I exclaimed, as the answer hit me between the eyes, 'there's only one obvious candidate: a man with a history of depression, alcohol abuse, and as volatile as they come. It's David Mackenzie, isn't it? The guy I plucked from Strathclyde, without ever realising that his colleagues through here were lining up to wave him goodbye.'

'I'm afraid it is.'

'Has he been under stress lately?'

'Self-inflicted, but yes. He's had trouble settling into Neil's old job, and he had to be more or less reprimanded at the weekend. Now Mario and I are blaming ourselves for putting him there.'

'Then stop bloody blaming yourselves,' I retorted. 'Blame me for making him your problem in the first place; I could have got rid of him, but my sheer stubborn pride wouldn't let me. What are you doing about the situation?'

'We're treating it as a suspicious incident,' Maggie replied, 'but keeping it confidential. We're not making any public statements or appeals, not until Thursday at the earliest. Ray Wilding's the investigating officer, working alone. Because of something that was found on Mackenzie's computer, he's looking at ferry terminals.'

'All of them?' I exclaimed.

'We'll have to. A computer check by all the major companies on bookings might lead us to him, but I'm not holding out any great hope. The security on outward Channel and North Sea crossings is a long way from perfect. In practice, you can book under an assumed name, without giving a vehicle registration. They, or he, if our worst fears are realised, could be out of the country already. They could be anywhere by now.'

'If.'

'Everything's "if" just now, Bob. If we can't find Mackenzie's details or registration number on the ferry companies' lists, Wilding's plan is to ask forces at each terminal to look at CCTV, without knowing they're searching for a cop. That's where I'd like your help.'

'You're wondering if he might have gone north, to the islands, rather than south, to Europe?'

'Either that or to Ireland,' she said. 'There's a route from Troon to Larne on your patch as well as all the CalMac ferries and lots of smaller ones. There are as many ferry routes within Scotland as there are to foreign countries from the entire United Kingdom.'

'I'll put people on it.' Two names came to me, a matched pair. 'In fact, I'll put my best on it. Tell Ray Wilding that somebody will be in touch. But there's one thing to consider, Maggie: this is David's old patch. I hear what you're saying about confidentiality, but people here will have known him and it might help if I share the name. Don't worry, I can trust the officers I plan on using to be discreet.'

'Whatever you think best.' I heard the worry in her voice, and sympathised. Every conscientious officer will fret about the job from time to time, but once you reach the chief constable's office it goes to a whole different level.

'Thanks, Bob,' she continued. 'Us cops, we're just ordinary people with a warrant card, so I'm still hoping that the pair of them will turn up with their tails between their legs and full of apologies, but we have to picture the worst, then act as if it's happened.'

'I know. The bugger is, it usually has. Anyway,' I told her, 'this is my day for doing you good turns. I'd like you to pass something on to Mario for me. Tell him that I've spoken to Bella Watson's landlord, and he's put a quite unexpected name in the frame, one that he will know from the days when he was fresh out of uniform . . . if he can remember that far back.'

I was frowning as I hung up, then walked the short distance to Sandra Bulloch's office.

'I want you to give someone a message from me,' I told her, 'but before you do, I'd like you to call Strathclyde University. Have them find Mr Jackson and ask him to call me back. They can tell him that I want to consult him professionally.'

I smiled to myself. 'Didn't I just tell him that we'd work together some day?'

Twenty-Five

'P eter Hastings McGrew,' Sammy Pye repeated, his eyes on the image on his computer screen, through its video call facility. 'Should I know him?'

'No,' Mario McGuire replied, 'that I wouldn't expect. Does his father's name, Perry Holmes, ring any bells with you?'

'One or two wee ones. I've heard it mentioned, but only by old-timers reminiscing.'

'Thanks, Inspector,' the ACC growled. 'He was still around when I joined CID. I'd suggest that you read up about him if you want to understand how his son might possibly relate to the Bella Watson inquiry. One of our former colleagues, a man called Tommy Partridge, wrote a book about him after he retired. That's as good a source document as any. Tommy spent his career chasing Holmes but never came close to nailing him. The book was only published after Perry died and couldn't sue anyone for defamation. Big Xavi Aislado, the owner of the *Saltire* newspaper, helped him write it.'

'I'll see if I can download it,' the DI promised.

'You can try, but you might not find an e-book version. While you're at it, there's something else you should follow up, something that had completely slipped my mind. Bella Watson had a grandchild.'

'What?' Pye exclaimed. 'How? Whose?'

'When Bob Skinner and I attended Marlon Watson's funeral,' McGuire replied, 'a girl turned up that we'd known nothing about. She was the dead man's bird, and she was noticeably in the family way, at least seven months gone. I remember that she was really upset, and that Bella took her away in the funeral car, although the kid had come with her pals.

'Bob got talking to her. He asked what her name was, and when she told him, it stuck in my mind, 'cos she was named after a pop singer, Lulu; that's all though, I'm buggered if I can remember her second name. I never heard of her again, but the child must be eighteen by now, assuming he or she arrived safely. It shouldn't be too difficult to trace.'

'We'll get on to it,' the DI promised. 'By the way, I've located its grandfather, Bella's ex-husband, but only after a fashion.'

'Clark Watson?'

'Yeah. He died two years ago, in Worthing, England. I've spoken to his widow, but she wasn't any help. She told me that Clark never spoke about his first family. The subject was off limits.'

'I'm not surprised. I remember Bob Skinner talking to him as well at the son's funeral, but being just a sprog DC then, I stood well back, being respectful and all, so I never heard what was said. Focus on the grandchild, Sammy. He or she, whatever, might be in Edinburgh, but he could be anywhere, in Australia even, for all we know.'

'Okay, sir. I'll keep Mr Mackenzie up to speed with anything we do turn up.'

Pye saw the on-screen McGuire shake his head. 'No. You'll

keep DCS Chambers in touch. Detective Superintendent Mackenzie is . . . non-operational, at the moment; he's taking some leave. Okay, Sam, so long. Give Ruth my best.'

'Non-operational?' Sauce Haddock exclaimed. He had been sitting to the right of Pye's desk, out of range of the built-in camera. 'What the hell does that mean?'

'Your guess is as good as mine, but from the look on the ACC's face it doesn't mean he's just having an ordinary sickie. I'm sure he got his arse kicked for jumping into our media briefing last week, but I wouldn't have thought it would have gone any further than that. If it has, fuck him; the guy was trying to use you and me as stepping stones. I don't know about you, Sauce, but I'm not having anybody's footprints on my shoulders.'

'No, me neither,' the DS agreed, 'but . . . I don't know, there's something up. I called Ray Wilding, up in Gayfield, about a golf tie we have to play and got Mavis McDougall instead. She told me that Ray's out of touch, working on an investigation. When I asked her what it was, she got very frosty, as our Mavis can, and told me I didn't need to know. My take on that is that she doesn't know either. Maybe it's secret squirrel stuff and Mackenzie's heading it up.'

'If it is,' Pye snorted, 'he'll be loving it. I hope it keeps him busy for a while. By the way, did you get anything more from Karen? Like who sent those cards?'

'Yes, I did. She's sent us a report; the intranet was down when she finished it last night, so she printed it out and had it delivered. I've just read it.'

'What does it say?

'Plenty,' Haddock declared. 'Karen's established that Bella Watson's mother had a sister, who was married to a man called Coulter. She had a daughter, a year or two older than Bella, and her name was Susan. Mr Coulter died late in the war, in Belgium, probably in the Battle of the Bulge, given the date.

'She's a class act, is Karen; I'd never have thought to do this, but she got on to the Registrar General's office. The census records for nineteen fifty-one won't go online for another forty years, but she was able to establish that Susan and her mother were living with the Watsons when it was taken, so the two girls were close, geographically and, it seems, personally.

'This Susan Coulter had a daughter, also named Susan, in nineteen sixty, when she was sixteen. The birth certificate shows the father as Victor Hart, birthplace Calgary, Canada, but he doesn't figure anywhere else in the story, nor does his name. Susan the second married a man named Eoin Riley in nineteen eighty-eight, in Edinburgh.

'A year later she had a daughter, named Victoria, and a year after that she and her husband were killed in a car crash on the coast road from Musselburgh to Prestonpans. Two years ago, Victoria gave birth to a daughter, Susan the third. The father's name is Patrick Booth, aged twenty-nine.'

Pye leaned back in his chair, beaming. 'Well done, Karen,' he murmured.

'Indeed. Her report says that Mrs McConnochie, her star witness, didn't fancy the look of Mr Booth. I've just run his name through the Police National Computer; it backs up Mrs McC's judgement. Booth has a record for housebreaking that goes back to when he was thirteen. He's also got a string of assault convictions, one of them serious; that got him three years, when he was twenty-three. I would say that makes him a person of interest, wouldn't you?'

'I would. Let's lift him and squeeze him; we'll see what pops out.'

'What about the grandchild,' the DS asked, 'and what about this man McGrew, that the ACC was on about?'

'I don't know what either might mean, not yet. You put DC Wright on tracing this Lulu and her kid, then dig out an address for Patrick Booth. While you're doing that, I'll get Googling and see what I can find out about this bloke Perry Holmes. From the way the ACC looked when he talked about him, he must have been something else.'

Haddock stepped back into the CID suite. There were two detective constables on shift, but one of them was engaged, interviewing the driver of a stolen car who had been arrested in Constitution Street the night before.

'Jackie,' he called out to the spare DC. She was the newest recruit to the squad, and had played no part in the hunt for Cramond Island woman's identity, and her killer. 'A word please.'

She looked up, eagerness in her eyes, her hair sparkling in a shaft of sunlight that came through the office window and fell across her desk.

'I need you to trace a couple of missing persons,' he said, and saw her enthusiasm fade. 'I only have a single forename,' he added, 'and no surname, but we need them found. It has to do with the Watson investigation.'

She beamed, and her enthusiasm returned.

Twenty-Six

'Is that DI Ray Wilding?' a woman asked, and even with only five contralto words in his ear, he knew that she was a Glaswegian.

'The same,' he replied, curious.

'This is DI Charlotte Mann, Strathclyde CID. My big boss, as in the chief, told me to call you . . . or rather his exec just told me, and that's as good as. Apparently you've got an all points out for somebody, only it's secret. The way he put it, via Sandra Bulloch, was that it's as sensitive as a haemophiliac wi' haemorrhoids. My DS and I are to give you any help you need on our patch.'

'Ah, thanks, Charlotte,' Wilding said. 'I've been expecting to hear from someone, but not this quick. Our head of CID's only just off the phone to tell me you'd been brought in.'

'Right. Now first things first; I answer to Lottie, not Charlotte. So, what do you need from us?'

'I'd like you to find him for us,' he responded, 'if he's in your part of the world. He, and his wife, have been missing for two days, and there are possible signs of violence in their house. We have reason to be looking at ferry terminals, but none of the carriers have a record of a booking by our man, or of his registration number. We also know that he hasn't used his bank card or a credit card to book a crossing.'

'None of that means he hasn't been on one,' Mann pointed out.

'Granted; he could have turned up at any port and paid cash. We know that on Sunday evening he withdrew over two grand from his bank account and credit cards, at various terminals in Edinburgh, and that he used one to fill his tank up at a wee garage on the south side of the city.'

'But those are the only transactions?'

'That's right. There's been no card activity since then. Also his car's a Honda CRV hybrid; that means that one tankful could get him to just about any port in Britain. Obviously there's a stop-on-sight order out on the vehicle nationwide. Maybe that'll be enough, but I doubt we'll be that lucky.'

'Does he have any other cards?' she asked.

'The wife has, but it hasn't been used.'

'Are all his blocked?'

'Of course they are,' Wilding said, his tone a little peevish, 'as of an hour ago.'

'All right, all right, keep your hair on,' she laughed, 'that's assuming you're not a baldy. I'm only establishing known facts. So, what you're telling me is that you suspect that this guy's killed his wife, put her body in the car and fucked off into the wide blue yonder, maybe using a ferry crossing.'

'That's one scenario, yes.'

'Right. Obvious question: what makes it so fucking sensitive, and why haven't you got the guy's name and face on every front page and TV screen in Scotland?'

He told her. 'My chief constable's given me authority to disclose that name to you two, and only you. She says that Mr Skinner's vouched for your discretion, personally.'

Her silence lasted for almost half a minute, but Wilding left it uninterrupted.

'Okay,' Mann said when she had absorbed his news. 'I'm with you; it's a CCTV job down at Troon to check whether he's off to Ireland. Fucking magic! Exactly how I like to spend my Tuesdays. But no worries, Ray, DS Provan and I will do that for you, and not a cheep to anyone, like you say. Give me the registration.'

She noted it down and hung up, then looked across her desk at the shabby, grey-haired, fifty-something figure who sat facing her. 'It's a fuckin' cop, innit?' he murmured.

'Yes, it is. And not any old fucking cop either. Did you ever work with Bandit Mackenzie?'

Dan Provan's eyes widened to the point of incredulity. 'It's him?' He blew out his cheeks. 'I've had that displeasure, although not that close. We were both in the same division when he was a DS, but we were never on the same investigation. I always thought he was unstable, but not that he'd go off his rocker. They're certain, are they?'

'Not certain, but from what Wilding told me, they think it's a bit more than likely.'

She pushed herself to her feet, suddenly, drawing herself up to her full, and not inconsiderable, height. Provan assumed she was ready to leave for Troon, until he saw that her eyes were on the door. He looked over his shoulder, then started out of his own chair.

'Sit down, the pair of you,' Bob Skinner said. 'I assume you've been in touch with Ray Wilding by now.'

'Yes, sir,' Lottie Mann confirmed. 'I'm just off the phone with him, and he's brought us up to speed. We're still taking it in.'

'Me too. Mackenzie and I have some shared history, so I'm taking this personally. I thought I'd drop down here to let you know that.'

'No pressure, eh?' Provan chuckled.

'Shut up, you insubordinate wee bastard,' Skinner retorted, but with a hint of a smile.

'Do you have any insight that would be useful to us, sir?' the DI asked.

'You mean did I ever see him as a wife murderer, Lottie? Hardly, not even as a wife-beater. I'm not sure I do yet, for the evidence they have isn't conclusive. The day that I'd even suspected as much, he'd have been on suspension and undergoing counselling. The day I'd been able to prove it, he'd have been in the dock.

'But . . . the fact is, the more intelligent someone is, the harder it is to see what's inside their head. Now you, Dan, I can read you like a fucking book, but Mackenzie, no I couldn't. For example, I never thought that he would bottle it on an armed operation, but he did.'

His eyes narrowed. 'The dangerous thing may be,' he continued, 'that he never thought so either. I've just had a conversation with a friend of mine, a consultant psychologist, one with a special insight, you might say. His view is that when someone as smart and ambitious as David Mackenzie finds that he isn't the person he believed he was, the consequences can be dramatic.'

'In which case,' Provan observed, 'if he's as smart as a' that, Christ, even if he's only as smart as me, and he has done something bad to his wife, he might not be at any ferry terminal yet.'

The chief nodded. 'I was wondering about that too, Dan. Why do you think so?'

'Drugs,' the dishevelled DS declared. 'These days, at any ferry terminal you're likely to find a dog or two, trained to sniff out all sorts of contraband, fags, drugs, even humans. Worst case, if he has done her in, as they're fearing in Edinburgh, turn up at one of these places wi' her in the boot of your car and you are seriously pushing your luck.'

'Absolutely,' Skinner agreed. 'And that ties in with something my psychologist said. If the Bandit has killed poor Cheryl, no way was it premeditated. He will have no getaway planned, he'll be in a panic. In that situation, my consultant says, people in a panic don't run away; either they sit tight and wait for the inevitable, or they go somewhere they know. We've all got a hidey-hole mapped out in our minds, people. We need to find out where Mackenzie's is, just in case he's heading for it.'

Twenty-Seven

'Did you find out anything interesting about the man Holmes?' Haddock asked as he slid into the passenger seat of his DI's car. 'The way the ACC described him made him sound like Al Capone.'

'Plenty,' Pye replied. 'There's a file on him on our intranet. From what I've read so far he was a lot smarter than Mr Capone. Scarface went to jail eventually, but Perry Holmes never did. I found Tommy Partridge's book too; it isn't on Kindle, as it happens, so I've ordered a copy from the library.'

'Have you ever met the man Partridge?'

'No,' Pye admitted, 'he was a bit before my time. He'll be pushing eighty now . . .'

'If he's still alive.'

'Oh, he is. I subscribe to an online magazine called *Scottish Review*. He's a regular contributor, like a wise old owl perched on a branch somewhere. He also has letters in the *Saltire* on occasion. He never has any trouble getting them published; the editor's his daughter.'

'He sounds like a crank,' the DS observed.

'Don't ever say that if Bob Skinner's around. Partridge was

one of his mentors, and if big Bob has a fault, it's that he's too loyal to his friends sometimes.'

'I'll bear it in mind . . . not that I expect to be seeing a lot of the big man from now on.'

'Where are we going, then?'

'Close by Wester Hailes; a street called Beeswaxbank Road, number fifty-three.'

'I know it,' Pye said. 'I had a few calls there when I was stationed in West Edinburgh as a young plod, before I got moved out to East Lothian. By the way, Karen Neville was there too around that time; in East Lothian, that is.'

Haddock glanced sideways, a cheeky grin on his face. 'Oh aye? And were you and she …'

'Wind it in, Sauce,' the DI growled. 'No we weren't; just friends, that's all. She and Andy Martin weren't either, not then. He was our divisional commander for a short while.'

Their conversation lapsed as Pye drove out of Leith, heading for the bypass rather than taking the straighter route through the ever-chaotic city centre. Initially his satnav protested his choice, insisting that he turn around as soon as convenient, but he solved the problem by switching it off.

Beeswaxbank Road was made up entirely of apartment blocks; fifty-year-old tenements that looked well overdue for refurbishment. On one side of the street, satellite dishes adorned their walls like acne on a teenager.

'Fifty-three,' Pye said as he parked in a bay opposite their target. 'We know that Mr Booth is on benefit. Let's see if he's in, or away job-seeking.'

Their destination was accessed via an open stairway, leading to flats above; as they moved towards the steps, Haddock pushed a toddler's plastic tricycle to one side. 'Quite tidy,' Pye remarked.

'Things have improved since I was here last. For a start, that wee bike would have been gone in thirty seconds.'

There were four doorways on each landing. The one that had a card with the names 'P. Booth' and 'V. Riley' in a doorframe holder was on the second floor. There was no bell push to be seen in the door, only an eye-level letterbox. Unusually, it had two mortise locks.

The detectives glanced at each other. 'Oh yes?' Haddock murmured. He tapped the door lightly with his knuckles. 'It's steel,' he said, 'and folk with steel doors always have something to hide. If they were a bit smarter they'd work out we're going to get in anyway, and not bother with all this.'

He pushed the letterbox ajar, and shouted, 'Police, open up!' into the space. 'Now listen,' he whispered, as Pye smiled. They heard the sound of rushing feet from within, then the sound of taps being run and a toilet being flushed. More than a minute later bolts creaked as they were drawn back, a lock clicked, and the door opened.

A young woman stood behind it, peering through the gap that a chain allowed. 'Good morning, Victoria,' Pye said.

'It's Vicky. Whitjiswant?' she demanded, aggressively.

'We want to talk to Patrick,' he told her.

'He's no' in.'

'We'd like to see that for ourselves.'

'Well, ye cannae.'

Pye shrugged and smiled down at her. 'Fine, Vicky. We'll just go, then, and leave you to explain to your man why you put his stock down the drain. We'll need to warn them down at Seafield that they've got another sort of shit coming their way. If they stand too close to that they could get high.'

She stood her ground, but uncertainty showed in her eyes.

'It was all a waste too,' Haddock told her. 'We don't have a search warrant, and we're not even drugs squad officers. We had no idea that your Patrick was the street dealer till we saw that door.'

'I dunno, Sauce,' the DI chipped in. 'That wee bike downstairs was a clue. Nobody around here would steal your kid's toy, Vicky, would they?'

'Well, what do yis want?' she asked. In the background a child yelled, 'Mammy!'

'We told you,' Haddock replied. 'We need to talk to Patrick. It's about your Auntie Bella.'

'What about Auntie Bella?'

'Do you not read the papers, or listen to the news?'

'I don't care about that. It's just the same old, same old, every day.'

'Not this time; this time, you're right in the middle of it. Your Auntie Bella's dead. Somebody stabbed her to death in her kitchen then put her body in the river.'

The young woman's hand flew to her mouth. 'My God,' she whispered. 'Does ma granny ken?'

'Not from us,' the DI said. 'Now are you going to let us in, or do we have to suspect that you and wee Susan are in imminent danger and act accordingly?'

She sighed, nodded, and unfastened the chain. The unoiled hinges squealed in protest as the heavy door swung open. The two men stepped into a carpeted hall. Haddock moved from room to room, five in all, opening cupboards and wardrobes, checking that Victoria Riley had told them true and that her partner was out. As he rejoined them in the hall he pocketed the extendible baton that he had been carrying, just in case. His left hand held something else: a jewel box.

He showed it to Pye. 'This was on a shelf in the fitted wardrobe in the kid's room. Susan says she wants her pottie,' he added, for the mother's benefit, but she ignored him. She was transfixed by the box.

'Go and see to your child, Vicky,' the DI instructed. To his slight surprise, she obeyed him.

'No way these are hers,' Haddock declared, opening his find and displaying the contents, half a dozen rings, inlaid with diamonds, sapphires and one emerald, several pairs of earrings, a string of pearls and other neckwear, including a gold heart-shaped pendant, on a chain. 'Our Vicky's a bling baby. This is an older woman's jewellery. And look at this.'

He took the pendant from the case, holding it up with only one finger, letting it swing round so that Pye could see the reverse side, and an inscription that read, 'Happy Birthday, Bella, from Tony'.

'Indeed,' the DI murmured. 'We really do need to have a serious word with the boy Patrick.'

The two detectives walked into the living room, where Vicky was in the act of handing her toddler a handful of Smarties. 'It's a reward,' she explained. 'She gets them every time she does it where she's meant to.'

'Smartie-pants, eh,' Pye said to the child, then showed her mother the jewel box, angling it so that she could see its contents. 'How did you come by this?'

She peered at it, and then up at him. 'It's no' mine,' she insisted. 'Ah've never seen that before.'

'No? It was in your spare room.'

'Well, Ah never put it there. What are yis trying to say?'

'We believe this was your Auntie Bella's. If you're telling us the truth, and we accept that, it means that your Patrick took it.

That begs a question. Did he kill her to get it, Vicky?'

'Patrick never took it,' she protested. The child was alarmed by her raised voice; she started to whimper. Haddock picked the Smartie box from the gateleg table on which it stood and gave it to her. She sniffed and beamed up at him.

'Are you certain about that?' he asked her, quietly.

'Aye, absolutely.'

'And you didn't take it?'

'Absolutely not!'

'So your story is that someone broke in here, got through your double-locked steel door and planted it, to incriminate you and Patrick in your Auntie Bella's murder. Is that it?'

'They must have. I never saw it before.'

'No,' Pye said. 'We don't buy that. Victoria Riley, we're arresting you on suspicion of the murder . . .'

He got no further. As he spoke he was interrupted by the squeal of metal upon metal coming from the hall.

'Vicky!' a rough voice boomed. 'What the fuck have I told you about no' lockin' the fuckin' door?'

'Patrick!' she called out in warning just as he stepped into view. 'It's the polis!'

For Pye and Haddock, time seemed to stretch; seconds became minutes as Booth stared at them, then reached behind his back. The DS went to his pocket, but his hand snagged in the lining. The detectives were helpless, exposed, as the newcomer brandished an automatic pistol, pointing it first at the sergeant then at the DI, wildly, with panic in his eyes. 'Freeze,' he yelled, theatrically.

Pye raised his hands, protectively, palms out. 'Easy,' he exclaimed, just as Haddock freed his baton, extending it as he dropped into a crouch and dived towards the gun, aiming a blow at the man's wrist as he swung it back towards him.

Booth fired, wildly, a fraction of one elongated second before the steel rod lashed across his hand and sent the pistol flying. The sergeant raised the weapon and made to strike again, but a Timberland boot caught him square in the genitalia before the blow was halfway there.

As Haddock folded, Pye went for the gun, but by the time he had recovered it, Patrick Booth was gone. He headed after him, turning into the hall just in time to see the massive door slam shut and hear it locked from the outside.

'Bastard!' he shouted, his heart pounding, thunderously. 'Vicky, we need a key, now!' he yelled as he turned . . . then stopped in his tracks.

Haddock was on his knees. His face was beetroot and twisted with pain, as he forced himself to his feet, but Pye's gaze passed him by. Behind him, the young mother lay stretched out on the floor, her left foot twitching slightly. The wall behind her was blood-spattered. Her daughter sat at her feet, her little face, stained with chocolate and something else, smiling up at the detective inspector.

'Come here, darling,' he said, gently, and lifted the child from the floor, letting her sit on the crook of his arm. 'You all right, Sauce?' he asked over his shoulder as he carried her through a door on his right and into the flat's narrow kitchen.

'I'm better than Vicky,' the DS hissed, through clenched teeth, 'but only just.'

'Check her out and then come in here.'

Haddock edged painfully across to where the young woman lay. Her foot had stopped twitching; she stared up at the ceiling with eyes that he knew would never see anything again. The shock of her last moment was written on her face, and a trail of blood came from a round red hole, right on her hairline. In a futile gesture, he placed two fingers to her throat, feeling for a pulse he knew that he would not find.

'She's gone,' he called to his colleague. He glanced around the room, and saw a key on the table. He picked it up, then joined Pye in the kitchen. He took his mobile from his pocket and held it up, one eyebrow raised in a question.

The DI nodded. 'Mary,' he said.

As a matter of routine, all detective officers of sergeant rank and above had the head of CID's number among their contacts. He found it and pressed, 'Call'.

'Chambers. What is it, Sauce?'

'DI Pye and I are at fifty-three Beeswaxbank Road. We came here to interview a man named Patrick Booth about the Bella Watson inquiry. We now have another homicide on our hands.'

'Are you collecting them?' the DCS asked, drily.

'I'm just glad I can still call it in, ma'am,' he said, then started to shudder as the closeness of his escape came home to him for the first time.

Pye read the signs, snapped his fingers and held out his hand for the mobile. 'This is Sammy, boss,' he snapped as he put it to his ear. 'The man Booth surprised us. He tried to shoot Haddock, but hit and killed his girlfriend instead. Then he legged it, locking us in here in the process. I'm assuming he had a car outside so we're going to need to get his number and put the word out as quick as we can. This all happened only a couple of minutes ago.'

'What do you need?'

'A full crime scene team, for starters, but this is a drug house, so that squad'll need to be informed as well. There's a child here, unharmed, thank God, and happily munching Smarties.

We'll need Social Services for her, and we'll need to trace her great-grandmother, whose name is Susan Coulter, probably aged seventy.'

'How do they relate to the Watson investigation?'

'Great-granny's Bella's cousin,' Pye explained. 'And Patrick Booth may have killed her.'

'I'd better mark him as approach with caution, then.'

'For sure, but the likelihood is he's unarmed. Sauce knocked the gun out of his hand after he'd shot the girl. It's still here, but I suppose, you never know, he may have another.'

'I'll make sure there's an armed response team handy when we trace him,' Chambers said. 'Well done, gentlemen. You stay there and wait for the cavalry.'

'Will do,' the DI said. 'But there's one other thing we're going to need, pronto: a gunshot residue test.'

'Sure, but let's catch him first.'

'No, boss. It has to be done on me. I picked up the weapon. My prints will be on it. I'll need to prove to Arthur fucking Dorward's satisfaction that I didn't shoot the girl myself.'

Twenty-Eight

'What the hell are we doing here, Lottie?' Dan Provan complained, as he watched the screen. 'He's not in fuckin' Ireland. A cop wouldn't run away to Ireland; he'd know it's too well watched.'

'This one would know that,' his inspector agreed, 'because he's ex-Strathclyde, but they might not realise that in Edinburgh. The man Wilding's coordinating this search, and he asked us to check the Troon CCTV. That's what we're doing. Anyway, the job's nearly done; this is the last possible crossing he could have taken within the time frame.'

The little DS grunted, then fell silent as they viewed the lines of cars boarding the high-speed ferry, bound for the Northern Irish port of Cairnryan.

'Nothing,' he declared, as the recording ended. 'You can tell your Edinburgh pal that he's just wasted half a day of our time.'

'I won't be putting it that way,' Lottie Mann said, 'but whatever, it's behind us now. Chances are he's not in this part of the world at all.'

'That's not what the chief's mysterious consultant psychologist thinks . . . and the chief seems to have bought into the idea.'

'That fact was not lost on me.'

'So what's our next port of call?'

'Nowhere tonight, for I've got to get home for my wee Jakey. But tomorrow we should look as close to home as we can. For a start, we'll talk to Human Resources, or we'll get Sandra Bulloch to talk to them, and see if we can get a look at Mackenzie's personnel file.'

'Won't they throw the usual data protection shite at us?'

'They might try, but we're on a potential murder inquiry and that should override any objections.'

'Okay, but like ye' said, that's only for openers, and the chances are there'll be nothing on it that takes us beyond where we're at the now. I think we'll need to dig a good bit deeper. While you're waitin' for that file, I'll speak to somebody I know that might have worked with the Bandit. I know that most people thought he was a bampot, but this fella might be able to help. The Mackenzie I remember, ye'd no choice but to listen to the sod, so he might have let something useful slip sometime or other.'

'Discretion, Dan,' Lottie warned.

'The guy I'll talk to, that's his middle name.'

Twenty-Nine

'What's going to happen to the wee girl?' Cheeky's expression was as serious as Sauce had ever known it. In fact he struggled to recall the last time he had seen her frown.

'That's a good question,' he admitted, pausing his forkful of coiled spaghetti halfway to his mouth. 'Daddy shot Mummy, so he's not going to be around to bring her up.'

'Didn't you say she has a granny?'

'No, I said great-granny. They traced her this afternoon. She's seventy, and she has arthritis, so she's not going to be any help.'

'They?' she repeated. 'Who are they? Why not you and Sammy?'

'The head of CID says that we shouldn't investigate the shooting. We were witnesses to the crime, so she wants an objective SIO. Jack McGurk's heading it up, with Karen Neville.'

'Have they got anywhere?'

'A traffic warden reported Booth's car, parked on a yellow line, just outside Waverley Station.' His face twisted into something that might have been a smile, had it been a little less vicious. 'You might say that was a wee bit of a clue, the first, as it happens. The second was when he used his credit card to buy a rail ticket to London.'

'Do you know which train he got?'

'It doesn't matter,' he said, his voice hard. 'It wouldn't even matter if he gets off at an earlier station. He'll leave the platform in handcuffs . . . and that's if he behaves himself. The transport cops are waiting for him at every stop, with armed support.'

'You sound as if you'd like them to shoot him, Sauce. That's not like you.'

'It wouldn't bother me one bit if they did,' he confessed.

'Why did he kill the girl? Was it just because she had let you two in?'

'I don't think he meant to kill her.'

'Then . . .' she stopped, and that rare frown returned. 'Was he shooting at you?'

'Nah,' he said, 'he was probably just firing wild, trying to scare us. That's what his defence QC will say, I'm sure.'

She reached across the table and turned his face up towards hers, forcing eye contact. 'I don't believe that.'

'Lucky for him you can't be on the jury, then.'

'Sauce, he tried to shoot you, didn't he, but he killed the girl instead. That's what happened, isn't it?'

'It all went off very fast,' he murmured. 'Although it didn't seem that way at the time; the after-effects of a kick in the balls stay with you for a long time.'

'And now you're all twisted up because the woman got what was meant for you. I know it, love. I can tell.'

'Not just that.' He shook his head. 'I hit him with my baton as he was trying to aim. I'm chewed up by the thought that if I hadn't, Vicky might still be alive.'

'And you might not.' She squeezed his chin, hard. 'Now you listen to me, Harold Haddock. That girl lived behind that steel door. She knew why it was there and she knew exactly what was going out through the letterbox. She lived with a dangerous man, she chose his lifestyle and she spent the money it brought in. You live by it, you die by it. Trust me, I'm an authority on the subject; look at my family background. My mother's a fucking thief, my Aunt Goldie's a monster, and my grandfather was Dundee's answer to the Krays, with a wee bit more menace about him than them, so they say.

'I could have been that girl Vicky, if Grandpa hadn't kept me out of the life. If I sound hard it's because it's in my genes, but if it takes a dead slut to bring you home alive, that's fine by me.'

'There's still a kid left with no parents,' he whispered.

'She'll be better off without them,' Cheeky retorted. She flashed a small smile his way. 'Maybe we could adopt her.'

Sauce winced. 'We may have to, if we want kids. I haven't been able to bring myself to look at my baw-bag yet.'

'Oh, you poor love.' Her eyes twinkled. 'Don't worry. I'll be gentle with you.'

'It'll still be like juggling hand grenades.' He stopped and his expression changed as a recollection came to him.

'Your grandpa,' he said. 'Maybe next time you speak to him you might ask him whether, in that other former life of his, the one we don't usually talk about, he ever had dealings with a man called Perry Holmes. If he did, it would be useful to know whether he ever met Holmes's son. He uses his mother's name; he's known as Hastie McGrew.'

She rose from the table. 'I'll ask him now. You go and switch on the telly, and I'll call him from the bedroom.'

'There's no rush,' he insisted.

'Rubbish. You've never asked me to get anything from Grandpa before. It must be important.' She headed for the door.

Sauce polished off the last of his pasta, then cleared the table, loading the used crockery and forks into the dishwasher. He had just switched on *EastEnders*, when Cheeky came back into the room, phone in hand.

'He wants to talk to you,' she said, holding out the handset. 'Grandpa never asks for anything either, so it must be important.' She saw his hesitancy. 'Please, love.'

Unsmiling, he took the phone from her, and muted the television sound. 'Mr McCullough.' He felt a shiver run through him. He had never spoken to his partner's grandfather before, but he might have been regarded as an expert on him, since he had read almost every word that had ever been written about him, in the media and on police intelligence files.

He knew that the man on the other end of the line was seen by many as the most influential person in his home city of Dundee, and by most of those who had known him in his younger days, as its most dangerous.

'Sauce, is it,' he asked, 'or do you prefer Harold? My name's Cameron, by the way. Only people who work for me call me Mr McCullough, and I don't expect you to be calling me Grandpa.'

'Sauce will be fine. I rarely get anything else these days.'

'First off,' Cheeky's grandfather began, 'it's good to be talking to you at last, although I understand why we haven't. Given what people say about me, it's a brave thing for someone in your job to have taken up with our lass, and I admire your for it.'

'I love her, Cameron, simple as that.'

'I know that, and I can see that you're making her happy.' Sauce heard the unspoken words, *Just as well for you.*

'That works both ways,' he replied.

'Good, good. Now, you asked her to ask me about Perry Holmes and his boy.' McCullough paused, as if words were being chosen carefully. 'Without going into detail about how we came across each other, yes, I did know Perry. He was what you might call a man of respect. Hugely intelligent and successful in everything he did; his legitimate business empire is still there, run by trustees on behalf of his son and daughter. I'm sure the police file on him is about a foot thick and that it's still stored in a Black Museum somewhere.'

'It still exists,' Sauce confirmed. 'There's a book about him too, written by one of our guys after he retired.'

'I've read it,' Grandpa said. 'The author didn't know all the story. Perry only ever made one mistake, and that was to be excessively loyal to his brother. He gave that head-banger Al far too much rope. The man was a liability, an animal, and the things he did got both of them killed eventually, although it took Perry a lot longer to die than it took the brother.

'It was widely assumed, and maybe still is, that when Perry was crippled, his criminal side came to an end, but in fact that wasn't the case.

'He never married the mother of his two kids, so nobody knew about Hastie. When his father got shot he came out of the army, and simply replaced his Uncle Al. He'd be about twenty-five when he came to see me in Dundee about a business deal that Perry and I had.

'He was a very formidable lad, although he didn't act hard. He'd his dad's brains, and as time proved, some of his uncle's tendencies, but because he was bright he was far more dangerous than Al ever was. I'd tell nobody but you this, but only two men have ever put a chill into me, and Hastie McGrew is one of them.'

'Who's the other, as a matter of interest?' Sauce asked.

'Somebody you know,' Cameron McCullough replied, 'the man who's right at the top of your game now, in fact.

'Anyway,' he went on, 'young Hastie ran the show for his old man, while the whole word thought he was just his nurse, until their luck ran out. Perry finally used up his extension, and Hastie was put away for killing two guys. His score was actually a lot higher than that, and I'm not talking about his army days.'

'I see.'

'So do I. The fact that you're asking me about him tells me that he must be out. He'll be due, given that it all happened almost twenty years ago. Let's see, he must be pushing fifty by now. Has his name come up in this high-profile investigation you're on?'

'Possibly,' Sauce conceded.

'Then take him very seriously.'

'We've got another name in the frame already, though.'

'Yes, Cheeky tells me that you had a close call with an idiot today. It's as well it wasn't Hastie. He never made mistakes. What makes you so sure the other one might be the right guy?' McCullough laughed, suddenly. 'Listen to me, asking a cop about a case. Forget it, son.'

'It's okay. I can tell you we found some stuff of the dead woman's in his flat, a box of jewellery. That, and traces of Class A drugs in the toilet bowl and around the place.'

'Was he a user or a dealer?'

'Oh, a dealer, definitely.'

'And the stuff you found, the jewels, was it valuable?'

'Mmm. Moderately so; four figures we reckoned, but well short of the five.'

'In that case are you really sure you're after the right man? Why would a drug dealer murder a woman just to steal a few baubles?'

Hell, that's a good question, Sauce thought, but he refrained from answering it.

'I'll tell you, lad,' Cheeky's grandfather said, '. . . and this is not me asking an indirect question, mind, because I really don't want to know . . . if this dead woman had any quarrel with Perry Holmes in the past, then don't rule out Hastie.'

Thirty

'This is an unexpected pleasure, Dan,' Max Allan told his visitor. 'You're the first of my old colleagues to look me up since I retired. But how did you know where to find me?'

Provan beamed up at the former assistant chief constable. 'For fuck's sake, Max,' he laughed. 'Everybody in the force knows you drink in a pub called the Hoolet's Nest. Why should that change just because you're no' a polis any more?'

'True enough. What are you for?'

'I'll have a bottle of Magner's, and that'll be me. I've upset too many uniforms in my time to take a chance.'

Allan nodded. 'I know that for a fact. Christ, the number of complaints I had about that tongue you've got on you. I hear you've landed on your feet, though. I wondered how you and Skinner would get on. I knew he'd either take to you or you'd be out on your arse in thirty seconds. Your homespun charm seems to have worked, from what I'm told. You and Lottie are his star CID turn, so Bridie Gorman said last week.'

He ordered Provan's cider, then glanced around the small saloon. 'You know why I like it here?' he asked. 'It's the most anonymous pub I know. The signs outside say "Barnhill Tavern", but nobody calls it that, ever. So if anyone wants to come looking

172

for me, searching for the Hoolet's, they're going to have a hell of a job finding me, unless they're local . . . and if they are, I'll see them before they see me. So, like I asked you earlier, how come you did? You're from Cambuslang.'

'I'm also a fuckin' detective,' the little sergeant retorted. 'I phoned your house before I left home. Your wife told me where you were and how to find it.'

'So much for security,' the retired ACC sighed. 'Now, what do you want?'

Provan feigned outrage. 'Why should I want anything? You and I go back over thirty years. You were my first sergeant in uniform.'

Allan laughed. 'And some impression I must have made on you. Look at you now. Do you practise being scruffy, Dan?'

'I don't have a wife to impress any more, Max. Not that I ever did impress her; she buggered off eight years ago, remember? Apart from that, though, yes I do. You were in uniform too long, or you wouldnae have to ask me. What's scruffy in the office is standard dress code in some of the places I have to go. I adapt it too. Skinner thinks I'm a Celtic supporter because I was wearing a shamrock lapel badge the first time we met. What he doesnae know is that I've got a Rangers badge as well that I wear when it's called for.'

He winked. 'You're right, by the way. Lottie and me, we do seem to be teacher's pets right now. He sent us off on a secret mission this afternoon. To come clean, that's why I'm here . . . not that it's no' nice to see you enjoying your happy retirement, mind.'

'So what's the secret?'

Provan glanced around the bar, checking that there was nobody within hearing distance. 'It's very secret,' he said, 'so anything I say's between us, kapisch?'

Allan nodded. 'Of course.'

'One of our professional colleagues has done a runner,' Provan continued.

'I see. And what district would this officer belong to? He's one of our own, I'm assuming, a Strathclyde officer . . . and a man.'

'No, he's Edinburgh . . . but it is a he.'

'So why are you in on the act? And why's Bob, for that matter?'

'Because he used to be one of ours: Bandit Mackenzie.'

Allan stared at him and his eyebrows rose. 'Indeed!' he murmured. 'No wonder the third floor's in a panic. What do you need from me?'

'Anything you can tell me about him that might give us a pointer to where he might run to. The investigation's bein' co-ordinated by a DI in Edinburgh, and he's got every force in the country with a coastline checking ferry terminals. They've been playing their cards close, but I'm guessing they found a ferry website open on his computer.

'If that's right he didnae go out òf Troon, that I know for certain, having spent the afternoon reviewing tapes down there. When I phoned the guy Wilding, he told me that there wis no advance booking, but there had been a possible sighting today in Hull, bound for Esbjerg in Denmark, right car, right colour, but a dirty number plate that couldn't be read on the CCTV. They won't know for sure till it gets there.'

'He never worked directly under me,' the veteran said, 'but there's one thing I remember about David Mackenzie, wherever he goes, he won't be able to speak the local lingo. I remember he applied for a secondment to Interpol, when he was a detective sergeant, but got knocked back because he didn't have a second language.' He took a mouthful from his pint glass. 'But you don't think he is on a ferry, do you, Danny?'

'I'm no' sure,' he confessed. 'Skinner, though, he's been talking to a psychobabbler; he didn't tell us who, but he seemed to rate him. His "expert" view was that he'd be more likely to run to somewhere closer to home, somewhere in his own comfort zone. Personally, I think profiling's all shite, but I'm just a common foot soldier.'

'That'll be right,' Allan scoffed. 'You're an anti-authoritarian little sod but there's nothing common about you, and there isn't a single idea you'd dismiss out of hand.'

'Maybe not,' Provan sniggered. 'I just don't like these boys coming out of university and spouting wisdom straight from their degree course. Just suppose the guy's right, can you think of anywhere that Mackenzie might head for?'

He frowned. 'There is someone you might talk to. I know a man, a priest in East Kilbride, and I've heard it said that he took the young David Mackenzie under his wing. He did that sort of thing. But not in the way that makes the headlines these days.'

'What's his name?'

'Tom Donnelly: Father Thomas Donnelly. He's quite a man; a pretty charismatic guy.'

'And I'll find him in East Kilbride, you say?'

'No, not any more: priests retire at seventy now, and Tom's a couple of years beyond that. The church owns some properties to house its own, and he lives in one of them, a nice wee cottage from the looks of the photo he sent me last year.'

'Is he likely to know where Mackenzie might go in a personal crisis?'

'It's possible, that's why I mentioned him. But the truth is, if he's had some sort of a breakdown, if he's not in his right mind, who knows where he'd go? I'm in your camp when it comes to psychology; I think it's all crap too.'

'We'll probably check the priest out anyway. Where is this cottage?'

'It's in Tighnabruaich.'

'Tighnabruaich! That's away in the back of beyond. Do ye no' have to get a plane to get there?'

'That wouldn't help; there isn't an airfield for miles around. The only realistic way is by car. But don't worry, you'll do it in a day easily.'

Thirty-One

'How far did he go?' Sauce Haddock asked, seated, with his feet planted on his DI's desk.

'He got off at Darlington,' Jack McGurk told him from his chair in the corner of the office cubicle. 'He strolled off the platform all nonchalant, with a rucksack over his shoulder, straight into a reception committee in the shape of two transport cops and an armed support team from the local force. They went on the assumption there was a firearm in the rucksack, and had him down in the ground in seconds. He's being brought up here this morning.'

'Are they sending him back on the train with an escort?'

'No, he's being driven up. The English are taking him as far as the border; I've got a car waiting for him there.'

'When do we get to interview him?' Sammy Pye asked.

His colleague shrugged. 'As soon as I'm done with him, Sam, but I can't tell you how long that'll be. He may be your prime suspect, but he's nailed on for the murder that I'm investigating, and the chief super says that gives me first crack at him. The drugs people will want to interview him as well, for sure, but they can wait. They're a bit embarrassed. Apparently they had no idea he was a dealer; he'd never appeared on their radar at all.'

'In that case they must be loving us, since we gave them the red faces by finding the stuff . . . even if it was by accident.'

McGurk smiled. 'Don't be looking for a Christmas card; that's all I'll say.' He glanced at Haddock. 'Oh, by the way, Sauce, when they cuffed Booth in Darlington, he screamed. They took him to the local hospital, straight away, so he couldn't claim police brutality later. He had an X-ray and they found a couple of broken bones in his hand.'

There was real malice in the young DS's eyes. 'That's the best news I've had for a while, Jack,' he said. 'I'm pleased that I left a mark on that bastard, 'cos he sure left one on me. You know that after he kicked me, Sammy made me get myself checked out in A&E?'

'I'm not surprised.'

'You're going to charge the man with serious assault as well as murder, I hope.'

'Too fucking right we are!' the acting DI declared. 'Of course that means the prosecution's going to need medical evidence about the nature and extent of your injuries.' He grinned. 'The doc was satisfied you were okay, I take it; you can never take too much care of the family jewels.'

'Aye, she was.'

'She? Did you tell Cheeky it was a woman?'

'Not a chance. We have no secrets, but sometimes it's best to leave out the odd fact.'

'Speaking of family jewels,' Sammy Pye said, 'we're going to need the box that we found in Booth's flat. It's central to the case we're building against him.'

'That's why I came down here,' McGurk told him. 'This is a very unusual situation. We're both investigating the same guy for different murders in different locations. We need to be bloody careful that neither of us contaminates the other's evidence chain.'

'That's true,' Haddock agreed. 'So give us the jewel box and Bella Watson's sparklers. They're our motive.'

'They surely are, and if you don't have them, you don't have the beginnings of a case against him.'

'So?'

Pye raised a hand. 'I see where Jack's going with this,' he murmured. 'If he gives us the jewels, just like that, we could be fucked. We didn't have a search warrant, so we're on shaky ground using them as evidence.

'Let's make some assumptions here. I doubt that Patrick Booth is a major drug importer himself; that means he's a rung on a ladder. In that racket, normally you'd expect that whoever's at the top of that ladder would brick it when he heard that the guy's been arrested. He'd be liable to do one of two things. He'd either try to have him killed while he's on remand . . . not the easiest thing to do, I don't care who you are . . . or he'd hire him a very good brief, probably Frances Birtles, or somebody of her stature.'

'Frankie Bristles,' the DS chuckled. 'We've met her before, haven't we, Jack, when we worked together?'

McGurk nodded. 'We have, so we know how sharp she is. If she does wind up representing Booth, none of us will need telling what she'll do as soon as you introduce those jewels as evidence. She'll want to know that they were legally obtained.'

'Granted,' Haddock argued, 'but we were invited in and we had reason to believe there were Class A drugs in the house, and when we looked for them . . .'

'And who invited you in?'

'Oh fuck,' he sighed. 'Vicky's hardly going to confirm that, not without a medium.'

'I couldn't have put it better myself,' Pye said. 'Without the jewellery box, we have nothing. Sure, Booth's prints will be at the scene of Bella Watson's murder, and we'll have his DNA there too, but we bloody well know he's been there, with Vicky and the child visiting her so-called auntie. We're got that from Karen's witness, Mrs McWhatsername, and I'm sure that Frankie Bristles or whoever it is that defends him will be able to prove, through her again, that the victim was seen alive after that visit.'

'In that case, what are we going to do, Sam?' Haddock asked. 'Do we need to do anything? He's done for killing Vicky, for sure.'

'For killing her, yes, but he's a long way short of being done for murder. My guess is that they'll try to plead that down to culpable homicide. Then, come the hearing, the defence will claim that we forced an illegal entry and that when he saw us there he panicked.'

'That's bollocks!' Haddock protested, righteously indignant. 'What about him booting mine? He's got to go down for that too.'

'Oh he will. He'll get a year to run concurrently with whatever he gets for the homicide, and what will that be? It won't be mandatory life, remember. Maybe six or seven, if it's a soft judge who takes pity on him for accidentally blowing the top of his sweetheart's head off. Hell, he could be out in two or three. I'm not having that.'

'How are we going to avoid it?' Sauce demanded.

'By making sure of our own evidence.' The DI looked at McGurk. 'Where is the box just now, Jack?'

'It's still at the scene. We haven't removed anything yet.'

'Good. Have the drugs squad been over the place?'

'Yes. There was plenty of residue in the bathroom basin and in the S-bend, plus they found a quantity that the girl had missed, hidden under the mattress of the wee girl's cot. They say it's not heroin or cocaine, but a synthetic drug. Whatever it is, they've got more than enough for him to be charged with possession with intent to supply.'

'Even better,' Pye said. 'I'll talk to Mary Chambers and make sure that they convict him on that charge first, so that it can be led in evidence in our case. That might well establish our right to enter. But just to be sure, you and I, Sauce, we'll get ourselves a search warrant, then we'll go back there, and we will find our evidence, legitimately.' He paused. 'Are you both okay with that?'

'All the way,' McGurk agreed.

'Yes, Master Luke,' Haddock said.

'Insubordinate fucker,' the DI grunted, but he was fond of his nickname. 'Right, Jack,' he continued, as the visitor unfolded his tall frame from his small chair. 'Thanks for coming down.'

'No worries. Let me know when you're going in there. It is my crime scene, after all, so Karen or I should be present.'

'Aye,' the young DS mused. 'It'll need to be done by the book, or our Mr Mackenzie will be all over us when he becomes "operational" again.'

'I detect a touch of sarcasm there, my young friend,' McGurk said. 'I've heard that he's on sick leave . . . suffering from a bad case of wounded pride, it's been suggested.' He lowered his voice. 'I think I speak for all of us when I say I hope he won't be back.'

'Amen,' Pye murmured. 'The man's an arse.'

'I had thought of a different anatomical analogy,' McGurk

countered, with a wink. 'See you later.' He headed for the door.

'You happy with that?' Pye asked Haddock as soon as they were alone.

'Sure. I wish we could get Booth right away, that's all.'

'No, it's better that we don't. It gives us time to get that warrant and make everything legit. Besides,' he added, 'Booth might have fallen into our lap, so to speak, but we do have another line of inquiry. We need to follow it up; if we didn't it would be sloppy and we'd get pulled up on it. Speaking for myself, I'd rather not have Mackenzie pull me up for anything, least of all a balls-up in a murder investigation.'

The DS frowned, but only for a second. 'Oh aye,' he exclaimed. 'The girlfriend of Bella's son's, and the potential grandchild. You're right; we need to find them and interview them, especially given the source of the information.'

Pye nodded. 'You get my drift. Off you go and see whether our Jackie's had any luck.'

Haddock nodded and stepped out of the cubicle office into the main CID room.

DC Wright was at her desk; she seemed to come to attention, although seated, as he approached. 'Sarge,' she began, until he raised a hand to stop her.

'Fuck's sake, Jackie,' he exclaimed, 'I know I'm a sarge. Call me Sauce; everyone else does and I wouldn't want you to feel left out.'

She smiled. 'If you insist.'

'How's your trace going, the one I asked you to do yesterday? Any joy?'

'Fine, but only up to a point. I used the date of Marlon Watson's death as a starting off point; approximately three months later, a girl called Marie McDonald Ford gave birth to a boy. Marlon was named as the father and the baby was called after him, with Ryan as his middle name.'

'Granny must have had a hand in that,' Haddock mused. 'Ryan was her other son's name, the one that was murdered when he was fifteen.'

'Mmm. Where did the name Lulu come from, do you think?'

'Real name,' he murmured, casually.

'What?'

'The singer Lulu; her real name is Marie.'

'Is that right?' The DC was impressed. 'Imagine you knowin' that. She's old enough to be your mother.'

'My mother told me. She's a fan . . . and yes, you're right. Mum's ten years younger than Lulu. She's always saying she wishes she looked it.'

'I'm sure she does look it. You've got a fresh-faced look about you.'

'That's not what my girlfriend says first thing in the morning. So,' he continued, 'Marlon Watson junior. What became of him?'

'That's what I meant by "up to a point". I've found a Registry Office marriage record for Marie Ford, two years later, to a man called Duane Hicks, a West Indian, from St Lucia. They had a child together, a girl they christened Robyn, with a "y". But that's where it stops. They no longer live at the address shown on the marriage certificate, and there's no record of either of the kids, Marlon or Robyn, ever attending school in Edinburgh. I've just been on to the Social Security department and there's no record of either Ford or Hicks currently paying National Insurance, or drawing benefit. The same goes for Marlon Ryan Watson; a number was generated for him automatically when he was sixteen, but it's never been active.'

'Does Duane Hicks have an NI number, given that he's not British?'

'Yes, he does, but he hasn't paid any contributions for fourteen years. When he did, he was employed as a marine engineer by a firm in Leith. I tried to contact it but it closed down, guess what, fourteen years ago. My assumption is that when Hicks became unemployed they left the country.'

'If that's right,' Haddock said, 'the first place to look has to be St Lucia, since that's where he's from.'

'Agreed, and I've called the High Commission in London. I gave them all the details I have but they say they'd need to check with the government office back home. They're four hours behind us, so they'll still be having their breakfast.'

'Maybe so, but the UK passport office won't be. How about checking whether Marlon Junior has ever applied for a passport?'

'Been there, done that. A passport was issued in his name in the year that Marie married Duane, but it's never been renewed. No passport has ever been issued for Robyn Hicks.'

'But she could have a St Lucian passport through her father.'

'Yes, but like I said,' she hesitated for a second, 'Sauce, I'll need to wait for St Lucia to wake up before I can check.'

'In that case, how about contacting the Home Office in the meantime, and asking whether a St Lucian would need a visa to get into Britain, and also whether one's ever been issued in the name of Marlon Ryan Hicks?'

The DC grinned. 'See? That's why you're a sarge and I'm just a plod.'

Thirty-Two

'How strong is this lead of yours, Dan?' Lottie Mann asked as they watched the ferry being secured to the Dunoon quayside. 'You know every bloody thing that happens in our force, or in Glasgow at any rate, or you know a man who does. So where did this information come from?'

'Just this once, Lottie, I'm not telling you.'

'I'll pull rank on you,' she threatened.

'You could pull my fuckin' ears wi' red hot pincers and it still wouldn't do you any good. And before you say it again, it's got eff all tae do with the Data Protection Act.'

'I still find it hard to believe, you know. The concept of David Mackenzie being taken under the wing of a priest, that is.'

'Why should that be so difficult to cope with?' Provan challenged. 'Are you saying you're surprised he's a Catholic just because he's got an old traditional Scottish name, one beginning wi' Mac rather an O'? All that Rangers versus Celtic stuff isn't typical of the whole country, you know; they're just a couple of wee cabals . . . okay, maybe no' so wee,' he conceded. 'Religion in Scotland was full of splits and schisms for centuries. We're a pretty ecumenical nation: there's nothin' in a name.'

'You and your philosophy and fancy words again,' she

mocked, but only playfully. Her junior officer happened to be her closest friend, and after an act of betrayal by her estranged and newly imprisoned husband, he had become her only confidant.

'I have my hidden depths,' he said, 'as somebody observed last night. But I'm as intrigued as you. If there's someone I would not have picked out as a former altar boy, it's Bandit Mackenzie.'

'Indeed,' she murmured, as the ferry's forward platform clanged down on to the stand, and as the dozen drivers on board returned to their vehicles. 'Father Donnelly. I've heard of him, you know. I've got cousins in East Kilbride, and they talked about him.

'He had a high profile in the town. Unorthodox, they said of him but quite a man. The feeling was that he should have been a bishop, but wasn't because the hierarchy were afraid of him.' She dug out her car keys from her bag. 'So, what time's he expecting us?'

'He's not. He doesn't know we're coming.'

'He what?' she boomed, loud enough for a van driver who was standing five yards away to turn his head and stare at them. 'Are you telling me we're going all the way to Tighnabruaich on spec? He could be on his holidays, away on a retreat, filling in for a sick priest. Retired guys do that sometimes.'

'The man I spoke to in the Archbishop's office says he hardly ever leaves the place, but aye, we're turning up unannounced. We don't just want to ask him where Mackenzie might go in a crisis, do we? We need to allow for the very realistic chance that he might have gone to the man himself. Unorthodox, you said. In my book that also means unpredictable; if our David is there, we don't want him warned off, do we, Lottie?'

Thirty-Three

'You are brilliant, Sauce,' Jackie Wright declared. 'Marlon Ryan Hicks applied for a UK entry visa four months ago. Apparently you need it if you're from there and want to work in Britain. In June, he applied for a UK passport in that name. They've got a file on him; he was told that he would have to change his birth surname legally before he could get one. He did that, and his application's now live. If you hadn't thought to check under Hicks, we might never have known.'

'Don't tell him he's brilliant, Jackie,' Sammy Pye called across the room. 'The last thing he needs is a seconder.'

'Ignore him,' Haddock laughed, as he perched in the edge of her desk. 'You only have to take orders from him on policing matters. Any other rabbits in your hat? For example, does his passport application have an address on it?'

'Yes it does, and surprise, surprise, it's in Edinburgh: number seventeen Port Glasgow Road. I've checked it out; it's a flat belonging to a property company, called Mycroft Residential Limited. The directors are Derek Drysalter, and Alafair Drysalter, but they don't own it; the shares are vested in a holding company called Rodatrop PLC.'

Pye had moved across to join them. 'Derek Drysalter?' he

repeated. 'When I was a kid, in my mid-teens, I remember a guy called Drysalter playing for the Hibs, and for Scotland. I'm pretty sure his first name was Derek. The Hibees paid Newcastle big bucks for him, but his career came to a sad end. He was a hit-and-run victim; his legs were so badly smashed up that he never played again. He did a wee bit on telly as a pundit, then he had a couple of jobs as a manager with Scottish Premier League teams. I haven't heard of him for a while, though.'

'The rebranded Marlon Hicks isn't a footballer, is he?' Haddock asked.

'If he is, he's not doing it professionally. I went on to the DSS again; he was given an NI number under his new name, and he's found himself a job as a mechanic, looking after a fleet of cars belonging to Sherlock Private Hire.

'Most people know about them. They're the biggest luxury car hire company in Edinburgh. If your daughter's getting married, that's where you go if you're out to impress the in-laws. Funerals too. There's an associated company, Sherlock Funeral Undertakers. It has offices around Edinburgh and the Lothians, but the car firm's based in Longstone.'

'Then let's go up there and have a word with the boy.' The DS rose and looked at the DI. 'You and me, boss, or will I take Jackie?'

'You take her; she deserves it. But hold on; bells are ringing here. Mycroft Residential, Sherlock Private Hire, Sherlock Funerals: those names tend to point in a certain direction. Have you checked these companies out, DC Wright?'

'Not yet, sir. I was just about to look them up on the Companies House website.'

'You do that, but I will bet you they are also subsidiaries of the PLC you mentioned, Rodatrop. Did you pick up anything about that?'

'There's very little different about it. It has the same directors. The only additional fact I was able to glean is that Derek Drysalter isn't a shareholder. Alafair is, though, one of two. The other's a man called Peter Hastings McGrew.'

Pye beamed. 'You little beauty! It's you that's the real genius around here.'

He turned on his heel and walked back into his office, closing the door behind him and leaving the others staring after him, Wright bewildered, but Haddock wide-eyed. As they watched, they saw him drop into his chair and snatch the phone from its cradle.

The DI was unaware of them as he dialled a number from a list on his desk. 'Sammy,' Mario McGuire said as he picked up, sounding a shade irritable. 'I thought I told you to go through DCS Chambers.'

'You did, boss,' he acknowledged, 'and I'll phone her as soon as I've spoken to you, but you're going to want to know this, soonest. You asked me about a man called McGrew. His name's just cropped up. We've located Bella Watson's grandson; he calls himself Hicks now, and it appears that he's working for a company owned by McGrew and his sister.'

He looked up, to see Haddock in the doorway. 'Loudspeaker.' The DS mouthed the word. Pye looked puzzled, but did as he asked.

'Are you sure about that?' the ACC exclaimed, his voice echoing in the small room.

'Certain.'

'But that's weird.'

'It sure is, sir,' Sauce intervened. 'Don't ask me my source,

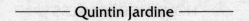

please, and Sammy, don't kick my arse, because I really was going to tell you, only things got in the way, but I've spoken to someone who knew Hastie McGrew in the old days. He told me that if he's around and Bella Watson's dead, the two could well be connected.'

Thirty-Four

Looking back, I find myself wondering whether I should have guessed how the story might develop when Mario called me that day.

Maybe, but it would have been a hell of a big mental leap, and even if I had made it, what could I have done?

McGuire was buzzing when he came on the phone; I could feel his excitement down the line, and knew that he was itching to tell me something. He managed to scratch it for a while, though, for he began with a question.

'Have your people come up with any intel on Hastie McGrew yet?' he asked.

'That's well-timed,' I told him. 'Sandra Bulloch, my assistant, just reported back to me. He's registered his sister's address with the probation service.'

'In Edinburgh, I take it.'

'Yes. You know it. You've been there, with me, a long time ago. Or had you forgotten?'

'Hell no!' He sounded offended by the very notion that he might have, then proved the depth of his recollection. 'We went there straight after we'd visited Derek Drysalter in hospital, didn't we, after he had his so-called accident. She'd had one too,

191

of the domestic variety; she was wearing big sunglasses to cover it. Their place was up near Blackford Hill. So they've never moved?'

'They're still there,' I confirmed. 'They must have a thing for crap nouveau riche architecture. I've heard very little of Alafair in the last few years. We kept an eye on her for a while after her father died, and what was then the national crime squad also monitored all Hastie's visitors, and all his communications from prison. We wanted to make sure they couldn't carry on where their father left off, but there was no sign of them trying to do that. Alafair doesn't have the brains, anyway, and Hastie, he's never had the opportunity.'

'Who did visit him?' McGuire asked. 'Did you ask your exec to find that out?' I could still sense that tingle.

'Of course I did,' I said. 'Do you think I'm slipping?' I wasn't sure of his answer, so I didn't wait for it.

'For the first three years, his sister was his only visitor. In his fourth year, she took Derek Drysalter with her. You probably remember that Derek didn't even know he had a brother-in-law, until Hastie went to prison. After that Derek came three or four times a year; sometimes with Alafair, sometimes on his own. In his sixth year, they brought their daughter; her name's Peri, spelt P, E, R, I, and she was two at her first visit.'

'So she'll be in her teens by now?'

'Yup, around the same age my Alex was when you and I first worked together, when all that shit with Hastie happened. Those three are all the family that McGrew has, and all the way through his sentence, he's only ever had one other visitor, a man called Vanburn Gayle.'

'That name's vaguely familiar.'

'It should be, if you remember everything about that case.

Vanburn was Perry Holmes's carer, his nurse-cum-masseur. He had two people looking after him; Hastie was the other.

'When I saw that name it opened a whole can of worms. I have never believed that Perry managed to drown himself, whatever the official verdict is. He had help. The investigators looked at Vanburn as a possible helper, but they found pretty quickly that he had quit and left town a few weeks before it happened, so he was crossed off the list . . . but it's interesting that he should show up a few years later, visiting his old boss's son in prison.'

'Are you saying I should reopen the investigation into Holmes's death?' Mario asked.

'Not for a minute,' I told him, emphatically. 'There would be no chance of a conviction, so it would be a waste of resources. Tony Manson was probably behind it, and he's long gone. Nevertheless ...'

'I know, you're wondering whether Hastie might have decided to put his old man out of his misery and got Vanburn either to do it or to set it up.'

'I am,' I admitted, 'but only wondering, mind. I don't actually care. If nobody'd been looking I might have drowned the evil fucker myself.'

McGuire let that one pass unremarked upon. 'How did McGrew behave in prison?' he asked instead.

'From what Sandra found out, he kept his head down, he did his time, and he got parole more or less as soon as he'd finished his tariff. He wasn't in much of a position to make trouble, even if he'd been of a mind to. Physically, he couldn't have.'

'Why not?'

'Think back again, Mario. Hastie was in the army, and saw a bit of action. He was wounded and it left him with a permanent weakness in his left hand and forearm. When we went to arrest him for those murders, he resisted and got shot in the right hand.'

'I remember that,' McGuire said, 'and I remember who shot him too.'

'That's by the by. The point is that the bullet destroyed the thumb joint and first knuckle, doubling his previous handicap. If he wanted to cut a pizza in the nick he had to get somebody to do it for him.

'My alarm bells went off when I learned that he could have found out where Bella Watson was living, but from what I've been told about how she was killed, it couldn't have been Hastie. You can ask Sarah, but I'm sure she'll confirm what I'm telling you, that it would have taken a degree of hand strength that he doesn't possess.'

'I see. That's very interesting.' I'd expected him to sound deflated, but he didn't. 'Now can I give you my news?'

I laughed. 'Could I stop you?'

'Probably not,' he conceded. 'I've been doing some reminiscing of my own, about Marlon's funeral, and who was there.'

No, you're not slipping, Skinner, I told myself, after it had taken me no more than a couple of seconds to spot where he was going.

'The girlfriend,' I said, 'Marlon's pregnant girlfriend. She came with her pals, but Bella took her away in the car when it was over. What was her name?'

'Marie Ford, but she called herself Lulu. The baby was a boy, christened Marlon Ryan, Lulu moved on and married a West Indian engineer called Hicks, and they moved back to his home island.'

'I like a story with a happy ending,' I remarked.

'So do I,' McGuire agreed. 'But this one's not over. I'm still trying to work out how Bella Watson's grandson, raised in St Lucia, came to be employed by and housed by, as he is, companies owned by the children of the man who ordered the deaths of his father and his uncle. Is that not the biggest coincidence you've ever come across?'

'McGuire,' I retorted, 'have I or have I not been telling you for going on the last twenty years that when it comes to murder I do not believe in coincidences?'

'You have indeed, Bob.'

'So what's your next step?'

'You know what it'll be.'

'I do indeed, Mario, I do. Let me know if I can help.'

Thirty-Five

Mary Chambers frowned as her phone rang in the car, at the very moment that she was manoeuvring into a tight parking space. She hit the Bluetooth button and snapped, 'Yes?' as she completed the move.

'Bad time?' Mario McGuire asked.

'Slightly, but it's okay now. Sorry.'

'Are you sure? You can always call me back.'

'No, boss, it's all right, honest. Let's deal with it.'

'It's a chain of command job,' the ACC said, 'a message I could pass on myself but if I did, you'd be out of the loop. I've just been speaking to Bob Skinner, and this comes from that conversation. I hope that Luke Skywalker's told you by now about a name that came up in the Bella Watson investigation: Duane Hicks, a St Lucian man who worked in Edinburgh long enough to marry Marlon Watson's girlfriend, and become stepfather to Bella's grandson.'

'Yes, I'm aware. Sammy gave me an update half an hour ago, when he asked me to get him a search warrant so he could find something he's already found.'

'Do I want to know that?'

'I think so. I had to weigh it up myself, but all he's doing is closing off a possible line of attack in a trial.'

'This is to do with the Bella investigation?'

'Yes. They have a strong suspect, a guy called Booth, and the thing that they're going to find again, on a firm legal basis this time, represents motive.

'As for the young man Hicks, he's part of a separate line of inquiry, but there's no reason to think it'll come to anything. It's an anomaly, that's all. Booth ticks all the boxes.

'That said, Sauce Haddock has a bee in his bonnet about Hastie McGrew. He says that he has solid information that in the old days he was more active than was known at the time, and that we should be taking him seriously now.'

'And I have solid information,' the ACC countered, 'that Hastie couldn't have done it, but let's not go there until we have to. Meantime, another name's cropped up, courtesy of big Bob. This man looked after Perry Holmes, with Hastie, until he was jailed, in the period leading up to his death. His name's Vanburn Gayle, he's also a West Indian, and I want to know whether there's any connection between him and Duane Hicks.'

'Okay,' Chambers said. 'Sammy has a clever little girl on his team; she traced Hicks, so I'll suggest that he puts her on it, while they're concentrating on Mr Booth.'

'How's that situation developing?'

'It isn't, yet. It's delicate, with Pye and Haddock as witnesses in one murder and investigators in another. I've decided that I'm going to sit in on both interviews, but not take part. That's where I'm bound now. Booth's back in Edinburgh and Jack McGurk's having first crack at him.'

'Go for it,' McGuire told her. 'If it helps, now that you're in the know, I can brief Pye's team myself.'

'I'd be grateful if you would.'

'Then it's done. Let me know how the first Booth interview goes.'

'Thanks.' She ended the call, switched off her engine, and stepped out into the car park behind the Torphichen Place police office. She had been stationed in the old building for a time, but the back entrance keypad code had been changed, and so she had to buzz for admission.

She bypassed the reception area, and took the stairs that led to the CID suite, where Jack McGurk and Karen Neville were waiting for her arrival.

'Sorry, folks,' she said as she breezed into the room. 'I'm a juggler at the moment with three major inquiries on the go. I just caught a call about one of them, hence I'm a couple of minutes late.'

'Three?' McGurk repeated, a question in the word.

The head of CID cursed herself for forgetting that Ray Wilding's mission was still clouded in secrecy. 'Slip of the tongue,' she replied, 'although the way this man Booth's going, who knows how many we'll wind up with. Are we ready to go?'

'Not quite,' the acting DI told her. 'Booth's with his solicitor. She asked for twenty minutes and she still has five to go.'

'She?'

'Birtles.'

'Frankie Bristles, eh. That was to be expected, I suppose. She's the go-to for nearly all of Edinburgh's wee hoodlums these days. Do we know who sent her?'

'Nobody sent her,' McGurk replied. 'Booth asked for her to be called, as soon as he was booked in here.'

'That's interesting. How are we handling the drugs aspect, Jack?'

'I don't want to know about that, ma'am. The drugs team were quite clear about that. Sammy and Sauce went there to interview Booth and his girlfriend as potential witnesses in the Cramond Island woman case. They had no reason to suspect that drugs were being dealt from that address . . . . not until they found the steel door, at any rate.

'With that line of inquiry discounted, Karen and I see no complications and we're not planning to go looking for any. He shot his girlfriend dead, we've got witnesses and we've got forensic evidence, his prints on the gun. That's all we need.'

The DCS nodded. 'Agreed. But I'm not dancing to Miss Birtles' tune, so let's get in there whether she's ready or not. What room are they in?'

'Interview two, ma'am,' Neville replied.

'Lead on then, Disco Queen.'

The DS grinned. In her younger days, before marrying Andy Martin, she had been a regular around the city's club scene. Her active social life had spawned the nickname, and it had stuck.

The three detectives walked the short distance to the interview room. When they reached it, Chambers stood aside. 'I'm just a fly on the wall here,' she said.

McGurk nodded, then strode into the room without knocking. Two faces, one male, the other female, turned towards him in surprise.

'Twenty minutes, I said,' Frances Birtles protested.

He smiled. 'You may have said, Frankie, but I never agreed. You've had time enough to persuade your client that he is as done as anyone you've ever seen and that he should be concentrating on keeping the judge happy.'

'You do your job, Jack,' she retorted, 'and I'll do mine.'

'Agreed, so let's get on with it. The quicker we're finished, the quicker the two of you can move on to your next engagement, with my colleagues down in Leith.'

'We'll see about that,' the grey-flecked lawyer snorted.

'Aye, we will,' Patrick Booth grunted.

'Who's doing this interview?' Birtles asked.

'Karen and me; DCS Chambers is just sitting in, that's all.'

'Fair enough. I understand why.'

They waited as Neville loaded the recorder and switched it on. When the red light was showing, McGurk identified the five people in the room, for the tape and the video camera, then cautioned the prisoner, formally.

'We're here to interview Mr Booth,' he went on, 'in connection with the murder of his partner, Victoria Riley, in their home at fifty-three Beeswaxbank Road, Edinburgh, and also with an assault on a police officer. Have you anything to say, Patrick?'

'No comment.'

'Oh dear,' Neville sighed. 'We have two witnesses to Vicky's murder, we have the murder weapon, an illegal unregistered firearm, with your fingerprints all over it, including a very clear one on the trigger. We're also confident of matching the lubricant used on the gun to traces found on your clothing, when the Transport Police removed it for examination.

'All of that means that we don't actually need any comment. You're going to be charged with murder, Mr Booth, be in no doubt about that, and you're going to be convicted. This is your opportunity to practise your plea in mitigation; in other words,' her voice rose, 'to tell us why you murdered that poor woman by putting a bullet through her head!'

'There's no need for that, Sergeant,' Frankie Birtles protested.

'Oh, but there is,' she insisted. 'I've still got the picture of

Vicky Riley fresh in my mind, at the scene and during her post-mortem, when the pathologist opened her up and found among other things that she was carrying your client's second child. I've got two kids of my own, so I do have a need, Miss Birtles. I need to hear him say why he did it.'

'I never done it,' Booth shouted, suddenly.

Jack McGurk stared at him. 'No? Then who did.'

'Yon fuckin' polis!' Booth brandished his right arm. His hand was encased in plaster.

The tall detective frowned. 'Elaborate, please.'

'The young lad, he did it. Ah never meant to shoot Vicky, but he hit me with his stick and the gun went off. He broke ma hand!' Booth pouted, as if to emphasise that he was a victim also.

'The statements that we have from the two police witnesses both say that the gun was discharged before DS Haddock's baton made contact with you.'

'It's no' true,' Booth protested. 'He hit me and that made me do it. I was never going to shoot her. That polis kilt her, no' me.'

'So who were you going to shoot? If not Vicky, it must have been one of the police officers. Right?'

'Ah never meant tae shoot anyone. The safety catch was on.'

McGurk looked at the solicitor, a faint smile twitching the corners of his mouth. 'Frankie,' he said, 'I assume that you've read the crime scene report. Are you going to tell your client he's an idiot or am I?'

She winced slightly, shook her head, and leaned towards Booth. 'Patrick,' she murmured, 'the firearm was an old Glock. It doesn't have a manual safety catch.'

'Do you have anything else?' McGurk asked her.

'Of course,' she responded, while glancing sideways at Booth.

'I have a client who has, let us say, an alternative lifestyle, which makes him feel the need for personal protection. Whether the weapon he carried was legal or not isn't the issue here.

'Patrick came into his home and found the door open; that alarmed him straight away. When he moved through to his living room, he found his partner and child being menaced by two unknown men. He assumed they were criminals and acted accordingly. Obviously, we'll plead to a charge of illegal possession of a firearm, but as for the rest . . .'

The acting DI smiled, with a degree of admiration. 'You're a fine advocate, Miss Birtles,' he said, 'but I couldn't help noticing that you weren't able to look me in the eye while you were explaining all that. The police witnesses both say that Miss Riley called out "It's the polis" while Mr Booth was still in the hall, then she was killed by his gun, in his hand.

'You and I both know that to have even a slim chance of an accidental death plea being accepted, he should have surrendered himself there and then, as soon as the gun was discharged. But he didn't. Instead he kicked DS Haddock four square in the privates and he legged it, as fast as he could. Why did you do that, Patrick?'

Booth frowned and fixed him with a deep, piercing stare. 'Because I was scared, mate, that's why,' he replied.

'Accepted, but assaulting a policeman and running away was never going to make you less scared. And, as I said to your solicitor, it's made your position even worse. You were never going to get away, man.'

'Aye, fine, but all Ah could think about at the time was gettin' the fuck away.'

'Even with your partner lying dead on the floor, and your child sitting beside her with her mother's blood all over her?'

'Even then. It wasnae you bastards I was scared of, or doin' some time. Have you any idea how much gear there was in the place?'

'We're not interested in the drugs,' McGurk said, quickly. 'That's a separate investigation, by other people.'

'Maybe you're not,' Booth wailed, 'but I fuckin' was! You guys'll only bang me up for a few years, but there's others would cut my feet aff wi' a fuckin' chainsaw. Look what . . .'

'Patrick!' Frankie Bristles exclaimed. 'Enough. Don't say another word. They have to prove you knew about the drugs.' She turned in her chair and looked at the detectives. 'If I advise my client to plead guilty to a reduced charge of culpable homicide, will you go for that?'

'It's not my decision,' the detective replied, 'but if the Crown Office agree to a plea deal we won't oppose it. I'm not dropping the police assault, though; Sauce Haddock would be seriously annoyed if I did. As for the gun, your man will have to take his chances there. If he's lucky, he might get off with no more than ten years, all in.'

'Fair enough,' the lawyer declared. 'In that case this interview's over. Charge him and let's go on to the next.'

Thirty-Six

'Is this it?' Dan Provan asked.

'My satnav says so,' Lottie Mann replied, as she drew her car to a halt and pulled on the handbrake.

'If ye believe her; I don't know how you can stand that bloody woman. If we'd followed her advice we'd be in Tarbert.' He paused. 'You are sure we're no' in Tarbert?'

'The sign we've just passed read "Tighnabruaich". If you'd been awake you'd have seen it.'

'I was awake. Who could sleep with you driving?' He blinked and peered across her at a terrace of white-painted cottages that stood above a raised embankment overlooking the wide flowing waterway on their left, and across to a hillside beyond.

'So that's the Kyles of Bute,' Mann said. 'I've heard about it often enough from my granny, but I've never seen it. She used to say that when she was a girl you could go for a sail on a paddle steamer that left the Broomielaw and came all the way here.'

'Where did it go after that?'

'Nowhere. It just went back to Glasgow.'

The little sergeant frowned, bewildered. 'What was the point of that?'

'They called it a pleasure cruise, Dan.'

'Was there a bar?'

'I have no idea. If there was, my granny wouldn't have been interested. She was a ginger wine woman.'

'Let's hope there was. It would have been no pleasure without one.'

'My God,' the DI muttered. 'No wonder your wife left. Come on, Dan. Let's go and see if the Father's in. What's the number?'

'Ah've no idea; Diocesan Cottages was all that I was told.'

They walked up a driveway, past an embankment until they reached an area in front of the quartet of cottages. Three small cars were parked, side by side, although there was room for more, and the red gravel was roughed up.

'Four houses, three cars,' Provan said. 'Maybe he is out.'

But as he spoke a door opened and a tall white-haired man stepped out, into the autumn sunshine. He was wearing blue denims and a short-sleeved shirt, with a red check pattern, and carried a rucksack, slung over one shoulder. He was tanned and although his skin had the striations of age, his arms were still muscular. 'Can I help you?' he asked.

'Possibly,' Mann replied. 'We're looking for Father Donnelly.'

He smiled, and both detectives felt its force. Even Provan, who prided himself on being the ultimate cynic, understood why Max Allan had described the priest as charismatic. 'That's me,' he chuckled, 'but I'm retired now, so I'm not really anyone's father. Benevolent uncle is as close as it gets these days. How do I address you?'

'I'm Detective Inspector Charlotte Mann, and this is Detective Sergeant Daniel Provan. We're CID officers from Glasgow.'

'My, my,' the emeritus priest exclaimed, 'and you're here looking for me? Did I need a licence to take the village lads out fishing in the boat?' His expression changed; the smile vanished, to be replaced by a look of sadness.

'Nobody's been making allegations, have they?' he asked. 'There's never been a reason why anyone might, but it's become fashionable these days. A tiny minority of my colleagues betray their calling and it's assumed that the virus infects us all.'

'It's nothing at all like that,' the DI assured him, looking up and into his eyes, trying to judge whether there was anything hidden behind them, but seeing nothing. 'As far as your boat's concerned, I wish I had someone to take my wee boy out fishing, but there aren't too many opportunities where we live.'

'If you're ever posted out this way,' Father Donnelly told her, 'give me a call and I'll find a space for him. Look, I was just on my way there, to the boat, that is. Would you like to follow me down, and we can talk there?'

'Aye,' Provan grunted, 'as long as we don't wind up being sold as slaves in the Carolinas.'

'Hah!' he laughed. 'So you're an admirer of Robert Louis Stevenson, Sergeant. You know, most people think of *Treasure Island* as his masterwork, but I've always preferred *Kidnapped*: there's so much more depth to it, more intrigue.'

The DS dissented. 'Nah, I don't buy that. Ye cannae beat Long John Silver. I've arrested a couple of guys like him in my time, although they both had two legs and nae parrot.'

Lottie Mann was astonished. 'You've actually read something longer than a betting slip, Dan?'

'You should ask your Jakey,' he said. 'Whenever I babysit for him, that's what he likes; it's his favourite story.'

The priest climbed into his car, a grey Ford Fiesta that dated back to the previous century, and the officers followed. He turned left out of the driveway and drove along by the waterside for little more than a mile, past a sign that read 'Port Driseach', where the detectives saw a few boats moored in a small cove. Father Donnelly parked at the roadside and, as they joined him, pointed to one of them, an eighteen-foot white day-boat that even the Glaswegians could see had not been built for speed. 'That's her. It'd take her all day to get to Rothesay, Sergeant, never mind the Carolinas.'

'How do we get tae it?' Provan asked. 'I'm no' a great swimmer.'

'Neither am I, so it's just as well we have a wee inflatable to get us out there.'

He led the way across the stony foreshore to a small dinghy floating at the water's edge and secured to a steel mooring ring by a heavy, padlocked chain.

'I share the boat with two of my neighbours, Father Smith and Father Edwards . . . they call him Father Ted in the village,' he chuckled, 'even though there's not a trace of humour about him.'

He held the dinghy steady as Mann stepped aboard and eased her large frame down into a seat. Provan joined her, more nimbly, and they set off, the priest in the bow, paddling the short distance to the boat. As they drew closer, the detectives could read its name: *Holy Orders*.

'It's more like *Last Orders* for my colleagues and me,' Father Donnelly joked, as they boarded via a steel ladder at the stern.

It occurred very quickly to Mann as she stood on the swaying deck that although the good ship *Holy Orders* was larger than it had seemed from the shore, it was doing strange things to her sense of balance. She sat down on a bench at the side.

Their captain noticed her discomfort. 'Have you ever been on a boat before?' he asked. She shook her head. 'And you're feeling a wee bit unsteady?' She nodded. 'Then find a fixed point, any fixed point, focus on it, and keep looking at it.'

She did as he advised, fastening her gaze on a building on the hillside on the Isle of Bute, while the priest busied himself inside the covered cockpit. Gradually she felt her queasiness subside, and by the time he reappeared, offering her a blue plastic mug, the threat of imminent sickness had gone. 'Tea,' he said. 'I always put a flask in my rucksack. There's enough for the three of us, but I can make some more if you want. There'll be no milk though.'

'We're polis, Father,' Dan Provan grunted as he seated himself alongside Lottie. 'We can drink it any way. Can we talk now?'

'Of course,' he replied, then flashed that dazzling smile again as he stood, mug in hand, looking down at them. 'In fact I can hardly wait to hear what's brought you all this way to do it.'

'We want to ask you about a colleague of ours,' Mann began, 'someone we believe you know.'

'I know several of your colleagues, past and present; some as parishioners, some as friends, some as both. For example, there's Max, Max Allan, your recently retired assistant chief constable. Max plays with the other team, he's Church of Scotland, but he was helpful to me when he was a young officer and I was in my first parish. We've been friends ever since. But I don't imagine it'll be him.'

So that's our Dan's mysterious source, the DI thought. *I should have guessed.*

Is he warning us not to push it with him? the DS thought, as Mann responded.

'No, it's not him,' she said. 'Actually it's a former colleague, at least he will be former until the forces merge: Detective

Superintendent David Mackenzie. I understand you've known him since he was a boy.'

'Ah, David.' He sat, lowering himself on to the bench facing them. 'Yes I have. He was a troubled lad when I met him; his childhood had been unfortunate, I'll say no more than that. I like to think I helped him in some way.

'David says I saved his life,' Father Donnelly admitted. 'I wouldn't go that far. The truth is his life was never in danger. His soul was, though, and if I've helped him save that I'll be happy to take some credit for it. When I met him he was heading down the wrong pathway at a fair rate of knots. I showed him there was another way.'

'How?' Mann asked. 'Forgive me, Father, but you have the air of a man who can handle himself in all sorts of ways. I believe you were a military chaplain in your twenties, isn't that right?'

There was a little less warmth in his smile. 'You've been checking up on me? Fair enough, I suppose; it's only reasonable to expect a police officer to do that. What you're really asking is whether I beat some sense into him. Am I right, Ms Mann?'

'It's Mrs,' she replied, 'and it's Lottie. Yes, I suppose so.'

'Then the answer's no.' He laughed, softly. 'You're confusing me with His Excellency Archbishop Gainer, through in Edinburgh. I've never done that with any young man, although I have invited one or two who were given to picking on the weak to take a swing at me and find out whether I had the moral courage to turn the other cheek. I also suggested that if I failed the test, something might happen that we would both regret, them more than me. I was never taken up on it.'

'Just as well,' Provan retorted. 'Behind a lot of these wee Ned hooligans are parents all too ready to complain about police brutality. I hate to think what they'd do if the priest gave their brats a thumping.'

'True,' he conceded. 'In any event, that would have been entirely the wrong way to go with David Mackenzie; his aggression was beaten into him. What's been implanted by violence can't be removed that way; it can only be made worse.

'No, when I met David, he was embarrassed by being highly intelligent, and proud of being tough. I tried to show him that he'd got it the wrong way round, and that changed him. Just like I got you to focus on that piece of hillside, Lottie, I got him to focus on what he was capable of doing for himself, rather than to others.'

'I don't understand any of that,' Provan confessed.

'The youthful aggression you've just told us about,' Mann murmured, nursing her mug in her hands, 'did it go away?'

Father Donnelly shook his head. 'No, I have to say that it never has, not completely. David still has a hair trigger. If you've worked with him you must know that.'

'DI Mann hasn't,' Provan said. 'I have, and sure I know it. You helped him show that he's clever, Father, and maybe you put him in the CID room rather than in a police cell, but God never made him a nice man, and you couldnae change what He had programmed.'

The priest laughed again. 'You're a bit of a spiritual thinker, Dan, aren't you? You're right, of course; it would be blasphemy to assert that I could. As for saving his soul, or helping him to do so, I suppose you would argue also that all I did was try to prevent him committing the sins that lay within him.'

The little cop nodded. 'I probably would.' Then he fixed him with an acute, questioning gaze. 'And if one of those sins was murder . . .'

Thirty-Seven

'What have you found out about this Vanburn Gayle? The day's wearing on and it's the ACC who's asking.'

Sammy Pye's tone was serious enough to make DC Wright's eyebrows rise. 'I thought I was a genius, boss,' she ventured.

'In this force you're only as good as the game you're playing, not the last one. When that's over, it's over.'

'In that case . . . no,' she admitted, 'I haven't found any links between Vanburn Gayle and Duane Hicks yet, but I have found Gayle.

'He lives in Makepeace Drive, Tranent. He's forty-eight and he was born in Trinidad, but he's lived in Britain for almost thirty years. Originally he qualified as a physiotherapist, but after he stopped being Holmes's carer, he did a three-year nursing degree in London. He worked there for another four years, then he moved back to Scotland, to Glasgow Royal Infirmary, and finally to the Western General, here in Edinburgh. That's where he is now.'

'Well done so far, Jackie,' Pye said, with a grin. 'Not genius level, but thorough. Whose passport does he hold?'

'British, for the last twelve years. On his first application, his father's name was given as William Gayle, and his mother's as

Lorraine Alcott, both Trinidadian nationals. He also has a UK driving licence; that's where I got the address.'

'What about Hicks? Any more information on him?'

'Yes, just in from the St Lucia Home Affairs department; Duane Hicks, aged forty-five, born in the town of Castries, the capital, parents' names Michael Hicks and Teresa Clay, both St Lucian nationals. As you see, boss, there's nothing there to link him and Gayle.'

'No, there isn't,' the DI agreed. 'I don't think you're going to get any further online, Jackie. The time's come to face them both up, him and Marlon Watson Junior. You and the DS can go and see Gayle, once he and I have finished with Mr Patrick Booth.' He glanced across at Haddock. 'Are you ready for that, Sauce? The front desk just buzzed me to say that he's here.'

'Oh yes,' his colleague replied, firmly. 'Am I ever ready. If he needs to go to the toilet, can it be me that takes him?'

'No, chum, I'm pulling rank. There were two of us facing that gun, remember, and you've already had one whack at him.'

He realised that Wright was staring at him, as if she was taking them seriously. 'It's all right, Jackie,' he said. 'If he needs to go, his lawyer gets to stand outside the door to protect us against any later claims that he was duffed up.'

'Karen Neville told me that his right hand's in stooky,' Haddock pointed out. 'She might need to go in and help him.'

The two investigators headed for the door, and walked downstairs to the interview room at the rear of the building. When they arrived, they saw the head of CID standing outside, waiting for them.

'Afternoon, ma'am,' Pye greeted her.

'Sammy, Sauce,' she responded, curtly. 'I thought I'd brief

you on the first interview. McGurk did a good job. He handled our Miss Birtles well too. As I thought, they tried to turn it against you two, but he wasn't having any of that. That strand of the investigation's pretty well locked up.'

'Plea to a reduced charge?' the DI ventured.

She nodded.

'Pleas to everything, I hope,' Haddock muttered.

Chambers treated him to one of her rare chuckles. 'It's all right, Sauce. Police assault stays in.'

'Did he say anything at all that had implications for our interview?' Pye asked.

'Only that he was scared of the people in his drug chain, but that's not a line for you to pursue.'

'What if he brings it up? I don't like being constrained in any interview, ma'am, least of all a murder investigation, when I'm the SIO. I don't want to speak out of turn, but we both know that I was given that role over the head of Superintendent Mackenzie, and that he'll be waiting for me to screw up.'

'I don't know any of that,' Chambers retorted. 'David Mackenzie's the city CID coordinator; he straddles all Edinburgh investigations, but he was never meant to lead any of them. He'd be doing what I'm doing with Booth, if he was available.'

'Where is he anyway, ma'am?' Haddock asked.

'Having time off for personal issues . . . that's if it's any business of yours, young man.'

'Sorry, boss; it's not,' he conceded.

'No.' She looked back at the DI. 'Sammy, I hear what you're saying about being handcuffed in there. All that I'm saying is that you're investigating the murder of Bella Watson, not Patrick Booth the drug dealer. I'll trust you to play it by ear. If something comes up that might help the drugs investigators, it'll be all right to follow it up as long as it doesn't obscure the main issue. I won't interfere unless I feel I have to; if I do, it'll be a tap on the shoulder, that'll be all.'

'Okay, that's fair enough,' Pye said. 'Let's get at it.'

He led the trio into the room. As they entered, Frances Birtles looked past him and focused on Haddock. 'Hello, Sauce,' she greeted him. 'I heard you were climbing the ladder.' She glanced at Chambers. 'Watch out for snakes, though.'

'They're all on your side of the table, Frankie,' he replied amiably. 'Good to see you, though.' His bonhomie vanished as soon as he took his seat facing Patrick Booth. 'But not you,' he added.

The prisoner brandished his plastered hand. 'See what you done?'

'Yeah,' the DS murmured, evenly, 'and I saw what you done too, what you did to that poor lass Vicky.' He looked into his eyes and was pleased to see him flinch.

'I never meant to.'

'Leave it out, both of you,' Pye snapped. 'That has nothing to do with our business here. Sauce, set up the recorder.' As soon as the machine was loaded and active, he went through the formalities. 'Mr Booth,' he continued, 'you're here to help us with our inquiries into the murder of Isabella Spreckley or Watson. Do you understand that?'

'He does,' Frankie Bristles replied. 'He also understands that he's here voluntarily, and that he can terminate this interview at any time.'

The DI nodded. 'Up to a point, but we'll get there later.'

'Pardon?' the solicitor exclaimed, but he ignored her.

'Can you tell us your relationship to the deceased, Mr Booth?'

'Aye,' Booth said, 'she was Vicky's auntie.'

'Vicky being Victoria Riley, the late Victoria Riley, your partner?'

'Aye.' He paused. 'I only knew her as Bella Spreckley, though, no' Watson. Ah met her first at Vicky's granny's place, a couple of times after that.'

'Did you ever visit her at her home in Caledonian Crescent?'

'Mmm. It was a nice wee flat, well kitted out. Vicky said it wasnae hers, but that some old boyfriend had set her up in it.'

'Why did you visit her?'

'Ah went to collect Vicky and wee Susan: that's our bairn.' He glanced to his left, towards his lawyer. 'Where is Susan anyway? I want tae see her. Make them let me see her, Miss Brittles.'

Haddock chuckled. 'That's a new variation on your name, Frankie. I'm sure you'll explain to your client that since he's been charged with shooting her mother dead, and that the child was in the room at the time, and got blood splattered on her, that might not happen any time soon.'

'He has a point, Patrick,' she admitted. 'Let's deal with this and I'll see what I can do later.'

'Aye all right,' Booth grumbled.

'Very good,' Pye continued. 'How often did you visit her?'

'Just the once, in February; Vicky took the bairn, to let her see her. No' that she was all that interested. Vicky only done it 'cos her granny told her to.'

'That would be Susan Coulter, yes?'

'Aye, that's right; Bella and she were brought up together. Bella wasnae Vicky's real auntie, ken.'

'So you just paid that one visit, right? Is that what you're saying?'

'To the best of his recollection, Inspector.'

He smiled at the lawyer. 'With respect, Frankie, your client doesn't seem like a complete idiot. He says he visited her for the first time in February. I accept that, because a neighbour had to tell him what floor Miss Spreckley lived on. That was seven months ago, tops. I'm sure that if he'd been there again since then, he'd know for sure. Isn't that right, Mr Booth?'

'Aye, that's right, just the once.'

'And you only went to pick up Vicky and Susan.'

'That's right.'

'Did you like Miss Spreckley?'

'Like her?' Booth repeated. 'There wasnae a lot to like about Bella. She might have been an old dear, but she was as hard as fuckin' nails, you could tell that. So no, Ah didnae like her.'

'Did she like you?'

'Bella didnae like anybody, apart from auld Susan.'

Frances Birtles leaned forward. 'Where are we going with this, Sammy?' she asked.

'Here,' he replied, then reached into the right-hand pocket of his jacket, which was bulging.

'I'm showing Mr Booth,' he continued, for the tape, 'a sealed plastic evidence envelope. It contains an ornamental jewel box.' He held it up, then placed it on the table, never taking his eyes from the other man, watching as his face contorted into a frown that was almost a grimace and as he hunched forward. 'I'm not going to open it, but I'm going to show you an image of an item that we found inside.'

He took a photograph from the same pocket and put it beside the box. 'It's a gold locket and it bears the inscription "To Bella from Tony". It's hallmarked and we've been able to establish that it was bought from Laing the Jeweller, in Edinburgh, seventeen years ago, by Mr Tony Manson. He was a heavy-duty criminal, and he and Bella had a relationship. The date of purchase suggests that this was a birthday present.'

The DI paused and looked at Birtles, half-expecting her to intervene, but she stayed silent.

'This box and its contents were found in your home, Mr Booth, during the execution of a search warrant relating specifically to this investigation. You've just said that you only visited the victim's home once, and then only briefly. Let's just take it for granted that she didn't give it to you in a grand gesture, or give it to Vicky, who wasn't really her niece. Let's save ourselves some time by you admitting that you stole it. Yes?'

Finally Frankie Bristles did open her mouth, but he stopped her with an upraised hand.

'He must respond,' he said. 'Either way, a one-word answer is all I need.'

Booth stared at the tabletop, and sighed heavily.

'Aye, okay. I stole it.'

'Right. Let me suggest two more things. One, if you stole it on that visit in February, there was no way that Miss Spreckley wouldn't have noticed its absence in all the time since. Two, she was not the sort of woman who'd have written it off to experience. "As hard as fucking nails," you said. Well, actually, we know that. So, Patrick, that leads us to the conclusion that I'm going to put to you now. You stole it after you killed her.'

He shook his head, violently. 'No,' he whispered, 'no, no, no.'

'Inspector,' Birtles began, trying to intervene again, but her client overrode her, finally meeting Pye's gaze.

'Ah took it, but Ah didnae kill her.'

'Then who did, if not you?'

'Don't ask me. All that Ah can tell you is that I didn't. Okay, Ah went back to her house again, but she wisnae there.'

'How did you get in?'

'From the street? Ah got in along wi' a neighbour.'

'No, into the flat,' Haddock said. 'If Bella wasn't there, how did you get in?'

Booth stared at him, scornfully. 'Please,' he retorted. 'There was only a Chubb lock on the door. No problem.'

'But if she wasn't there,' he paused, 'why did you go in?'

'Ah needed to see her.'

'So badly that you broke into her house?' Pye exclaimed. 'Come on, Patrick, you went there to rob her, and you wound up killing her.'

'Sammy,' the lawyer protested, 'you've got no evidence of that.'

'Don't be naive, Frankie,' he laughed. 'I've got the jewel box in his house, I've got him agreeing that he took it, and I've got him describing how he broke into the dead woman's flat. We're still doing DNA analysis, but now that I'm able to take a sample from your client, I'll put him in the room where she was killed. I'd go to trial on that. Would you fancy your chances of an acquittal?'

'A jury might look for more proof of murder.'

'That would be a jury of fifteen people, with a majority verdict acceptable to the judge. You reckon you could persuade eight of them to see it your way?'

'It's happened before. There is a Not Proven verdict available remember.'

'Sure.' He turned his attention back to the prisoner. 'There you have it, Patrick, a frank assessment of your chances, from your own lawyer: they are not good. I can charge you with murder now and walk out of here. By the time you get to trial your list of convictions will include culpable homicide, police

218

assault and firearms offences, on top of everything else, and so the six or seven years you're looking at now, allowing for parole, will go up to, oh, I'd say a minimum of twenty. D' you fancy that?'

'Ah didnae kill her!' Booth shouted, so loudly that even Chambers, seated away from the table, reacted.

Birtles put a hand on his arm but he shook her off. 'Ah needed tae see her because she was my contact for the gear, okay? She had been for a few months, ever since we started dealing.

'That day in February when I was at her house she asked me if I was up for some business: high-quality crystal meth, no' smack, or cocaine, from a small supplier, no' a cartel, low profile, low risk. Ah said I was, and we got started.'

'Patrick!' Birtles snapped a warning.

'Shut the fuck up!'

'Sammy,' the DI heard Chambers murmur. He leaned forward as if to avoid a tap on his shoulder.

'Ah met Bella once a month,' Booth continued, 'in a different place every time, tae give her the take. She'd give me my cut, and take the rest.

'She never handled the gear, though. I always picked that up, also once a month, from somebody else, a driver in a van wi' Spanish plates. It had all sorts in it: household stuff, like, furniture, computers, suitcases. Sometimes it was full, sometimes near empty.

'Bella always told me where tae go, and it could be anywhere. One time it was Wigan, the next Scunthorpe, the next Stoke; anywhere . . . but never big cities, Ah noticed that, and never in Scotland. Anyhow, the system worked fine until last month.

'Ah was supposed tae meet Bella in the Seabird Centre in North Berwick, but she never turned up. Afterwards Ah realised there was a big problem. I had the supply Ah'd picked up in Durham a couple of weeks before that but the source would be out a month's money, and Ah don't have to tell you how well that goes down wi' these people.'

He stared at Pye and Haddock, looking for affirmation. The DS nodded. 'Go on,' he whispered.

'That's why Ah went tae see Bella,' Booth said, 'to find out where the fuck she'd been and gie her the money but when Ah got in, there was blood all over the kitchen.

'I was shitting myself at that, I tell you. All Ah could think of was that Bella had been skimming off the take and that the folk up the chain had done her for it. So Ah took what I could, the jewel box and a few quid she had lying about, then got the hell out of there.

'Ah thought it would be me next, no kiddin'. I started packin' all the time. That's why Ah had the gun when Ah walked intae the house. When Ah found your guys . . . aye, okay, Vicky shouted that they were polis, but tae me they could have been anybody. I thought my turn had come.

'That's what happened, honest. Ah never killed Bella, and Ah never meant tae kill Vicky either.'

He stopped, then sagged in his chair as if exhausted. Pye allowed the silence to linger for a while, and the tension abate.

'What happened to the money?' he asked, when he was ready.

'Well, Ah didnae leave it there, did Ah?' Booth exclaimed. 'I took it away and put it back in ma hoose, in a bag behind the bath panel.'

The DI paused again, to absorb what he had been told.

'For the sake of this discussion,' he resumed, after a while, 'let's say I buy into that. Miss Birtles is bound to advise you to cooperate with the drugs squad. Frankly, so would I, but my job is still to find out who killed Miss Spreckley, whatever the motive.

'So, leaving other issues aside, is there anything you can tell me about the flat that might help me do that? Take all the time you need to think about it. Remember, all you've done so far is spun me a story. Years of your life could still be hanging on what you say to me.' He paused. 'Would you like a coffee? I could probably use one.'

Booth nodded.

'Me too, if you're buying,' Frankie Birtles said. 'Can I have five minutes with my client?'

'Yes, but not alone, unless he's cuffed; I'm responsible for your safety and he is a dangerous man.'

'I don't believe he is, Inspector, but okay, you can have a uniform in the room.'

Chambers, Pye and Haddock withdrew, leaving a constable behind with instructions to watch over the pair, but forget any conversation he might hear. In the corridor, after the DS had been despatched to fetch four coffees and a diet Sprite, the head of CID . . . who was on a weight-loss campaign . . . leaned close to the DI.

'That was okay in there,' she said, 'as it turned out. You can hand a copy of that tape to the drugs team, and they'll thank you for it, but sunshine, you came close to ignoring an order. A nice conviction here will do your promotion prospects no harm, but crossing me could have the opposite effect.'

'I know, boss,' Pye conceded, 'but I could see his eyes, and you couldn't. I knew he was going to give up everything he had.'

The DCS nodded, then winked at him. 'And you were right, you jammy bugger. What do you make of this supply chain he talked about? Ice, he said, methamphetamine, not heroin. That was news to me; our drugs team are going to hear about it too. They never bloody told me! They never mentioned any money either. If Booth's telling the truth, they've either found it and not said, or it's still bloody there! Either way,' she growled, 'somebody's in trouble.'

Pye shrugged. 'They're on a separate investigation, boss, as everyone keeps hammering home. Obviously they didn't see the need to share.'

'They share everything with me, like you do. Them's the rules. Well, fuck 'em,' Chambers declared. 'You keep that tape to yourself for a while, Sammy. If Bella's death is linked to drugs, your investigations have crossed paths. You've made progress, they haven't, so you carry the ball.' She flexed her square shoulders, shaking out stiffness. 'What do you think?' she asked.

'About the chain? Methamphetamine's not like Class A opiates. It's synthesised, it's highly addictive, and it's fashionable. It's quite plausible that someone with the know-how could set up a wee factory in a quiet place and operate under the radar. The next step in the investigation is to get as much as I can out of Booth, then see if we can find that van driver.'

'How?'

'We'll have dates and locations of the pick-ups. That'll be a start.'

'True,' she agreed, just as Haddock returned with a tray, looking miffed by his relegation to coffee boy. She read his expression and smiled. 'Good for the soul, Sauce,' she said, as she opened the interview room door for him.

'My client wishes to cooperate as fully as he can,' Frances Birtles declared, as the refreshments were distributed, and Haddock made a show of giving one specific mug to Booth. The prisoner looked at him suspiciously, as if he suspected him of spitting in it . . . exactly as the DS had intended.

'However,' she continued, 'he has to know who he's dealing with. You know what I mean, Sammy. He wants to be assured that if he offers you assistance you don't then hand him over to the drugs squad, to face charges that will get him longer inside than the culpable homicide that he's already up against.'

'He's dealing with me, Frankie. If his information results in an arrest for Bella Watson's murder, and if it leads further up the drug supply chain, he'll be a Crown witness in both cases. That'll mean he can't be charged with selling anything.'

'Do you understand that, Patrick?' she asked.

He nodded. 'Will Ah have to go in the witness box?'

'Probably,' Pye said. 'There's a limit to what I can offer. As a minimum I want a list of all your meetings with the van driver, dates, times and places. The registration number would be a bonus. Did you note that, or can you remember it?'

'Ah don't even remember what make of van it was, only that it was white, and didnae have any names on the side. It was about Transit size, but I don't think it was a Transit, ken.'

'Okay, write down all you can and we'll take it from there. It's the best deal that's going, make no mistake, and you're in no position to haggle. Now let's go back on the record.'

He restarted the interview, formally, repeating the introductions and reminding Booth that he was still under caution. 'You've had time to think,' he continued. 'I want you to describe again what you saw in Miss Spreckley's house after you broke in.'

'Like Ah said, there was blood in the kitchen, on the walls, the floor, the worktops. It was like she'd been pulpin' tomatoes and the lid had come off the blender. That's what Ah thought it was at first, tomatoes, till Ah realised it wasnae.'

'What made you realise?'

'Ah stood in it. It was sticky and that's when I kent what it was.'

'What did you do next?'

'Ah went into the bathroom and washed it off ma shoes. Somebody'd ripped up the carpet, by the way. Then Ah looked round for anything that might be worth having. Ah found a purse, and had a few quid out of that, and some other money in a drawer. The jewel box was in the bedroom, on the dressing table.'

'How many rooms were you in?'

'All of them.'

'Was there anything in any of them that you remembered not having been there before?'

Booth frowned, and his eyes narrowed. 'No,' he said. And then his face seemed to brighten as if a light had gone on. 'But there was something wasnae there, apart frae the carpet. When Ah was there before wee Susan was sleepin' in her buggy when Ah went to collect her, and she was in Bella's bedroom. The pram was right up against this long broon chest thing at the end of her bed. When Ah went back in there, after the jewels and stuff, it wasnae there any more.'

'Was it strong, this chest?' Pye asked slowly.

'Fuckin' solid. Ah banged my knee on it when Ah tried to move the buggy. It was wood, wi' big handles at either end.

'Did it extend the full width of the bed?'

'Aye.' He gave a small, nasty smile as if he had seen a mental image that had pleased him. 'Deep too; big enough for a body if it was jammed in there . . . even wrapped in a rug.'

'But too long for one person to handle?'

'He'd need to be a gorilla.'

'You're sure about this?' Pye asked. 'If you're trying to lay a false trail, we will know.'

'It's the truth.'

'Okay, it's a new line of inquiry and it answers a big question. You've got some points on the board. But you'd better not be kidding us about this van driver bloke either.'

Booth stared at him. 'Ah never said it was a bloke,' he exclaimed. 'The van driver's a woman.'

Thirty-Eight

'Please tell me you're going to have something positive for me, DI Mann.' In all his life, Ray Wilding had never come as close to begging. 'I've got my top floor watching me on this, and I've never felt so exposed.'

'No positive leads yourself then?' Lottie asked.

'None. Mackenzie's vanished off the face of the earth.'

'Does anyone outside our circle have a sniff of it yet?'

'I don't believe so. The official line is that he's having time off to deal with personal issues. That's holding, not least because he's just had a run-in with the ACC; most people within CID believe that he's been benched till he cools off. They'll be benching me if I don't come up with something soon. What have you got?'

'I don't know. My nee'bur and I ...'

'Your what?'

Mann laughed. 'Ah sorry; that's a Glasgow term. I meant, my colleague and I have just spoken to his priest, out in the arse end of Argyllshire. We left him ten minutes ago and now we're sitting in a hotel car park, getting ready for the long road home.'

'I didn't know Mackenzie was a religious man,' Wilding said. 'He's never given me that impression.'

'I don't know how religious he is, but the man we've spoken to has been a major influence in his life. How much have they told you about him?'

'I've seen his service record, and had a very quick look at his HR file, that's all. I've also spoken as discreetly as I could to some of his neighbours . . . his real neighbours, that is, not the Weegie kind, and it seems he never mixed with them. The upshot is that still I know very little personal about him. I would have spoken to his friends within the force, the problem being that he doesn't have any.'

'The same was true when he was a Strathclyde officer,' Mann told him. 'I never worked with him, but Dan Provan, my sergeant, did. He says there was something about him that grated on everyone; he was arrogant, a glory-hunter, and he was anti-authority, when authority wasn't listening, that is. Dan describes him as a Ned with a warrant card, a bandit with a sheriff's badge. But he got results, very good results, and he got promotion.'

'He sounds like the original mystery man,' Wilding observed. 'He's certainly been an outsider here, a boss's man when Bob Skinner was around, but without a patron since he's been gone.'

'We can unravel some of the mystery, thanks to the man we've just left.'

'The priest?'

'Yes.' She explained who Father Thomas Donnelly was, and how he had come into the troubled life of the young David Mackenzie. 'He took him under his wing, and to paraphrase his words, he put him on the right pathway.'

'A pathway that led him into the police force.'

'Yes. But something from his childhood wouldn't necessarily have kept him out.'

'Granted, but it happened, and I'm just gobsmacked that you

and I are hearing about it for the first time from a priest up in Auchna-wherever-it-is. We've been fearing something bad, but not really wanting to believe it. Now, it looks as if we might have to.'

'Not according to Father Donnelly,' Lottie Mann said.

'Why not?'

'Well, when we talked to him we got round to asking him whether or not Mackenzie was capable of murder.'

'Was that not a bit risky?'

'No, we were on his boat. Clearly, he's at his most comfortable there; he regards it as a sort of confessional. He didn't laugh off our question, not quite, but he did say that for all they might have squabbled like any other couple, Mackenzie cares for Cheryl, and he dismissed any thought that he might have harmed her. He was emphatic about it.'

'That's why you'll never find a priest on a jury,' DI Wilding retorted.

Provan chuckled. 'That's gey cynical, chum. Sounds to me that you've been hanging around Bob Skinner for too long.'

Thirty-Nine

'Is one pleased with oneself?' Sauce Haddock asked as he closed the door of the small office.

'Dunno what you mean,' Pye murmured.

'Not fucking much! We went in there handcuffed and you wind up getting to drive the whole bloody train.'

The DI permitted himself a small smile. 'There is that,' he conceded. 'Mary's a good boss. She's constructive, and not obstructive, like fucking Mackenzie. By the way,' he added, 'you never heard me say that, or that I'm not looking forward to him sorting his personal issue.'

'I don't think anyone in Edinburgh CID is, Sammy. He's a strange man, is our superintendent.'

'Well, at least he's not here to get in our way. Priorities, Sauce. We've got Booth's list of meetings with the van driver. This is not going to be easy, but I want you to contact all the petrol companies, including the supermarkets, and ask them if they can identify all sales of fuel made on and around those dates and in those localities that were settled with a Spanish credit or debit card. They should be able to do that.'

'But will they do it for me? I'm just a humble detective

sergeant . . . and a very junior one, as the boss pointed out when she made me get the fucking coffee!'

'Just drop your voice an octave or so,' the DI suggested, 'and they'll think you're a grown-up. Ask Jackie to help you. Going by the results she's been getting with her phone research, nobody could say no to her.' He looked up. 'And speaking of DC Wright . . .'

The glass-panelled door opened and the young detective stuck her head into the room. 'Excuse me, Inspector,' she began, 'but I was wondering, do you still want me to go with the DS to interview this man Gayle. It's just that I've . . .'

'Got a date tonight?' Haddock ventured.

She flushed. 'As it happens, yes . . . not that I can't cancel it.'

'No,' Pye replied. 'Your love life's secure. The game's changed; I've got another task for you and Sauce. I'll talk to Gayle myself.'

'Thanks, boss,' she said, a smile lighting up her face. 'In that case, I've established from the Western General that he's working today, until ten o'clock, when the night staff come on. I thought I should check that, rather than go all the way to Tranent only to find out that he wasn't in.'

'Did you get me a parking space as well?' the DI asked, deadpan.

'Oh no, boss,' she gasped. 'I'm sorry; I forgot.'

He grinned. 'Don't let it ruin your day. You probably forgot also that the Western General is bang next door to our head-quarters building. I don't think my car's going to be a problem.'

Forty

I confess that I couldn't see further than my own embarrassment and wounded pride after Detective Inspector Mann's phone call had updated me on the David Mackenzie situation.

Although she and Provan were helping out in what was a confidential Edinburgh inquiry, I wasn't going to be kept out of the loop. At the same time, I didn't want to be seen to be leaning on my former colleagues, hence my instruction, no, my informal request, that everything she reported to Ray Wilding should come to me as well.

I thought back to my first meeting with the officer then known as Bandit, a DI at the time, in North Lanarkshire. He'd run away with the idea that Ruth, my then secretary, now Mrs DI Sammy Pye, might have murdered her uncle.

In the course of an interview during which, as Ruth described it, he had 'sprayed the room with testosterone', he'd made some unfortunate remarks about me, off tape. They might have been true, but they were unfortunate for him, as Ruth had her own recorder running, and they found their way back to me.

I paid him a private visit, and gave him what I will describe only as 'a good talking to'. I had the power, then, to finish him in CID, forever, but I didn't because a good friend who knew him and had worked with him gave him a half decent reference. In fact, Willie Haggerty described him as the cockiest, most conceited bastard he had ever met but added that he had the potential to become a great detective officer.

Of course, yours truly, the great Bob Skinner, who could probably have outdone Mackenzie in the conceit department any day of the week, I decided that I was the man to straighten him out and release that potential. So I poached him from Strathclyde, never once wondering why Jock Govan, his chief constable, took it so well, and I put him in charge of our drugs squad.

He was pretty good in that role; with hindsight I should have left him there, but I didn't. Instead I promoted him into a division. It was unfamiliar territory, and his manner didn't go down well. Soon afterwards, he found himself with a gun in his hand and in a situation where his courage was tested. It failed, and I had a problem on my hands.

To paraphrase something Lennie Plenderleith said, there's nothing worse for a tough guy than the realisation that he isn't actually all that tough. Bandit took it hard; in fact, he stopped being Bandit altogether and became a candidate for early retirement on health grounds. If I had left the decision to Sir James Proud, the chief, or even to the ACC, Brian Mackie, he'd have been gone, but I didn't.

No, I couldn't face up to my own flawed judgement, so I stuck him in a uniform and made him Command Corridor exec. In that role he managed to piss off most people in his circle, even getting himself into Mario McGuire's bad books. That's very hard to do, but if you succeed, you find that it's not a place anyone would want to be.

As I sat in my office contemplating Lottie Mann's briefing, I was forced to face up to a few truths. It wasn't that I'd misjudged Mackenzie; I'd always seen him as a mix of intelligence, arrogance, and aggression. He'd displayed the last two of those traits in his confrontation with Ruth. I'd thought I'd knocked the aggression out of him when I'd sorted him out, but as I looked at the situation Edinburgh was facing, it seemed likely that it had only gone into hiding, to re-emerge with a vengeance.

I thought more deeply about the man. His intelligence; that would always be there. His arrogance? From what I'd heard, Mario had put him in his place, well and truly, forcing him into a fairly public climbdown, a serious loss of face for a person to whom front was all-important. Would that have been enough to make him potentially violent? Possibly.

Christ, Skinner, I asked myself, what have you done?

I'd have given myself a more severe mental kicking but for one thing. Mackenzie's back story had been complete news to me.

When Lottie told me of Father Donnelly's remark about Mackenzie's troubled childhood, it was only the priest's name that convinced me to follow it up. In my own teenage years he'd been quite a famous man in Lanarkshire for his progressive work with young people, in a diocese that was on the right of conservative.

If he'd been Mackenzie's mentor, well, it fitted what I'd read about the man back then, a dog collar who took no nonsense, a bit like my friend Archbishop Gainer, only he'd been a rough diamond himself in his younger days.

It wasn't difficult to come up with his phone number; it couldn't have been because it took Sandra Bulloch all of ninety seconds to find him.

I dialled him myself, before realising that he might still be on the boat that Mann had told me about. I was about to hang up when my call was transferred to a mobile number. As the retired cleric answered, I could hear seabirds in the background.

'Father Donnelly,' I began, 'my name's Bob Skinner. You've just had a visit from two of my officers.'

'Hello, Mr Skinner,' he replied. His voice was younger than I'd been expecting. 'I know who you are. As a matter if fact, I've known for years. I kent your faither, as we say in Scotland. I was involved in a youth initiative in Motherwell way back when, and he was one of my financial backers.'

'That surprises me,' I said. 'My father wasn't Catholic.'

'No, but he was a good man. He told me that if I could prevent kids from growing up to be defended in court by the likes of him then he was happy to help me take the burden off the legal aid system.'

Fucking hell, Bob! Another entry in the long list of things you never knew about your dad.

'You must have been around ten then. I remember him talking about you. He said you were a very quiet, withdrawn boy. You seem to have got over that.'

'With the help of a good woman; no,' I corrected myself, 'two good women. Did he ever mention my brother, Michael?'

'Not really; I remember him saying that he was a bit of a mystery in his own way too, but that's all. Now, young Bob, what's all this about? Are you checking up on your subordinates?'

'Check up on DI Mann? How brave do you think I am?'

'No, maybe not. What can I do for you then?'

'I want to ask to you some more about David Mackenzie. How did you come across him?'

'Is this important, Mr Skinner?' he asked.

'Yes it is, Father. And please call me Bob.'

'Thank you, Bob. How much do you know about David?'

'As a police officer,' I replied, 'everything. As a man, very little.'

'Ahh well,' he sighed. 'In that case I'd better tell you the full story. I had assumed that it was known within the police service, at senior level, at least. I'm more than a little surprised that it isn't.'

There was something in his voice that made me grip the phone a little harder.

'David Mackenzie, the boy David,' he began, 'spent half his childhood in a children's home in East Kilbride. His father was a long-distance lorry driver who put his truck down a mountainside in Italy when David was only four years old. His mother never got over it and took an overdose a year later.' He paused. 'This is all news to you?'

'Completely,' I said, flabbergasted. 'He was orphaned?'

'Yes, but it got worse.' Father Donnelly continued. 'The child was taken in for a while by an aunt, his mother's sister, but her husband turned out to be a very bad lot.

'He abused the boy violently; he thrashed him mercilessly for every small infraction, while all the time he was spoiling his own kids. The social workers should have spotted it during the supervision process that followed his mother's suicide, but they must have been asleep on the job.

'They woke up when David, then aged nine, threw the contents of a bubbling chip pan over his uncle, as he was taking off his belt to lash the kid again.'

'Bloody hell,' I couldn't stop myself from whispering.

'There may have been metaphorical chips in it,' the priest said, 'for one of them stuck to the boy's shoulder, and permanently.

'In those days, the age of criminal responsibility was only eight, but when the investigating officers saw the scars on his back and buttocks . . . for the man drew blood most times . . . and a couple of old rib fractures on X-rays, things got turned around.

'The uncle recovered well enough from his burns to go to jail for a couple of years. The aunt was prosecuted too, but she only got probation. Young David got the children's home.'

'That's tragic,' I exclaimed in my astonishment. 'How did he get on there?'

'That depends on the measurement you apply, Bob. He was a bright boy, so he did well academically, but he was never out of bother. He was always fighting, in and out of the home. He'd a real hair-trigger temper, and it got him in trouble a couple of times in his early to mid teens.

'The most serious thing he did landed him in front of the Children's Panel. He chucked a brick at a kid who'd been razzing him, outside the school. He was lucky, for it caught the boy on the forehead and didn't do any more than superficial damage. Even at that, he might well have wound up in a secure unit if the chair of the Children's Panel hadn't been persuaded to take another line.'

'How did they straighten his act up?' I asked.

'That's where I come in,' the priest told me. 'I'd been chaplain at the home for a while. The Panel chair made him enrol in a local inter-denominational youth club that I ran at the time, not unlike the one in Motherwell, and made me responsible for his care.

'I took no crap from him, mind, but I challenged him intellectually rather than physically, and started him using his brain rather than his fists. I made him buckle down at school too, so well that he left with a good group of Highers.

'By that time he had moved out of the home and was living with me in the chapter house. When he left I found him a clerking job, and I got him set up in a flat of his own.'

'And you kept in touch after that?'

'Of course I did. We've never lost touch. David joined the church when he was eighteen, his own choice, not at my request. I married him and Cheryl, and I baptised both their children, Alice and Zach, the younger one just before I retired.'

'How did you know,' I asked, 'about this chip-pan attack, if you only met David as a teenager?'

'Initially, from the manager of the home; she told me about it and showed me the boy's file. Not that there was much detail, mind; all it mentioned was a violent response to abuse. I didn't know the full circumstances until Max Allan told me about it.'

'Max? As in ACC Allan, recently retired from the service?'

'Yes. Max and I drank in the same pub, the Hoolet's in High Blantyre, for the same reason, basically: we both wanted a place away from our day job. He had heard about the Children's Panel reference at work. He was stationed in East Kilbride then, and he'd been in Uddingston when the blow-up with the abusive foster parents happened.'

'Foster parents, you say?'

'Yes, David was never formally adopted.'

'And Max told you the full story?'

'Yes. He was the investigating officer. He said that he first learned about it from the hospital, when the uncle was admitted. As I remember . . . it's a long time since I heard this, mind . . . he told me David's aunt claimed that it had been an accident. The uncle wasn't in a position to say anything at that point. The A&E doctor didn't believe her for a moment. He assumed that she'd done it herself, and he called the police.

'Max thought the same thing . . . until he spoke to David. He assumed that he'd confirm the unanimous conclusion, but instead, this nine-year-old boy looked him dead in the eye, and said, "She never done it, it was me. He was going to leather me again. She would have let him, like she did every other time. If there had been two chip pans she'd have got the other one."

'He was proud of himself, too, so Max said. He got the doctor to examine the boy there and then, and he found those scars from beatings, inflicted over a period of years, and three fractures to his ribs that clearly had never been treated, or reported, according to his medical records.'

'And David was definitely nine years old?' I said.

'Yes. He was nearly ten when he was placed in the home; I recall that from his file.'

'That means he was old enough to have been charged with serious assault, yet he never was.'

'No. Max told me that when he started to recover, the uncle wanted him prosecuted, but that he talked him out of it.'

Knowing Max, I could imagine how he did that. 'What sort of a kid was he in the children's home, Father?' I asked.

'He was one among quite a few troubled kids in that place. The manager was a sincere woman but, to be frank, I don't believe she was up to the job. She never had any real control: that was evident to me, although not to my fellow chaplain, from the Church of Scotland; he was as weak as her.'

'There were two of you?' I was surprised; I'd assumed that it was a Catholic home.

'Yes, there were. David was really his "client" in that he'd been baptised as a Protestant, but he had no influence over him and when the assault thing happened, he washed his hands of him. So did the manager; Mrs Meek, her name was. Ironic, eh?

'The Children's Panel hearing took place in the home. She said that he was beyond her control, and my clerical colleague agreed with her. I was there, you see. I went, because I was afraid the lad would wind up in a secure unit and that would be the end of him.

'When the Meek woman said what she did, I'm afraid I lost my temper. I told her that she'd never bloody tried to control him or influence him in any way, and that her only interests were in feeding him, and getting him to school on time.

'The Children's Panel chair asked me if I'd like to have a go with him, and I said I would. So she made him enrol in my youth group and made me responsible for his behaviour, from then on.'

'How did you get on?' I asked him.

'It wasn't too difficult, actually; I won his respect. Nobody had ever done that before; they'd only gained his suspicion and resentment.

'As soon as he turned sixteen, he came to live with me in the chapter house. In this day and age that wouldn't be possible; the bishop would foul his trousers at the very idea. Back then, though, it worked.

'David never really had a proper parental relationship, you see, or quasi-parental, and he seemed to appreciate it. He really was formidably clever as a young man, and that helped.'

I was amazed by what I was being told. 'Did he ever flare up?' I wondered.

'With me, no; I was a proper authority figure to him. But he wasn't with me twenty-four seven; I'm sure that he did, from time to time. He'd learned that chucking bricks at other people was not a clever thing to do, but he still had an air of self-confidence about him, and that could be provocative.

'He annoyed one or two of my parishioners, I admit. By that time, though, Cheryl was around and she may have been a moderating influence on him.'

I was surprised. 'They go back that far? I had no idea.'

'Oh yes. The Austin family moved to East Kilbride when Cheryl was about fourteen. She's only a year younger than David; they met at school, and they were close from the start. Indeed, it may well be that she had more to do with him keeping out of trouble than I did. She may also have been why he was so keen to have his own flat at such a young age. He was only nineteen when he moved into a wee place I found for him.'

'Was that when they got married?'

'Oh no, they didn't marry until a few years after that. Cheryl's parents were sensible people. They never interfered with the relationship, but they did insist on her getting a qualification. She went to university in Glasgow and did her pharmacy degree, while David was making his way in the police. They finally tied the knot when they were twenty-five, and didn't have children until they'd both turned thirty.'

'Having been a couple for fifteen years?' I observed. 'That must have been a bit of a culture shock.'

'I suppose. I'm not sure why they waited so long.'

Possibly because David liked being the centre of attention, I thought. I didn't put that to the priest, for I wanted to get to what had been originally the reason for my call.

'Father,' I said, 'I'd like to ask you about the time when he joined the police. Were you involved in that?'

'Closely. As I said, David left school with a good group of Higher passes. They were enough to get him into university, but he didn't want to go there, not straight away. He said that he wanted to work for a couple of years, to get some money behind him. He'd been left a small sum when his parents died, a few thousand, but his aunt and uncle had stolen it. When I asked the aunt about it she claimed they'd spent it on him. She was lying, of course, but there was nothing to be done about it.

'I helped find him a clerical job with South Lanarkshire Council, and he got on fine there. He worked hard and his bosses couldn't fault his performance, but the feedback I was getting was that he could be hard to manage, that he always knew better than them.

'He and Cheryl had quite a combustible relationship too; when she started university he saw a lot less of her, and he didn't like that. There were rows, and eventually an incident one Saturday when he found her with a group of fellow students in a café in Buchanan Street, and threatened one of the boys.

'Eventually Cheryl asked me for help, and David and I had a heart-to-heart. I told him that he needed to work on his self-discipline or he was going to lose his girl and a hell of a lot more.

'He must have been listening, because a week later, he came to see me, and he had a police application form with him. I helped him fill it in.'

That was what I wanted to hear. 'You did?' I said. 'Can you remember any of the detail?'

'Pretty much all of it.'

'How much of his personal history did you include?'

'That was the sensitive part,' Father Donnelly replied. 'I don't have to tell you that applicants are expected to make full disclosure. I insisted that David do so, even though technically he needn't have declared the chip-pan incident, and he might even have argued that the Children's Panel hearing didn't record a finding of guilt. We drew up a memorandum together and attached it to the application form. It set out his entire life history and we both signed it.'

'Are you certain that he submitted it? I'd heard none of this until you told me.'

'David didn't submit it. I did. I posted his application myself. When he was accepted for the service, I assumed that it had been taken into account.'

'It may have been,' I admitted, 'but I can find no record of it.'

'What would you do, Bob,' the priest asked me, casually, turning the tables, 'if such an application landed on your desk today, with those same circumstances?'

I thought about that one, then gave him an honest answer. 'I'd probably reject it. A police officer's stability needs to be unquestionable. I know now that David's never has been. At the very least, such an applicant would need a rigorous psychological evaluation.'

'I see.' All at once, Tom Donnelly sounded his age. 'I thought I was doing the best I could, for everyone,' he sighed. 'For David, for Cheryl and for the police service.'

'You did,' I told him. 'As you said, you made full disclosure, and obviously your name on the form was enough to overcome any doubts the people who handled it may have had. Any mistake was ours, not yours. Incidentally,' I asked, casually, 'when the application was made, did you mention it to Max Allan?'

'No, I did not.'

'Okay.'

I was about to thank him and hang up, when he broke into my thoughts. 'Will you do one thing for me, Bob?' he said. 'During my visit from DI Mann and DS Provan, and during this discussion, nobody has actually told me what David is supposed to have done. There have been hints but nothing more. Can you tell me, straight out, in confidence. of course.'

And so I did. 'David Mackenzie is missing. He's suspected of having murdered Cheryl.'

I heard a huge sigh, right in my ear. 'I thought you were heading in that direction,' he murmured. 'In that case, I can tell you, categorically, that he did not. I can't tell you how I know this, but he didn't.'

Forty-One

Sammy Pye was not a big fan of Edinburgh's Western General Hospital. He had no complaints about its clinical standards, his mother having been treated there, successfully, for breast cancer, but its layout was confusing, and also he believed that its site was overdeveloped, with too many buildings on too small an acreage.

Fortunately, finding Vanburn Gayle was not going to be a problem. Jackie Wright had established that he worked in Ward One, the chemotherapy unit, which was on the southern entrance road.

As he had told the DC, his warrant card enabled him to park at the rear of the police headquarters building, which was destined to become a regional office after the impending unification, and walked the short distance to the hospital precinct.

His mother's experience there made him realise it would be insensitive simply to walk into the ward. Instead he went to the Oncology Centre reception and showed his badge to the woman behind the counter. 'I'd like a word with Staff Nurse Gayle,' he said, 'about an investigation that he might be able to help us with. I understand he's on duty just now.'

'He is,' she replied, 'and you're in luck. He's on a break just now.' She pointed to her left. 'He's just round the corner there, past the kiosk.' She smiled. 'He's West Indian, and he's kind of hard to miss.'

He thanked her and walked towards the lounge area that opened out past the refreshment bar. One glance round the corner told him that the receptionist had understated things. The man was impossible to miss. He was dark-skinned, with frizzy grey hair, and even seated, reading a copy of the *Metro*, he looked massive, with weightlifter shoulders and huge forearms that protruded from his short-sleeved blue tunic.

'Mr Gayle,' he said.

The nurse looked up, blinking in his surprise.

'Detective Inspector Pye, Leith CID.' His warrant card was still in his hand, and he held it out for inspection. 'Do you have a minute?'

'Sure,' he replied, in a deep mellow voice, 'but for what?'

'I'd like to talk to you about a current investigation.'

Suspicion crept into his brown eyes. 'Current?' he repeated.

'Yes, it concerns the murder of a woman in Edinburgh. It took place a couple of weeks ago, but her identity was only confirmed at the weekend.'

Suspicion became alarm. 'Why do you want to talk to me?'

'Relax,' Pye murmured, with what he hoped was a reassuring smile. 'It's peripheral to the main investigation, just something that's come up. Be assured that you are not a suspect; if you were I wouldn't be alone and we wouldn't be talking here.'

The big man nodded. 'Okay, if you say so. Let's do it; I have ten minutes or so, but then I must be back on the ward.'

Pye lowered himself on to a seat facing Gayle. 'Thanks,' he said. 'I want to ask you about two people. The first is a man named Duane Hicks. He lived in Edinburgh for a while in the nineteen nineties, but moved back to St Lucia, where he's from.'

The nurse shrugged. 'Duane? Sure, what's he done?'

'Nothing, as far as I know,' the DI replied. 'But you do know him, yes?'

'Sure, he's family of sorts: his mother and my mother are cousins. My mum's from St Lucia, like him. She couldn't get a job at home so she moved to Trinidad, and stayed there after she met my father. I only met Duane for the first time when he worked here, and I haven't seen him since, not face to face. We speak from time to time.'

'Did you know he married in Edinburgh?'

'Yes, I think my mother told me at the time, but I'd moved to London when that happened. I've never met his wife; I know nothing about her, except Mum said she was a local girl, and she had a kid.' He frowned. 'You're not going to tell me Duane's dead, are you?'

'No, I'm not. As far as I know he's alive and well.'

'Then what . . .'

'Bear with me,' Pye said. 'I want to ask you about someone else, a man named Peter Hastings McGrew, known commonly as Hastie. Mr McGrew was jailed for murder, around about the time you left Edinburgh. I'm advised that you were one of the very few people who visited him in prison.'

'Hey, man,' Gayle exclaimed, 'you really been checking up on me. Yes, I visited Hastie. He and I looked after his father, Mr Holmes . . . only I didn't know at that time that Hastie was his son. They kept that secret, the pair of them. I still don't know why they did that; I asked him, in prison, but all he would say was they had their reasons.'

'But Mr Holmes's daughter was no secret.'

'Alafair? No, I knew about her.'

'It never occurred to you that Hastie had the same surname?'

The big man stared back, surprised; genuinely so, the DI read. 'I never knew that; I just assumed her family name was Holmes. She was married to that footballer guy with the funny name, Drysalter, and that's how I knew her . . . as Alafair Drysalter. Why'd they do that anyway, man; not use their dad's name? Do you police know?'

'Can't you guess, Mr Gayle? Their parents were never married, and given Mr Holmes's business, they thought it better that Hastie and Alafair use their mother's name.'

'What business? Mr Holmes was a property developer; plus he had a limo company, a funeral business, and he was in the leisure and security business. He also owned a big chain of care homes. It was that company paid me when I looked after him.'

'Sure, he was all those things, but much more. He was also . . .' He stopped to consider his words. 'Let me put it this way; if the Scottish police had a list of public enemies, in his time Perry Holmes would have been number one. He was a quadriplegic when you looked after him. Didn't you know how he got that way?'

'I know he was shot,' Gayle replied. 'His doctor told me the story, and of course I saw the scars. A former employee went crazy, and ambushed Mr Holmes and his brother.'

'That's only one-third true. Billy Spreckley never worked for the Holmeses, not formally anyway, and he wasn't crazy. He shot them because they had his brother and his nephew killed.'

'Mr Holmes? Are you serious?'

'I never joke on the job,' Pye assured him. 'Mr Gayle, correct me if I've been misinformed, but you were there when Hastie was arrested, were you not?'

'Too true,' he admitted, 'and I'll never forget it. Hastie had a gun but that policeman, Skinner, he shot it out of his hand. I'll never forget him either: he was a very scary man, in a quiet way. Those murders that Hastie went to jail for,' Gayle continued, 'they had nothing to do with his father. A girl he knew was attacked and the police were going to do nothing about it, so he went after the guys who did it. That was the story; that's what he told me.'

'And that's what the court accepted, but there were other murders that he was never charged with and they definitely had to do with your patient. Tell me,' the detective went on, 'why did you leave him when you did?'

'I went to do a nursing degree, in London,' the man replied. 'Didn't you find that out when you checked up on me?' he added, with a faint hint of sarcasm.

'As a matter of fact we did, and this isn't part of my investigation; I'm just curious, my cop's nose is twitching. You can imagine why, since Mr Holmes was drowned in his treatment pool not long after you left. Why did you go? Were you scared by Hastie's arrest?'

'Yeah,' he conceded, 'sure I was. You woulda been too if you'd been there.' His own recent experience with Patrick Booth made Pye admit privately that he was right. 'But that wasn't why I went then. I was given money, quite a lot of money, and I was able to afford to go.'

Pye felt a surge of excitement but hid it. 'And who gave you the money? There's a school of police thought says it was a man called Tony Manson.'

Gayle chuckled. 'Then they ain't thinking straight, Inspector. I never heard of that man. No, it was Alafair gave it to me.'

'Alafair?'

'Yes, she said it was compensation for the stress of Hastie's arrest. And it was her who found me the course in London. It was all official, man. I paid tax on it, the money. I know this, 'cos it said on my form when I left.'

Bloody hell. This is not history as it was written. I need to report this.

When the nurse continued, Pye was so distracted that the words sailed over his head. He excused himself. 'I'm sorry, could you repeat that?'

'I said, what does all that have to do with Duane Hicks?'

The DI replied, 'I was getting there, and I will, but let's stay with Hastie for now. Why did you visit him?'

'Because he and I were friends when we worked together; it felt like the thing to do. Then there was the money, I suppose. Without it, I'd never have been able to take my degree, and I'd never have been here. I felt grateful to the family, and that was the only way I could show it.'

'When you saw him, what did you talk about?'

Gayle smiled, revealing perfect tombstone teeth. 'All sorts of things, man. Books, music, movies I'd seen. Sport, of course; we talked about cricket a lot. He's a fan, and it's part of my culture.'

'Did you ever talk about the old days, about Edinburgh?'

'Some, but not much.'

'When you did, did Hastie ever mention a woman called Bella Watson?'

'As a matter of fact, he did. One day, not long before he was released, I asked him about the other guys in the prison, whether any of them were famous. He said there was a guy called Lennie something, about his own age, from Edinburgh. He told me that he'd never met him on the outside because . . . how did he put it . . . they were from different parts of town, but he'd got to know him inside.

'He said he was very much a reformed guy, that he'd spent all his sentence studying, but that in the old days, he'd had a ferocious reputation. I asked him if he was the most dangerous person he knew, and he said no, that he wasn't dangerous any more, and that even when he was, he didn't come close to a woman called Bella Watson.

'He told me that inside Lennie there was always a kind heart, but that this Bella woman, she didn't have no heart at all, just pure evil inside.'

'Have you seen him since he was released from prison?' the DI asked.

'No. He said he would look me up when he felt like a free man again. He expected that would take time. I've promised to give him physio treatment. He has handicaps, you know.'

'Yes, I've heard that. Now,' Pye said, briskly, 'let's get back to Duane Hicks. Have you heard from him recently?'

'Recently? This year, certainly; he called me out of the blue, in early January, and asked if I could do him a favour. He said his boy Marlon . . . now I think about it, that must have been his wife's kid: they have two of their own, but they're still at school . . . Marlon, he had trained as a mechanic and was lookin' to come back to Edinburgh to work. My mum had said to his mum that I knew people; last time I was home I told her about Hastie and Alafair and the businesses they own.

'A week or so later, I saw Hastie in Kilmarnock, and I asked him if they had anything going. A couple of days on, Alafair called me and said they'd hire him. She even fixed him up with somewhere to live, as a favour to me. Once the kid was settled in he dropped by to thank me. I haven't seen him since.'

The DI nodded. 'Okay. Now, once again, you're saying you don't know anything about Duane's wife.'

'Her name's Marie, but that's it. Why, man? Why's it so important?'

'It may not be, but a bookie would give you rotten odds against. Bella Watson, the woman I asked you about: it's her murder I'm investigating, and young Marlon Hicks is her grandson. You can bet that if Hastie McGrew thought Bella was pure evil, she felt much the same way about him.'

Forty-Two

I didn't blame Lottie for getting less out of the priest than I did. I could have told her to go harder with him, but there was no certainty that would have worked. Tom Donnelly had felt a personal connection with me, through my father, and that may well have persuaded him to open up as much as he had.

He'd given me enough food for thought to send me into a mental meltdown, and some of it, I decided, I was keeping to myself. As for the rest, I was prepared to share that, and even to swap it.

I thought through my options; when I was ready I picked up the phone and called Maggie Rose . . . sorry, Maggie Steele; my old habits die harder than Bruce Willis. 'Hi, Bob,' she greeted me, sounding less than cheerful.

'Who stole your scone?' I asked.

'And my birthday cake,' she retorted. 'I've got Mario with me; we've just had a visit from Mary Chambers, briefing us on the Bella Watson murder inquiry.'

'How's that one going?' I don't think I sounded too interested; Bella's demise was poetic justice in my book, and so as an outside observer I couldn't summon up too much enthusiasm.

'She's got more lines of inquiry than a spider's web. The

unfortunate thing is that they all lead in different directions. The DCS has called a case conference for tomorrow to try to pull them together. Just to add a fresh complication, she had a call from Sammy Pye in the middle of our visit. He's just picked up a piece of information that might mean we have to reopen a very cold case: the death of Perry Holmes.'

That got my attention. 'Indeed? I wouldn't be spending too much money on it. Lennie Plenderleith reckons that Manson had him done. You'll be struggling to convict him, since he's as dead as Perry.'

'No, not him.'

'Still, think carefully,' I advised. 'It's been a long time and there were no witnesses. It could even have been an accident . . . although I admit that I have never bought the fiscal's dodgy wheelchair theory.'

'Don't worry,' Maggie said, 'that's not a top priority. Right now, the two of us are contemplating the prospect of holding a press briefing tomorrow, to go public on David Mackenzie's disappearance, and to announce that he's wanted on suspicion of murdering his wife. I'm going to get crucified.'

'No,' I heard McGuire say loudly in the background. 'I am; you're not taking the rap for this.'

'It's my rap to take,' Maggie declared, for his benefit and mine; her voice echoed, telling me that she'd put me on speaker-phone. 'I'm the chief constable; I can't get out from under. That forty-eight-hour silence isn't going to look too clever under questioning.'

'Just hold on,' I told her, 'before you get into a warm bath and open your veins. Have you set up this suicide mission yet?'

'No, we're leaving it until the morning. Why?'

'Because you need a rethink; Mackenzie might have done a

couple of things in his time that he didn't want anyone to know about, but he has not murdered his wife.'

'What?' she shouted in my ear. 'How do you know that?'

'It comes from an unimpeachable source. When I was a boy in Motherwell,' I added, in explanation, 'there was a guy on the council who was the local bishop's mouthpiece. That was what he used to say when he was quoting his master's voice.'

'Did you get that from the bishop, then?' she asked, with a trace of sarcasm that I must have left in her office when I moved out.

'Almost as good as; I got it from David's priest.'

'From his what?' McGuire exclaimed. 'I never knew Mackenzie was a Catholic.'

'There are lots of things none of us knew about Mackenzie, chum. He wasn't born into it, as far as I know; he signed up as a teenager.'

'You trust this clerical informant, do you, Bob?' he asked.

'Yes I do.'

'He told you Cheryl is still alive?'

'Not directly, but that's what he meant.'

'Do you know this guy?' I'd never been cross-examined by McGuire before. I wasn't sure I cared for it.

'My father knew him,' I replied, well aware how lame that sounded.

'That doesn't fill me with confidence,' he drawled. 'I seem to remember you telling me once that you hardly knew your father yourself.'

'Mario!' I heard Maggie snap.

'No,' I said, 'that's a fair point. But Tom Donnelly told me categorically that Mackenzie is not a wife-murderer, and I will go with that. If you two don't want to, then fine, let the media vultures pick your bones tomorrow. But be ready to look like a couple of Charlies when Cheryl shows up alive and well in the tabloid of her choice.'

'If this goes pear-shaped, Bob . . .'

I acknowledged her hesitancy. 'I know. You've both got careers to protect, especially with the new unified force well over the horizon, whereas I don't give a shit about mine. It's your call, and it has to be based on your judgement.'

'But yours is that we should hold fire?'

'Mine is that you have no evidence other than a few blood-stains on a towel, and they don't prove violence. There are any number of possible explanations for that; a sudden nosebleed, as I said before. Sarah had one when we were in Spain last week, but nobody thought about locking me up.'

'What about the duvet, Mags?' McGuire asked. 'Does Bob know about that?'

'Sorry, Mario,' she replied, after a short pause, 'I'm still processing the news that he and Sarah were in Spain last week. Yes, the missing duvet from off their bed.'

'Again, that proves nothing,' I pointed out. 'You've got a couple who've disappeared at the same time, leaving their kids behind, safe with her mother. That's all that you know for sure. I take it you've checked their financial situation. Do they have money problems, debt collectors knocking on the door, that sort of thing?'

'Yes we have, and no they don't. They're as comfortable as you'd expect a couple to be with two good salaries coming in.'

'Is there anything in Mackenzie's past career that rings any alarm bells, villains with a grudge, and so on?'

'No, we've eliminated that as a possibility.' She sighed. 'Okay, this is about judgement, as you said earlier. We've both followed yours from the start, and I'm going to follow it again. We'll do nothing about a media conference, and reconsider on Monday. If there's flak when it does come out . . .'

'If it comes out,' I interrupted. 'They could return tomorrow, penitent and unharmed.'

'Okay then, if it leaks, and the media go on the attack, we can argue that there was no danger to the public, so we had no obligation to them. Agreed, Mario?'

'Agreed.'

'A deal, then; we come back from the brink. Thanks, Bob, for your input and your advice.'

'Don't mention it,' I said. 'I hope it works out for you; something's happened between them, that's for sure.'

I know what you're thinking. Why isn't he sharing everything he knows with them, two people he's known and trusted for much of his career and most of theirs? I should have but I chose not to, for I had a scent in my nostrils. It wasn't a very pleasant odour, and I wanted to get to its source on my own.

'Mags,' I said, 'the way this is turning out it's almost as much my investigation as yours. Could you do something for me?'

'Name it, oh master,' she chuckled. 'Why is it all your requests still sound like orders?'

'This is a request, honest. I've been looking for Mackenzie's personnel file, but my people tell me that everything was sent to Edinburgh when he moved. Any chance I could see it?'

'If you want to; but I warn you, Ray Wilding's looked at it and found nothing.'

'Nevertheless.'

'Okay, I'll have it sent to you tonight.' She paused. 'Where do I send it?' she asked, provocatively. 'Your place or Sarah's?'

'Mine, thanks,' I replied, po-faced. 'I'll let you have it back when I'm done.'

'What do you expect to find in it that Wilding didn't?'

'Nothing, Maggie, absolutely nothing,' I told her, and I meant it.

Forty-Three

'Well,' Mary Chambers began, as she gazed around the conference table in the Edinburgh police headquarters building, 'this is quite a team to be investigating one disreputable old woman's murder. Is that why we're not making any progress? Too many cooks, is that it?'

Five police officers gazed back at her: Detective Inspectors Sammy Pye and Jack McGurk, Detective Sergeants Harold Haddock and Karen Neville, and Detective Constable Jackie Wright, who had not been summoned but had been included by Pye in recognition of the sound work she had done. There was a seventh person in the room, a slight, earnest woman in her late twenties; she was a newcomer to them all and had introduced herself as Anna Jacobowski, a senior scientist with the Scottish Police Forensic Service.

Jack McGurk frowned. 'I don't see that, ma'am,' he protested. 'We've all had distinct roles in an investigation that was complex from the very beginning. Speaking personally, I don't think my team have stepped on anybody's toes. If Karen hadn't been on the ball and thinking clearly, it would have taken us much longer to match the blood in the Caledonian Crescent flat to the Cramond Island remains.'

'Maybe so,' Chambers admitted.

'I've even got a bonus to report,' he added. 'Karen and DC Singh were diverted there by Mr Mackenzie when they were on their way to investigate a hit and run in Gorgie Road. Tarvil went back to that investigation and spoke to the witnesses. They told him that the car that hit the girl was going like a bat out of hell, "Like a getaway car", according to one of them who'd been sober enough to give them the make and model of the vehicle . . . it was a Nissan Qashquai . . . and a partial number that showed it was five years old, registered in the city.

'He cross-checked all possibles with the DVLA, and Patrick Booth's name jumped out. We've got the vehicle impounded, so it was plain sailing after that. We can do him for that as well.'

'And we will,' the head of CID said. 'How's the victim?'

'She'll live. Tarvil gave her the name of a lawyer, so she can sue Booth for compensation for her injuries. She won't have any problem there; the one legal thing the guy did was keep his tax and insurance up to date.'

'Does Booth know yet?' Sauce Haddock asked.

'Not yet,' McGurk replied. 'No rush.'

'It'll be a nasty surprise for him.' Sauce laughed, vindictively. 'Another few years down the road just when he thought he was getting off lightly for shooting wee Vicky.'

'You have to play it by the book, Jack,' Chambers declared. 'I'm not messing with Frankie Bristles. If you have enough to charge him, do it, and disclose to her.' She nodded, then continued.

'Okay, you've made your point, Acting DI McGurk. This is a bugger of an investigation and I can justify the resources we've devoted to it, whoever asks me. My main concern was that most of it's gone off in the absence of the CID coordinator. He should have been doing all along what I'm doing this morning but I'm happy that we are where we'd have been if he had been here.'

'No comment.' Haddock's voice was barely more than a whisper, but she picked it up.

'No,' the DCS growled, 'and there'd better not be, or you'll be getting the coffee for the rest of your effing career.'

'Sorry, boss,' he muttered as Pye reached out and cuffed him lightly round the ear, while nodding towards Jacobowski, who was seated next to him, staring determinedly at the table. *Strangers present*, he mouthed.

As if she had picked up on it, Chambers turned to the scientist. 'Anna,' she said, 'thanks for joining us. You're a welcome change from Arthur Dorward.' *Pretty little thing*, she thought. 'You're also the lynchpin of this investigation. Without your work we'd have nothing, so it's appreciated. What have you got for us?'

'Thanks, Chief Superintendent,' the civilian replied. 'What I don't have is a full picture, but we're getting there. However, it is very difficult. The Caledonian Crescent flat is like a DNA stockpot. When we went in there we were told that the victim has lived alone, and had a small circle of friends, so we didn't expect to find evidence of the presence of any more than a dozen individuals; the dead woman herself, the police officers who attended, four in all, the meter reader, the law office clerk, the niece, her child and her partner, and the lady downstairs, since DS Neville said she'd claimed to have been in there to borrow sugar.'

'And have a general nose around,' Karen volunteered.

'No doubt,' Jacobowski agreed, 'and she did. We found her DNA and fingerprints in the kitchen, the living room, and in the main bedroom.' She paused. 'It's amazing what personal traces can survive, you know. I say this because of the major problem that we encountered. When we started to analyse the samples we took, at least half of them didn't match up with anyone . . . and we're a long way from being finished with our analysis and comparison.'

'Maybe she had a party we weren't told about,' Haddock suggested.

Karen Neville shook her head. 'No way; Mrs McConnochie would have known, and she'd have mentioned it.'

'She's not infallible,' the scientist said. 'She didn't tell you about the flood.'

Neville frowned. 'What flood?'

'The one the lawyers told us about when we asked. We noticed early on that the kitchen and the bathroom had been completely refurbished and that the living room had just been redecorated. Mr Dorward said we should ask the property administrators about it, rather than bother you. They told us that the flat directly above had a burst pipe, about three weeks before Miss Spreckley disappeared.

'The damage was quite extensive; the ceiling came down, the kitchen units were warped and the bathroom carpet was ruined. Miss Spreckley kicked up a huge fuss, they said, and demanded that everything be put right.

'Rather than wait for the neighbour's insurers to get the finger out, the administrators acted straight away. They called in plasterers, plumbers, painters, carpenters and carpet fitters, and the job was expedited. It was completed the Friday before the estimated date of the woman's death, apart from the new bathroom carpet, which hadn't arrived.

'We still don't know for sure how many people were in there, far less who they were.'

'What do you know?' McGurk asked.

'We can put Booth, Vicky and the child in the house. Specifically we have Booth's prints on the surface of the victim's dressing table and on every drawer and cupboard door in the place. He gave it a real going-over. Now we have his footwear we can prove he stood in the blood as well; he didn't do so when it was fresh, though. Only after it had congealed.'

'Why was Booth so thorough, Sammy?' Chambers asked. 'What's your thinking on that?'

'Drugs,' Pye replied, instantly. 'Booth told us that Bella never handled the merchandise herself, only the money, but I reckon that when he found the flat in the state it was, he decided to make sure there was nothing there that would excite our narcotics people.

'Speaking of whom, boss,' he added, 'I've been thinking, it's one thing me running an investigation within our own force, but from what we know, this is a new supply route into Scotland of a factory-made drug. Should we not be telling the Drug Enforcement Agency?'

'Yes, we should,' she replied. 'Next question: have we done so? Answer, yes we have. The ACC's briefed Mr Martin, informally, to find out whether they've been holding out on us, as much as anything else. His response was that it's the first they've heard of it. He's happy to let us carry on but he wants to be kept informed. What have you got to tell him?'

'Nothing definite; but we do have Booth, singing his heart out in exchange for not being charged with Bella's murder. Now we have the hit-and-run to hold over him as well, maybe he'll sing a little louder . . . if he knows any more of the song, that is. Meantime, DC Wright's been looking for Spanish credit cards in the area where he told us that he met the van driver. Jackie, tell the DCS how it's been going.'

The young detective flushed, and clutched her notebook to her like a comforter. 'I've been surprised by how many Spanish people there are in Britain, ma'am,' she began, 'even with a search centred on places like Durham, Cheltenham, Wigan, Stoke and Scunthorpe.

'Given what Booth told us about the van having goods in it, our thinking is that the driver's a person who does deliveries of furniture and other stuff to and from Spain for ex-pats and people with Spanish holiday homes, and that the locations for the meetings were dictated by wherever she happened to be picking up or dropping off. I checked with the British Consulate in Madrid; they told me there are hundreds of people doing that sort of thing, not just Brits but French, Belgians, et cetera, and that none of them register as businesses.

'I've been looking at time periods two days on either side of each meeting; that's thousands and thousands of transactions, but I've had eighty-two different hits of people using Spanish chip and pin cards in those vicinities. Seventeen of them have been British names, and I've been most interested in these.

'The problems are that no individual's shown up twice, and even more significant, not one of them has been a woman.'

'Nevertheless,' Chambers countered, 'can you check those seventeen British names through the card issuer?'

'In theory, yes,' the DC replied, 'if every card links to a bank account. Road tax in Spain's paid to the local council, not the state, so the bank will have direct debit records that show the vehicle make and registration number. In practice, not in a hurry and maybe not at all: the Spanish are as keen on data protection as we are, and we'd need a court order, in Spain.'

'Leave that with me,' the head of CID told her. 'Drug Enforcement may be able to help us. Keep looking for those names; if someone shows up twice, flag it up. The woman could be married; she could be flashing her husband's plastic. That's the trouble about chip and pin, too bloody easy to do that. Good work so far, Jackie.' The girl beamed and turned an even deeper shade of red.

'Sammy,' Chambers continued, 'has Booth been able to tell us any more about the driver than he did when I was there?'

'Not a lot,' Pye replied. 'Their meetings usually lasted less than a minute. She's middle-aged, he said, white but tanned. She wears a parka or a hoodie in the summer, and a woollen hat as well so he can't help with hair colour. Also, he said she always wears big glasses.

'As for her language, he says he wasn't sure; she said very little. Sometimes in English, sometimes in Spanish, which he understands a wee bit, thanks to a cellmate from Valencia last time he was inside. The one thing he did say was that she sounds husky; not like a smoker he said, but deep, throaty, sexy-like.'

'He's sure it is a woman?'

'Certain, he says. But I don't think he fancies her somehow. I asked him why he was so spooked. "You haven't fuckin' met her, pal," was what he replied.'

'Hopefully we will, before too much longer.' She stopped, as she saw Jacobowski, hand raised like a child in school. 'Yes, Anna.'

'About the drug,' she replied. 'I haven't been involved personally, because I'm up to my ears in Caledonian Crescent, but another part of the service has been working on the traces that were recovered from Booth's flat. His poor girlfriend really didn't make a very good job of getting rid of it.

'They can confirm it's methamphetamine and that it's pretty good stuff. The principal ingredient is ephedrine, rather than pseudoephedrine, brewed up in combination with red phosphorous, iodine and water. If you know what you're doing, crystal meth can be produced in your garden shed, or it can be made, and is made by criminal cartels, in industrial quantities. If you don't know what you're doing . . .'

She paused and her eyes went somewhere else for a second or two, then fixed on Haddock. 'Do you like Bruce Springsteen?' she asked, suddenly.

He smiled at the unexpected question. 'The Boss? Absolutely: he's a hero.'

'Do you know a song called "Sinaloa Cowboys"?'

'Yeah, I think so.'

'Then listen to the lyric. It's about two Mexican brothers synthesising methamphetamine in a shack, and it doesn't end well. The process is very dangerous, and some of the chemicals used are highly volatile. Explosions and fires are common. This stuff, though, it's pretty refined; it's been made by a proper chemist . . . or someone with similar skills.'

'Where are you going with this?' McGurk asked, his curiosity evident.

'Spain,' she replied. 'In our analysis, we found something that just shouldn't be there, traces of grape residue. This is how good we are, people.' She ventured a small smile of pride. 'We've identified it as a variety known as Pedro Ximenez, unique to Spain and used in one of its best known exports. If you want to trace this stuff to source, you should be looking in Andalusia, in a facility that's been used, and maybe still is, in the production of sherry.'

'Indeed?' Chambers said. 'If we're meant to be impressed by that, Anna, then we are.'

'Thank you.'

'Have you told the SCDEA?' she asked.

'Mr Dorward's doing so this morning. My colleagues only completed their analysis last night.'

'Then I'd better speak to them, since we're looking for the same people.'

'Provided,' Pye intervened, 'that Bella Watson's murder is related to her involvement with the supply of drugs. That was Booth's immediate assumption when he saw her flat, and it's been ours too, but the van driver is the only person in the chain that we know about.'

'It's still a reasonable assumption, boss,' Sauce Haddock countered.

'Granted, but it doesn't preclude other options. Bella had a historic feud with the Holmes family; Perry Holmes's son's just been released from jail.'

'And Bella Watson's grandson's working for one of the Holmes companies,' Chambers observed. 'What the hell's that about?'

Pye laughed, shaking his head. 'I do not know, boss, but it's time we found out.'

'I agree, Sammy. But it's not necessarily part of the murder investigation, and I want you and Sauce focused on that. You concentrate on Hastie McGrew; find him and invite him to have a chat with us.'

'Will do.'

'Jack, Karen, I want you to have a word with young Mr Hicks, but without his employers finding out that they've got a Watson in their nest. They might not take too kindly to that.'

'Yes, ma'am,' McGurk said. 'We'll come up with a spurious reason for interviewing him.'

'We can be heir hunters,' Neville suggested. 'You know who

I mean, those people you see on telly looking for relatives of folk who've died without leaving a will, then signing them up and taking a cut of the proceeds.'

'That sounds like a plan,' Chambers agreed, 'as long as you identify yourself properly as soon as you've got the kid on his own.

'Right,' she continued. 'In the meantime, I've been thinking. It's time I contributed something positive given that I'm supposed to be leading this department. We know that Bella Watson was murdered in her own kitchen. We have the plausible assumption that she was removed from the flat in a trunk that Booth said was missing from her bedroom, and that he said it would take two people to move. Agreed?'

Pye and Haddock nodded, in tandem.

'Good. So there they are, these two people, downstairs with a bled-out corpse in a makeshift coffin . . . in the middle of the night, I would guess, otherwise the woman downstairs with the built-in radar would be bound to have heard them. What do they do next?'

'They have a vehicle,' Sauce murmured. 'And not a saloon car, maybe not even an estate, because the ottoman thing is going on for five feet wide and at least a couple of feet deep. Possibly a van.'

'Possibly the same van that Patrick Booth saw?' Chambers continued. 'It's a long shot, but we'll never know unless we prove it or eliminate it. I'd suggest that you go looking for Spanish bank cards in Scotland and as far south as Newcastle around the time we believe Watson was murdered. And while you're at it, if the traffic CCTV tapes are still available that far back . . .'

Forty-Four

HOUR OF DARKNESS

Maggie was as good as her word. A parcel was waiting for me when I arrived home from Glasgow, dropped off, Trish, the children's carer, told me, by a police motorcyclist. I imagined that the guy had been grateful for the run down to Gullane.

I left it unopened. In the aftermath of Aileen's departure I had made an absolute rule. When I was at home, my time belonged to my three kids, and most of all to Seonaid, my youngest. It had been brought home to me earlier in the year that my second daughter didn't know me nearly as well as she should, and since then I've been making up for lost time with her. She's five and newly started primary school. Her day had thrown up lots to talk about, including a new app for her iPad Mini that one of her classmates had insisted she couldn't live without.

I did supper, pasta with a fish sauce, followed by a fresh berry dessert, and we all ate together. Trish cooks for the brood when she has to, but not for me, or for Sarah when she's at her place; our rule, not hers. She's been with us for a while now and we value her.

Once that was done, and Seonaid couldn't blag any further extension to her bedtime, I read her a story. We'd started *The Hobbit* the night before . . . a little advanced you might think, but she has mature tastes for her age . . . and she wouldn't let me stop until Gandalf had seen off the trolls.

Almost as soon as they'd been turned to stone, her eyelids grew as heavy as theirs would have been and within a couple of minutes she was asleep. I sat by her bedside for a few minutes more, just looking at her, and holding on to the thought that nothing that happened during any of my working days came close to being as important as that which happened at home.

After that, I couldn't bring myself to let David Mackenzie intrude into my evening in any shape or form. Instead I called Sarah and asked her if she fancied breakfast with me and the kids. Happily, she did.

Because of all that, Maggie's package didn't get opened until next morning in Glasgow, once my briefing with my assistants was over.

There was a covering note inside. 'This is the file you wanted,' Maggie had written. 'I think you'll find it lives up to your expectations.' That puzzled me for a second or two, until I remembered that I'd told her what those expectations were. She hadn't understood quite what I'd meant.

I opened the folder and flicked through the papers, looking for anything that was not on an official form, but seeing nothing, at first glance. I nodded in provisional satisfaction and began to go through it.

The file had been maintained meticulously, by personnel departments in both Glasgow and Edinburgh. Some of the documents I knew I would find, for I had sent them there myself. It was arranged in descending chronological order; the first item was a note of Mackenzie's transfer from uniform back into CID, setting out his duties as coordinator of the Edinburgh divisions, and signed by Mario McGuire.

'I wouldn't have done that,' I murmured to my empty room, although on reflection I might have, on a kill or cure basis, if the guy had pestered me enough. I don't think so, though. I'd suspected the Bandit of being a closet homophobe, and I'd have thought three or four times before putting him in a direct reporting line with Mary Chambers, who is gay.

I turned the entry over and came to a performance review for the previous calendar year, compiled by Maggie Steele, then an ACC. She'd given him a good score, in every category, and yet her summary was slightly at odds with that, suggesting that his overall effectiveness was marred by what she described as 'an inability to demonstrate anything resembling humility'. In other words, 'He's good, but he's arrogant.'

The previous year's appraisal had been completed by Brian Mackie, and ended in much the same way. 'His outwardly respectful manner fails to hide the impression that sometimes he feels he is suffering fools, and not particularly gladly.'

The next document was a note of his promotion to superintendent, and after that, a report by Kevin O'Malley, the Edinburgh force's favourite shrink. It had landed on my desk when I was deputy chief, and I confess that I'd skimmed it, focusing only on the conclusion, that David Mackenzie had recovered from an episode of post-traumatic stress exacerbated by alcohol abuse and was fit to return to duty, albeit in a less stressful role.

If I'd read it more carefully I might have given more weight to Kevin's note that the subject had refused to discuss any aspects of his early life or his domestic situation and that he had 'reacted with rude aggression when pressed'.

There it was. I'd been told and I'd ignored it: the Bandit was a man with a secret past and he did not want it revealed.

You're a fool, Skinner, I thought. *You're more arrogant than Mackenzie.*

I swung round in my chair and looked out of the window, westward across the evolving skyline of a city that I'd never been able to like, and thought about what had brought me into my lofty office.

The more I considered it, the more I concluded that I was too like the man we were trying to find, far too like him for comfort. His faults were my faults and they had clouded my judgement.

If that old priest was wrong, and the man I'd brought into my team had killed his wife because of the pressure of a job he should never have been in, I knew that it would weigh heavily on me for the rest of my life.

I took a bottle of water from my fridge, then returned to the file, picking my way backwards through David Mackenzie's career, through years of appraisals, by different officers, yet with remarkably similar observations, through several commendations, through successive and rapid promotions.

Finally, there was only one document left: his application to join the police service. It was free-standing, unsupported by any other papers. The memorandum that Father Donnelly had described was missing from the folder. I was fairly certain that it had never been there.

I looked at the form. It was neat, each entry printed in firm capital letters: date and place of birth, parents' names, both deceased, schools attended, educational achievements, and work experience. It was supported by two referees: Father Thomas Donnelly, parish priest, and Magnus Austin, engineer. Each had signed beneath his name, and before David had signed and dated the form himself.

Every section had been completed, save one: that which

requires applicants to list any court appearances, even those where an absolute discharge was granted, and any involvement with a police investigation. I had looked at hundreds of these forms during my police career. A minority had disclosed offences and charges, but in every other that I could remember the applicant had written 'None'. On Mackenzie's form that section was blank.

A long time ago, at a CID dinner that took place just after I'd made a particularly high-profile arrest, my colleagues presented me with a magnifying glass. The gift was a joke, but it actually worked, so I kept it. When I'd emptied my desk in Edinburgh, I'd brought it with me. I took it out and held it over the empty section, studying it for as long as it took for me to be certain.

There was no other sign of erasure, but the paper within the rectangular box was lighter than the rest of the sheet, than the rest of the document. A very effective chemical must have been used to dissolve the ink that had been there, for the surface was absolutely smooth, but it had been doctored, for sure.

I closed the folder; the prediction I'd offered Maggie and Mario had come to pass. I'd been confident that it would and so I'd known what I was going to do before I started. I reached for the notepad that I keep on my desk, scrawled out a note and ripped it off, then walked the few yards to my exec's office.

I handed her the sheet of lined paper, and the folder. 'Sandra,' I said, 'take this to Arthur Dorward in the Forensic Service, please, give him my compliments and ask him to do what I ask in that note. Beg the so-and-so if you have to, but get him to make it his top priority and tell him I need his findings on my desk first thing tomorrow morning.

'If he wants to know what it's about, give him my compliments again and tell him to mind his own bloody business.'

Forty-Five

'This is fascinating,' Marlon Hicks said, as he settled into a booth in the café in Nicolson Street, where he had agreed to meet the woman from the unclaimed inheritance agency who had called him at work that morning. If he was surprised that she had with her a very tall and very serious colleague, his expression gave no hint of it.

Karen Neville smiled. 'That's what they all say,' she replied. 'Descendant research is a very interesting occupation, looking into people's family trees, and finding new branches that you never knew existed.'

'Just like being a detective, eh?'

'You're spot on there, Mr Hicks. Sometimes I think I should take it up professionally. I'm trained for it and I could set my own working hours.'

The young man was taken aback. 'You mean you don't get paid for this?' he exclaimed. He was an odd mix. Facially he could almost have passed for an older version of one of the boys she had seen in the faded photograph in Bella Watson's flat. Vocally, a blind person might have taken him for a West Indian.

'No, we get paid for something else. We are detectives, the

orthodox kind. I'm DS Neville, Edinburgh CID, and this is my colleague, acting DI McGurk.'

Hicks stared at her. He sat bolt upright on his bench seat, then his eyes went to the café door, as if he was contemplating being on the other side of it as soon as possible.

'It's okay,' she said, keeping her tone as calming as she could, and laying a hand on his, gently, but ready to hold on tight if he did decide to make a run for it.

'You're not in any trouble here,' McGurk added. 'We're involved in a very complex investigation, and we need your help. We apologise for being a bit devious. That's not how we work, usually, but we know you haven't been in your job for all that long, and sometimes, if the police turn up in the workplace looking for a new employee, the bosses can get nervous.' He produced his warrant card, and Neville followed suit. 'Take a look, in case you doubt us. Proof that we are who we say we are.'

The youth leaned forward and peered at them. Then he nodded, seemingly reassured. 'So,' he responded, 'what do you want from me?'

'We'd like to talk to you about your father,' Neville told him. Instinctively, both officers knew that Hicks would respond better to her, and McGurk was happy to lean back and let her lead.

'My father? What's he got to do with anything in Edinburgh?'

'How much do you know about him?'

'I know he's a super bloke, and I love him. He's the reason I'm here; he taught me my trade and then he got me a job in Scotland, 'cause like he says, there's a limit to the experience you can gather in St Lucia. Like today; I'm working on a Rolls-Royce. Tomorrow it could be a Mercedes limo, or a Bentley; there aren't too many cars like that on a little island. I'm going to go back, though; my dad has his own business, and I want to work with him, so he can retire when he's ready.'

'I'm not talking about Mr Hicks, Marlon,' the DS said, gently. 'I mean your natural father, Marlon Watson.'

He frowned, and in an instant his bright, open face was clouded by anger. 'Him? I don't think of him as my father. All he ever give me was his name and I'm changin' that. My dad is Duane Hicks, nobody else, and you're right, Hicks is my name too. That other man, he left Mama before I was born, left her alone. He hurt her so bad she won't ever talk about him.'

'But she named you after him,' Neville pointed out.

'I never knew that,' he retorted fiercely, 'not until I had to see my birth certificate so I could change my name all legal, for my British passport. I'm happy to be St Lucian, but Dad said no, I should have a British passport too.'

'She never told you that you were named after him?'

'Never. She told me she called me after a boxer, Marvellous Marvin Hagler, only she got his name wrong. Sure, I know now she was kidding, but I'm still happy with that. I don't want to be called after him.'

'Whatever, it's your choice. What about your grandmother? Have you ever had anything to do with her, that you can recall?'

He stared at her, and a mile-wide smile spread across his face. 'Grandma? Of course I have. She was the first person I went to see when I got here. Grandma's cool. She's kinda old, but she likes Beyoncé, and the Rolling Stones, and Bob Marley. She's got Wailers albums that I never heard of, and she even knows who Pete Tosh was.' He chuckled. 'She likes the volume loud too; Grandpa Ford, he's always tellin' her to turn it down some, but she never listens.'

'No, Marlon,' Neville said, quietly. 'Again, I wasn't asking about your Grandma Ford; I meant your Grandma Watson.'

The sunshine vanished as quickly as it had arrived. 'What you saying?' he protested. 'I ain't got no Grandma Watson. I got Grandma Ford and Grandpa Ford and Grandma Hicks. I never heard of no other grandma.'

'Are you sure? You knew that Mr Hicks wasn't your natural father . . .'

'Sure I knew that,' he snapped scornfully. 'Just by looking at him then looking in the mirror, I'm gonna know that. Duane's black, lady, and I'm pale.'

'Yes, but if Marlon Watson's your natural father, then it stands to reason that . . .'

'I don't give a fuck about no reason,' Marlon exclaimed, loudly enough for the lady behind the counter to throw a meaningful look in his direction. 'I don't know the man or anything about him and I don't want to know.' He gazed at McGurk. 'Look, Mistah Acting Inspector, can I go now? You get me here thinking you were someone else and you ask me all these crazy questions, but you don't tell me what it's about. To be truthful wit' you, I don't care what it's about, so I don' see why I should sit here any longer. I got to get back to work.'

The big detective nodded. 'Okay,' he conceded, 'you're right. We should tell you what our inquiries are about, but I warn you, it may shock you. Yes, it's true that your father left your mother before you were born, but he didn't have any choice in the matter. He left her because he was murdered.

'From what I've been told about him, he wasn't a bad man, but if you don't know anything about your Watson family you're probably lucky, and I can understand why your mother and your dad have protected you from the truth.'

As McGurk spoke, Neville studied the young man's expression

as the words sank in, seeing shock, incomprehension and in equal measure.

'This ain't true,' he whispered.

'I'm sorry,' she countered, 'it is. Your father, his brother and their uncle were all murdered, by or on the orders of the same people. It was an underworld thing.'

'Are you telling me my father and his kin were all gangsters?' Marlon gasped.

'The uncle thought he was, but he was out of his depth. Your father's brother was a stupid little boy, fifteen years old, but he wanted to be one. As for your father, he was somebody who kept the wrong company, and it got him killed.'

'Fifteen years old?' Marlon repeated. 'What happened to him?'

'He dealt drugs for his uncle to kids at his school, and they were caught; to the people who supplied them, that was a capital offence.'

'Who were these people? The ones who killed them?'

'That doesn't matter,' McGurk told him. 'It's ancient history now.'

'And what about this grandma you say I've got?'

'Well, that's the thing,' Martin said. 'I'm afraid that she's followed the pattern. It's her murder we're investigating. Her remains were found in the river a couple of weeks ago.'

'You mean the dead woman who's been in the papers? The body on the island? That was her?'

'I'm afraid so.'

'God!' he gasped.

'That's why I have to ask you again. Did you know of her, and have you ever visited her?'

'No,' he insisted, 'never. Honest,' he added. 'Why? Has somebody said I did?'

'No,' McGurk replied, 'but just in case our bosses ask us to prove that to their satisfaction, we'd like you to give us a sample of your DNA. Would you agree to that?'

'What? You mean like blood?'

'No,' Neville reassured him, 'just a saliva smear from your mouth. We can take it right here.' She reached into her bag and took out a sealed spatula, and a plastic envelope.

The young man glanced around, checking that no one was watching.

'I can take it from you in the toilet if you'd rather,' McGurk offered.

'No. Let's do it here.'

Following the sergeant's instructions, he opened his mouth and let her swab the inside of his cheek, then watched as she bagged the sample and put it away.

'Do you tell me when you get a result?' he asked.

'No, it's not like that,' she replied. 'You're giving it to us for elimination only and you haven't committed a crime, so it won't be kept on the national database.'

Marlon shrugged. 'It's nothin' to me. As long as it don't mean I have to be a Watson, that's okay.'

Forty-Six

'There was a time,' Sammy Pye said, as he looked at the white building through its slatted stainless-steel gates, 'about thirty years ago, when this was the cutting edge of modernist architecture.'

'If that was so, it's got a bit blunt over the years,' Sauce Haddock observed. 'That gate's never thirty years old.'

'No, it isn't. It looks fairly modern. From Mario McGuire's description I was expecting something solid. Let's see if the doorbell works.'

In fact, there was no bell, only a buzzer, with a camera above. He pressed and they waited, Haddock muttering, 'One quick spray of a paint aerosol and that's fucked.'

'Smart people put a layer of cling film over the lens,' the DI countered.

'Yes?' A male voice came from the speaker grille.

'Police,' the DS said, holding up his warrant card for inspection.

'Put it closer to the camera, mate.'

He did as he was asked.

'What brings you here?'

'A murder investigation,' Pye snapped, 'so open the gate, please.'

'I don't know if I will. This family's got no reason to like you guys.'

'To whom are we speaking?'

'Derek Drysalter.'

'And this is your house?'

'My wife's and mine, yes.'

'It's also the registered address of Peter Hastings McGrew, a life sentence prisoner released on licence.'

'So what?'

'So have you any idea what "on licence" means? If not, then get the door open, or you'll find out.'

'Hastie's not here.'

'Doesn't matter, open up . . . please.'

The background crackle of the speaker stopped, and the light above the camera went out. A few seconds later the steel gate slid open, and the two detectives stepped into the grounds.

A long driveway led up to the house; by the time they reached the front door, it had been opened and a figure waited there, not a man, but a woman. Pye had done his homework and knew that, once, she had been a model; twenty years on she had retained a certain grace, but added two or three sizes, emphasised by the a black onesie that she was wearing.

'I'm Alafair Drysalter.' It sounded more of an announcement than an introduction.

'DI Pye, DS Haddock.'

'I suppose you'd better come in.'

'Thank you.'

She stood aside for them and then ushered them through to a huge galleried living area, with a glass wall and two centred patio doors that opened out into a garden boasting a small swimming pool. It would have enjoyed a fine view up Blackford

Hill, Haddock reckoned, but for a line of tall leylandii.

Derek Drysalter was waiting for them there, glaring as they entered. The former footballer had gained much more weight than his wife, and had given up the fight against male pattern baldness, shaving his remaining hair close to his skull. He was standing, but supporting himself on a Malacca cane with a silver handle.

'Darling,' his wife said, 'I can handle this on my own. Unless these gentlemen want you here, why don't you go and surprise Peri by picking her up from school. You know the bus from Mary Erskine can be a bind, and she does have the Olly Murs concert tonight. Is that okay, Inspector?' she asked.

'Yes, it's fine by us,' Pye replied, fixing his eyes on the man, and his cane. 'Do you have a mobility problem, Mr Drysalter,' he grinned, 'or is that a weapon?'

'My second knee replacement,' he answered, unsmiling, 'a month ago. I'm only just back on my feet.'

So you won't have been walking upstairs at Caledonian Crescent, Haddock thought, *far less helping to carry a body down in a trunk.*

'I'm okay to drive, though,' Drysalter added, as he headed towards the hallway, with a careful shuffling gait. 'My car's an automatic.'

'Now,' his wife said, briskly, as he left, and as they took seats on a long curved sofa facing the garden, 'what's all this about? A murder inquiry? Really, guys, I thought those days were long gone. Hastie did what he did and he paid the price, more than he should have, in the circumstances.'

'Who says we're here to talk about your brother?' Haddock shot back.

'What else would it be?'

'It could be a couple of things,' Pye said. 'For example, there's the matter of your father's death. That was investigated at the time and no conclusion was reached.'

'Yes there was,' she exclaimed. 'The procurator fiscal decided that it had been a tragic accident.'

'Actually, he didn't. He decided that accidental death was a possibility. Alongside that, he had no solid evidence to proceed against anyone. I read the investigation summary before we came here. The established facts were that your father's agency carers left him asleep in his powered chair and went off to the kitchen for a break. When they came back they found both him and the chair in the hydrotherapy pool. There was nobody else in the house at the time.

'Perry Holmes having been what he was, obviously the carers were treated as suspects, but they had impeccable records, and the stuff that the investigators found in the kitchen, dirty plates, et cetera, tended to support their story. The building was secure, and there were no signs of forced entry; the caring agency worked in shifts, and there was only one set of keys to the premises. In fact there were only two sets in all and you had the other one.'

'Fine,' Alafair snapped. 'And I was at home when it happened, miles away from Dad's place. Derek wasn't that long out of hospital after his hit-and-run, and we had friends for dinner to celebrate, one of Derek's Scotland teammates and his wife.'

'High-profile witnesses, no doubt about that. So, a machine malfunction was the only feasible solution, since your father was completely paralysed and couldn't have driven himself into that pool even if he had been suicidal . . . which he wasn't since on the day of his death he'd called his bookie and put ten grand on the favourite for a big race that was due to be run in three days' time.'

Pye paused. 'I can see why the fiscal went with the possibility of an accident. And I can even see why the investigating officers were happy to accept that conclusion. But there were far more who weren't, including a not long retired detective, Superintendent Tommy Partridge.

'He spent much of his career trying to put your dad in jail, and he wrote a book about him after he was dead. I'm in the process of reading it. He claimed there was an anomaly. He claimed that your father's house had security that included cameras all around the place and movement sensors. A month before he died, you reported that it was faulty and that you'd shut it down. The firm that monitored it tried to make an appointment to repair it, but they couldn't come up with a date that suited you.'

'So?' she retorted. 'Derek was in hospital at the time. He was my top priority.'

'Tommy Partridge thought that a man called Tony Manson was your top priority at the time, although he never put that in his book.'

'Then how would you know that?' she snapped.

'Mr Partridge told me,' the DI replied. 'I spoke to him this morning. He has a theory and I'm going to put it to you. He believes that when Hastie, your brother, went to prison, he was afraid that since he wasn't around to manage the criminal side of your father's business, and protect him in the way that your Uncle Alasdair had done, he was vulnerable, both to his rivals, and to the police.

'With asset seizure looming on the horizon, he decided that the old man had become a liability, and that he had to go. The swimming pool accident, so the theory goes, was his idea and you set it up, probably through your gangster on the side, Tony

Manson. Old Tommy spent years trying to prove that, but the fiscal didn't want to know.'

'I'm not surprised,' Alafair sneered.

'Me neither,' Pye admitted, 'but if Tommy had discovered what I now know, that you paid your father's previous carer, Vanburn Gayle, a serious sum of money as a so-called bonus and found him a place on a nursing degree course down in London, then the prosecutor might have taken a very different line.'

He was staring hard at the woman as he finished. After a while she met his eyes.

'Then,' she whispered. She continued, more loudly. 'That was then and this is now. Vanburn was paid a legitimate bonus from a legitimate source. Anyway, why would I pay him off?'

'Because he would never have left your father alone?' Haddock suggested.

'Supposition,' she protested. 'Anyway, the fact is that Derek and I were here, having dinner, when my father died, and you could never come close to proving that I gave my keys to anyone else.'

'Because Manson's dead?' the young DS murmured.

For the merest fraction of a second Alafair might have been about to betray herself with a nod, but if she had she mastered the voluntary reflex, and contented herself with a cool stare back at him. 'Really, sonny,' she sighed, 'you can do better than that.'

'Until very recently we might have,' Pye said. 'You weren't Tony's only woman. He had another on the go; when your father went into the pool and the bubbles stopped coming up, the pair of them were on a Mediterranean holiday together.

'Her name is Bella Watson, and if you know anything at all

about your own family history . . . and I'm sure you know every-thing . . . you'll be aware that the Holmeses pretty much wiped hers out, one way or another. You couldn't get to her, though, not as long as Manson was alive. When he wasn't she went back to her maiden name and moved into a place that was bought for her.'

He paused, looking for another reaction, but he saw none. 'She probably thought she was safe there,' he went on, 'but fate can be a real bastard. By a sheer accident, not long before he was released from prison, Hastie was given a clue to her whereabouts, and shortly after he was released, somebody stabbed her to death and put her body in the Firth of Forth.'

'Well, it wasn't Hastie,' she exclaimed. 'I can tell you that.'

'We know that. Physically he couldn't have inflicted the injuries that killed the woman; he doesn't have the strength in his hands.'

'He doesn't have the strength anywhere,' she retorted. 'He's in a nursing home. He went into our limo hire business a couple of weeks after he got out. He has to show the probation people that he's working, and he decided to get involved with that as a starter. He'd only been there a few months when he had a funny turn; he was taken to hospital from there and he's been diagnosed with a brain tumour. Go on; go and check if you doubt me.' Her face twisted into something very unattractive. 'And they said the Watson family was hard done by,' she exclaimed.

'Yes, they did,' Pye agreed, ignoring the irony, 'and they still do. Your brother might be out of commission, and your husband too, but you're a big strong woman, and I'm sure Hastie could have found you a helper from his hospital bed. I'm going to require a DNA swab from you, Mrs Drysalter, and your finger-prints . . . for elimination of course,' he added. 'DS Haddock has all the kit. We can do them here, and if we hurry, we'll be done before your daughter gets home. If not, and you have to explain, I'm sure the story will give her bragging rights at Mary Erskine for a long time. You know what kids are like. You used to be one, after all.'

Forty-Seven

Friday was the day I'd meant to do something about the decision I'd reached while Sarah and I were in Spain. I had faced a straight choice: embrace the future and shape it to my will, or look to maintain as much of the status quo as I could. Either way would have to be best for my family, among whom I included Sarah, for me, and for the police service, in that order.

I knew how I'd jumped and I was sure it would please at least two of those, and maybe all three.

It was the day I was going to tackle it, but it was sidetracked, because I found myself up to my oxters . . . that is, my armpits, to those who don't speak Scottish . . . in events that ran pretty quickly beyond my control.

I'd been at my desk for just over an hour when Sandra knocked on my door and stepped into my room without waiting for an answer. I was with my deputy, Bridie Gorman, at the time, talking about the practicalities of the handover to the new unified Police Scotland, or rather its impracticalities, as far as Bridie was concerned, so neither of us minded the interruption.

'I'm sorry, sir, ma'am,' Bulloch said, 'but you did say that when this came back you wanted to see it right away.' She handed me a package, about the same size and shape as the one Maggie Steele had sent through from Edinburgh.

I thanked her and told Bridie that it concerned a sensitive matter that I had to deal with on my own. I could tell that she was miffed that I didn't trust her enough to share, but I decided to apologise later.

I tore the package open and found the Mackenzie HR file, and an added bonus, a second envelope containing a handwritten note from Arthur Dorward . . . it couldn't have been from anyone else; his style is unique.

*You asked me to dust the first entry document in this extensive file for fingerprints, and to run comparisons of all the results through the national fingerprint library. You did so, in your usual cryptic and enigmatic ******* [his asterisks, not mine] way without giving me any clue about who I was ******* looking for. As usual, you assume that I can work blindfolded at one hundred per cent efficiency. As usual I have proved you right.*

From seventy-three fingerprint traces in total, I've managed to find three matches in the library. All three relate to individuals whose prints are held for purposes of elimination, and not as convicted persons.

Not unnaturally, one of those sets is your own. Jesus Christ, Chief Constable, will you ever learn to wear disposable gloves? Another belongs to one David Mackenzie, currently, as I am advised, a detective superintendent in Edinburgh. Since the document is his employment application, that's hardly a surprise. The third and final set, left thumb, partial left palm print, right thumb and right index finger, belong to the recently retired Assistant Chief Constable Max Allan.

I have no idea what any of this means. Maybe one day you'll tell me, maybe you won't, but whatever, you can go to court on it.

Arthur D

Was I surprised? Was I hell. Max had professed little knowledge of Mackenzie's background to Dan Provan, and yet he had told Tom Donnelly that he was the investigating officer when the boy had chucked the chips at his uncle.

I thought about sending the file back to Arthur and telling him to dust every entry looking for Max's prints, but that really would have been pushing my luck. I reckoned that I had enough to go on, so I left it at that. Instead I called the head of Human Resources, direct.

'Chief Constable here,' I said; I was thinking too hard to exchange pleasantries. 'I want to see the HR folder on ACC Max Allan. I know he's retired, but if you tell me that you've destroyed it I won't be happy.'

'Then you can relax, Chief,' she said. 'We've just finished processing his pension, and because of his rank, it came to me to be signed off. His file's still in my office, awaiting return to storage. You'll have it in five minutes.'

Forty-Eight

'Boss, I've been thinking,' Haddock said.

'Glad to hear it,' Sammy Pye retorted. 'Sometimes I wonder. Did it produce a pearl of wisdom?'

'Up yours . . . with respect, of course. I'd love us to be able to put Alafair Drysalter in Bella Watson's kitchen and find a strand of her hair stuck in the blood, but I don't believe it's going to happen. She's a spoiled selfish woman, and she has that dim sod of a husband on a string, but I don't see her with a knife in her hand.'

'Me neither,' the DI admitted. 'I only did the test out of thoroughness, not expectation . . . and to rile her a wee bit as well. I'm quite convinced we hit the nail on the head over her father's death, and it's possible she could have paid people to do the job on Bella Watson, but the timing's wrong for me.

'We know from the feedback from the ACC that Hastie McGrew picked up a clue to where she was living while he was still in prison. If they were that desperate to get rid of her, would they have waited until Hastie was released? I don't see that.

'To be honest, I got the impression that if Alafair ever knew of Bella's existence, she'd forgotten about her, and the same may well have been true of Hastie. Which reminds me, did the hospital confirm his condition?'

'I spoke to his probation officer,' Sauce replied, 'and she was able to fill me in. She's entitled to know, since he's a lifer on parole. She's been advised by the hospital that he has not one, but two brain tumours, and that surgery isn't an option. Nothing's an option really; they could try radiation but he'd almost certainly wind up like his father, and even then not for long. As it is, the probation officer says he has motor difficulties and his speech is starting to go. They're about to move him into a specialist nursing home.'

'Poor bastard.'

'Huh!' Haddock snorted. 'That poor bastard murdered two men in Edinburgh, and there were three more in Tyneside that the CPS knew he did but never charged him with because there was a one in four chance of an acquittal. If ever there's a case of poetic justice, it's him.'

'Would you feel that way if it was Cheeky's grandpa with the tumour?' Pye asked, quietly.

'Probably, but I'd keep it to myself.' Sauce paused. 'In a roundabout way that leads me back to Perry Holmes. What are we going to do about his death and Gayle's evidence, that Alafair paid him to go away?'

'Us? We're going to report it to the fiscal's office and that's all. I spoke to the DCS and that's what she says.'

'What if they kick it back to us?'

'She won't let them. She'll send it to the cold case unit. But it won't come to that, Sauce; we're pretty sure what happened, but pretty soon, when Hastie goes, Alafair will be the only one of them left alive. There's nobody to incriminate her; even the fiscal will work that one out.' He frowned. 'Let's not get side-tracked on that any longer. Mary Chambers is keen to know how we're getting on with her bright idea, looking for Spanish plated vans near Caledonian Crescent around the time of the murder.'

'I was afraid she would be,' Haddock said. 'I've got the City Council's monitoring department on to it. You can guess how pleased they were when I asked them. So far, nothing; I'll stir them if you like, but they know already that it comes from the boss.'

'It's all right, I'll tell her. It was a shot in the dark and Mary knows it.' He was in the act of reaching for his phone when it rang.

'DI Pye,' a bright female voice sang on the other end of the line, 'this is Anna Jacobowski from the Forensic Service. I've got something rather intriguing for you on your murder inquiry.'

'Just intriguing? Not case-breaking?'

'That's down to you guys, isn't it?' she chuckled. 'We've just analysed one of the dozens of DNA samples from Caledonian Crescent. It's different from all the rest; it demonstrates a second generation familial relationship with the dead woman.'

'What does that mean, in plain Scottish?'

'It means it's her grandson.'

'Her grandson?' Pye repeated, switching the phone to speaker mode. 'You're on broadcast, Anna. DS Haddock is with me.'

'That's very interesting,' Sauce remarked. 'Jack McGurk and Karen Neville interviewed Marlon Junior yesterday and he denied even knowing that he had a Granny Watson. I think you and I need to talk to this lad ourselves, boss.'

'Maybe you do,' the scientist intervened, 'but I haven't got to the really interesting part yet. I've tested the Marlon Hicks swab that I received from your two colleagues, and from the very first analysis I can tell you that the other one isn't his. Bella Watson had two grandsons, gentlemen . . . at least two.'

'How?' Pye gasped.

'How many ways are there, Inspector?' Jacobowski laughed. 'I'll send you a written report by email.'

'There's IVF,' Haddock observed, as she hung up, 'but somehow I can't see Marlon Senior leaving any frozen sperm behind him.'

Pye frowned, looking up from his chair at the ceiling. 'Could Lulu and Marlon have had another son, one we never knew about?'

'No. If they were brothers, Anna would have said.'

'Of course, but Bella had another son, remember. He died when he was fifteen, but I suppose, in theory . . .'

'I'll get on to the General Registers Office; see if Ryan is named on any birth record . . . other than his own. Any son of his would be pushing thirty by now, so I'll know where to look.'

'Get Jackie to do that, Sauce, I've got another task for us. We know from Marlon Hicks that Lulu's mother's still around. Let's find her, and ask her how much she knows about the Watson family.'

Forty-Nine

The HR person was as good as her word; Max Allan's file made it from her office to mine within five minutes. It extended to three folders, Max having enjoyed a long career that had ended in the carnage of the assassination of my predecessor in the Strathclyde chief's chair a few weeks earlier.

'Why the hell couldn't all this have been computerised?' I grumbled as I contemplated forty years' worth of documents. 'Then I could have entered "David Mackenzie" in the search window and pushed a button.'

But it hadn't so there was nothing for it but to start the process. I decided to discard some of the material, since Mackenzie hadn't been born when Max had joined the force, and so I skimmed through his career until I found his posting to Uddingston, in Lanarkshire, as a detective sergeant. The name rang a bell with me, and not only because Myra and her family had lived close by. Tom Donnelly had told me that was where the chippan incident had happened.

I went through the documents one by one, from that point on, and pretty soon I had a result. I hadn't expected to find a report of the affair on Max's file, as that would have been in CID records rather than personnel, but I did find a summary. It was attached to a note of an official commendation by the chief constable of the day, acknowledging Max's exceptional performance in uncovering the abuse of the child and framing charges leading to a successful prosecution. The boy had been identified in the commendation document, but his name had been redacted.

I wondered about that; indeed I was curious enough to pick up the phone and ask the head of HR about it. 'Would your department have done that automatically, thirty-odd years ago?'

'No,' she replied at once, 'not then. Nowadays yes, but back then, in a confidential file, no. The published notice of commendation wouldn't have included the attachment, you see.'

'Was there ever a time when you'd have gone back and done it retrospectively?'

'If we had the manpower to do that . . .' she began, leaving the rest unsaid.

'Could ACC Allan have had access to his own file?'

'In theory everyone has a right to see all information held about them but, Chief, when you're an ACC, there isn't a door in the building that's closed to you . . . apart from your office, perhaps.'

'Mine? No, it isn't, in fact.'

'It hasn't always been that way, I assure you.'

I laughed. 'I'm sure. And who knows what the future will hold?'

I thanked her and got on with my self-imposed task, taking another step forward to the year in which Mackenzie had applied to join the force. By that time, Max was back in Glasgow, back in headquarters in Pitt Street. He was a chief super by then, and back in uniform, as he had been for most of his career, in a desk job supervising the traffic department. Nothing to do directly with staff recruitment; it was the responsibility of one of the ACCs of the day, but he reported to that guy, and he would have been on the same floor. If he'd wanted to . . .

'But why, Bob, why?' I asked myself. 'Why would Max want to smooth Mackenzie's way into the force and remove anything that wouldn't have pleased the recruitment panel?'

I went through the rest of the file looking for an answer, but I saw nothing. Why was I bothered? Because the man had denied knowledge of someone who was a fugitive and he had lied about it.

At that point I could have gone straight to him. I could even have extended the traditional invitation to Pitt Street, 'to help with our inquiries'. But, like anyone skilled in cross-examination, I prefer to have the answers before I put the questions, and there were none in that file.

I decided on another tack, another, informal line of inquiry. I have a pal, a man who's been useful to me on several occasions. His name is Jim Glossop; he used to be a civil servant but he retired at sixty and became a consultant genealogist. I found him on my contact list and selected his number.

'Bob,' he ventured, the mobile signal sounding a little other-worldly, 'is that you? I thought you'd moved on to great things.'

'You mean I wasn't bloody great before, Jim?'

'Right,' he said firmly, then laughed. 'Let me rephrase that.'

'No, mate, it's out there now. It's a pretty good judgement, too.'

'What can I do for you,' he asked. 'I don't imagine this is a social call, not from a man who's as busy as you must be.'

'Not exactly,' I admitted. 'It's not exactly a police matter either, not yet, at any rate. I want to know about a man named

Maxwell Allan, parents' names, wife's maiden name, siblings, anything there is.'

'He's Scottish, I take it.'

'Yes.'

'You got a date of birth?'

I read it from the file.

'It shouldn't be a problem, then. I take it you need it yesterday.'

'The day before if possible. And Jim, the bill comes to me, not the police service.'

'What bill?' He hung up.

Fifty

Finding Marlon's Grandma Ford was much easier than the detectives had feared it might be. They checked the address shown on the young man's birth record and discovered that she still lived there. Two calls later they had discovered that she had a job as a dinner lady at one of the city's schools, and that her working day had just ended.

The Fords were council tenants, in the city's sprawling, nineteen fifties, Clermiston estate. It had been regarded as a showpiece in its time and retained an air of gentility.

'Not bad,' Haddock remarked, surveying number twenty-seven Clermiston Grange. 'There were schemes in Edinburgh built well after this that aren't there any more.'

The house was a mid-terraced villa with a large front garden that was maintained better than most in the street. A close-mown lawn was surrounded by rose bushes, all of them neatly trimmed. 'I wish mine looked like that,' Pye muttered as they walked up the path towards the white front door.

The DI was reaching out to push the buzzer when the door swung open, and a woman stood looking at them, severely. The detectives knew that Gina Ford was sixty-two years old, and that had created an image in their relatively young minds. Their stereotype was short, stocky and with grey hair, possibly wearing an apron; they did not expect a five-foot eight-inch ash blonde who could have passed for fifty, wearing a loose Bob Marley T-shirt that did little to disguise an impressive bust and jeans that might have been painted on.

'I've been expecting you guys,' she said. 'It's as well you came to me, or I'd have come lookin' for you.'

'You'd go looking for Jehovah's Witnesses?' Haddock exclaimed, wide-eyed.

The stern expression cracked, and a small smile took its place. 'Bloody comedian,' she said, grudgingly. 'You look no more like Witnesses than I look like Beyoncé Knowles. Do you do a line as a female impersonator as well, son? I was told one of you was a woman.'

'Different officers, Mrs Ford,' Pye replied, identifying himself and his sergeant. He made to show her his warrant card, but she waved it away.

'Come on in,' she ordered. 'I don't like the polis on my doorstep. Pye and Haddock,' she added. 'You sound like the menu in a fuckin' chippie.'

As they stepped into a well-decorated hallway, Haddock nodded over his shoulder. 'You've got a nice garden. Do you look after it?'

She shook her head. 'Still he makes with the funnies. This boy must keep you in stitches, Inspector.' She waved a perfectly manicured hand. 'Do I look as if I've got manure under my nails, Sergeant? No, that's all my man's work; I take care of the inside, he does the rest. It keeps us out of each other's hair . . . no' that he's got much, mind. One of the secrets of a happy marriage, lads, you should remember that.'

'I'll bear it in mind,' Pye said, drily, as she led them into a neat living room, well-furnished and sparkling with cleanliness. He was still smarting from her menu wisecrack. 'Now, tell me,' he continued, declining the offer of a seat, 'why were you going to come looking for us?'

'Why the hell do you think?' Her initial anger resurfaced. 'Who do you people think you are? What gives you the right to go upsetting my grandson? He came to see me last night, in a hell of a state. His mother and I have spent the whole of his lifetime protecting him from the truth about his father, and your two bloody colleagues go and spill it out in the middle of some bloody café!'

'I'm sorry,' the DI retorted. 'His name came up in the middle of our investigation and he had to be interviewed. It wasn't possible to do it without telling him exactly why.'

'Why not?'

'I can explain that, Mrs Ford. We're investigating his grandmother's murder, and we found that Marlon is working for the family that police believe ordered his father's killing.'

Gina Ford stared at him, rocking slightly back on her heels. 'What the fuck are you talking about?' she whispered.

'How much do you know about your grandson's father's death?' Haddock asked her, more gently than Pye.

'The same as everybody else,' she said. 'He was found battered to death in the old Infirmary Street Baths. A few weeks later the papers said that the men the police suspected of doin' it had been found dead themselves, in Newcastle. They said it was a gangland thing.'

'That's more or less how it was,' the DS agreed. 'The investigators at the time believed they were silenced by the man who ordered it.'

'All that's no surprise,' she told him, 'given that the Watsons were involved. Fucking lowlives, that family. That Marlon was the biggest mistake my Lulu ever made . . . the only mistake, God bless her. He wasn't a bad lad as such, always quite cheery, but the man he worked for was. And as for his mother . . .' Finally, she sank into an armchair and insisted that the detectives seat themselves.

'Bella Watson tried to take over our lass after she found out she was pregnant by Marlon. But Robert and I, we weren't having it, weren't letting her have any influence over the child. We told her to stay away from our family. She didn't like it, even threatened us, but my Robert's no soft touch. He's been a bus driver for thirty years, and he takes no nonsense. He went to see the man Marlon had worked for and told him what was happening. He said not to worry, and Bella never came near us again.'

'But you know she's dead?' Pye asked, his earlier annoyance forgotten.

'Oh aye. I saw it in the *Evening News*. No surprise really, and I suppose no surprise that you folk should want to talk to the laddie. But to tell him about her, that's something else. I'm not happy about that. We all decided very early on to tell wee Marlon that his dad had run off. Then Duane came along, he and Lulu got married and had Robyn, and then Kyle out in St Lucia, and we more or less forgot all about what had happened. So, why did you have to upset him?'

'There was no option,' the DI explained. 'I know, Marlon said he had no idea he had another grandmother, but we're simply not able to take someone's word in a serious crime investigation. We needed his DNA to prove that he'd never been in her flat, and the officers who interviewed him had to tell him why they wanted it. As for doing it in a café, it's a discreet process, so they thought it was better to see him there than going to his work or having him brought into the police station.'

'I suppose,' Mrs Ford conceded. She was silent for a while as she replayed the discussion in her mind. 'What you said earlier,' she went on, when she was ready, 'about Marlon working for the folk that killed his dad. What did you mean by that? Who ordered it?'

'His name was Perry Holmes,' Pye told her. 'He was the top man in organised crime in Edinburgh and probably in Scotland, at the peak of his career. He had a run-in with the man who employed Marlon Senior.'

'The guy Manson?'

'That's right.'

'And the laddie was killed in the crossfire?'

'More or less. He was targeted, to send a message to Manson, because Manson was having an affair with Holmes's daughter.'

'They killed the boy for something his boss done?' She was incredulous.

'Yes.'

'Animals, the lot of them. So how does our laddie come to be working for them?'

'As far as we can see it's purely accidental. Perry Holmes was in a wheelchair. He had a carer, who happens to be Duane Hicks's cousin, and who still works in Edinburgh. Duane asked him if he could help young Marlon find a job.

'Perry Holmes had a lot of legitimate businesses, as well as the criminal side, and when he died his son and daughter inherited them. Vanburn, the cousin, was on good terms with the son, and that's how it came about. They even gave him a flat to rent, I believe.'

'That's true,' she affirmed. 'These people, do they know who Marlon's father was?'

'I don't believe they have any idea, and it will stay that way as far as we're concerned.'

'How much does he know about them?'

'Again, nothing. He was told the circumstances of his father's death and his family history, but that's all.'

'And that's enough. He must never know about these Holmes people.'

Pye nodded. 'We couldn't agree more.'

'Thanks. We'll get the boy out of there. Robert'll find him a job in the bus garage, and he can come and live with us.' She leaned back in her chair and looked at them. 'But that's not all that brought you here, is it?' she observed.

Haddock smiled at her perspicacity. 'Not quite,' he admitted. 'We wanted to ask if you know anything else about the Watson clan. To be specific, did Lulu ever mention Marlon having had a child, a son, by anyone else, before her?'

'I doubt it would have been after her, son, given that she had a few weeks to go when they buried him. But no, she never did. If you're really asking whether he had an earlier kid with Lulu, the answer's no. She wasn't off the rails much longer than it took her to get knocked up.'

Pye leaned forward, rejoining the discussion. 'What about the rest of the family? You see, we know that Bella had another grandson, but we can't work out how.'

'I see.' Gina Ford paused, pondering the question. 'Well,' she ventured, 'as I recall, the last time I saw our Marlon's dad, when he dropped Lulu off from a hospital appointment, he was all excited. I asked him why. He said that he was going to meet his sister, and he hadn't seen her for twelve years.'

'Sister?' Haddock exclaimed as he stared at the DI. 'What bloody sister?'

Fifty-One

I hadn't expected Jim Glossop to get back to me before the following Monday afternoon, at the earliest, but I've always underestimated his skill and his tenacity. I was on the point of leaving the office for a weekend with my family, when Sandra buzzed me to say that he had called.

I was ever so slightly vexed. On the basis of Father Donnelly's firm assurance, in my mind I had downgraded the search for the missing Mackenzies from a potential murder hunt to a domestic situation that had got way out of hand and for which there would be hell to pay when eventually they turned up.

Monday would have suited me fine; at that moment my mind was fixed on Gullane's Number Three golf course and the evening round that I had promised James Andrew, my younger son, who shows significant promise for his age. (Mark, his older brother, is a whiz at the computer version of the game. He can find no serious console opposition in our house, but sadly he has no aptitude on grass.)

I took the call nonetheless; I could have asked Sandra to lie and say I'd just left, but that would have been churlish. She might also have refused, and that would have been awkward. On top of all that, Jim was a mate, doing me a good turn.

'Jim,' I said, making myself sound as enthusiastic as I could. 'You need more information?'

'Not at all. It was dead easy really. There's no twists and turns in your subject's recent history. He was born exactly when you said, in Houston, Renfrewshire. His parents were Alastair Gourlay Allan and Wilma Maxwell Allan, maiden name Adams, both schoolteachers, married in Glasgow University Chapel on the thirty-first of August, nineteen forty-three. One sibling, Jonathan Allan, born on the second of February nineteen forty-four, no comment.' He paused for a chuckle.

'Maxwell Allan married Julie Austin,' he continued, 'on the seventh of April, nineteen seventy-seven, in High Blantyre Parish Church. They listed their occupations as police officer, and physiotherapist. They had two children, a son called Gourlay and a daughter called Rosina, but she died in infancy. How's that then?'

'A sad ending, but bloody brilliant as always.' I hadn't known about Max's lost child; but some things are too painful to mention, so that didn't shock me.

I'd been scribbling as he spoke, and had all the salient details noted down. From the list of names, one was familiar. 'Hold on, Jim,' I said, as I delved back into Mackenzie's file. I was looking for confirmation and I found it.

'That's great,' I said, 'but I need one more thing . . . well, two more actually. Can you find out whether Julie Austin has, or had, a brother called Magnus, and whether he had any kids?'

Fifty-Two

'No,' Mary Chambers declared. 'I have never heard any mention of Marlon Watson having a sister. After you called me I even checked with the ACC. He was involved in the murder investigation, albeit as he says he was brand new in CID, but he swears blind that nobody ever made any mention to him of any sister. Are you sure this woman's memory is up to it? She is a grandmother, after all.'

'My granny never looked like that,' Pye countered, 'or was half as sharp. It's a line of inquiry and we'll check it out.'

'You do that,' the head of CID said, 'but it's not your top priority. The council CCTV monitoring people have been on, looking for Sauce. When they were told you and he weren't in, they came on to me. They want to see you, pronto. They've been bursting their braces for you and I got the impression they're looking for a bit of public credit for it.'

'We're on our way back to Leith,' the DI said, 'but we'll divert there. As you say, boss, the sister can wait.'

The Bluetooth call went dead just as they reached the traffic lights in Great Junction Street. Haddock, who was at the wheel, made a last-minute lane change and flashed a right turn signal, drawing a horn blast from the driver behind. The man followed him into Leith Walk, and sat on his rear bumper, big in his mirror, headlights flashing and horn still blaring.

'Fuck this!' the sergeant declared, slowing.

'Ignore him, Sauce,' Pye ordered. 'If he follows us all the way to the council offices we'll do him there.'

They never found out whether he would have gone that far, for they were stopped by a red light at the next junction. Immediately their pursuer leapt out of his vehicle and ran up to Haddock's door. The DS rolled down his window, holding up his warrant card.

'Can you read that, sir?' he asked. 'If not, it says, "Get back in your motor or we'll do you for breach of the peace." Understood?'

The red-faced man uttered not a word; instead he weighed up his options and chose correctly.

'I was in Traffic in my second year in the force,' Sauce said, as the lights changed and he drove away. 'I hated having to be polite to people like him.'

When they arrived at the City Council headquarters in Market Street, they had a second argument, with the car park supervisor, but once again the warrant cards won the day. The office was on the point of closing as they made their way inside, but the receptionist had been briefed to expect them. 'Second floor, gentlemen,' he said. 'It's the door facing the lift.'

The second instruction proved to be unnecessary. As they stepped out of the elevator, a man was waiting for them; a very fat man, in shirtsleeves, with the council logo on his tie. 'Johnny Halliday,' he announced, extending a podgy hand to Pye. 'I'm the team leader here. The front desk let me know you were on your way up.'

'You've got something for us, our boss told us,' the DI said.

'Indeed we have,' Halliday replied, with evident pride. 'Come and see.'

He led the way into an open-plan work area with more video monitors than either detective could count. Each one was live, with a different view of the city's streets, displayed four to a screen. 'This way,' he said, leading them to the far corner, which was partitioned off from the rest. 'This is my domain,' he announced, grandly. 'Sit yourselves down.'

Three seats were arranged at a table, in front of a flat-screen monitor, on which an image was frozen.

'What we have here,' the team leader explained, 'is the view from the camera that looks up Orwell Terrace. As you probably know, that leads up to Caledonian Crescent. The time is five minutes past midnight on the day after your review window. Now look here.' He pressed a control on a black box on the table and the screen became active.

As Pye and Haddock looked on, they saw a dark-coloured saloon drive towards the camera, and then pass out of sight as it took a left turn into Dalry Road.

'Okay?' Halliday murmured, eagerly. 'Now.'

As he spoke another vehicle appeared on screen, travelling in the opposite direction, making the same turn, but right, into Orwell Terrace, much more awkwardly than the car had done. It was a light-coloured van, without markings.

'That's a Renault Master, long wheelbase,' their host advised them. 'Now look.' He touched another control and the screen froze. 'I think you'll find that the registration number is quite legible.'

Haddock leaned forward and read aloud. 'Eight, zero nine five H N J.'

'Exactly,' Halliday agreed. 'And I think you'll find that that is a Spanish plate. That's what you wanted, isn't it?'

'Absolutely,' Pye told him, feeling his day take a turn for the better. 'Not just that, it's when we wanted it, and where. Thanks, Johnny.'

'I'm not done yet. Hold on.' He pressed some more buttons and a second view appeared on screen. 'We don't have a camera in the crescent itself, I'm afraid, but there is one at the exit of Caledonian Road, and this is what it shows looking up towards Haymarket. This is what it showed fifty-seven minutes later.'

He activated the player; within a minute the same van swung into view once again, heading away from the camera.

'Outstanding,' Haddock exclaimed. 'We're pushing our luck, I know, but do you have a shot that lets us see the driver?'

'Unfortunately not.' The man was slightly crestfallen, but only for a few seconds. 'However,' he continued, 'I can tell you where it went. We have footage of it heading along Queensferry Road and then later in Granton. We lose it in Marine Drive, but I'm confident that it didn't come back into the city after that.'

He leaned back. 'I read the newspapers, chaps,' he said, familiarly, 'so I know what this is all about. If you in turn know that area, you'll be aware that there's a walkway along the foreshore that runs off Marine Drive. In theory it's pedestrian and cyclists only, but the gate is a bit loose and it can be accessed by a vehicle, even one as large as a long wheelbase Renault Master van. If you're trying to work out where that poor woman's body was dumped, my guess is that you've found the very spot.'

Fifty-Three

There were times when Karen Neville reckoned that she had been too generous to her ex-husband during the negotiations over their split. She had no complaints with the generosity of his child support payments to Danielle and Robert, and he had agreed to her taking all of the substantial profit from the sale of their house in Perth. Yet as she settled into a work routine that involved constant weekend shifts, she had moments when she thought how pleasant it would be to be a full-time mother, at least until both children were at school. When these moments came she wondered whether if she had been a little more aggressive, a little less reasonable when they agreed that their marriage was terminal, she might have secured personal alimony that would have made it possible.

But those feelings never lasted for long. The truth was that she liked her job. The truth was that she had been a full-time mother and had found it trying and frustrating. The truth was that she had come to believe that she had as much right to a career as Andy and had become resentful that he had assumed without discussion that she should be the one to make the sacrifice. The truth was that their relationship had begun in the workplace and had thrived there. Domestically, whenever they were vertical rather than horizontal, they had bored each other witless.

And so, when he came to collect the children on a Friday evening, the only topics in their brief conversation, beyond the deeds and needs of their daughter and son, were usually professional.

As he stood in her kitchen watching Danielle putting on her jacket, unassisted, Andy asked the inevitable question. 'So, what sort of a week have you had?'

'I'm in the middle of it, remember,' she replied. 'So far it's been relatively unproductive. I've only caught one bad guy, and I didn't really catch him, I just did the interview with Jack.'

'What was that about?'

'It was a man called Booth. You must have heard about it, even in your network. He walked into his flat and found Sammy Pye and Sauce Haddock there talking to his girlfriend. He pulled a gun and she was shot. He denied meaning to shoot her; his main line of defence seems to be that he was trying to shoot Sauce, and I don't think that's going to get him very far.'

Andy laughed. 'It bloody well will; probably as far as Peterhead Prison. You're right, I have heard of Mr Booth, but not through your investigation. Sammy and the lad went to interview him about the Bella Watson murder and accidentally came across a chain of crystal meth that neither we in the SCDEA nor the Edinburgh drugs team had known anything about.'

'So you're involved now?'

'Only in trying to trace the source, which, thanks to the forensic scientists, we know is in Spain, and probably in a specific region. My people are helping the Guardia Civil to track it down. As you'd expect, Booth's singing his head off, but he doesn't actually know that much. It's a well put together operation, and the late and unlamented Bella was a part of it. She handled the money, Booth collected the gear from someone else and sold it in and around Edinburgh.'

'I know all that,' Karen told him. 'I'm involved in the investigation. It was me that identified Watson, remember, when Tarvil and I were sent to her flat by our esteemed coordinator.'

He grinned. 'You don't like Mr Mackenzie, then.'

She frowned back. 'You could say that. Don't tell me you do.'

'I can't tell you anything, Karen. The fact is I don't care about the man. I'm told he has a down on me for some reason. If so, he's welcome. Been making waves in the city, has he?'

'Not this week. He's on leave. Actually it's a bit odd; you'd expect that the divisions would have known about it in advance, but none of us did. "Sorting out some personal issues" is what we've been told, but there's a whisper that he's had his arse kicked by the ACC and been sent to cool off.'

'Rather him than me; Mario's a formidable arse-kicker.' He glanced at his daughter, then back at his ex-wife. 'You said you're involved in the Bella investigation?'

'I am this weekend, standing in for Sammy and "the lad", as you call him. Don't underrate him, by the way. He's got "future ACC" written all over him.'

'That's if his choice of partner doesn't get in the way.'

'What do you mean?'

'Never mind; no gossip between us, Mario said. Ask McGurk if you want to know. What have you got on your plate with the Watson thing?'

'Plate. A good choice of word. I've just had a call from Sammy.' She paused. 'Actually, now that I think of it, it might interest you. If you know all about Booth's drug route you'll be aware that the deliveries were made in random locations by a woman driving a van with Spanish plates. Sammy says he's placed the van, through CCTV, in Caledonian Crescent on the night that we think the murder happened. My big task tomorrow is to trace the owner.'

'Too right it interests me,' Andy said as Danielle tugged at his sleeve. 'It lets us track down this crew from both ends.'

'Take it over by all means,' she offered.

'No thanks, you're doing fine as it is, and besides, I don't want to make an enemy of Sammy Pye. But let me know what you find out, as soon as you do.'

'I will do,' Karen promised, 'but I do have other things on my plate. A couple of days ago I took a mouth swab from a kid who was born in Edinburgh but thinks he's West Indian.' She smiled. 'I suppose he is in a way, more than Scottish, since he's spent most of his life there. His name's Marlon Hicks, but he was born Marlon Watson Junior. He's Bella's grandson.'

'That's interesting.'

'But not nearly as interesting as this. The boy denied ever having heard of her, and his maternal granny says that's true. But forensics ran his DNA profile anyway.'

'And placed him in Bella's flat?' Andy asked, intrigued, as he picked up his daughter and let her sit in the crook of his arm.

'No. They did find grandson DNA there. But it wasn't his.'

'So? He has a brother?'

'Yes he does, but not by Marlon. Bella has another grandson, but we have no idea where he came from. It wasn't from Ryan, Marlon's brother, we know that.'

'I don't suppose the stork brought it, so have you looked at the daughter?'

She stared at him, blank-faced. 'What daughter?'

'Jesus,' he gasped. 'And Sammy Pye's supposed to be bright. Bella Watson had a daughter.'

'Then nobody's ever mentioned her to me. Are you sure?'

'Sure?' he repeated. 'I've met her, my dear. I was part of the team that investigated Marlon's murder. It's going on twenty years ago, but I remember Bob taking me with him when he went to tell her about it. She was a presenter on a local radio station, called Airburst. It doesn't exist any more, but that's where we went.

'Yes, I remember now; she was estranged from her family, she told us. She was just about to go on air, but she said she'd be all right, and that she wouldn't break down or anything, because she hadn't seen her brother for twelve years.'

He frowned. 'There was something else. Before we saw her, we went to visit Bella in that Wild West street where she lived at the time. She talked about her but I noticed that there were no photographs of her in the house.'

'It was the same in the Caledonian Crescent flat,' Karen told him, 'so time didn't heal anything. Where is she now, do you know?'

'I have no idea.'

'What was her name?'

'Mia. She had a professional surname; I can't quite recall it but that was her real Christian name. She was bloody gorgeous,' he murmured, 'I remember that much about her.' Then his eyebrows rose. 'And something else.'

He put his daughter down, on a worktop. 'Danielle, sit there for a minute please. Daddy has to make a phone call.' He looked at Karen as he took out his mobile. 'I'm going to put this on speaker.' He held the phone in his left hand as he found a contact and called the number.

'Andy.' Alex Skinner's voice, given a metallic tone by the small speaker, sounded in the kitchen. 'What's up? Are you stuck somewhere? Do you need me to collect the children?'

'No,' he replied. 'I'm at Karen's. This is a professional call.'

'Your profession or mine?'

'Ours. It relates to something Karen's working on. Do you remember Mia Watson, from when you were a kid?'

'Mia Sparkles?' She paused. 'That's one from the past.' Andy had the odd feeling that she was talking to herself rather than them. 'Oh yes, I remember her. I was her number one fan.' She hesitated again. 'Well, number one equal, maybe,' she murmured, as if to herself.

'Do you know what happened to her?'

'Only that she left. She didn't turn up for her programme one day and she was never on that station again.'

'Did you ever hear of her again?' Karen asked.

'No. Not that I've ever tried to find her, mind you. Someone else came on the radio and I moved on, like you do when you're thirteen. Besides . . .'

'Besides what?'

'I'd gone off her by then,' she said, abruptly. 'I was a fickle child, as Andy will tell you.'

'You said you were fan number one equal. Who was the other?'

'Oh,' Alex replied, casually, 'that was just me being waspish; the other was probably Mia herself.'

'Okay, thanks,' Andy said. 'See you tomorrow, yes?'

'Yes. Are we still going to the Botanics?'

'Sure. So long.'

'So long, Alex,' Danielle echoed, just as the line went dead.

'There you have it,' he said. 'Mia Watson, Mia Sparkles; take your pick, but she does exist and she's all yours. She'll be mid-forties now, I think.'

'Thanks,' Karen murmured.

He read something unsaid in her eyes. 'What?' he asked.

'Oh, it's nothing, just . . . I'm not looking to pick a fight and you know her much better than I do so you'll probably say I'm talking nonsense, but I'm standing here thinking that there's something your lady never told us.'

Fifty-Four

I made it home from Glasgow in time to keep my word to my boy. The weather was fine and there was enough light in the day to let us play a full eighteen holes on Number Three.

In fact we made it round in under two and a half hours; James Andrew hits it pretty straight and I was playing only iron clubs to match his distance, so there was no time spent searching for balls in the rough. I gave him two shots a hole and he beat me, no problem. He might have only just turned nine, but he's a better putter than me already and he always will be.

We'd been playing for a fiver . . . five pence in his case, five pounds in mine . . . and so Sarah, watching from a window, could tell the outcome as soon as he stepped out of the car. Incidentally, he gets very pissed off these days about having to use a child seat, but until he outgrows it physically, which will probably be soon, that's how it will be.

'How many?' she asked me as I came into the kitchen. When she returned to Scotland from her sojourn in America she bought a place in Edinburgh. The arrangement was that the kids would stay with me on schooldays and be with her at the weekends, but after the reconciliation that had taken both of us by surprise, that was beginning to go by the board, and Sarah was spending more and more time in Gullane.

'Little bugger beat me four and three,' I confessed. 'He wanted to play for another fiver over the last three holes, but I drew the line at that. Just as well; he won them all.'

'You might have to start hitting proper shots,' she suggested.

'It'll make no difference. In another five years he'll be giving me shots.'

'And you'll be very proud of him when that happens.' She kissed me and handed me a bowl of chilli con carne. 'You had a phone call,' she said.

'Just the one?' (So had my life become.)

'Yeah, it makes a change. Maybe people have other things to do on a Friday night than bother you. It was your friend Jim, the guy who used to work in New Register House. He said you should call him back.'

I did, on the phone in the garden room, as soon as I'd finished my chilli. And that was the start of my weekend from hell.

Jim answered so quickly that I suspected he'd been beside the phone waiting for me to ring.

'Have you got something already?' I asked. 'On a Friday night?'

'The impossible I do at once,' he replied, then spared me the punchline. 'It took me no time at all. Julie Austin. Mrs Allan; she does indeed have a brother called Magnus. He's married to a woman named Julie Smith, which must make family dinner parties a little confusing, and they have issue, two of them, Richard Edward and Cheryl Mary. Does that give you all you need?'

'Oh hell yes,' I said. 'I'm in your debt. And you must send me a bill; to my office in Glasgow. This is now a police matter.'

'In that case,' he replied, as cheerfully as ever, 'I'll do so as quickly as I've answered all your questions.'

As I'd told Jim, I did have all I needed. Through his wife, Max Allan was Cheryl Mackenzie's uncle. Cheryl's relationship with David went back to their teens.

They were all bloody family, and beyond any reasonable doubt . . . in my mind at least . . . Uncle Max had smoothed the way for young David's entry into the police force, by concealing a history that might well have ruled him out, even with Tom Donnelly's name on his application.

I could have let it lie there undisturbed, and forgotten about the whole business. Indeed I might have, if Mackenzie had been a stable, reliable officer doing a job that was of value to his force. But he was none of those things, and to cap it all off, he was missing.

I thought about calling Maggie straight away. Mackenzie was on the Edinburgh payroll, not mine, and she had a right to know. But I put it off, and took out my mobile to look up a number. I was about to call it, when Sarah came into the room, and read the look on my face.

'Trouble?'

I nodded.

'As in weekend-screwing-up trouble?'

'I fear it might be.'

She smiled. 'And I said not so long ago that it had been a quiet night. I should a known.'

I made the call, and Father Donnelly answered; there was background noise, of the pub variety. 'Bob,' he said his voice raised, 'hang on. I'll have to go outside.' I waited, then heard a sound that might have been a door closing, and the babble disappeared. 'That's better,' he said. 'What can I do for you?'

'You could begin by telling me how you know that David Mackenzie hasn't harmed his wife,' I suggested.

'No I can't,' he replied, 'I really cannot; not even after a couple of pints of Coors.'

His insistence was enough stop me pressing any harder. 'Fair enough,' I conceded. 'But can you tell me how long you've known that Max Allan and Mackenzie are related, through his wife being Cheryl's aunt, her father's sister?'

'I've never known that, I promise you. Mrs Allan was godmother to their older child, but at no point was I told that she was family.'

'What about their wedding? Weren't the Allans there?'

'No one was there, other than Mr and Mrs Austin and myself. They wanted it private because David didn't have any family, none that he'd acknowledge anyway.'

'I see.'

'Bob, what's this about?' the priest asked.

'This is one where I really can't tell you,' I assured him. 'We all have our ethics and our duty.'

'I understand.'

'I need to ask you about the application form, Father,' I continued. 'You told me that you helped David compile it. I'd like you to think back, and tell me if you can recall whether the box relating to declaration of court appearances and police involvement was left blank.'

'No it wasn't,' he declared. 'I do recall that very well. I insisted that he put "See separate document" in there, because I didn't want it rejected on a technicality.'

'Right, now finally, I ask again: Max Allan was not involved in its completion and there was no way he could have seen or handled the form before you posted it. Can you confirm that?'

Part of me was hoping that he'd say 'No', so that the old guy would at least have some wiggle room, but he didn't.

'Absolutely,' he replied.

'Okay, Father,' I sighed. 'Thanks. Go back in there and have one on me.'

'But don't call Max, that's what you're saying, Bob, isn't it?'

'I'm afraid so.'

I let the priest return to his Friday pals, and then made the call I'd postponed earlier. Maggie Steele listened to what I had to tell her without interrupting. But got to the point as soon as I'd finished.

'What you're telling me,' she said, 'is that I've got a detective superintendent who's a police officer because of a dishonest application.'

'Exactly. And I have evidence that a recently retired ACC played an active part in that fraud.'

'Nightmare,' she sighed. 'What are we going to do about it?'

'Not we, Maggie, me. A criminal act was committed in Strathclyde. It's my jurisdiction and it's for me to pursue it.'

'Not personally, surely.'

'Absolutely. I kicked this game off, so I'll play it to the whistle. Who knows? I might even find Mackenzie in the process.'

Fifty-Five

Karen Neville had only just begun to ponder the anomaly of Bella Watson's daughter as she walked into the Leith police office. She had set that consideration aside not long after Andy had left, to concentrate on her first serious date since their divorce.

She had met a widowed single father, a self-employed architect, a few weeks before, on the nursery school run. They had started to talk while waiting for their children, and had met for coffee the next day, then lunch the following week, and the week after that, and . . .

When Nigel had invited her to dinner at his house, at first she had been a little uncertain, but he seemed like a nice guy, so she had accepted. She had even put an overnight bag in her car, just in case.

The evening had been a disaster.

He'd turned out to be a lousy cook, but she had made allowances for that, since he had over-reached himself, clearly, with the menu. It was Karen's firm opinion that no man, other than possibly Albert Roux, could make a proper soufflé, but she gave Nigel credit for trying.

The small talk that had come easily in public places had

been stilted over his dinner table, but she had made allowances for that, given their unspoken agenda. There had been some kissing, and brief, schoolboyish fumbling on the sofa afterwards, until she had taken him gently by the hand and said, 'Nigel, show me where your bedroom is.'

The only saving grace, she told herself later, was that she had not been completely naked when he had started to cry.

He had, though. When she had stepped out of his en-suite shower room, in the Anne Summers bra and thong she had chosen for the evening, he had been sitting on the edge of his bed, his clothes neatly folded and laid on a chair. He had been gazing up at her, and it had occurred to her that the last person who had looked at her in such a desolate way had been Danielle, when her kitten had been run over in Perth.

'Karen, I can't do this,' he had moaned. 'It still hurts too much.'

And then the tears had come, a few at first and then the flood. The sobs had followed, not quiet, full-blown, heart-rending.

She might still have made it through, and helped the poor guy through his crisis, and then recover his sexual confidence, if the bedroom door had not opened, and his three-year-old daughter had not come stumbling in, awake enough to stare at her in fright and shout, 'What are you doing to my daddy?' before starting to scream, loudly enough to trigger a fresh paroxysm from the hapless, no, make that hopeless, she decided, Nigel.

She had grabbed her discarded clothes, dressed in the hall downstairs, then vacated the premises before the damn kid's yelling woke the neighbourhood.

She had been half expecting a call in the morning but none had come, and so Nigel had been written off to experience.

There might be an awkward encounter on the next school run but she could live with that.

The business of the weekend was finally back on her mind as she stepped into the unfamiliar CID office. There was one other person in the room, female, mid-twenties, dark hair, plain clothes.

'Good morning, DC Wright,' Karen said. 'DI Pye told me you'd pulled the overtime this weekend.'

'Yes,' she replied, so bright-eyed and brisk that the DS almost winced. 'He said our priority is that number plate the monitoring people found for us. I've been looking at how we go about tracking down the registered owner of a Spanish vehicle. It's not going to be easy.'

'The older I get,' the DS murmured, 'the more I realise that nothing in life is as easy as you think it's going to be.'

Her colleague grinned. 'Ouch! That's pretty cynical for a Saturday morning. Man trouble?'

'You would not believe it, so let's not go there. What's the problem?'

'It's that Spanish numbers don't work the way ours do,' Wright told her. 'You'd think that in this day and age there would be a standardised European system, but there isn't. They tell us in Brussels we can't buy food in pounds and ounces, but they let us do our own thing in areas that really need centralising. You know how with our number plates the first two letters tell you the area where a car or a van was registered?'

Neville nodded.

'Well, it's not like that in Spain.' She pushed an image across her desk for the sergeant to inspect. 'That's the van,' she said. 'Look, you've got four numbers, and then you've got these three control letters, H, N and J. In the real world, that would tell us roughly where this van was bought and first registered, but not in Spain, it doesn't.

'Their system is national. The initial control letter, H in this case, is used until all the possible letter and number combinations are exhausted, then they move on to the next. But when it comes to registration, that's done with the local authority and you pay your vehicle tax to them.'

'Where did you find all this out?'

'From the consular section of the Spanish Embassy. They say that the number can be traced, but it'll take a while. And they won't be able even to begin before Monday.'

'Bloody hell! Is there no way we can short-circuit it?'

'I'm afraid not,' Wright sighed.

Neville swore softly, in frustration, picking up the image from the DC's desk. As she did so, her mobile vibrated in her pocket. She took it out, and checked the caller's name on screen. 'Nigel'.

'I think not,' she murmured, and rejected the call. As she did so, her eye was caught by something in the picture. 'Jackie,' she said, 'do you only have a hard copy of this?'

'No. It came as an email attachment.'

'Can you blow it up?'

'I should be able to.'

'Then do it, as big as you can. There's a sticker on the back of the van, on the lower right quarter, and I'd like to be able to read it.'

'Give me a minute.' The young DC pulled her computer screen closer to her and reached for her mouse. She called up the image and opened an edit programme, frowning with concentration as she went though a series of on-screen adjustments.

When she was ready she nodded . . . and then laughed out

loud. 'I don't know if this will do us much good. It has to be a joke: look.'

Neville leaned forward, over her shoulder, and read, 'www.moronrenault.es. What the hell is that?' she wondered. 'I think you're right,' she decided, 'it's a Spanish boy joke, but let's make sure. Google it.'

She straightened up as Wright went to work, and returned to her phone, finding 'Nigel' in her contact list and deleting the entry. As she finished, she felt the young DC tugging at her sleeve.

'Look at this, Sarge,' she urged. 'It isn't a joke after all. There is actually a place called Moron de la Frontera; it's in Andalusia, between Seville and Marbella, and it has a Renault dealer. It's all there on its website, along with a phone number. If they supplied that van, they can tell us who bought it.'

'Well done, Jackie, well done us. There's only one small problem: language. Where are we going to find a Spanish speaker on a Saturday morning?'

Her younger colleague smiled, diffidently. 'You're looking at one. I did Spanish in my degree. I was hoping it would help me in my police career . . . I'd like to join Interpol eventually.'

'Then put it to work,' Karen told her. 'Give them a call.'

She left her to her task and installed herself behind Sauce Haddock's desk, where the Bella Watson murder book was waiting for her. She opened it and started to speed-read through entries that she thought might be relevant, focused on the word 'Daughter', doing her best to ignore the flow of Spanish from a few yards away.

Fifteen minutes went by, and yet she was no more than a third of the way through when Jackie Wright hung up her phone and turned to her with a look of triumph on her face.

'Gotcha!' she exclaimed, giving a small fist-pump. 'The dealer came up trumps. The van was bought two years ago, by a woman called Maria Centelleos. She lives in a town called Utrera, closer to Seville, in a street called Calle Mar del Coral, number one hundred and seventeen.

'Hey,' she exclaimed, suddenly, 'that surname's familiar. Can I have a look at the file, Sarge?'

She came across to Neville's desk and flicked though the murder book, until she found the page she had sought.

'Yes,' she murmured, pressing her index finger to an entry. 'The trawl we did of the areas near Patrick Booth's drug drops, looking for fuel bought with Spanish cards: it threw up one payment, made in a filling station just south of Durham, on a card in the name of Ignacio Centelleos, issued by Cajamar, a rural savings bank. We haven't sourced the details of the holder, but it can be done.'

'Then do so. Ignacio; that's a man's name, isn't it?'

'Yes, and quite common. The surname isn't, though; it's very unusual. If I remember right, it means "Sparkles" in English.'

Karen stared at her. 'Repeat that, please, Jackie. You're telling me that Maria Centelleos in Spanish is Maria Sparkles in English?'

'Yes.'

'Oh, you beauty!' She snatched her mobile from the desk and called the first name on her list of 'favourite' numbers.

'Karen,' Andy responded. 'What's up?'

'Absolutely nothing, my dear. You don't know what you got till it's gone,' she laughed.

'What the hell are you on about? Did you get laid last night and want to crow about it?'

'Close but no cigar. That's not to say that I did get laid,

but . . . och, to hell with him. My ingenious Spanish-speaking DC and I have traced the owner of that van.'

'Yes, her name's Maria Centelleos.'

'You know?'

'Yes, I'm sorry to spoil your triumph but I just had a call from the Guardia Civil national drugs team. We've been working with them trying to trace the source of manufacture, and thanks to our forensics people they've found it.

'It's a small sherry-producing bodega near a town called El Cuervo, and she's listed as the owner. However, the only thing it seems to have been producing lately are methamphetamines.

'The feedback I'm getting is that the place was only ever marginally profitable, and that it went tits up at the start of the recession. They seem to have fought back by changing their product line. There's one small problem, though. The place was burned to the ground, a couple of weeks ago. They found the meth traces in a vat, but it'll be difficult to prove physically who made the stuff.'

'Have they arrested her?'

'No. The Centelleos woman and her son have been away from home for quite some time, according to their neighbours. Unfortunately, tracing them doesn't figure very high on the Guardia Civil's list of priorities. They're looking, but not very hard. It was small-time and the place is destroyed. They have much bigger targets and limited manpower, so if anyone's going to catch her it'll have to be us.'

'The son's name is Ignacio, yes?'

'So I'm told. The kid's some sort of genius chemist, the Guardia people say. He must be if he can synthesise crystal meth at the age of eighteen without blowing his fucking head off.'

'And that's all you've got, is it?' she asked.

'So far, yes. Your tone tells me you think you have more.'

'Indeed I have. A pound to a pinch of pig shit, leave out a couple of letters and translate her surname into English and you've got Bella Watson's missing daughter, and with her, from the sound of it, the mystery grandson that we can place in her flat.'

'Hey,' he said warmly, 'good for you guys. It's amazing what you can do on a weekend. Are you going to break it to Sammy Pye?'

'No, I'll let the head of CID do that. She's my very next call.'

Fifty-Six

'Is there any slight chance that one day, your phone won't ring on a Saturday?' Paula Viareggio asked her husband.

'That could happen,' he told her, 'if I'm made redundant after the start of Police Scotland.'

He was frowning when he said it: she took him seriously.

'They wouldn't do that, would they?' she exclaimed. 'Not with Bob Skinner in charge, surely not.'

'Work it out, love,' he suggested. 'There are going to be four deputies and six ACCs. Andy Martin's a cert to be one of the deputies, Maggie's odds on to be another, and probably Brian Mackie. That'll leave a lot more people at that rank than there are vacancies. Some will retire, sure, but I'm no cert to get a slot.'

'You will, though.'

'Let's wait and see.'

'It'll be a disgrace if you don't.'

He laughed and hugged her. 'No, it'll be fate. That's what happens when you let politicians run the country.'

'Don't talk to me about them,' Paula muttered. 'Who was that on the phone?' she asked.

'Mary Chambers, dropping a bombshell. One I must ask Andy about.'

He left her to attend to baby Eamon's latest demand and called his one-time colleague.

'I know what you're on about,' Martin exclaimed, before McGuire had a chance to ask him. 'Bella Watson's daughter, right?'

'Dead right. Mary's just told me about her. She says they're absolutely sure. Are you guys?'

'It looks nailed on. It was her van, in her mother's street and she's using her old radio name, or nearly all of it.'

'Andy,' McGuire said, 'I was on the Marlon Watson investigation, remember, and I had no idea that a daughter existed.'

'Oh, she did, I promise you; short dark hair, drop-dead gorgeous, eyes you could drown in; she looked a bit like Audrey Hepburn. If you doubt me, ask Alex; she says she met her too, although she was vague on how. Understandable, since she was only a kid at the time.

'But Mario,' he added, 'she was never a suspect, not for a moment, so after that first meeting, that I was in on, there was no need to talk to her again. It's no surprise you never heard of her. After all, you were only the CID gopher at the time.' He laughed. 'I remember you turning up for your first day in plain clothes in an Armani suit and Bob having to tell you, not too quietly, to dress like a cop.'

'Yes, I remember too. At least I can wear what I like now, unless uniform's called for. I might wear it when I visit my CID team on Monday, to read the fucking riot act! I'm going to want to know,' he said, 'why we're only finding out about Mia Watson now, and why it takes somebody's granny and the head of an outside agency to tell us. I've already torn a strip off Mary . . . unfairly maybe, with Mackenzie being missing. When that man turns up he's fucking toast, I tell you.'

'Hey, calm down, big fella,' Martin urged him. 'Don't get too steamed up. As I understand it, your team might have done a more thorough family check on Bella at the start, but they did trace the daughter, the hard way, and they did find out that her son, the anomalous grandson, existed. That said, when I see Karen tomorrow night to deliver the kids I'll tell her to wear her iron knickers on Monday morning.'

'She's exempt,' McGuire said, quickly. 'It's Sammy and Sauce I'll be after . . . although again that's probably unfair, since Mackenzie appointed himself SIO at the start of the investigation till I told him otherwise. That'll be another can he's carrying.'

'He'll be weighed down. What's this about him being missing anyway?'

'Slip of the tongue. I never said that; he's on personal leave, okay?'

'Noted. Now,' Andy asked, 'what's the story?'

'He and his wife have flown the coop. We don't know why and we don't know where they've gone. There were some forensics in the house that had us a ball-hair off launching a full-scale murder hunt, but Bob's assured us that he hasn't harmed her.'

'Bob has? How's he involved?'

'We felt we had to tell him,' McGuire explained, 'because of Mackenzie's Strathclyde background, plus we needed his force's help in the early days.'

'And because of their personal history?'

'Partly.'

'So Bob's investigating the business himself?'

'I haven't a clue what Bob's doing.' McGuire paused. 'You don't, do you?' he asked.

'No,' Martin replied, 'but I can tell you this. If he is on the trail, God help Mackenzie.'

Fifty-Seven

I'd known Max Allan for as long as I'd held chief officer rank. We'd met at the first ACPOS (Scottish chiefs' association) meeting I'd attended as an ACC and had regular contact from then on. But in all that time I'd learned very little about his personal life. I knew vaguely that he and his wife were regular customers at one of Paula Viareggio's delicatessens, but that was all.

I'd expected Sarah to blow a gasket when I told her that I had to go through to Lanarkshire to see him, but when I explained why, she understood.

As I'd told Maggie, having uncovered the potential scandal, I felt that I had to see it through, but it was more than that.

Yes, I could have walked into Bridie Gorman's office on the following Monday, dumped everything on her and told her to get on with it, but it would have been awkward for her, as she and Max had been side-by-side colleagues in Strathclyde.

He and I hadn't; he'd been gone, to all intents and purposes, when I had moved into Pitt Street, so our relationship had been at one remove.

The thought did occur to me that perhaps I should call in an outside force to investigate, but on reflection I decided that was inappropriate because Max was no longer a serving officer.

And so it was yours truly who rang his doorbell, at his house in High Blantyre, to find myself face to face with a woman I'd never met, but whose close family background I knew.

'Mrs Allan,' I began, 'I'm Bob Skinner, the chief constable.'

She gasped, and smiled. 'I know who you are, Mr Skinner,' she said, 'although I have no idea why you're here. Is Max getting that knighthood at last? Have you come to break the news?'

'Not exactly, Mrs Allan,' I replied, 'but I do have something I need to discuss with him.'

'And you've come all this way? That's a pity, because Max isn't at home . . . not at this one, anyway.' She stood aside. 'But please come in nonetheless. Let me offer you a cup of tea at least.'

'That would be kind of you,' I told her and let her usher me indoors.

Mrs Allan was of the generation who show guests automatically to the best room, and so she did. In their case it was a bay-windowed lounge looking out on to the front garden. There wasn't a single crease on any of the chairs, nor was there a television in the room, so I guessed that Max and his Mrs spent very little time there.

When my hostess returned, she was pushing a trolley, with two cups in saucers, and a Picquot Ware teapot and water jug with a matching sugar and cream set, the like of which I'd seen auctioned on *Bargain Hunt* a few weeks earlier.

'What a pity,' she repeated as she poured, through a tea strainer. 'Max will be so upset.' She passed me a cup, then dropped the question I'd been expecting. 'Can I tell him what it's about?'

'Actually it's about your nephew,' I responded.

She frowned quizzically. 'Richard? What's he got to do with the police, for goodness sake? He's an engineer like his father was.'

I set my tea on a side table and turned back to face her, and the plate of Penguin biscuits she was offering me.

'No thank you,' I murmured politely. 'No, not Richard; David. David Mackenzie.'

Her round matronly face seemed to cloud over for a second, and her eyes became a little distant as if she'd taken a couple of steps back from me mentally.

'David,' she said, her lips slightly pursed. 'Cheryl's husband. I never quite think of him as my nephew.'

'You don't care for him?'

'It's not my place to say. He's married to my niece and I'm dear wee Zach's godmother. It's just that I find him, well, a little brash, to be honest.'

'Brash?'

'Yes, I'm afraid so. A little coarse, too much so for my liking. His background isn't his fault of course, but it's unfortunate to say the least. That business with the hot oil!' She gave a little gasp. 'I know he was very young, and they did say he was ill-treated, but I have my worries about anyone who could do a thing like that, for any reason, at any age.'

'So you know about it?' I probed, gently.

'Oh yes. Max told me all about it. He told me when it happened, and then later when Cheryl took up with David, he told me it was the same boy.'

'How did Max feel about it, them getting together?'

'I don't imagine he was too happy. In fact I know he wasn't. But he's extremely fond of Cheryl, he always has been. At the end of the day, anything she sets her heart on she can have as far as Max is concerned.'

'Did that include David joining the police force?'

'Oh yes.' Mrs Allan gave me a small nod, as if to infer that she was reading my mind. 'I know,' she said. 'I wondered at the time whether the police would want him. I said as much to Max, but he said that it would be all right. He'd put in a word for him and he'd be accepted. And of course he was. I believe he worked for you in Edinburgh, Mr Skinner, did he not?'

'Yes, he did.'

'How did you find him?'

I hadn't expected that one, but I improvised. 'Almost too conscientious,' I replied.

She nodded. 'Yes, I can see why you would say that. Eager to please the bosses. He was always eager to please Max, that's for certain.'

'And eager to please Cheryl?'

'Hmph!' Mrs Allan snapped. 'If only that were so. Their marriage was volatile, to say the least. My sister-in-law, Julie . . . we have the same name, you know . . . told me once that she believed that David had abused Cheryl, that he'd been violent. I was going to tell Max, but Julie persuaded me not to. As well for him,' she added. 'That would have been the end of his career, I can tell you, if my Max had known that.'

'Now that I know it, Mrs Allan,' I pointed out, 'I may have to think through what to do about it, even though he isn't under my command any more.'

'Oh dear,' she exclaimed. 'I hope I haven't said anything to get him into trouble.'

She meant the opposite, of course, but all I did was shake my head and say, 'No, no, you haven't said anything of the sort.'

I finished my tea in a gulp and rose. 'Thank you very much,' I said. 'You've been very kind but I must go. I'm sorry to have missed Max, but I'm sure I'll catch up with him.'

She was about to say something else when my phone sounded. 'Excuse me,' I told her, fishing it out. 'In my job, you'll understand, every call might be important.' I checked the caller before answering; to my surprise it was Lottie Mann.

'Inspector,' I murmured, 'you must have a good reason to be calling me.'

'Of course I do, boss,' she replied, in her own special blunt way. 'I thought you'd want to know this, right away. I've just had a call from Ray Wilding in Edinburgh. Apparently Cheryl Mackenzie's just walked into her mother's, and now she's wondering what all the fuss is about. So, panic over, it seems.'

'I'm not so sure about that,' I told her, 'but thanks.'

I turned back to Mrs Allan. I thanked her and as we shook hands she ventured, 'Eh, what can I tell Max if he asks?'

'As it happens, nothing,' I replied. 'It looks as if the matter's been overtaken by events.'

But has it? I thought as I drove away.

Mrs Allan had given me the address of the Lanark Cottage; I had been intending to go there, but second thoughts overtook me. Instead I used voice dial . . . after years of trying I've finally mastered the art . . . to call Maggie Steele's mobile.

'You've heard,' she said, statement, not question.

'Yes. Your DI called my DI and she called me.'

She seemed to read that as a criticism, for her tone turned defensive. 'I was just about to call you myself, Bob,' she protested.

'I know, I know. I wasn't getting at you. Sorry if I sounded testy, but Cheryl Mackenzie's reappearance doesn't affect the line of inquiry that I'm following. And since I told you she was safe, it doesn't surprise me either. What are you planning to do about her?'

'I've told Ray Wilding to have a chat with her, to get more out of her. It was her mother who called Ray; he'd given her his number and told her to use it any time. Cheryl's story is that she and David had a big argument and she stormed off in the huff, telling him that he could look after the kids for a while and run a job at the same time and see how he liked it.'

'Do you buy that?'

'Not at first time of asking. That's why I've asked Ray to interview her; not under caution or anything, just an informal chat.'

'I'd like to make it slightly more formal,' I told her. 'And I'd like to sit in on it.'

'You would? That's a bit heavy, is it not?'

'I won't bite her, I promise. I'm not after her; it's her husband and Max Allan that are in my sights.'

'Okay,' Maggie agreed. 'I'll tell Ray to hold off going to see her until you can join him. I take it from the background noise that you're on the road.'

'Yes I am, but Mags, I'm not for going to see the woman. I've had officers chasing after her and David all week. She can come to see us, if that's all right with you. Ray's in Gayfield, yes? I'll meet him there, and she can join us. I'm sure her mother can look after the kids for a wee bit longer.'

'That makes it more formal than I'd envisaged.'

I laughed. 'Listen, Chief Constable, if this was a man that we were talking about, if the roles were reversed and it was Mackenzie who'd come swanning in after being missing for a week . . . would you be treating him so gently? Like hell you would.'

'Maybe not,' she conceded. 'All right, I'll send a car for her. When can you be at Gayfield?'

'Give me an hour. That'll do it.'

I ended the call, then turned off the music, just as it kicked back in; I had plenty to think about and the Drive-By Truckers were not conducive to that.

I was passing Harthill services, and my conversation with Cheryl Mackenzie was pretty much planned out, when the phone rang.

'Yes,' I said, to accept the call.

'Pops,' my older daughter said, 'can you talk?'

'Last time I checked, kid, sure.' I was casual but she sounded anxious. 'What's up?' I asked her.

'It's this investigation into the woman Watson's murder. I haven't been following it very closely, but last night I had the strangest call from Andy. He was at Karen's picking up the kids and he rang me . . . or rather they did . . . to ask me about Mia Watson. I don't know why, and he's said nothing since, but it worries me.'

I was glad she wasn't in the car with me so that she couldn't see the effect of her news.

I waited until I was sure I could keep my tone under control, then I asked, 'Why should it worry you, love? Her mother's been murdered, it's quite natural that her name should come up. I'm surprised that it hasn't before now.'

'But Pops, Mia's trouble. Remember how she just disappeared all those years ago? Remember how . . . ?'

'Remember you were only thirteen at the time,' I countered. 'Impressionable, volatile and full of emerging hormones. Your recollections of that time may not be one hundred per cent accurate.'

'Maybe not,' she persisted, 'but I do know this. You talk a lot about the past, especially to me. It's always "Remember this?" and "Remember that?" It's the way you are. Yet, since Mia disappeared, you have never mentioned her name, not once, not ever. So please don't tell me her turning up means nothing to you. You've never lied to me before. Please don't start now.'

'Okay,' I replied, 'I won't. It's true; I hoped I'd never see her again. But it's not my investigation and it's not my force that's looking into her mother's death, so there is no reason why I should. So don't you worry . . .'

'If you say ". . . your pretty little head" I will scream. I'll stop worrying when they lock up whoever killed her mother so that she can stay wherever the hell it was she went off to!'

Me too, kid, I thought when she'd calmed down, and hung up, *me too*.

Fifty-Eight

Karen Neville and Jackie Wright enjoyed basking in the warmth of their triumph in the unmasking of Bella Watson's unsuspected daughter, for as long as it lasted.

It ended with a phone call from Sammy Pye, asking for an immediate update after having his Saturday interrupted by the head of CID, wanting to know why it had taken the accidental intervention of the director of the SCDEA to unlock the secret.

'Mary's being good about it,' he said. 'She's blaming it on Mackenzie, but the way she feels about him at the moment, she'd blame him for global bloody warming. But I slipped up, no doubt about it; it never occurred to me to check whether the victim had any other children. What I haven't told her, though, is that Sauce and I actually heard about her last night, from young Hicks's granny.'

'You did?'

'Yes, but then we were sidetracked by a call to the monitoring unit, so we didn't have a chance to log it in. It was on my to-do list for Monday.'

'Your secret is safe with me,' Karen promised him. 'But don't take it all on yourself; that photograph in the flat kidded me too. We weren't the first to be fooled either, either. Andy told me that

341

when he was in Watson's house twenty-odd years ago, with Bob Skinner, it was the same. There were pictures of her and the boys, but no sign that there had ever been a daughter. They wouldn't have known about her, he said, if Bella hadn't mentioned her.'

'And Andy met her then?'

'Yes, but just the once. She made an impression, though. She was on radio, but from what he said she should have been on telly. Mind you, he was impressionable then,' she added.

Pye chuckled. 'I'll let you into a secret; I am not so old that I don't remember Mia Sparkles myself. I must have been about sixteen when she was on the radio, on that Airburst station.'

'She passed me by,' she commented, 'but then I was a Radio Forth girl.'

'Andy's right about her looks,' the DI said, softly. 'I remember her face was on billboard posters for a couple of weeks, and it was a traffic hazard. She had a big audience among teenage kids in and around Edinburgh. She used to talk about things that they were actually experiencing, voice-breaking, periods, wet dreams, that sort of stuff.'

'From what you're saying,' Karen laughed, 'there must have been a few wet dreams about her.'

'I'm sure there were. And then she just disappeared. I actually remember tuning into Airburst that day, after school. They trailed her programme as usual, but when the time came she wasn't there. The previous presenter just carried on, saying that Mia Sparkles had been unavoidably detained, but she never did turn up.'

'So I gather. Did it make the papers? I can't recall.'

'Yes. It was a one-week wonder. The rival radio stations

rubbed it in big time, as you'd expect. It was the beginning of a very short end for Airburst. It folded not long after that.'

'I wonder if she was ever listed as a missing person,' the DS mused.

'I've been wondering the same,' Pye told her. 'To tell you the truth, in my early days in CID, I actually looked her up and she wasn't. But of course, I never knew her real name was Watson. In fact that makes me think; it might be worth checking again, under that surname. If she was reported missing, and she's never been found, she should still be on a list, even going that far back. Could you do that for me, now?'

'Yes, I will,' Neville said, 'but what will it tell us?'

'It'll tell us who reported her. That might be interesting.'

'True,' she admitted. 'I'll get on it and let you know.'

'No!' he protested, laughing. 'I'm off duty, remember.'

She left him to the rest of his weekend, and called the missing person records office. It was on skeleton staffing, and as she expected, her request for a trace on a report going back three decades was greeted unenthusiastically.

'I'll get back to you,' the civilian clerk sighed, after he had noted the details.

'Within half an hour,' she added.

'Oh, I don't know if I can do that,' the man warned.

'I do. This is a live inquiry. So pull your finger out, please.'

She left him to it and made herself a coffee from the CID room supply, being careful to drop a pound coin into the kitty tin. She would have made two, but Wright was deep in conversation.

She took it back to her temporary desk, and was wondering whether there was a doughnut shop within walking distance of Queen Charlotte Street, when she was interrupted by another call.

That guy must have taken me seriously, she thought, smiling, as she took it, but the voice on the line, although male, was much older.

'Is that the officer in charge of the Watson investigation?'

'For today only, yes. Detective Sergeant Karen Neville.'

'No DI there?'

'Afraid not,' she replied, mildly annoyed. 'I'm as good as it gets over the weekend.'

'Of course, sorry, Sergeant.' The man was contrite. 'Don't mind me. My name is Tom Partridge, detective superintendent, retired for more than a few years. There's something I think I should report to you. I had a visit yesterday from a young man, a very young man indeed. He turned up on my doorstep, wanting to ask me about a book that I wrote after I handed in my a warrant card. It was about the life and times of a villain called Perry Holmes. Have you heard of him?'

'Yes I have, and I've heard of you too, Mr Partridge.'

The old man laughed, softly. 'The old crank with the bee in his bonnet, eh?'

'No,' she contradicted him, 'a well-respected officer, who left a lot of good things behind him in this force.'

'You can flatter me any time, Sarge; I love it. Anyway, this kid introduced himself as Marlon Hicks, and it became obvious he was quite upset. He said he'd tried to get a copy of my book from the Central Library . . . it's either that or the charity shops these days . . . but the librarian there told him the only copy was out. As it happened, I go there quite a lot and the lady knows where I live, so she sent him along to see me.'

'Was it wise for her to do that?'

'Aye, it was fine,' he replied. 'I've got no problem with it. I know who to let over my door and who to keep on the step. This boy I let in and I talked to him. He told me a very strange story, and a sad one too. He'd just found out the day before, he said, that he was the son of a man called Marlon Watson.'

'I know,' Neville said. 'It was me who told him. We had to interview him in connection with the Bella Watson murder inquiry . . . I'm assuming you know about that . . . and there was no way I couldn't tell him why.'

'Of course not,' Partridge agreed, 'but how much did you actually tell him?'

'Only what was necessary for the investigation.'

'You didn't tell him who the police think killed his father?'

'Absolutely not.'

'No, I thought not, because that's what he wanted to know from me. Can I ask you, do you know who did it, Sergeant, Karen if I may, and I'm Tommy, by the way?'

'I think so, Tommy. If I recollect correctly the evidence suggested that Perry Holmes had him killed.'

'That's right. Bob Skinner . . . he led the investigation . . . proved that beyond a doubt. But the case never came to court, see, because Perry's son, Hastie McGrew, made sure there was nobody left alive who could tie his father to the crime. I never flat out accused him in my book either, but only because the lawyers wouldn't let me.'

'Did you tell young Marlon any of this?' Neville asked.

'No, I didn't. I just felt it wouldn't be prudent, because the boy was very wound up. He said that he'd misjudged his father all his life, and that now he realised that he was a victim and not a bad man at all. He was angry, Karen, disturbed . . . unquiet, to use an old word, a characteristic that I observed for many years in the genes of the Watson family.'

'Are you saying that we should have another word with him?'

'At the very least,' the old detective replied. 'All the more so because I've just had a call from my daughter. She's the editor of the *Saltire* newspaper. She told me that this morning the boy came into their front office looking for old issues. He told the laddie there that he'd been to see me and that I'd advised him to check all the old cuttings about the Marlon Watson murder.'

'And did he?'

'Aye, he did. The lad in the office just happened to mention it later to my June, by chance, after he'd gone. I remember those cuttings, Karen; my June wrote some of the stories and they must have had better lawyers than me because they didn't leave much room for doubt that Perry Holmes was behind the killing and that his son was involved too.'

'I'm with you,' Neville murmured.

'Good, 'cos I still keep tabs on that crew, and I know that Hastie's out of jail and back in Edinburgh.'

'We're on it, Tommy,' she said. 'Thanks a lot.'

'Don't mention it. It takes me back to the old days. I wish you luck; he seemed like a nice boy, and I'd hate him to do something daft. There's been enough of that in his family.'

'So I gather. Just one more thing,' she added. 'Do you know what Hastie McGrew was actually jailed for? All I know is that it was a couple of murders, but no more. What was it about?'

'I know up to a point. He pleaded guilty so there was no trial, and no evidence led, only statements. The Crown said that he'd killed the two men because he believed they'd been involved in the rape of a family member. Now Hastie only had the one female family member, Alafair, his sister. I assume it was her, but if you needed to know for sure, you might have trouble. The lead detective in the case was Alison Higgins and she's dead now, so that line's closed off.

'Bob Skinner's the only one left who could tell you,' he added, 'but don't hold your breath. I asked him myself once, and, even though he used to call me "sir", he refused point-blank to tell me.'

'I won't be pushing him,' Karen chuckled, 'but I don't see that it's relevant, just curiosity in my part. Thanks again. I'll get on with tracing the boy.'

She hung up and was about to dial Mary Chambers' home number, when Jackie Wright held up a hand to stop her.

'This just in,' she exclaimed, 'as they say on Sky News. I've had a call from Anna Jacobowski. They're still working flat out on those DNA traces and they've come up with a hot one. They can place somebody new in Bella Watson's flat, but only in the living room: Hastie McGrew.'

'Say that again?'

The DC did as ordered. 'Is that significant?' she asked.

'Hugely, if the history between the Holmes and Watson families teaches us anything at all. But I have another priority.'

She made her call to Chambers, and reported Partridge's call. The chief superintendent understood its meaning at once. 'If the boy knows that McGrew had his father killed . . . Karen,' she continued, 'could he know that Hastie's in a nursing home?'

'He works for him; indeed recently he's worked with him, with Hastie having been about the place before he fell ill. If there's been talk on the shop floor, yes, he could know.'

'Let's assume he does. Look, I'm at my partner's place just now; I think you know where that is. Pick me up from there. While you're on your way, I'll find out where McGrew's being looked after, then call ahead to say he's to have no visitors. I might be overreacting, but rather that than the other way.'

'Too true. We need to keep him alive; I've got some questions to ask him. See you shortly, ma'am.'

Neville was in the act of putting on her jacket when the phone rang again. 'Take that, Jackie,' she shouted, but seeing as she looked up that the DC was on another call. 'Bugger,' she snapped, but snatched up the handset.

'I hope this is quick enough for you,' the missing persons clerk sniffed. 'Yes, there is a missing person's file on a woman called Mia Watson. She was aged twenty-seven when it was opened. That's not yesterday, so we class it as historic, but it's still open.'

'Who notified us, do you know?'

'Yes, it was filed by someone called Alafair Drysalter, and the relationship's shown as sister.'

'Sister? Are you sure?'

'I can read, Detective Sergeant Neville,' he sniffed.

'Okay, sorry. Thanks. Nothing else on the file, is there? No notes.'

'Only one; it was added a few weeks after the file was open. If the person is traced, we're instructed to advise a Detective Superintendent Skinner, whoever he might be.'

Fifty-Nine

The news from Alex was what I'd been dreading, ever since I heard that someone had finally sent Mia's appalling mother to her long home. I was surprised that it had taken so long for her name to emerge, but I hadn't been about to make the suggestion that they should look for her.

Nobody else could ever read me like my kid, not even her mother, and so her point about me blanking Mia Watson from my recollections struck home hard. Thinking back, she was right; from the day after I watched her drive off into the metaphorical sunset from the Radio Airburst car park, her name had never passed my lips.

But that wasn't to say I hadn't thought about her in all those years; oh yes, I had, and often. Mia was gone; to where I didn't care, but it was where I'd wanted her to stay. I'd even taken steps to make sure I was warned of any reappearance.

A few weeks after her disappearance, I did a quiet check to ensure that nobody had reported her missing. To my surprise and slight consternation, I discovered that someone had; to be specific, Alafair Drysalter. She had described herself as 'sister' in her report and that was fair enough. From the age of fifteen, Mia had been raised alongside Perry Holmes's daughter.

Mia had been a young lady with places to go, in her time, but she could never quite shake off her varied upbringing, and so she had never fulfilled that star potential. Instead she had got herself in what could have been a very large jam, from which she had been extricated by someone with influence.

Me.

I forced the woman from my mind as I parked in Gayfield Square. Like any good citizen, I put money in a meter, since I no longer had an 'Edinburgh Police: on duty' card with my signature on it, or the local clout to have a parking ticket pulled with a single phone call.

I'd made it five minutes faster than I'd told Maggie, but Ray Wilding was waiting for me nonetheless. I'd been quietly impressed as I'd watched his rise from detective constable. He was one of the younger members of the group I thought of . . . I still do, in fact . . . as 'Skinner's People', and one of the brightest. I see him and Sammy Pye making it to command rank, but maybe not before young Haddock overtakes them both.

I had never imagined David Mackenzie making it to the top floor, though, not in his own right rather than as an exec, not even when I spotted him in North Lanarkshire and thought he might have been able to bring something new to the Edinburgh party.

He had, for a while, until the bad outweighed the good. Naturally I blamed myself. My assessment of the man hadn't gone beyond the superficial. I should have seen through him, no matter how effectively his background and his character had been kept under wraps by dear old Uncle Max.

Tom Donnelly's belief that violence and aggression had been beaten into him was probably correct, but all I'd learned about him and observed made me pretty sure that for all the old priest's advice and counselling, he had never removed it. He had taught him to manage it, that was all.

'How do we play this, sir?' Wilding asked me as I joined him in his office.

'It's your territory,' I pointed out. 'You're coordinating the investigation.'

'Maybe, but I'm not taking the lead with you in the room. Also, to be honest, I'm not sure why we're doing this in the office. I was just going to have a chat with her at home, till I was told to bring her in here.'

'Okay, let me explain. I've been looking for Mackenzie from a different angle, through the man himself, and I've uncovered some stuff I don't like. That stuff is potentially criminal, and while it may not involve Cheryl, it's not appropriate for cosy fireside chats either. That's why she's here and that's why we're going to talk to her in an interview room, and video the conversation.'

That was nearly all of the truth, but I had something else on my mind that I decided not to share in case it affected Ray's approach.

'To answer your question,' I continued, 'we're going to play it by ear. If you're happy, I'll lead and set the tone. You can chip in whenever you feel the need. She should be here in a minute. Meantime, I must make a phone call.'

I was ready and waiting in the interview room when Cheryl Mackenzie arrived. I asked Wilding to greet her in reception and bring her through, but without telling her I was there.

We had met before a couple of times, immediately after she and David had moved to Edinburgh, and again when I visited him after he had his breakdown. When she saw me her eyes widened and she gave a very small gasp. I smiled, in an attempt to put her at her ease, and told her that it was all right, that I wasn't the bearer of bad news.

'I've been concerned about you,' I said, as she took a seat, in a group of three that I'd set out, away from the usual interview table, 'and so have other people in Strathclyde.'

'Thank you,' she replied, then added, 'and I'm really sorry you have been. My mum started to cry, you know, when I walked through the door this morning. It took her all her time to ask me where I've been.'

'And where have you been, Cheryl?' I asked.

'I've been away, by myself. I just had to, Mr Skinner.'

'Why?'

'Because I just couldn't take any more of David's intensity and his anger. I've had twenty years of it and I can't take any more. I thought he was okay, but he's not. He's paranoid, he thinks that life's one big conspiracy against him. He hates everybody; he hates you, he hates Mrs Steele, and he loathes ACC McGuire especially, I think because he's afraid of him.'

Her remark didn't surprise me . . . anyone who believed McGuire was after him would be entitled to be afraid . . . but her next did.

'You know what I think?' she asked, rhetorically. 'I think he associates him with his uncle.'

I made myself frown. 'His uncle?' I repeated, quietly.

'Yes.' She hunched her shoulders, leaning forward a little, in the way people sometimes do when they're telling you a secret.

'When David was young, he was brought up by an aunt and uncle, after his parents both died. The uncle was very cruel to him, so much so that David was taken away from them and brought up in a children's home.' She paused and looked at me. 'But you must know that, Mr Skinner.'

I nodded. 'Yes, I do, but carry on.'

She hesitated, finding the right words. 'Well, I suspect that Mr McGuire makes him think of that uncle . . . I don't mean that he's ever threatened him in any way, I just think he associates the two of them in his mind.'

'Then he's wrong,' Wilding assured her. 'Speaking as someone who works under ACC McGuire's command, I promise you that he's a very fair and considerate boss. He can be blunt, but everybody likes him.'

'Are you afraid of David, Cheryl?' I asked.

'No!' she protested. 'We've been together for ever.'

'Then what made you go off so suddenly? People don't become paranoid overnight, and as you've just said, you've been a couple since you were in your teens. Yes,' I added, 'I know that too.'

'Nothing,' she replied. 'I told you, I just had enough. I needed a break from him.'

I sensed that she was trying to evade my gaze but I wouldn't let her.

'He thumped you, Cheryl. Didn't he?

She shook her head, tearing her eyes from mine. 'No,' she whispered.

'Look at me and say that,' I challenged. 'He did. Your blood was on a towel in your bathroom. Please, tell me the truth; this isn't about a prosecution for assault. If it was I wouldn't be here, and neither would DI Wilding. You'd be talking as a witness to DCS Chambers and ACC McGuire.'

She sighed. 'Okay, yes he did. He had a blazing row with Mario McGuire over the telephone last Saturday morning and that set him off. It set me off as well. I told him I'd had enough of him blaming everybody but himself whenever he screwed something up and he just turned and hit me.

'He split my lip and gave me a black eye in the making.' She wiped some cosmetic from her face, revealing a fading bruise on her left cheek. 'It was all over in a few seconds and he was full of remorse, but I had to get away from him.'

'Did you ever think, even for one second,' Wilding asked, 'of calling the police after he thumped you?'

'No,' she replied without any pause for thought. 'That would have been the cruellest thing I could possibly have done to him. The police force is all that's been holding David together for a while now. If I'd got you involved that would have gone.'

'So you left,' I said, 'to give him some cooling-off time?'

'Yes. I packed a bag and I left.'

'Where did you go?'

'I just drove. I wound up in Tarbert, and booked into a bed and breakfast. I stayed there until I was ready to come back.'

'Without calling anyone? Without calling your mother even, to let her know you were all right? Without calling into your work?'

'I didn't want to speak to anyone; I assumed David would look after the children. The fact of the matter is, I wasn't sure I would ever come back.'

'How did you pay for the trip?'

'Cash. I pulled as much money as I could out of ATMs, about two thousand pounds. I put some of it on one of David's credit cards, just to punish him.' She threw me a small smile.

'Was that the only reason you drew the cash? To piss him off?'

She sighed, and the smile went away. 'No. I didn't want David to be able to find me. He's a police officer, so I knew how easy it would be for him if I used cards later on.'

That was the moment when all my thoughts and suspicions

coalesced, and when I became close to certain that I knew what had happened. I considered stopping there and then, but decided to go a little further, until the legal ground was too shaky beneath my feet to continue.

'But he didn't, Cheryl,' I said, 'for the problem is, David's disappeared too. He hasn't been seen since last weekend either.'

She chewed her lip, nodding. 'Yes, I know. My mum said. That was why she went so frantic when I turned up. I don't know why he's done that, Mr Skinner. I don't know where he's gone.'

'Where do you think he might have run to?'

'I don't know,' she murmured. 'I'm afraid, though.'

'Afraid of what?'

'Afraid he might have harmed himself. Afraid he's dead.' Her face crumpled and she looked close to tears.

'But how would he do that? You took his car, yes?'

'Yes.'

'Why did you do that?' Wilding asked her, staying so casual that I knew he, too, had picked up a vibe. 'Yours was parked in front of your house. Why would you take David's?'

'To punish him again, I suppose.' A moment of spite flashed across her face, and for that instant I was looking at a different woman.

'So how did David go anywhere?' I continued. 'He didn't take your car, so how did he run off?'

She shrugged. 'I don't know. He must have got a taxi, then a train.'

'I've got a problem with that, Cheryl,' I confessed. 'I'm asking myself, how did he pay for it? His cards haven't been used either, and no money's been pulled from your accounts other than that two grand you took.'

'I don't know,' she protested. 'Maybe he stole a car. Maybe he had a card you didn't know about. Maybe he got a fucking Wonga loan!'

'Calm down, Cheryl, please,' I said, quietly. 'I'm concerned about him, just as you must be.'

She composed herself. 'I'm sorry. I know. I'm just out of my mind with worry.'

'I'm not surprised. Answer me something else, about David, if you will. If he was in real trouble, where do you think he would go . . . or rather to whom? I've been wondering about that and given what I've found out about David's background, I could make a guess. I'm wondering if it would be the same as yours.'

Her eyes narrowed, as if she was looking a couple of questions ahead, then she replied to the one in hand. 'Father Donnelly,' she murmured.

'That's his priest?' I added for Wilding's benefit. 'The man who more or less adopted him in his teenage years?'

'Yes, that's him.'

'But he hasn't gone there,' I told her.

'That's a pity,' she said.

'You're right. It is. I know he didn't because just before you got here I called Father Donnelly, and I asked him that point-blank. He told me that he hadn't.'

I let that sink for a second or two before I went on, to what by then she knew was coming.

'But you did, Cheryl,' I murmured, lowering my voice, because I didn't want to frighten her. 'You went to see Father Donnelly on Monday, in Tighnabruaich, where he lives now. When we check with your bed and breakfast I think we'll find that you checked in there on that same day, having taken the ferry to Tarbert from Portavadie. It's not that far from Tighnabruaich.

'That answers another question: why someone had been checking out ferry routes on your computer. It begs another, of course. Did that person check so many just to confuse Ray here?'

'I wouldn't know,' she whispered.

'I'm afraid that I think you would, that you know all too well. I'll tell you what else I've worked out. You must have slept in David's Honda on the Sunday night. If you slept at all, that is; it must have been pretty challenging in that confined space, all things considered.'

'I don't know what you mean,' she snapped.

'Yes you do, Cheryl. Father Donnelly couldn't tell me what you and he talked about. Couldn't, I repeat, not wouldn't, which can only mean that he took your confession, as a priest, and is bound to keep it secret.'

She sagged in her chair and I knew that we had gone as far as we could.

I rose from mine. 'I'm going to stop there, Mrs Mackenzie,' I said. 'DI Wilding will now arrest you on suspicion of the murder of your husband, and you'll be formally cautioned. You'll be re-interviewed by other officers, no doubt. What you've told us here won't be offered as evidence, but we will be able to use it to put together a complete picture of your movements.'

I stood, and she looked up at me, nothing much in her eyes any more other than exhaustion.

'I have one more question, Cheryl,' I concluded, 'but I think I know the answer already. I expect we'll find that you checked out of your B and B on Wednesday or on Thursday, at the latest. After that, did you visit your Uncle Max?'

Sixty

Karen Neville was still more than puzzled by the news from Missing Persons as she drove into Stockbridge. So much so that she had almost called her former husband once again, only staying her hand when she realised that he would probably be with Alex Skinner, not wanting to be suspected of phoning him at any excuse.

Mary Chambers was waiting on the pavement when she pulled up outside her partner's flat. The whole force knew that the DCS was involved with the sister of Griff Montell, a fellow Edinburgh cop. He had taken the news badly when he had found out, but a transfer to Special Branch, which operated outside the CID network, had been the diplomatic solution.

'It's called Oakmount,' Chambers said as she buckled herself into the passenger seat, 'and it's in the Grange. I've got the location on my phone. Head for the area and I'll find it when we get there.'

Neville obeyed, staying silent for a while as she concentrated on navigating her way through three sets of the temporary traffic lights which had become a curse of the city. The head of CID left her to it, uninterrupted, until they had crossed the Meadows, and were heading up Kilgraston Road.

'What's this boy like, Karen?' she asked.

'I found him okay,' she replied, 'but what Jack and I told him changed his whole lifetime thinking about his father, and made him part of a family he never knew existed. When Mr Partridge said he seemed disturbed, that was enough for me.'

'Me too. I've got a car up there, with orders to stop anyone other than family from getting to McGrew. Mind you, from what I heard from DI Pye, we're only postponing the inevitable by keeping him safe.'

'More than that, ma'am,' Neville said. 'I've got some questions to ask him.' She told the DCS about the latest finding from the DNA trawl of the Caledonian Crescent flat.

'Was he, by God?' she hissed. 'But we were told he's physically harmless.'

'Himself, perhaps,' the DS conceded, 'but he might not have been alone. There's so much DNA he could have had a platoon of known heavies there without us finding them. The only questionable thing is, the DNA was found in the living room; that wasn't affected by the burst pipe from above, so it wasn't redecorated. He could have been there at any time and not just in that short window between the workmen finishing and Watson being killed.'

'Then we do need to have a serious chat with Hastie; maybe he was meeting the folk in the Spanish van.'

'There's a thought,' Neville murmured as she stopped for a red light, and as Chambers' phone rang.

As the head of CID took the call, she seemed to straighten up in her seat as she listened to what she was being told. 'Yes, ma'am,' she said, and her sergeant knew at once who the caller was. 'As soon I've wrapped up the urgent matter I'm on at the moment, I'll be there. Allowing for the weekend traffic, I should be at Gayfield in an hour.'

She whistled as she took the mobile from her ear. 'Fucking hell!' she exclaimed. 'That was the chief. If this here gets complicated I might need to haul in Haddock to join you. I've just been ordered to meet ACC McGuire at Gayfield, to do a formal interview with Cheryl Mackenzie. Ray Wilding's just arrested her for murdering her husband.'

The bombshell was still reverberating in Neville's mind when her boss called out, 'Take a right here,' as she approached a junction. 'Second on the left next,' she continued as they made the turn, into a quiet suburban street, in which only a single pedestrian could be seen, 'and we should be there.'

She had barely finished speaking before her driver slammed on the brakes. 'That's him,' Karen shouted, as she freed herself from her seat belt and jumped from the car. 'Marlon Hicks.'

By the time Chambers' feet hit the pavement the DS had pinned the lightly built youth against the wall of the house he had been passing. 'Don't run, Marlon,' Karen warned him. 'There's no point and there's no need. We want to talk to you, that's all.'

'What about?' he retorted. 'I ain't done nothin'.'

'That's true, and we want to make sure that you don't. What are you doing here?'

'Just walkin', lady, that's all. I got a right.'

As he spoke she patted him down. Her hand came upon something in a pocket of his hoodie; she reached in and withdrew a kitchen knife.

'You don't have a right to carry that,' the head of CID said, as she reached them. 'Give us some sensible answers, son, or we'll arrest you.'

'We know where you were going, Marlon,' Neville told him. 'And I don't like the fact that you were going there with a knife in your pocket.' She dropped her hands to her sides, freeing him, but ready to stop him instantly if he tried to run again.

'I wasn't going to use it,' he murmured. 'I only brought it to scare him.'

'I don't think it would,' she replied, fingering the blade. 'You could barely cut butter with this thing. Why did you want to frighten him?'

'I wanted to make him tell me why they killed my father. They took him from me before I was even born, those people.'

'Didn't the newspaper stories explain it?' the DS asked. 'Your father was murdered because the man he worked for was having an affair with Hastie McGrew's sister Alafair.'

'They killed him for that?'

'They did. McGrew's father paid the men who did it; he was a ruthless and evil man, and his son's no better. When the police looked like tracing them, Hastie killed them to keep them quiet. That's who you were on your way to try and frighten with a blunt potato peeler. I don't think it would have worked, Marlon.'

Tears filled the young man's eyes. 'Why did my mum and Duane keep it from me?' he moaned. 'I grew up hating my father.'

'I'd imagine they did it to stop you from growing up to fuck up your life by doing something as bloody stupid as this,' Chambers replied. 'Fortunately you didn't, so this is what's going to happen. You're going to buy a kitchen knife to replace that one, because we're keeping it, then you're going to pack in your job with the McGrews' company and you're going to move in with your granny. I'm told she's a good woman. Is all that agreed?'

Marlon nodded. 'Yes, lady.'

'Good. I shouldn't need to say this but I will, just in case you take another daft turn. If you come anywhere near the Oakmount Nursing Home again, you'll be lifted and I'll charge you with the first thing that comes into my head. Now go on, son, and think yourself lucky that DS Neville saw you when she did.'

They watched him as he walked away, until he reached the junction and passed out of sight.

'Do you think he'll behave himself?' the head of CID asked the DS as they returned to their car.

'I'm pretty sure he will. He's a nice kid at heart. I wouldn't like to have a shock like he's had.'

She drove on, taking the second turning on the left as she had been instructed, and seeing the nursing home immediately, a modern three-storey building taking up half the street on which it stood. She swung into the car park and slid into a bay next to a police patrol car. Its occupants, two constables, were waiting for them in the home's reception hall.

'You can stand down,' the DCS told them. 'The panic's over. But wait for me; I'm going to need a lift to Gayfield Square. Do you happen to know which floor McGrew's on?'

'He's in room one eleven,' the older officer told her, 'first floor. Not that we went up there: I heard a woman asking for him at reception a few minutes ago. She said she was his sister. There was a guy with her, a baldy fella. He'd a walking stick; looked as if he belonged in here himself.'

'That's handy,' Chambers observed. 'It might save us a second visit.'

The two detectives took the stairs up to the first floor. 'The baldy guy will be the husband, Derek Drysalter,' Neville said.

'Mmm,' her boss murmured. 'I saw him play for Scotland once. He had hair then. And speak of the devil . . .'

Drysalter was standing in the corridor, outside room one hundred and eleven. He frowned as they approached him, warrant cards in hand. 'Jesus Christ,' he exclaimed. 'At a time like this? What do you think you're doing?'

'Visiting the sick,' Chambers replied, sharply. 'We need to talk to your brother-in-law.'

'You'll have a job,' Drysalter snapped, trembling with anger and tension. 'He went into a coma two hours ago; my wife and I have just seen his doctor. She says he'll probably not come out of it. Tough shit, eh. He does nearly twenty years and then gets only a few months on the outside.'

'Life's a bitch and then you die,' the DCS said. 'Look at it this way: in another era, they'd have dropped him through the floor with a rope round his neck. Anyway, a man can do a lot in a few months; possibly even enough to earn him another twenty years, him and anyone involved with him.'

'Listen,' the former footballer protested, 'I know nothing about any of that stuff, any of it. I didn't join the family firm when I married Alafair.'

'In which case we'll need to talk to her. You know,' Chambers told him, as she moved past him, 'I used to have a Scotland shirt with your name on the back. Pity about the hair, by the way.'

There was music playing in Hastie McGrew's room, just loudly enough for Alafair Drysalter, who was standing at the end of her brother's bed, not to hear the detectives as they entered. When Neville coughed, she gave a little jump and spun round.

'Who the . . .' she began, stopping short as she saw the cards. 'Oh no,' she sighed. 'Do you people never stop?'

'We tend not to,' the DS said. 'We came here to interview

your brother, but it looks like we're going to have to talk to you instead.'

'About what this time? Are you still on about my father's death?'

'No, it's not about that, for now at any rate. The situation is that we can put your brother in Bella Watson's flat. So far your DNA hasn't shown up there, but it won't surprise me if it does.'

'Look,' she exclaimed, 'Hastie couldn't have killed the bloody woman. I thought you'd established that.'

'But he knows people who could.'

'In which case he'd have been bloody silly to go with them while they did the job, and silly, Hastie is not. And by the way, you can stop looking for me there, because I wasn't.'

She nodded towards the still, pale, hairless figure on the bed. 'As for my brother, look at him. What's the point in pursuing this any further?'

'Because a woman's been murdered,' Chambers replied. 'She might not have been a very nice woman, a monster in fact, and she might have been involved in the drugs trade, but she was still murdered, and whether we can be arsed or not, it's our job to find out who did it. So, why was your brother in Bella's flat? Was it because he was involved in the methamphetamine racket with her?'

'No!' Alafair snapped. 'It's because he wasn't. That's all I'm prepared to say.'

'In that case we'll be charging you with obstructing justice. You don't want that, Mrs Drysalter, do you? Up to now you're the clean one of your family. My officers tell me you have a child at Mary Erskine. How's she going to take that?'

'Are you threatening me?'

'Are you really that naive?' Karen Neville laughed. 'Of course we're threatening you. And we'll follow through on it unless you tell us what the bloody hell's been going on here.'

'Okay,' she sighed in defeat. 'The fact is that Hastie was approached almost as soon as he got out of prison and offered a deal to import and sell methamphetamines. He told me about it and said it looked pretty foolproof. The quantities would be very profitable but there would never be silly amounts in circulation.

'He reckoned it could stay under the radar for quite some time if it was handled properly. Well, I went bat-shit, let me tell you. I said that I'd done my last prison visit, and I forbade him to have anything to do with it. Believe it or not he does listen to me. He said okay, if I was that set against it he'd pass it on to somebody else.'

'To Bella Watson?'

'Yes. He told me he'd found out by accident from a guy in the jail that she was living somewhere in Edinburgh, and that he'd been able to track her down. He went to see her and offered her the deal; he told her it was compensation for what happened to her boy. Hastie always did think Dad went too far with that,' she offered in explanation. 'That's why he was in Bella's flat, to set up the drug route. The old cow went for it, but for security, Hastie didn't tell her who the supplier was.'

'Not ever?'

'Not that I know of. I told him never to mention it to me again.'

'Who approached him? Who was the supplier?'

'He never told me that, and frankly I didn't want to know.'

'Is that the truth, Mrs Drysalter?' Chambers asked.

'Yes it is. There's no point in holding anything back. What can you do to my brother now?'

Sixty-One

When Karen Neville walked back into the Leith CID room she was surprised to see that the DI's cubicle was illuminated by the faint glow of a computer monitor. She opened the door to find Sammy Pye seated behind his desk.

'Excuse me,' she said, 'has it suddenly stopped being Saturday?'

'It has for me. I called Jackie for another update; when she told me everything that had happened, I couldn't sit on my arse at home any longer. Have you traced Marlon Hicks?'

'Yes. He isn't a threat any longer . . . not that he ever was really. The way it is now with Hastie McGrew, the only threat to him will come from the angry souls waiting for him on the other side.'

She explained that the man had been comatose when they had arrived at his nursing home, and that no bets were being placed on him seeing out the weekend.

'Bugger!' Pye moaned. 'I'd been hoping . . .'

'. . . that he'd wrap up the murder investigation for you? Come on, Sammy, that was never going to happen. The visit wasn't a total loss, though. We couldn't talk to Hastie, but we did find his sister there. She's still nervous about being implicated in her father's death, so she was very frank with us.'

Neville related Alafair Drysalter's account of how the methamphetamine had found its way into Edinburgh and how her brother had involved Bella Watson in its distribution.

'Do you really think he gave her the deal because he had a guilty conscience?' Pye asked sceptically.

'Let's say I'm not convinced,' the DS replied. 'I think it's more likely that he didn't want to be hands-on himself . . . his father never was, from what we're told . . . and that he took it to Bella because having been away since the mid-nineties, she was the only person he knew from those days who was still around.'

'I'll buy into that. But Alafair wouldn't tell you who it was approached Hastie?'

'No, she said she didn't know.'

'Did you believe that.?'

'Not for a second, but it doesn't matter. We think we know anyway. Did Jackie tell you about the name of the owner of the Spanish van?'

'Yes.' Pye grinned. 'Nice one. Maria Centelleos, equals Sparkles, Mia Watson's old radio name.'

'And more than that. Andy's people have established, subject to chemical testing, that the methamphetamine was made in a place owned by her.'

'Wow. That really does land it at her door. Has she been arrested?' he asked, hopefully.

'No.' She explained that the bodega had been destroyed, and that the Centelleos mother and son had vanished.

'There's a son?'

'Yes. So, unless there are other young Watsons scattered around Edinburgh, we now know whose DNA we've found in Bella's flat.'

'But I'm investigating a murder, not a family reunion,' the DI pointed out.

'Forget the murder for now,' Karen told him, 'focus on the drugs.'

'Okay, I will. What you're suggesting is that Maria Centelleos made them. But why would she, of all people, approach Hastie McGrew with a drug deal? That's what I don't understand.'

'Neither did I but I do now. The DCS had to leave, but I stayed on and the pair of us went for a coffee, leaving Derek to watch over his brother-in-law in case he decided to croak.

'I had something else to ask Alafair, something I only discovered today. After Mia Sparkles disappeared, Alafair filed a formal missing person report and in it she claimed to be her sister.'

'Did she?' Pye's eyebrows rose. 'Are you sure about that? I mean why the hell would she? We know who their parents were, both of them.'

'She did, though, and my first thought was that it was a simple matter of the last of the Holmes family wanting to eliminate the last of the Watsons. I guess the same must have occurred to Bob Skinner, for he had the report flagged up for him to be notified as soon as Mia was traced. But we were wrong. Alafair told me that the two of them were brought up together for a few years.'

'They were what? How the hell did that happen? In their day, those two families were the local equivalent of the Hatfields and the McCoys.'

Karen contradicted him. 'Not always. If you go far enough back, Bella's brother Gavin used to work for the Holmeses. He was their dealer in his housing scheme, one that's long gone, thank God. Alafair told me that dear old Gavin, before he came to a sticky end, pimped his niece Mia, then well underage, to her Uncle Alasdair, who was notorious for liking them young. Bella knew about it and wasn't bothered. But when Perry Holmes found out about it, he was; he was very bothered indeed.

'He took Mia away from Alasdair, and from Edinburgh altogether, and installed her with his own kids, in Hamilton, where they lived with their mother, Miss McGrew. He looked after Mia all the way through university. So you see, to all intents and purposes, a Watson became a Holmes.'

'Ele-fucking-mentary,' Pye murmured. 'But why should she vanish? Did Alafair tell you that?'

'She doesn't know, but back then she feared the worst, that Mia might have been murdered too. So she filed her formal missing person report, in the hope that her disappearance would be investigated.' She frowned. 'Now that I think about it, Bob Skinner couldn't have thought she was dead, since he had that note put on it. Leaving that aside though,' she continued, 'that makes sense to me, Sammy. It explains why Hastie didn't tell Bella who was the source of the crystal meth and how the route was set up so that the two of them never met. Remember, Patrick Booth always collected and dealt the stuff; Bella always handled the money.

'I've spoken to our drugs squad leader,' she added, 'to pass on what Alafair told me. Booth's given them the rest of it, how the money thing worked; he got his cut then she'd take hers, and send the rest to the supplier, to Mia.'

'How? Did he tell the squad that? Did he even know?'

'Yes, he did. He said she used a money broker to transfer it to a Euro account in Gibraltar.'

'Could there be someone else involved? Could this Mia woman be a front for someone?'

'There's no trace of anyone else. Her van was seen approaching her mother's flat, her son's DNA was in the place.'

'So why did it all blow up?' the DI asked. 'What brought them over here . . . assuming it was her driving the van, and that she didn't let the lad come on his own?'

'There's only one person can tell us, and that's her,' the DS pointed out. 'When it comes to finding her, it looks as if we're in the hands of the Spanish. Once they do, though, we've cracked it.'

'Not quite,' Pye pointed out. 'Proving she was in the flat . . . and we haven't done that yet . . . that's one thing; linking her to the murder, that's another. Before she can even become a viable suspect, we need to tie her, evidentially, to the body. If we can do that, we'll be in business.'

'Yes,' Neville agreed; then she smiled. 'It's too bad you'll miss out on the glory.'

'That's not why I'm in the job,' he insisted, 'but what do you mean?'

'If I were you,' she advised him, 'I'd get Mary Chambers' okay to have a press conference today. No, we haven't made an arrest for Bella Watson's murder, but you can tell the media that we've got a strong suspect, and we've broken a drugs ring in the process.'

'Why should I rush it?' Pye asked, intrigued. 'The investigation's been going on for weeks.'

'Maybe so,' Karen said, 'but I think you'll find that a story is going to break very soon that's going to blow it right off the front page.'

Sixty-Two

There was a time in my life when I'd have been as high as a kite walking out of that interview room, a time when I'd have thought that any result was a good result, regardless of the feelings of the innocent caught up in the backwash. After Myra died, I'd spent years making myself impervious to my own pain, and been so successful that the hurt of others had meant nothing to me.

I knew that my intensity could scare people; I'd even been proud of the fact and prepared to use it as a weapon. It's still there, but not to the same extent. Too much has happened to me over the years, and too much has happened to others. I've hurt too many people close to me, most of all, Sarah.

It took my own wounding by Aileen, Sarah's successor in my life, now gone to wreak, her havoc on English politics, to make me understand how much harm I'd caused Sarah. I've made both of us a promise that I'd never do so again.

That's why I told her about Mia Watson, after Alex's phone call, told her all about her, and why I'd hoped she'd stay away for good.

Sarah thought about it for a while, and then she asked, 'If I'd been around at the time, would the outcome have been any different?'

'I'd like to think so,' I replied, honestly, 'but given the man I was back then, I can't be certain.'

She kissed me and said, 'Well, I have faith in the man you are now, and that's enough for me.'

How tragic it was, I thought as I drove, that David Mackenzie had never experienced such self-discovery. He had died, as I knew for sure by then, as he had lived, self-centred, uncaring and ultimately self-destructive. It was an even greater tragedy that he had destroyed three other people alongside himself.

Cheryl was bound for a life sentence. Their children, Alice and Zach, faced one that would be even longer, as they would discover. They would carry their parents' story with them for life, and they might even be condemned to an institutional upbringing, unless the uncle that I knew they had was big-hearted enough to take them on . . . always assuming he wasn't a clone of the one who had blighted David's life.

Yes, I was more than a little depressed as I drove west. I hadn't gone in there with Wilding intending to unmask a murderess, although the information that Father Donnelly had finally got round to giving me had made that a highly possible scenario.

No, I'd gone in there hoping against hope that Cheryl would tell me that her volatile husband had pissed off to cool down in Benidorm and work off the jealousy that he harboured towards everyone he encountered in his professional life.

My optimism had faded when she said that she had withdrawn all that cash, not David. She hadn't been trying to throw him off her scent; she'd been trying to fool us.

Even then, though, it wasn't until I told her that I knew about her confession to Tom Donnelly, the secrets that he could not, rather than would not divulge, and I saw the look on her face, that the last doubt left me.

The Allans' cottage wasn't actually in Lanark, but in the surrounding countryside, near to Hyndford Bridge which crosses the River Clyde, near the old Winston Barracks, a place I'd heard my father mention. There was a car parked just along the road when I arrived, but I ignored it. Instead I turned into the short drive that led into Max's place.

The old ex-ACC wasn't surprised to see me when he answered the summons of the big brass knocker. 'Come in, Bob,' he said. 'Julie told me you'd been to see her.'

He led me through the house and out into the back garden. Actually 'garden' was an understatement; it was more of a paddock, and there was an old building at the far end that might have been a stable.

'Sit yourself down,' he insisted, pointing to a green metal table, with a couple of folding seats. 'Would you like a beer?'

At that moment I would have loved a beer, but something stopped me from accepting; it wouldn't have tasted right. 'No thanks, Max,' I replied. 'The tap water's nice in this part of the world, though.'

He disappeared back indoors, returning with a jug and two tumblers, all blue plastic. 'This'll be about Mackenzie,' he murmured, as he poured.

'Yes, Max,' I told him. 'And don't tell me you weren't expecting me, even before your wife called you. I'm too good for that.'

'I never made any secret of the fact that David was married to my niece,' he said, anticipating my first accusation and denying it, all in one breath.

'Come on, Max,' I sighed, probably sounding as sad as I felt. 'That's exactly what you did. You never declared it, and you should have. I've asked around and I can't find a single officer who knows about the relationship. In my book that's secrecy. You could have volunteered it when Dan Provan came to see you in your local, but you held it back, even then.'

'I didn't think it was relevant,' he said.

'Aw, man,' I protested, 'please don't insult me, or yourself for that matter. A police officer, a former colleague, and his wife had disappeared. There were clear signs that he might have harmed her, possibly even killed her. Everything you knew was bloody relevant.'

'But how was I supposed to know all that had happened?' he countered. 'Wee Dan was very circumspect when we had our chat.'

'Not that bloody circumspect. I know that he told you Mackenzie was missing, yet you virtually denied knowledge of the man.

'Let me ask you something, Max. Your wife, and her sister-in-law, the two Julies, do they not get on? Do they never speak to each other? Sorry, chum, I believe that you knew from early on that Cheryl was missing too and that the worst was feared. When you heard you panicked.'

'Why would I do that? Are you going to tell me that?'

'Sure,' I retorted, 'and before you ask, yes, I can prove it. You were scared because you intercepted David's application to join the police, with its accompanying document and the full disclosure that would have ruled him out, almost certainly in those days, as a candidate. In doing so you saddled the force with a guy who was emotionally unstable, and borderline psycho. That's criminal, and I'm duty bound to report it to the fiscal.'

My old friend threw back his head and gave a short laugh. 'Aye, fine,' he exclaimed. 'You do that. You'll look like a clown at the trial, though.' He peered at me, over the top of his reading glasses. 'When you took him off my hands, Bob, one of his line managers was insisting that I refer him for psychological assessment. I had no grounds for refusing that, but you turned up and took the problem away. So yes, go ahead, report me to the Crown Office and see if you like the way you come out of it.'

I sensed relief in him, as if he'd just dodged a bullet. So I fired again.

'I wouldn't hesitate, Max, but I'm not really here about that. I'm here about Cheryl. We know, chum. She's been charged.'

It happened in an instant. The light left his eyes, the colour left his face and his cheeks seemed to collapse as he turned into a very old man, far older than his years.

'I'm sorry,' I told him, sincerely. 'There's no triumph in this.'

'I love that lass,' he whispered. 'All the more since our wee Rosina was taken so young. I warned her about David right at the very start. If you've found out about his past, you'll know I was involved right at the very start.' He looked at me again. 'You do know all of it, I take it?'

I nodded.

He frowned, deeply. 'David had taken some terrible beatings from that uncle of his,' he continued, 'but he never showed a scrap of remorse for what he did to him in revenge. It's easy to assume that his nature was beaten into him but maybe it was there all along.

'I told Cheryl to be careful when she took up with him, but she had her heart set on him. So I did what I could. I pushed Tom Donnelly towards him, you know. I thought his influence would make him better, and it did, or I thought it did.'

'Why did you tell Provan about Father Tom?'

'Because at the time I thought that David would go there. When Julie told me, I thought what you all did, that he'd finally snapped and done something terrible to the lass. In sending Dan to Tom, I thought I was sending him after David. It never occurred to me that it would be Cheryl who'd turn up on his doorstep. It never occurred to me then either that our relationship need come out, or that it would be seen as relevant if it did.'

He looked me in the eye. 'You're right of course, I did change his application form. Cheryl made me promise to help him get into the force, and that was the only way I could be sure of it.'

'She told us he knocked her about,' I said.

'Aye, she told me that too, but only lately. The abused became the abuser, and not just physically; there was mental cruelty there too. It's not that he didn't love her; he did, no question, but as you said, he was borderline psycho, Bob, and sometimes he strayed over on to the other side.' Max buried his face in his hands and rubbed it, vigorously, almost violently.

'If only she'd told me about that sooner,' he moaned, 'but she didn't because she knew I'd have finished him in the police, and without the police, he'd have had no restraint, none at all. She put up with it, until she snapped herself. She did to him what he did to that uncle years ago, only she was better at it.'

'How?' I asked, as horrific visions flashed through my mind.

He must have read them in my eyes, for he exclaimed, 'No, no! Nothing as cruel as that. You know she's a pharmacist?' I nodded. 'She had some stuff in the house that she probably shouldn't have, diazepam, sedatives that she gave him when he got really disturbed, that time he had his serious breakdown. She ground enough into a bottle of beer to knock him out and then she suffocated him with a plastic bag.'

He removed his specs to wipe away tears. 'I think she sees it as something of a mercy killing,' he said. 'She told me he was raving about your man McGuire, and about Andy Martin; he said that given half a chance he'd kill them both. She believed he meant it, so in the end she killed him to save him from himself.'

I gazed at him, directly. 'Where is he, Max?'

He stamped his foot on the ground. I looked down and saw that some of the paving on which we sat was new, or had been replaced. The concrete grouting between the slabs was much less weathered than the rest.

'I'm sorry, Bob,' Max sighed. 'I know. After forty years as a police officer, I shouldn't have had a second thought. I should have called you as soon as she turned up here on Thursday evening. She phoned me, you see, and told me she needed my help. She needed my help,' he repeated. 'I love the lassie like a daughter. What was I going to do?'

I couldn't answer him. A long time ago, I disregarded my own duty, even if it wasn't on such a serious scale.

'What next?' he asked.

'Lottie and Dan are outside,' I replied, quietly. 'They'll take you into custody, then we'll get the excavators in. Your house is now a crime scene.'

'Tell them to put it back the way they found it, Bob, please. My Julie loves this garden.'

His Julie. Another life shattered.

I couldn't look at him as I phoned Lottie Mann, telling her to join us.

I couldn't bring myself to hang around either. I didn't want to see him being put into the back of a police car with the ridiculous over-precaution of an officer's hand on his head. I didn't want to see the paper suits crawling over the place looking for samples of the bleach Max said he'd used to scrub out the luggage compartment of the Honda that his niece had used as a hearse.

He'd asked me if I thought she might be able to plead to a reduced charge. I mumbled my way round that one, but it must have been as clear to him as it was to me that her flight, and the things she'd done in the aftermath to conceal her crime, had to mean, inevitably, that she'd be done for nothing less than murder.

I wanted out of there and so I got out of there, heading back to Sarah and my lovely, normal, well-adjusted family unit, that I'd determined was going to be the centre of my life from that moment on.

But I didn't get halfway home before I had another call from Alex that kicked the ball right up on the slates once again.

Sixty-Three

It made Alexis Skinner very sad that she had no memory of her mother, only a vision in her mind put together on the basis of photographs, stories her father had told her, and the shockingly self-revealing diaries that had been discovered after her early death in a car accident that she would probably have survived in a modern vehicle.

Alex was under no illusion that Myra Graham Skinner had been an angel, but her dad had loved her. More than that, he had liked her; he had told her when she was old enough for mature discussion that when she had died, it was as if he had lost three people, his wife, his lover and his best friend.

It was only as an adult that she had come to appreciate what a sad and lonely man her father had been through her childhood. He hadn't been monastic, not at all; there had been women, for sure, and even a semi-domestic relationship with another detective called Alison that had lasted for a couple of years, until it dwindled to nothing.

The Mia Sparkles thing . . . she always thought of her by her radio name . . . had been very short-lived . . . if it had ever lived at all, for maybe she'd been wrong about a strange phone conversation she'd had with her father after he'd been away overnight . . . but it had made an impression on her.

He had met Mia in the course of an investigation, and somehow, after he'd told her she had a big fan in Gullane, he had wound up bringing her home. While Alex had been impressed as any thirteen-year-old would have been by a star figure twice her age, and had taken to her, she had known instinctively that she was not stepmother material, and so she had not been heartbroken when she had gone, as surprisingly as she had arrived.

She thought of the years between her mother's death and the arrival of Sarah as her father's Dark Ages. She believed firmly that they should stay unlit, and so, when Andy had brought up Mia's name, she had been unusually uncommunicative.

She and he had been a couple on, off and then on again for a decade, and they had a 'no secrets' policy. However, if Mia was a secret, she was her father's, not hers, and not one to be shared with anyone. He hadn't pressed her on it; indeed, he hadn't discussed it further, and that was good.

As she watched Andy's daughter running through the first few fallen leaves of autumn in the Royal Botanic Gardens, with her younger brother staggering after her, she wondered what her mother would have thought about her lack of desire for children of her own.

She and Andy had broken off their engagement over his discovery that she had terminated a pregnancy without his knowledge. She had done so because she had believed that having a child at that point would have disrupted the formative years of her legal career.

She stood by her decision; it had worked out for her. She had become a partner in her firm, Curle Anthony and Jarvis, in almost record time, and was one of its key earners. She had reached a position where if she chose, she could take a couple of years out to start a family, then step back in exactly where she had been before.

But she felt no urge to make that move, and with no pressure from Andy, she was beginning to doubt that she ever would. They might marry, they might not. Either way they would be happy . . . just like her father and Sarah, who seemed more content and confident the second time around than they had ever been before.

She was smiling at the thought, as she ran to retrieve a ball that Danielle had kicked down a sloping path, smiling as her mobile rang.

She reached the ball, stood on it to stop its progress, and checked the phone. She saw her own number on screen; her position in her firm meant weekend calls and because of that she put her landline on divert every time she went out.

'This is Alex,' she said, cheerily.

'I think I would have known that,' a woman replied. 'You had a mature voice for a thirteen-year-old. This is Mia, Mia Watson, Mia Sparkles, if you remember that name.'

'Yes,' she whispered. 'Yes I do. What do you want?'

'I need to speak to your father. I'm sorry to be calling you, but his number is ex-directory and probably monitored, so this is the only way I could think of to contact him.'

'What do you want me to do?' she snapped. 'I won't forward this call, if that's what you're thinking. It'll be his choice whether he speaks to you or not.'

'Understood.' Alex was struck by the change in her voice. There was none of the old vivacity; instead there was a coolness, and an underlying tension. 'I'd like you to ask him to call this number. It's a Spanish mobile.' She recited nine digits, then repeated them. 'Have you got that?'

'Yes; I've noted it. Okay, I'll do it, but I warn you, he may not want to know you. It's been a long time, and his life's a lot different now.'

'So's mine,' the woman said, 'believe me. Tell him it's very much in his interests to call me . . . to call me, and nobody else, that is. It has to be between us, and us alone.'

The line went dead. She found herself staring at the phone.

'Who was that?' Andy asked, approaching, with Robert riding on his shoulders. 'The ghost of Christmas yet to come, by the look on your face.'

'Business,' she answered, sharply. She kicked Danielle's ball back towards him. 'I'll catch you up,' she said. 'I have to make a call.'

Sixty-Four

'I can't get my head round this,' Sammy Pye said.

'I have trouble myself,' Karen Neville admitted, 'but it's true nonetheless. I called Jack McGurk and asked him if he knew about it. He didn't but he rang me back half an hour later, after he'd spoken to DI Stallings . . . I don't know her, she came in after I'd gone to Perth with Andy, but I'm told she's Ray Wilding's other half . . . and managed to get something out of her, on a colleague-to-colleague basis.'

'These are heavy grapes, even for the force vine.'

'Tasty metaphor, Sam,' she acknowledged. 'It seems that Ray's been coordinating a national search for the Mackenzies since Monday, after they both disappeared. The fear was that he'd done her in, not the other way around, but from what Ray said, she turned up safe and sound this morning, claiming no knowledge of where her husband was.

'He was called in by the chief to talk to her, but not at home, in his nick. Even then, no alarm bells were ringing with him. But when he got to Gayfield, Bob Skinner turned up and more or less took over the interview. Next thing Ray knew, he was being told to arrest her on suspicion of murder, and turn the thing over to Mary Chambers and the ACC.'

'But only suspicion of murder?'

'At that point yes, but Stallings . . . what's her first name?'

'Rebecca . . . Becky.'

'Right. She told Jack that Ray had just been sent by Maggie Steele to an address in Lanarkshire, where a second, related, arrest had been made by Strathclyde.'

'Does Becky know who it is?'

'No, Ray wasn't told. But he did say that the chief sounded very tense indeed.'

'Jeez,' the DI whistled. 'You were right. This is going to be top of the news cycle when it breaks; we'll get blown out of sight.'

'Don't get too down about it. If the Spanish can't trace this Mia woman, that might be a good thing.'

'Yes, but even if they do, Karen, it's her mother's death that we're investigating. I know, if what Alafair told you is true, there's no love lost between them, but even so, her mother . . .'

'Is that so different from Cheryl Mackenzie murdering her husband?' She frowned. 'We've been friends for a long time, so I can say this to you. I'd say it to Andy as well, for it's true of him too . . . of all of you really. You guys, in your heart of hearts, you want to be Bob Skinner, but he is what he is because there's no evil beyond his comprehension, nothing so dark that he can't see its detail.'

'I don't know if I fancy that,' he admitted. 'Maybe I'll settle for being Sammy Pye.'

'That would be a good choice,' she told him. 'When you go to the other place, there's no way back.'

'Hey,' Sammy exclaimed, 'that has the sound of personal experience about it.'

'Probably, but I don't want to talk about it. All I'm saying is that when it comes to homicide, nothing's off limits.'

'Okay but there's this too. Everything has to be proved in court, however obvious it may be to the likes of us.'

'That's true,' she agreed, 'and it's what I really meant about Mia not being traced being a good thing. We can put her van in Caledonian Crescent at the time of Bella's death, but we can't put her in it. Who knows, we might find her DNA in the flat, eventually, but as we've just discovered with Hastie McGrew, and as you said yourself a few minutes ago, that won't prove anything, other than that she went to see her mother.'

Pye yawned. 'And with that discouraging word,' he pushed himself to his feet, 'I'm out of here.'

The DS checked her watch. 'Me too, in half an hour,' she said, 'but I might just go and investigate a break-in in Costa Coffee that I thought had been reported.'

'Got big plans for tonight?'

She shot him a raised eyebrow glance. 'Big plans and I don't go together. I've forsworn them, for ever.'

'Oh dear,' he chuckled, 'sorry I asked.'

'Not your fault. Just when I thought it was time to go back in the water, I found it was too salty for my taste.'

'I won't even try to understand that. There are always dating sites you could try.'

'Online poker, maybe. Online dating, never.'

Pye turned towards the door of his office, to find that it was open and that Jackie Wright was standing there.

'I've just had a call from the Fife police,' she began. 'Remember we put out an appeal for any sightings of a wooden blanket chest along the coast? There was one found a few days ago, washed up on the beach at Kinghorn.

'It's in the local nick; they weren't sure what to do with it.

They were going to give it to a local antique dealer. They said if we want it, it's ours, but we'll have to collect it.'

The DI looked at the DS, and smiled. 'That could be your evening taken care of,' he said.

Sixty-Five

Trepidation is one of those words that has never really figured in my vocabulary, nor even in my adult life.

If I'm honest, it was a big part of my childhood, although I couldn't have put that name to it at the time. It was what I felt whenever my bedroom door opened at home. If my mother came into the room, or less frequently, my dad, that was all right. If it was my brother, Michael, that agitation turned into fear, or even terror, depending simply on the expression on his face.

It has occurred to me on occasion that maybe I should have sought him out while I had the chance, not to give him some more of his own back, but to thank him. Reason being, having survived him, I've never really been afraid of anything else that might happen to me.

More than that, he left me with an acceptance of some of the things I've encountered as a police officer that few other cops have. The notion, 'surely he couldn't have done that to another human being', has never held me back. Thanks, brother.

Yet I might have gone the other way. It was clear to me that David Mackenzie hadn't survived his abuse. I understood the boy who had thrown that superhot oil over his uncle. Part of me even admired him. He did something about his awful treatment; I didn't.

My revenge could have been a lot simpler than his. I could have told my father, but I was too scared by Michael's promise of the consequences, specifically, the amputation of my thumbs with garden shears, ever to do that. Instead I bore it and waited for my growth, turning myself gradually into someone far more formidable than he had ever been, making myself the one to be feared.

I went on to become, I reckon, a properly functioning adult. I learned how to love, rather than despise. I don't believe that David Mackenzie ever did the same. He's been accused by many of being in love with himself, but when I talked to Lennie about him, afterwards, he was convinced that the opposite was true, and that ultimately the man had been consumed by self-loathing.

But I wasn't thinking of David as I dialled Mia's number, from a lay-by on the outskirts of Edinburgh. As those bedroom door butterflies returned to my stomach, I was thinking of Michael.

'Hello, Bob,' she said, before I had a chance to utter a word.

'Hello, Mia,' I replied. 'How did you know it was me?'

'Nobody else has this number. It's a throwaway, bought with cash and a false identity.'

I surprised myself by laughing. 'How many have you got, for fuck's sake?'

'Three. I still have the paper version of my Mia Watson UK driving licence, and a Tunisian passport in another name, the one I showed when I bought the phone. The Spanish need an ID for all phones these days. Officially, though, I'm known as Maria Centelleos. But I suspect you know that by now.'

'No, I didn't,' I told her truthfully. 'I haven't been part of the investigation into your mother's murder. I know none of the details, none at all, but I knew your name had come up. You should contact the police in Edinburgh, not me. I'm not part of that force now.'

'I know you're not,' she told me. 'I know most of what there is to know about you, Bob. You have a very high profile on the internet; key in "Robert Morgan Skinner" and all sorts of stuff comes out.

'For a start, your wives, including the most recent one dropping her knickers for that actor Joey Morroco. Then there's Alex's progress . . . I thought that kid would go far; she could play you like a Stradivarius. Stories about your big cases, your rise to the top, to the very top.' She paused, for breath I thought, but no, for effect. 'Which I could have halted with one phone call, at any time.'

Trepidation? Yes, it was back well and truly, but I cuffed it round the ear and sent it scurrying.

'You reckon? How would that work out?' I asked.

'It would work out because the only thing that you can't Google is you and me, and what happened between us when you were investigating my brother's killing.'

'One night, lady, that was all. One night of admittedly pretty good sex, and then you brushed me off in the morning.'

'I didn't brush you off,' she claimed indignantly. 'You went psycho on me when you woke up.'

'I had a bad dream, Mia,' I protested, suddenly aware that we were having an argument that had been postponed from one century into the next. 'I'd been at a crime scene in Newcastle the night before,' I went on, agitated by the memory. 'Christ, I'd seen a guy with his tripes out on his own kitchen table! Of course I was fucking jumpy!'

'It wasn't just that,' she said. 'All your dreams weren't bad. You kept calling me "Alison" when you were talking in your sleep.'

If I'd been standing, that might have cut the feet from under me, but she wasn't to know that.

'Are you sure it wasn't "Myra"?' I snapped. 'Or maybe "Madonna". I fancied her at one point. Either way, this is not "career ending with one phone call" kind of stuff.'

'Maybe not, but tipping me off that I'd become a suspect in my brother's murder and warning me to get out of town, that might cut some ice.' She had a point there, I must concede . . . but it wasn't conclusive.

'The way I read the press,' she continued, 'that First Minister guy doesn't like you much.'

'Then read again. Clive Graham and I get on okay.'

'If you do, it's out of necessity on his part. This new single force he's setting up: with you in the top job you'd be as powerful as him. No politician wants that. Yes, he'd be very interested in what I have to say.'

'Then go ahead,' I challenged.

'No, because there's more than that, something that you could not possibly survive professionally. You help me and it will stay a secret. I'll tell you what it is, but it has to be face to face.'

Her intensity got to me. What the hell, there would be no harm done, and maybe even a little good.

'Suppose I agree to meet you. Where? Starbuck's in George Street. The Sheraton Hotel lobby, where we met once? Your old place in Davidson's Mains, so we can go over old times?'

'Nowhere as convenient for you, but not completely inconvenient. Your favourite family restaurant, you called it, so you'll know the place I mean. I'll meet you there.'

'When?'

'Tomorrow. Eight thirty, dinner. You're paying; I got the lunch in the Sheraton, remember.'

'You're kidding me,' I gasped. 'It's in another country.'

'I'm not kidding in the slightest. I've checked, and you can do it. Hell, you're Bob Skinner, you can do anything.' She gave a small laugh and then her voice seemed to be younger, that of the Mia I'd known. 'Apart from remembering the name of the woman you're sleeping with, that is.'

Sixty-Six

Maggie Steele believed that she would not have survived as a person, far less a chief police officer, without her daughter. She had been in the middle of her pregnancy when she had been hit by two piledrivers, the sudden and unexpected death of her husband Stevie, and her own cancer diagnosis.

At one point she had been given a likely choice between her own life and that of her child, but she had delayed the surgery until Stephanie Rose Steele had been safely delivered, and they had both pulled through, mother and daughter together.

It had been a fecund couple of years in her force, she had observed one evening to her sister, who lived with her and did much of the daytime child caring. 'First Stevie and me, then Mario and Paula; now Ray Wilding's gone and got Becky Stallings up the duff.'

Bet had reacted with a smile 'That's nice, though, isn't it? That you all have something at home to take your mind off your jobs, especially the detectives.'

'That's easy for you to say, sis, but you don't have to manage a team around maternity and paternity leave. Bloody nightmare!'

'You set the example,' Bet had pointed out.

'Maybe, but I never thought then that I'd wind up as chief.

Mind you, there were lots of things I never thought.'

Stephanie was playing happily at her feet as she faced Mario McGuire across her round kitchen table, the one that Stevie had built in when he had moved into the place, before they had been as much as a lustful gleam in each other's eye. Her mug of green tea was warm within the circle of her hands. She had asked Mario to phone her after the interview of Cheryl Mackenzie was over, but he had called on her in person.

'Were there any glitches at all?' she asked.

'No. She gave us it all without any pressure. They had a fight, over the way he'd reacted to an argument he and I had, and he hit her. He went crazy, she said. She thought he was insane, and maybe he was.

'However, she may not be too attached to reality herself, because she's decided it was a mercy killing. She talked us all the way through it, repeating for the tape all of the stuff that Bob uncovered in the first interview.'

'Her lawyer was happy?'

'As happy as you can be when your client's confessing to murder, but yes; he didn't raise any objections.'

'I'm glad about that, for I was worried,' Maggie confessed. 'I thought Bob might have gone too far with her earlier.'

'Me too,' Mario murmured, 'and that's interesting. In all the years we worked under Bob, you and I never questioned the way he did things, never doubted his judgement. Yet now, even though he's barely out the door, here we are second-guessing him.'

'Welcome to command rank,' she told him. 'We are him, now. Back then he was responsible for everybody else's mistakes, along with his own. Now we're in that position, carrying the can for everything that's done in our territory, by everyone . . . including him when he goes on one of his solo missions.'

McGuire laughed. 'He'll never stop doing that; doesn't matter which office he's in. That reminds me, is everything done and dusted on his patch?'

'Yes, they've begun recovering Mackenzie's body, and Max Allan's been taken into custody. He's being held in Pitt Street over the weekend, for court on Monday.'

'Will they be tried jointly or separately, him and Cheryl? What do you think?'

'That,' Maggie said, 'is the Lord Advocate's problem, not mine or Bob's. I'd guess they'll be in court together, but the way things are just now, a trial looks unlikely. Max has a separate charge to answer, though, if the fiscal in Glasgow decides to go ahead with it.'

'Poor old bastard. He'll spend the first part of his retirement under lock and key.'

'Maybe not,' she suggested. 'He wasn't a party to the killing, only the concealment, and from what Bob said, Cheryl was like a daughter to him. With a good advocate, and a sympathetic judge, maybe one of the ladies on the Bench, he could get a suspended sentence.'

'Yes, sure.' Mario's voice was smeared with sarcasm. 'And maybe I'll apply for the top job in Police Scotland and you'll all be working for me in a few weeks. There's no chance of any of that happening. He was a cop, Mags. I can't think of a single judge who'd brave the media storm that not jailing him would cause.'

She was about to concede his point when she noticed Stephanie's face going red, and rushed to pick her up. 'Steph,' she cried out, 'you're supposed to tell me when you need to poo. Get used to this, Mario, it's coming your way.'

'News for you, it's here already.'

As he spoke, the door chime sounded. 'Get that, please,' Maggie asked. 'I've no idea who it might be.'

'Sure.' He went down the few steps from the hall, wondering what casual caller would choose an early Saturday evening, and threw the door open.

A red-haired man stood on the threshold, confusion stamped on his face.

'Arthur?' McGuire exclaimed.

'Mario?' Dorward countered.

'I'm here on business,' the ACC said quickly, 'before you get any ideas.'

'Me too, before you do. But it's maybe as well you are.'

'You'd better come in, then. Maggie's attending to some paperwork, you might say.'

He led the way up and across to the sitting room. 'It's Arthur Dorward,' he called, 'and I don't think he's come to sell you tickets for the Forensic Service dance.'

'Minute,' a voice replied from the nursery.

One stretched into two before Maggie appeared, carrying her refreshed child on her hip. 'Mr Dorward,' she said, 'to what do we owe?' Then she looked at his expression and her smile vanished.

'Something's come up in our analysis of the samples from one forty-two Caledonian Crescent,' he began. 'You'll recall we found a trace of grandfamilial DNA, and established that it wasn't from the lad you thought it was. Well, to try to identify it more clearly, we followed standard practice and ran it through the entire male database looking for a match.'

He stopped, and took a brown manila envelope from under his arm. 'Most things I do over the phone. Some I send by email. But this one, this has to be done in person; it's for your eyes only, and it's bloody dynamite.'

Sixty-Seven

Mia was right; I could get there and I did. I went online as soon as I got home, and found a flight that evening from Edinburgh to Barcelona. I booked it with about half an hour to spare, and also a room for the night in the gastronomic hotel in Placa Reial that Sarah and I had enjoyed on our homeward journey.

Naturally I told her, about Mia's phone call and her strange insistence. When I was finished, she looked up at me and said, 'This woman meant something to you, Bob, didn't she?'

'I can't deny that,' I replied, 'but it wasn't for long. Sure, I had the hots for her, but I was glad when she left.'

'No secret longings afterwards?'

'None at all. Then or now. I wanted her gone, and I hoped she'd stay gone.'

'Was she right about Clive Graham?' she asked. 'Would he like you out of the picture?'

'Probably,' I told her. I'd been asking myself the same question. 'But that won't be his decision. He set this Police Scotland thing up, against the wishes of most objective senior cops. Now he has to live with the consequences; if he doesn't like them, fuck him.'

'What do you think this secret of Mia's is?'

'I have no idea. Maybe she bought a lottery ticket in my name and it came up.'

She frowned. 'Bob, don't be flip. I'm worried about this.'

'Then come with me,' I offered, even though I was standing in the hall with my travel bag in my hand, ready to leave. 'I'll book another seat.'

'I can't,' she said. 'I've got three autopsies booked for Monday. Sweetheart, what if this is a set-up?'

'If I thought that for a millisecond, would I have asked you to come with me just now? Mia wants to meet on my turf. If she had bad intentions, she wouldn't be doing that.'

'If anyone calls and asks where you are, what do I say?'

'Nothing. Whoever it is, tell them I'm going away for a couple of days, and can't be contacted. I'll do my best to get back on Monday.'

I kissed her, said goodbye to the kids and hit the road. I was on my way to Spain, but my preparations weren't complete. One phone call from the car took care of the rest. It was to Sammy Pye; I asked him to have an overview of the Bella Watson murder investigation emailed to me the following morning.

I knew he was surprised by my request, and wondering whether he should comply. 'I may be able to contribute something, Sammy,' I told him, 'so I'd like to see what's been happening. But I may be wrong, so I'd rather this stayed confidential between us for now. There'll be no flak over it, I promise.'

He agreed. Pye and I go back to his earliest days in the force. He was efficient even then, and so conscientious that he once tried to deny me entry to a crime scene.

I had no bags to check in when I arrived at the airport, and so I went straight to the gate. I was on the steps up to the airport and on the point of switching my phone to flight mode when it sounded, in my hand. I looked at the screen and saw that Maggie Steele was calling me from her home number.

An update on Cheryl Mackenzie, I guessed; frankly, I'd had enough of that saga, and the queue in front of me started to move just at that moment, so I rejected the call and went offline.

I have a confession to make here. I don't like eating alone in a restaurant nor do I like spending a night alone in a hotel. I had to do both in Barcelona, and when I awoke in the middle of the night, I felt unhappy and anxious.

I had gone charging off in answer to Mia's summons, lured by her secret, without having the faintest idea of what it was. What if Sarah's fear was right after all? What if it was a set-up? The woman was a combination of Watson and Holmes, after all, and maybe that added up to a Moriarty.

What we call 'the small hours' in English, the Spanish call '*madrugada*'. I spent most of that time thinking about Mia, questioning my decision and my judgement and wondering whether she'd go through with her threat if I didn't show up.

After all, I owed her nothing, I didn't give a damn about her dead mother and I no longer gave a damn about her. Our relationship had lasted all of one night and ended in acrimony, so what the hell was I doing there, I asked myself in the Barcelona darkness?

And yet I knew I had to go. I had to find out what it was that I 'could not possibly survive'. If it was real, I couldn't let it do me in unknowingly.

I went back to sleep eventually, and I woke late. My body clock was set to UK time, and it's pretty reliable. I showered, then went out for breakfast in a café on the Ramblas. My taxi driver from the airport had described it as a street '*muy peligroso*', very dangerous. That's an exaggeration, but it's always been a mecca for pickpockets and the Spanish economic crisis has made it worse.

I wasn't bothered though; in fact part of me was hoping that somebody would try to dip my wallet, for my *madrugada* edginess had given way to annoyance, and I was feeling pretty dangerous myself. What the hell right did Mia think she had to summon me with a cack-handed blackmail threat?

I fuelled myself with a chorizo sandwich, and an espresso . . . I was sure that Sarah would have allowed me one in the circumstances, although she's been keeping a close eye on my intake . . . then walked back to the hotel. As soon as I reached my room, I retrieved my iPad from the safe and checked my email inbox.

The report was there, waiting for me. I read it slowly and carefully, taking in every step and every detail of the investigation, and when I was finished I knew why Mia wanted to see me . . . or I thought I did.

I caught a train from Passeig de Gracia, one of the slow ones that stops at Camallera, not far from my Spanish town. There was a taxi parked outside the bar across the street from the station. I found its driver inside, and once I'd satisfied myself that he'd been on coffee rather than brandy, I had him drive me home.

I had almost five hours before my meeting with Mia. I spent one of them swimming, thinking unrelated thoughts, and wondering in their midst how Cheryl Mackenzie and the uncle who had ruined himself for her had handled their first night in custody.

I'd begun to doubt whether Max would survive any term of imprisonment and so I'd decided to do what I could to try and keep him out. It wouldn't be easy, but the least I could do was talk to the Lord Advocate, a golf buddy of mine. If that didn't work, there was always the possibility of a word with Archie Nelson or Phil Davidson, two of the most influential judges on the Scottish Bench.

When I came out of the pool and back into the real world, I checked my emails once again. There was only one, another missive from Pye, updating the stuff he'd sent me earlier. I'd been wondering how I was going to play my meeting with Mia, and specifically, what I was going to do when it was over. Sammy's message more or less made my mind up for me.

I dressed for the evening, in slacks and a light cotton jacket, then made a couple of phone calls on my landline. (The mobile had stayed switched off all day; I didn't want any interruptions.) The second of them was to Sarah.

'How are you?' she asked me anxiously.

'I'm missing you like hell,' I told her, truly, 'but otherwise I'm okay. The sooner this is over and done with the better.'

'Maggie Steele called last night. She said she needs to see you, about something very important. I said she'd have to wait for a couple of days. She wouldn't tell me what it was about, but she sounded really uptight about it.'

'Uptight or not, she's still going to have to wait. I may call her once this business is done, or I may leave it until tomorrow. I just want this woman out of my hair. I can't look at anything else until she's dealt with.'

'You'll call me when she is, yes?'

'Promise.'

I wanted to walk to my dinner date. Normally it would take me half an hour, but I had a call to make on the way, so I left early. Summer was over, but the evenings usually stay warm until well into October.

How had I known for sure that Mia had meant us to meet in La Clota? She had more or less quoted directly from an interview I gave to the *Herald* newspaper in Glasgow, after I'd been confirmed in the Strathclyde job. That's how closely she'd been tracking me. I had a vague and slightly ridiculous feeling of being stalked, but I laughed it off.

I paid that call en route, spoke to the people I'd arranged to see, then went on my way. I've never been any good at strolling, and so I arrived at the port area five minutes early. I didn't want to be there first so I killed that time by taking a detour along the marina, admiring some of the larger boats that were moored there. The majority flew Catalan flags and pennants, but there were several other nations on show, French, German, Italian, British, and one single Scottish saltire.

I walked up to it for a closer look . . . and my stomach flipped. It was big by comparison with most around it, at least forty feet long, but it was the name that reached out and seized me.

Palacio de Ginebra. A Scottish boat with a Spanish comedy name, *The Gin Palace.* It was no joke of a yacht, however, but a serious open-water vessel, that needed proper crewing.

I knew that because unless there were two of them, and there weren't, for the closer I looked the more familiar it became, I had been its deckhand myself for one glorious weekend. By one of those bizarre coincidences that make life completely unpredictable, Sarah had mentioned it not long before, and there I was looking at the very same vessel.

It was mothballed, its binnacle and hatches covered, so there was no clue to its current ownership, but when I sailed it . . . I know I should say 'her' . . . it had belonged to Alison Higgins' brother, Eden, a Scottish furniture magnate.

She and I and Alex had been invited for a weekend on the

Firth of Clyde with Eden and his son Rory. It was a catharsis for me, that trip. Doing things that were completely new, being part of an entirely different kind of team, had made me think in an entirely different way. By the time we got back to Inverkip after our round trip to Campbeltown, I had decided that I was going to jack in the police, buy a yacht as big as Eden's and sail it myself, for fun and commercially.

That notion lasted for a few minutes, until my next phone call, one that dragged me back into the live case I had then, at the heart of which was . . . Mia Watson. By the time that was over, the spell was broken.

I encountered Eden on a couple of occasions after that, the last being at Alison's funeral. We haven't kept in touch subsequently, for Ali and I had been ancient history by then, but he'd loved that boat, so I couldn't imagine him having sold it. On the other hand, he'd loved his sister too. Had there been too much of her left in it?

I resolved to find out. It's an intention that I still have, but that night I had other matters in hand.

I slipped into the restaurant through the back door in the decked, marquee-like outdoor section, rather than entering from the seafront as most people do. My thinking was that I'd rather see Mia before she saw me.

I looked around the place; half the tables were occupied, some by familiar faces in twos and fours, and as many unfamiliar. But there were no unaccompanied people, and definitely no Mia . . . unless she'd aged very badly since last I'd seen her, and acquired a fat Gauloise-smoking husband with a ludicrous Errol Flynn moustache.

'Bob!' John, the owner, called to me from the doorway to the main restaurant. 'What you do here?' He's Catalan, but his mother is Scottish, so his English is pretty good; better than my Catalan, that's for sure.

'I'm meeting somebody,' I replied. 'It's business; a lady.'

He nodded. 'Ah, I understand now. The lady's Scottish, yes. She call last night and book a table for three. She spoke Spanish good, but her accent is just like my mum. That's you there.' He pointed to a table with the best sea view in the place, with a 'Reserved' sign. As he'd said, it was set for three.

'What do you want to drink?'

'Vichy Catalan.'

He chuckled. 'Fizzy water? You? This must be a serious meeting.'

I chose the middle of the three seats, on the side of the table that looked out across the marina. There had been a little wind, so John had rolled down the canvas wall. Its plastic window obscured the view slightly, but that didn't stop me from spotting a woman. She was sitting on the other side of the road that runs in front of La Clota, on the wall near the water's edge, but she wasn't looking out to sea. No, she was looking around her, and I could read caution in it.

When she was satisfied, she stood up, and started to cross the road. I didn't watch her. Instead I poured some of the water that John had put on the table. I stood as she reached me, extending my hand, to ward off any attempt to kiss me on the cheek.

'Hello, Mia,' I greeted her.

'Hello, Bob. It's good to see you. Thank you for coming.'

'You didn't give me much choice,' I observed.

She had taken care of herself, no mistake about that. Mia has one of those elfin faces, high cheekbones, pointed chin, big expressive eyes, the sort that never seems to age. She looked pretty much as she had the last time I'd seen her, and if I'd got her out of her simple, cream, square-shouldered dress, I'd have bet that her body would have checked out just as well.

'How have you been?' she asked.

'You should know already,' I replied. 'You seem to know everything about me, right down to this place.'

'Don't be offended,' she pouted. 'I have a special interest in you. I always did, ever since we met.'

'I'm sorry to be brutal,' I retorted, 'but my interest in you ended when you drove out of the Airburst car park all those years ago.'

'Really? Why?'

'You know why. You set your brother Marlon up to be murdered, Mia; my people found a text on his phone from you, sent on the day he died. It invited him to your place, at nine that evening. When he got there, the two hoods from Newcastle that Perry Holmes had hired were waiting for him.' I paused, but only for a second.

'You know what happened next,' I went on. 'They took the poor lad down to the old Infirmary Street Baths. The council had closed them down by then, but the equipment was still there. They threw Marlon off the high board into the empty pool, and they kept on doing it until he was dead. I was there afterwards,' I told her. 'I spared you the details at the time, but let's just say it remains one of my more vivid memories.'

'I owed Perry,' she whispered, then fell silent as John appeared with his order pad.

'You ready to order,' he asked, 'or you want to wait for the third person?'

'No,' Mia said. 'We'll eat. We'll be joined later. I'd like fish.'

'Me too,' I added.

'The sea bass is best today. I do two of them, okay?'

'Okay,' I agreed, 'in the oven, and a nice white wine, an Albarino, maybe.'

She waited until he had gone before taking up her story once again. 'Perry Holmes saved my life,' she said, frown lines appearing around her eyes. 'You have no idea what that brother of his was like, that Alasdair. I was thirteen or fourteen, Bob, not much older than your Alex was when I met her, when my uncle, my very own uncle,' she hissed, 'first forced me to go with him. You spared me the details, you said. I'll do the same for you but only because I can't repeat them, not even to myself.

'I think Al Holmes would probably have killed me in the end, if Perry hadn't found out about it. For all the things they say that he was capable of himself, he was a very moral man when it came to children. He burst in on us one night when Al had me tied to the bed, face down for a bit of variety . . . get the picture? . . . and he beat him like a dog. He threatened to castrate him, and he promised he would, if he ever caught him with a kid again. And then he untied me and took me home with him.'

She paused as a waitress arrived with the wine, opened it and poured.

'Nice,' Mia said, after she'd tasted it. 'I know a bit about wine, you know.'

'So I've heard.'

She didn't react to my remark. 'To be honest,' she continued, 'when Perry took me away I expected more of the same, but I couldn't have been more wrong. He asked me about my family life and I told him about Uncle Gavin and how he'd pretty much sold me. He asked me about my mother and I said she'd known and hadn't cared.'

If I hadn't known her better I'd have thought she was going to cry. 'I don't know why my mother hated me, Bob,' she whispered, 'but she did, always. Years later when I was on the radio she found out about it, and extorted money from me. You must remember that; you put a stop to it.'

Yes, I remembered. Mia told me about it during one of our first meetings, and I had given old Bella a serious talking to, one that Alf Stein would have been proud of.

'As vicious as Al had been,' she said, 'Perry was the absolute opposite. He bought me a lot of new clothes, then he took me through to Hamilton and gave me a room in his wife's place. I know they weren't married but that's what he called her. I went to school with Alafair and I got to know Hastie too, whenever he came back from the forces on leave. I had a decent home, for the first time ever, not one that was full of hate, and violent boys and men. I did well at school and then Perry put me through university. Yes, Bob, I had a new life and my mother never knew where I'd gone.

'So yes, I owed Perry and when he asked me to set up a meeting with my brother, because he wanted to ask him some things about Tony Manson, I did it without a second thought.'

'I never asked you this at the time,' I said, 'maybe because I thought I'd be better off not knowing, but I will now. Did you know about the hoods from Newcastle?'

She shook her head and winced. 'No,' she whispered. 'They arrived just before nine, and told me Perry had sent them to take Marlon to him.'

'Did you know that Manson was porking Alafair at the time?'

'No, she didn't tell me that; she wouldn't, the way things were between him and Perry.'

'How did you feel when you heard what had happened to Marlon?'

She sipped her wine then looked me straight in the eye. 'How do you think? I was gutted, because I'd been deceived. Was I overcome with grief? Honestly, no, because Marlon had chosen that sort of life, in spite of what happened to Gavin and to Ryan, my other brother. He knew what Tony Manson was.

'And this too,' she added. 'My brothers were always the best loaf in the house; mother's pride. They treated me like shit as well; I was their servant too.'

Silence fell between us as the sea bass arrived, and it stayed there, more or less, as we did it justice. Any talk was merely that of a renewed acquaintance, and all of it came from Mia. She asked me about my kids, although I sensed that she had no real interest.

'Do you still have that cottage in Gullane?' she ventured. 'I loved that place the first time I saw it. For a very short while, I imagined what it would be like to live there with you.'

'What?' I said, with more than a little derision. 'Me and Perry Holmes's foster-child? Get real, Mia.'

Yet even as I spoke and saw the flash of hurt in her eyes, I thought of Sauce Haddock and his partner, the granddaughter of a criminal who'd been . . . I hoped my tense was right . . . almost as big a player as Perry.

Then I recalled the young woman who'd hooked me and I thought, *Maybe, just maybe.*

I kicked that notion into touch and focused on the present as we finished our meals.

'Okay,' I said when I was ready, 'you think you've got a hold over me that you can use in some way. Back then, you might have, but this is now. Claim that I tipped you off, and I think you'd find that you'd be asked to prove the allegation. Not just that, Mia,' I added, 'you'd find that nobody cared. The truth is, I didn't tell you to get out of town to save you from being arrested for Marlon's murder. You've just told me you didn't know those guys were going to be there, and I believe you. I'd have believed you back then, just the same.

'You wouldn't have been an accused, you'd have been a witness, but that case was never going to come to trial, 'cos you can't put dead people in the dock, and by that time, Hastie had taken care of the Newcastle end.'

'So why did you warn me?'

'I did it to protect you. Not from Tony Manson, for he'd never have crossed me, but from Bella. She was another animal altogether.'

'You mean she knew that I'd invited Marlon to my place?' she asked, her eyes narrowing.

'Yes.'

'How?'

'I told her.'

'You told her,' she whispered, incredulous. Her expression froze. 'Why, in God's name, did you do that?'

'Because I wanted her to know,' I said. 'I wanted her to see how she'd destroyed her children, I wanted her to see what an evil cow she was. That's why I told you never to come back to Scotland, and to forget that you ever had a mother. You were so much better off without her.'

'Jesus,' Mia gasped. 'You told her. Bob, you don't know what you did.'

'What do you mean?' I asked.

'I'll get there,' she replied, 'but first tell me, how much do you know about her death?'

'I can only tell you what the Edinburgh investigators have pieced together. As you know, it's not my force any longer. But why should I do that? Let me guess. You want to know whether they've found out about you and the methamphetamine supply. Right?'

She nodded and offered a small grin.

'What's so fucking funny?' I asked her.

'Nothing,' she said quickly. 'I'll deny any involvement in that.'

'Sure, because you were smart enough to burn your bodega to the ground before you did a runner from the Spanish drugs cops. Yes, they know about it in Edinburgh. Why, for God's sake, Mia, did you get into that racket? Tell me; it won't go any further.'

'I don't know,' she sighed. 'You know the old saying about taking the boy out of the ghetto? Maybe in my case it runs along the lines of, you can take the girl out of the family, but you can't take the family out of the girl.'

She picked up her glass in both hands and took a sip. 'Let me tell you how it was with me, Bob,' she murmured. 'I struggled for a few years after I moved to Spain, getting by on presenter jobs on English shows on local radio, until my Spanish became good enough to get me into the mainstream stations. It was tough, but over the years I managed to put a little money together.

'Then I did something fairly daft. I bought a sherry bodega in a place called El Cuervo. It's not quite the end of the earth, but probably a stopover on the way there. The guy I bought it from stayed on for a while, to show me the ropes, and we ran profitably for a while. Then, about two years ago, he died, very suddenly, just as the recession was starting to bite. That's when Ignacio came in.'

'Ignacio being?' I asked, although I knew from Pye's file.

'My son.'

'I don't recall him in Edinburgh.'

'No, he was born in Spain, eighteen years ago. He told me that he knew someone who had a brother who could put the place to good use, if we didn't ask any questions. I could see myself being penniless again, so I said yes, and I didn't ask. Sure enough, reasonable money started to roll in, and there was no comeback . . . for a while, that is. Then, about nine months ago, Ignacio came to me again and said that his pal wanted to quit, as the local markets were becoming a bit risky, not so much from the police but from other people, a crew of Mexicans who didn't like what he was doing.'

I recalled a note I'd read on the file, by Karen Neville, after an unofficial chat with Alafair Drysalter. 'So you had the bright idea of creating another route?'

'Yes.'

'And you approached Hastie McGrew, fresh out of the nick?'

'Yes,' she admitted. 'At first he was suspicious; I'd had no contact with either him or Alafair since I left. He doubted me at first; he was worried that the cops might be trying to set him up again, but I was able to tell him some family stuff that convinced him I was who I said I was.

'Hastie said he'd think about my proposition. A week or so later he came back and told me that he'd set something up, although he could not get anywhere near it himself. You understand why?'

I nodded. 'Of course. But he never would have. He must have learned from Perry: never let anything be traced to you, anything that can be proved.'

'Just so,' she agreed. 'It was simple,' she continued. 'I couriered the drugs across to Britain in a van loaded with stuff I was taking back home for the ex-pat Brits that are bailing out of

Spain in the thousands. That was my cover. I always hid the drugs in their items, never in the van, so that if I was caught . . . unlikely as that was on the crossings I used . . . I'd be able to claim innocence.'

Good thinking, Mia, I thought. *You're the smartest Watson of them all . . . not that that would be too hellish difficult.*

'I was met,' she went on, 'wherever I said, by a guy I knew only as Patrick. He took the consignment, and that was that. The money flowed to me by a different route.' She leaned forward, looking at me earnestly. 'That's the truth, Bob.'

'No,' I said, 'not quite. At least it's not quite as the Spanish drugs police see it. They believe that Ignacio synthesised the stuff himself, that there never was any pal. They checked his school records and found that his chemistry results were off the scale.'

'Shit,' she murmured. 'Then I need your help even more.'

'How do you imagine I can help you with all this?' I protested. 'I have no jurisdiction here, and as for Scotland, it's gone too far for that. Remember my young DC, Andy, the blond boy with the green eyes? He's now the head of our Drug Enforcement Agency, and he takes his job very seriously. I can't call him off.'

She stared hard at the tablecloth.

'The guy Patrick,' I went on, 'if you'd been checking up on him in the Edinburgh online papers as well as on me, you'd know that he was busted last week. In the process, he shot his girlfriend dead, instead of the cop he was trying to kill. As you can imagine, he's singing his fucking head off.'

'Oh Jeez,' she sighed. 'It never rains, eh? Bob, I'm not too worried about the Spanish police. They're too busy chasing the Mexicans and the Colombians to bother about little old me. But

your people, they're different. You couldn't tell them the route's
closed down now, could you?'

'They know that already, Mia. But they're not going to send
you a letter of thanks, and they can't just forget it ever existed.' I
thought for a second or two. 'However . . . if they stuck you in a
line-up, what are the chances of Patrick Booth identifying you?'

'As long as I'm not the only one there wearing a poncho, a
woolly hat and shades so big they almost cover your face, I'd say
they were pretty poor.'

'Then maybe you don't need help,' I suggested; then I
frowned. 'But something tells me that's not your biggest worry, is
it?' I ventured.

'No.'

'That has to do with this deep dark secret, I guess, the one
you say will hole my career below the waterline.'

'Yes,' she said, 'and I suppose it's time you found out what
it is.'

She took a mobile from her small gold handbag, keyed in a
text and sent it, then leaned back in her chair. I did the same,
catching up with the Albarino in the silence. If I hadn't glanced
to my left I wouldn't have seen the look on John's face, the
surprise in his eyes as he looked at a point behind me and
exclaimed, 'Nacho?'

And then he was standing beside me, the newcomer, the
third place at the table. I'd seen him in a similar position before,
but then he'd been wearing a waiter's uniform.

'This is my son,' Mia said, 'Ignacio Centelleos.'

I looked at him as he took his seat, and all sorts of things
clicked into place, dates, details of a night three months off a
year before the kid was born, the way he looked almost exactly
like a photograph I have at home of another teenage lad: me.

'This is our son,' his mother added.

'I don't know if I should say, "Hi, Dad,"' Nacho murmured. 'It is very new to me too.'

Mia took something else from her bag, a document, folded down to quarter size. 'If you doubt me,' she said, 'that's a DNA analysis report. If your Spanish isn't good enough to read it you can have it officially translated. Either way, it'll tell you definitively that you and I are Ignacio's parents. If you still doubt it we can run another test, no problem.'

I couldn't help smiling, as if I was admiring my son's ingenuity, as in fact I was. 'You stole my swimming trunks from my garden,' I chuckled. 'Didn't you?'

'I'm sorry,' he replied, solemnly. 'I had no choice.'

'Don't worry about it, kid.' I almost called him 'son', but I couldn't. 'I'd probably have done the same.'

Then I turned to Mia, no longer smiling. 'Why did you have him do that?'

'I had to,' she insisted. 'You see, Bob, I'd never been absolutely certain that you were his father. Do you remember that not long before we met I was raped, by three men in Edinburgh? Three bastards who were carrying a grudge from my schooldays.'

'Yes,' I said, 'and I remember what happened to two of them. Hastie McGrew served his life sentence for killing them.'

'Exactly. I've always been sorry about that, sorry for Hastie; nobody asked him to, not me, not Perry. He just did it, as if I really was his sister.'

'But you must have told him who they were,' I pointed out.

'Yes,' she admitted, 'but I never thought for a moment he'd do that. I didn't think any man cared that much.' As she spoke I could see something new in her eyes, a real depth of misery.

'I've been abused by men all my life: by that beast Alasdair and then by those three drunk, ugly brutes. You were the only man who ever treated me gently, and even you tried to throttle me when you woke out of that dream. Believe this or don't believe it, I don't care, but I've never been with anyone since you.'

She paused to compose herself. 'They gave me a morning-after pill at the hospital, when I was treated, then you and I . . .' she looked at me, avoiding Ignacio. 'You only used a condom the first time, remember. After that we got a little . . . overenthusiastic.'

That is true; I've never forgotten any of that night.

'When I fell pregnant,' Mia continued, 'I thought it must be yours, but I could never be one hundred per cent certain. Maybe that pill hadn't done the job properly, for all I knew. I never talked to our son about his father, not until it became necessary for me to find out for sure. I told him, then when I saw that *Herald* article, I asked him to come here and by hook or by fucking crook get a testable sample from you.'

'This was the first place I come,' Ignacio said, taking up the story, 'and I was lucky, John was looking for a waiter. He gave me a job and I waited on you when you came here.

'My idea was to steal a glass you had used, and I did, but some clown bumped me in the kitchen and it broke in my pocket. So I went to your house, I wait for you to go out, and I get lucky, I find your trunks and they have hair, lots of it on the inside, with the roots; that you need for testing. I'm sorry, it was very intru . . . I don't have the word in English.'

I supplied it. 'Intrusive, Ignacio, but you're forgiven. You want a drink?'

He nodded. 'A beer, please, sir.'

'Don't call me sir. No, don't call me Dad either, at least not till it's sunk in.' I called the waitress over and asked for two canyas.

'So why, Mia?' I asked. 'Let's strip all else aside, why did it suddenly become necessary, as you put it?'

'Because of my mother.'

'Go on,' I invited her, although by that time, I knew what was coming.

'The drug route worked well for six months,' she began. 'I would send an email to a UK email address from a Hotmail account I created in Spain, giving the time and place of the next handover point. It was secure,' she explained. 'I always sent them from open Wi-Fi zones, never from my home IP address.

'My payments hit the bank, I supplied more product and so on; a nice little cycle, with either end of the chain anonymous so that nobody could shop us if someone was caught in Edinburgh.'

'And Booth was caught.'

'It was all over by then anyway,' she said. 'A few weeks ago, my money didn't arrive. I sent an email asking where the hell it was, and got a message back saying I'd have to come to collect it, that things had changed and that the Edinburgh end wasn't happy to go on without knowing who they were dealing with. I tried to get in touch with Hastie, through the limo firm . . . that was how I'd contacted him before . . . but I was told that he'd collapsed and was in hospital.

'I had to go. They . . . I thought it was they . . . had my money and they were the outlet for my product. I sent an email agreeing and I was told to go to an address in Edinburgh, in Caledonian Crescent. I didn't want to fly and leave a trail on an aircraft passenger manifest so I drove. We drove, rather; Ignacio insisted on coming with me, to share the journey.'

'And because I did not want Mama to go alone,' the boy added. No, scratch that; not 'the boy', the young man. Ignacio is a solid lad and could have passed for early twenties, as could I when I was around eighteen.

'You should have stopped her going altogether,' I snapped. Listen to me, lecturing him already.

'He couldn't have,' Mia said, 'any more than he could have stopped you. So we got in the van and we drove, across Spain and France and through the tunnel.'

'Eight zero nine five H N J.'

Both of them stared at me. 'Fucking amateurs,' I murmured, sadly. 'There are far more street cameras now than there were in your time in Edinburgh, Mia. They picked you up early on. Not in Caledonian Crescent, though. There isn't one there. So, what happened?'

'We found the address,' she continued, 'just after midnight as ordered. Ignacio pressed the button for flat one stroke one as we'd been told. A woman's voice came through the speaker, telling us to come up, and we were let in.'

She paused, to take another drink, and I saw that her hand was shaking. Her voice was steady, though.

'I was behind Ignacio when she opened the door, so I didn't see her properly at first. And she didn't get a look at me either, as I was wearing night driving glasses and my woolly hat. I took them off as we were following her into the kitchen. When we got in there and we got a good look at each other . . .'

'*Una pesadilla*,' Ignacio whispered. Yes, I could see that it would have been a nightmare to him, when the women of the Watson family came face to face.

'It was my mother,' Mia said. 'I couldn't believe it, and neither could she. She was as surprised as I was. Then her face just twisted into something awful, it just filled with hatred.

'She picked up a meat cleaver and she came for me, swinging it at my head. I threw an arm up to protect myself; the cleaver hit me but it didn't cut all the way through my jacket. She'd have killed me, Bob, if Ignacio hadn't grabbed her from behind and hauled her off.'

She looked into my eyes, searching for belief. I tried to show her nothing.

'When he did, though, she tried to hit him with the thing, waving it behind her . . . until I picked up a knife and stabbed her, again and again, until I hit something vital and the blood started pumping everywhere, and she gurgled and her eyes rolled and she died.'

I looked at her for a while, not knowing for sure what to make of her. 'You'd just killed your mother. How did you feel?' I asked.

'I'd just saved my son,' she retorted. 'I felt pleased.'

'It won't always be that way, Mia. You're not done with those *pesadillas* yet. I doubt if you ever will be.' I didn't dwell on the thought. 'So, that done and dusted, how did you get the body into the river?'

'Ignacio found a big blanket chest in her bedroom. It was big enough to take her, so we crammed her in there. We checked there was nobody around, then between us we got it downstairs and into the van. We took the money too; she had that in a supermarket bag in the kitchen.'

'Why? Why did you do all that? Why not just leave her there?'

'Now, I don't know for sure,' she admitted. 'I suppose we hoped it would give us time to get out of the country before she was found. And it did.

'There's a road beside the river where I used to go running when I was on Airburst. We took the van down there and got

417

lucky. It was high tide; we took her out, stripped her clothes off so there was nothing to identify her, and dropped her into the water off some rocks, then we heaved the chest in after her. Then we headed home. We took the clothes and burned them on the way.'

'As you burned your old bodega?' I held a hand up, stopping any response. 'No, don't answer that. That happened here in Spain, so I don't want to know, just in case I'm ever asked whether I do or not.'

I picked up my beer and drained most of it, then looked at them, first at my son, and then at his mother. 'What's the bottom line, Mia?' I asked her. 'What do you want from me?'

'I want you to protect Ignacio. And I want you to give me a head start. If I'm arrested, it all comes out, and your career will be over. You couldn't possibly be appointed to that big new job.'

I looked back at her and felt utter despair wash over me. 'So fucking what?' I hissed. 'When Sarah and I were over here,' I told her, 'I decided that I'm withdrawing my application. I don't want the job. It's not for me. If that means my police career is over, so be it. My job doesn't get me up in the morning, not any more. Sarah does, and my children do. Earlier you said to me that I didn't know what I've done. Well, neither do you.'

'Yes I do,' she protested. 'Exactly.'

I shook my head. 'No you don't. You could have protected him eighteen years ago, by telling me about him. Do you think, seriously, that I wouldn't have acknowledged him? Of course I would; I'd never have considered otherwise.

'You and me, that might not have worked, but as his mother, you would have been untouchable, by Bella, by Tony Manson, by anyone who feared my wrath descending upon them.'

I had to pause to stem my rising anger.

'But you didn't,' I hissed at her. 'Instead you've destroyed our boy.'

'How?' she protested.

'Your story is flawed, Mia. It doesn't work. My wife did the post-mortem examination of your mother. She will stand in the witness box at any trial and say under oath that the angle of Bella's wounds prove that she was killed by the person, a much taller person than her, who restrained her from behind. You couldn't have done it; you're no taller than she was, and you're probably not strong enough. It was Ignacio that killed her, not you, and all three of us here know it.'

I looked at him and he nodded. '*Perdon*, Papa,' he whispered. '*Lo siento*.'

'I'll confess to it, Bob.' Mia's protestation turned to pleading. 'I have done, to you, and I'll stick to it.'

I'd have been happy to let her, but I was forced to set her straight.

'You can confess until they make you a saint, but proof of guilt is still required in Scotland, and if your story can be disproved forensically, the worst thing that can happen to you is five years for obstructing justice. It won't help Ignacio. Because there's more.'

'How can there be?'

'The ottoman. The blanket chest. You should have taken it away with you and burned it as well,' I said. I was angry with her, and that confused me as, after all, I was sitting with a murderer and his accomplice.

'The fucking thing washed up on the other side of the Firth,' I said. 'The local bobbies thought nothing of it, but Edinburgh asked about it and it was handed over. The Fife people hadn't even bothered to look inside. When the investigators did, they found your mother's blood, and they found a kitchen knife with two sets of DNA traces on it. They've been able to match them to Bella and to Ignacio. And just to put the tin lid on it, they found other blood traces in the box. There was a nail on the inside, with skin fragments on it.'

I turned to Ignacio. 'The last time we met you had a plaster on the back of your left hand, isn't that right?'

He nodded, extending it towards me, so that I could see a scar, healed but still vivid, and recent.

'You tore the back of your hand open when you put your grandmother's body in the chest, or when you took it out. Either way, it's crucial, incontrovertible evidence. And it's done for you.'

Mia reached out and caught my arm, gripping it hard. 'Surely you can do something about that. In your position you can destroy evidence.'

'Do you know what I did yesterday?' I asked her. 'I spent much of it destroying what's left of the life of an old man, an old friend, an old colleague, because he did just that. Now you're asking me to do the same thing.'

'Yes,' she acknowledged, 'I am. Will you?'

Would I have? I hope not, but I'll never know for sure, because the question was academic by then.

'Even if I tried,' I sighed, 'it's too late. Sammy Pye and his people in Edinburgh have proved beyond the faintest, most unreasonable doubt that Bella Watson was killed by her grandson.

'They know that she had two grandsons, and that the other one did not do it. Because of that . . .' I took my iPad from a pocket of my jacket, activated it and showed her a document that appeared on screen. 'That's a European arrest warrant, sworn out today in Edinburgh, in Ignacio's name. They don't issue those just to pick up suspects, only for people who will be charged with a specific offence, in this case, murder.'

I pointed through the plastic screen and across the road. Neither Mia nor our son had noticed the car that had been parked there for several minutes, or the two men who were standing beside it.

'See those guys?' I said. 'They're detectives of the Catalan police force. When I saw that warrant, I was duty bound, as a serving police officer, to seek to enforce it. I arranged for them to be here, Mia, because I had a suspicion that I would be meeting the man named on it. However, I had no suspicion that he was my son. So, my dear, you have put me in the position of being forced to hand him over.'

'You could say it isn't him,' Mia suggested, hopelessly.

'But John knows it is,' I pointed out. 'He'll have his name on his employment records. Those cops know John; everybody in fucking L'Escala knows John.'

'He could run for it.' She was desperate.

'No way. Those cops are armed; I'm not having him shot trying to escape.'

'They could take me instead.' She was starting to cry.

'No, they couldn't. Mia, you didn't leave any DNA in the apartment, and you were never photographed behind the wheel of your van. Any traces you might have left on the outside of the chest were washed off in the water. There is no evidence that you were ever there.'

I glanced across the road again, and saw the two detectives begin to move towards us.

'This is what's going to happen,' I said, quickly. 'They'll take Ignacio into custody, and I will ensure that he's extradited to Scotland at once. I can have two guys on a plane tomorrow.

Once he's there,' I promised, 'I'll arrange for his case to be handled by the best young lawyer in Scotland, who just happens to be his half-sister.

'Mia, you'll get yourself to Edinburgh and you'll tell the story of what happened . . . the true story, mind, all of it . . . to Detective Inspector Sammy Pye.'

I took Ignacio by the arm and drew him to his feet.

'You've done some stupid things in your life so far,' I told him, 'but as far as I can see you did them to protect your mother, and I respect that.'

I did and still do, but one question disturbs me. If I had brought Ignacio up, or been around to influence him, would he have turned out as he has, lumbered at age eighteen with a back story that will follow him all his life? Of course that's another way of asking, if I had been in his shoes, if I had experienced the same circumstances, would I have done anything differently?

Lately that's been dominating my *madrugada* thinking, and so far I haven't been able to persuade myself that I would. But one thing I do know: from now on, as James Andrew grows, I will be watching him like a hawk, remembering my father's words, with his dying breath, 'Blood will out, always.'

'When you're in Scotland,' I promised Ignacio, 'I'll use all the influence I have to get the best result I can for you. Whatever the outcome is, I promise you this. You're my son and you'll always be under my protection.'

I rode with him in the cops' car, back to the Mossos d'Esquadra station, and I saw him booked in, all the way to the holding cell. I made it very clear also, to the officer in charge, that I'd be back to see him next morning, and that if there was a single scratch on him, their head man in Barcelona would hear all about it.

When I came out, Mia was waiting.

'Have you got a car?' I asked.

'Yes.'

'Then you'd better run us back down to La Clota. If I left without paying the bill, John would never let me forget it.'

'What's going to happen to Ignacio?' she murmured as she parked beside the restaurant. I could see that her cheeks really were stained with tears, and that pleased me in an odd way. I had doubted that she was capable of them.

'Worst case, life,' I replied, harshly. 'Best case, an acquittal on grounds of self-defence. I'd guess somewhere in between. I was going to ask for a sentencing favour for someone else, but that'll have to go by the board now. I'll use all the influence I have, call in all the debts I'm owed, for the boy.'

Tough luck, Max, but I'm sure you'd understand.

'What will happen about the drugs,' I continued, 'I don't know for sure, but if Booth can't identify you, there's a good chance you may be in the clear. If so, you're a lucky little idiot. Honest to God, Mia, I wish it was you in that cell and not him.'

'Lucky? You think I don't wish that too?' she retorted, bitterly. 'Bob, what should I do now?'

'Are you in a hotel here?'

'Yes.'

'Then stick around until Ignacio's on the way to Scotland. They'll let you see him, I'm sure; I've squared that. Once he's gone, follow him, as I told you. You'll probably be arrested, but I'm pretty sure I can get you bail. Stay with Alafair, if she'll have you. Actually she might welcome your support. I'm told that Hastie died this morning.

'Hey,' I exclaimed, unashamedly cynical, 'that's even more luck for you. He'd have been pressured into giving evidence against you in the drugs thing. Another secret gone to the grave.

As it is now, unless Booth can identify you in a line-up, and unless the Spanish decide they're interested after all, you'll probably be in the clear.'

I got out of her car. As I watched her drive into the night, I couldn't help wondering what future part she might play in my life. None, if I can help it. On the other hand, if she had come to me when she found out she was pregnant . . . Who knows?

But I do know this, a man can't have so many children that he can afford to miss a single moment in the life of any of them. Mia robbed me of eighteen years of Ignacio. I'll be damned if I'm going to miss any more, whatever really lies inside him, whatever his terrible genetic mix has put there.

I went back to La Clota, squared up with John, and told him what had happened, leaving out the family side of things. Then I had another beer, sat on a couch in front of the restaurant and called Sarah, my place of safety in my hour of darkness. I knew that some more tough, sleepless time was looming, and I wasn't looking forward to it.

The place was almost deserted by then and I was glad, for I got pretty emotional. So did Sarah. When we were done, I don't believe we've ever felt closer to each other.

I made one more call before I headed home, to Sandra Bulloch's direct line, dropping a message on her voicemail to tell her I wouldn't be in the office before Wednesday, and instructing her to call the Police Authority first thing in the morning and advise them that they would soon be receiving formal notice of the withdrawal of my application for the exalted post of Chief Constable of the new Police Scotland.

It had nothing to do with Ignacio, and his situation. I had decided, before I ever knew about him, that if the politicians wanted to make a stupid, unnecessary mistake, I wasn't going to help them make it work.

I left then and started the walk home, the first steps of a longer journey. I have no clear idea where it will take me. My future may be within the police force, it may be outside. Whatever, it'll be on my terms.

Who knows? As I reflected that night, as I passed the Palacio de Ginebra once more, this time I might even buy that damn boat.

Now you can buy any of these other bestselling books by **Quintin Jardine** from your bookshop or *direct from his publisher*.

FREE P&P AND UK DELIVERY
(Overseas and Ireland £3.50 per book)

Bob Skinner series

Fatal Last Words	£8.99
A Rush of Blood	£6.99
Grievous Angel	£8.99
Funeral Note	£8.99
Pray For The Dying	£7.99
Hour of Darkness	£7.99

Primavera Blackstone series

As Easy As Murder	£7.99
Deadly Business	£7.99
As Serious as Death	£7.99

Oz Blackstone series

Unnatural Justice	£6.99
Alarm Call	£8.99
For the Death of Me	£8.99

TO ORDER SIMPLY CALL THIS NUMBER

01235 400 414

or visit our website: www.headline.co.uk

Prices and availability subject to change without notice